SKYSCAPE

SKYSCAPE

Michael Cadnum

Carroll & Graf Publishers, Inc.
New York

Copyright © 1994 by Michael Cadnum

First Carroll & Graf edition September 1994

Carroll & Graf Publishers, Inc.
260 Fifth Avenue
New York, NY 10001

Library of Congress Cataloging-in-Publication Data

  Skyscape / Michael Cadnum.—1st Carroll & Graf ed.
    p. cm.
  ISBN 0-7867-0135-8 : $21.95 ($30.95 Can.)
  1. Television personalities—Californis—Fiction. 2. Married people—California—Fiction. 3. Psychiatrists—Californis—Fiction. 4. Artists—California—Fiction. I. Title.
PS3553.A314S54 1994
813'.54—dc20   94-25078
                                                 CIP

Manufactured in the United States of America

for Sherina

I would like to thank my father, Robert Cadnum, for the abundance of aviation lore he shared with me throughout the writing of this novel, and I would like to thank him, too, for his enduring enthusiasm for books.

I would like to thank the kind people at KTVU, Oakland, for their cheer and advice.

This novel is dedicated to the memory of Craig Hoffman, a man whose love of life was a force of nature.

If only one could possess it all and keep it, one would be a god.

Bernard Berenson

SKYSCAPE

PART ONE

BURN HEAVEN

"What a beautiful day," we say. But what of that emptiness, the sky?

Bruno Kraft, *Essays*

1

The big dead lake was glowing.

The sun was up, but Patterson could look right at it without hurting his eyes. He held on to the dash, the armrest, anything he could reach. There was no road, nothing but rubble. Bishop worked the Range Rover back and forth over the sharp rocks, the jagged boulders and the splinters.

It was hard going. They were crazy to be this far out. The vehicle lurched, rocked to one side, recovered with a whine from all four wheels. Even within the air-conditioned cab Patterson could feel the heat coming, the hard heat.

They swung up, and balanced on a ridge. The vehicle teetered, Bishop fighting the wheel. The man was brilliant with machinery, but he was battling the folds and wrinkles in trackless stone, struggling to avoid tearing out the bottom of the Rover. By now they were miles away from the oasis.

The reason Patterson was having just a little trouble being patient was that Bishop was a man who did not like to say much. He just did what he was told. But Patterson would like to ask. He would like to know what they were doing.

The sun was too bright to look at now.

The vehicle lunged downward, almost out of control. Bishop gunned the engine, and brought them full power to the top of yet another ridge. Bishop slipped the gear into neutral and let the engine purr.

The stillness was a relief. They both enjoyed it for a moment. Then Bishop said, "I think it's over there."

3

Patterson hadn't been able to come down to his estate in the desert for months. The first chance he had and what happens—Bishop has a discovery, something bad, something that can't wait.

"I can't see anything," said Patterson.

There was nothing but rock, and the expanse of salt flat off to the north. The truth was, he didn't really want to look very hard.

Bishop didn't say anything more.

And Patterson was reluctant to ask. "You could see it from the air?"

"I was flying the Vega," said Bishop. "I could see a reflection off a window. Circled down to take a look. I had a bad feeling."

"I still don't see it."

"Between those big black rocks."

Patterson squinted. He tried to tell himself that he didn't see it, but he did.

It was a light pickup truck, sand-white, resting there with an air of expectancy. Maybe there was a little hope. The driver was off relieving his bladder or taking dawn photographs or just soaking all of this in.

Except it was virtually impossible to get where the truck was, and if you did it was even more difficult to get out. Even with a practiced eye and skill with machinery it would be luck alone that would see the Rover back at Owl Springs without a ruptured tire, and the Range Rover had off-road steel-belteds. Nobody got this far out into Patterson's land. Nobody at all. And yet there was this little truck, this life-size toy. What made people think they'd be safe in a thing like that?

"People are fools," said Patterson. The down-sized pickup was at the edge of the salt pan, stuck.

When Patterson made no further response, Bishop said, "The lake is so hard you wouldn't see any tracks."

"It's like pavement," said Patterson. "Salt and boric acid."

Bishop worried Patterson by switching off the engine. Patterson never turned off his engine out here.

"The Vega's a real airplane," said Patterson, as though they had struggled all the way out there to talk about vintage aircraft. But it was true: it was better to talk about airplanes and the lake bed and hope that there would be a sign of life from the little truck.

Who could they be? Who would have the blind ignorance to churn across the Naval Weapons Testing Center, a vacant, silent expanse, all the way to this empty place. It was summer. Patterson routinely worked with people who seemed impervious to common sense, people who planned murders, molested children, played around with lethal, mind-twisting chemicals—people who were certain nothing bad could ever happen. But this was different. The cute truck was perched there like an ad for Japanese imports.

"It can't be them," said Patterson.

There was a touch of exasperation in Bishop's voice. "It has to be."

"Then why didn't you call the sheriff?"

Bishop had the slightest smile, a grim purse of the lips. "I knew what you wanted."

Bishop had come far in recent years. Once, he had been a haunted man.

Patterson gave him a nod. Bishop was smart.

"I know how much you have on your mind," said Bishop. "How you need your rest."

"Rest is what I need," Patterson agreed.

Patterson picked the canteen off the floor. Then he put his hand on the latch and popped the door.

Desert hit him. The soft hush of the air conditioner vanished and he was surrounded by It, the way he always thought of this beautiful waste in the Eastern Mojave: It.

Each footstep rumbled. Each breath was loud. It was so quiet here the silence itself was blaring. The sun was climbing now, and it was white, the heat pushing Patterson, solar wind from the core of the solar system colliding with his body.

Patterson loved it here, but not so far out, not out by the dry lake. This was a bad place, this was where you could sweat out two liters an hour and be beef jerky by sundown. Patterson hitched the canteen to his belt, taking his time, and then he called out.

It was the puniness of his voice that stopped him. He was used to body mikes and sound checks, and was not accustomed to hearing himself sound small.

"Can anybody hear me?" Patterson shouted, and the air soaked up his voice, the dead walls of air killing the sound.

Bishop tugged a billed cap down over his head, shading his eyes. Patterson had left his hat in the car. Patterson loved desert because it made you think about simple things: water, headgear, shoes.

It made you think: make a mistake and I won't make it until dark.

Patterson had seen a lot, but he wasn't looking forward to this.

Bishop had seen some things, too, and he didn't want to lead the way. It was Patterson's land, Patterson's life, really. Bishop was just an adjunct.

They found the first one leaning against the front bumper. Patterson even spoke to him. As he did he realized the absurdity of his effort, so his "Hey there" came out very quiet.

The man's teeth were white and exposed in an exaggerated smile. His skin was blackened, and the light wind stirred what was left of the blond hair.

And to think, mused Patterson wryly, that I was ready to use my neglected skills as a physician. Look, he wanted to tell this unhappy camper, I brought you some water.

The other one was in the bed of the pickup, fetal position, sunebony, auburn hair fastened behind with a fourteen-karat clasp. Her expression was that of a woman gazing into sun, eyes all but shut, lips parted with the effort of concentrating against the light.

Patterson had seen this in photos of Rommel's Afrika Corps. A few men wandered off, lost in the North African desert, and were found years later, preserved like this. It was wrong to talk. Not just pointless—the human voice violated this place. Better to stand there and let everything be just the way it was.

"I remember when they were lost," said Bishop.

The canteen was in Patterson's hand, the weight of the water potent, like the heft of a pistol. The water tasted vaguely of the plastic lining of the container. Bishop took a pull, too. The line from a dozen old Westerns occurred to Patterson: don't drink it too fast.

"The sheriff's department Cessnas circled around for a few days," said Bishop. "Then they forgot about it."

They forgot, Patterson told himself. People were good at forgetting.

"Remarkable preservation," said Patterson. Only he didn't say it. There was an awe that kept him from speaking, the way he felt when, as a boy, he had seen a stallion servicing a mare. Majesty and obscenity were sometimes one. These corpses had a kind of beauty.

"Four years ago," said Bishop.

Four years. For four years this couple had been at rest, all the while my own life, my career, have been so hectic I have scarcely had a single day of absolute peace in months. Years. Maybe for the entire four years these sleepers have been here. It was chilling—he found himself envying them.

The couple had covered the pickup with a large plastic dropcloth in an effort to buy shade. It was this plastic sheet that had kept overhead aircraft from spotting them, although the likelihood of being observed from the air was slim anyway. Patterson tugged the plastic covering back into place, and anchored it with two heavy chunks of igneous rock. Carefully, he added a few chunks more. Then he turned away. Sometimes that's how it was. You did what you could, and then you walked. Bishop's voice had no hint of an apology when he said, "I wanted you to see."

Sometimes there was something quietly independent about Bishop. Patterson did not respond until they both sat in the Range Rover. Patterson had a devilish insight: the engine wouldn't start. If the world is just the engine won't start.

It started.

"What's the craziest thing you ever did in an airplane?" asked Patterson.

"I don't do crazy things," said Bishop. "Sometimes I fly down below sea level, over at Salton Sea."

"So do I. That's not crazy," said Patterson. "That makes sense. Maybe these people deserve what happened."

The desert had them, bodies committed to it lost and preserved at once.

Bishop tried to back up, tried to go forward. Beautiful, thought Patterson. We're stuck. Pebbles and sand churned up into the air outside.

Then, with a lurch, they were moving. Gradually they worked their way around the scattered boulders.

Patterson did not say anything more. He held himself steady as the Range Rover rocked and the air conditioning fought the heat.

What the desert has it can keep, he thought. We don't want a bunch of people out here looking around. You never knew what else they might turn up.

2

Margaret stepped into the studio and stopped, putting a hand to her throat.

The new, empty canvas was huge. It was so white, so completely empty, that it radiated an airy, fresh color back into the room, and it would have been a cheerful presence except that Margaret knew what it meant.

Curtis had been working in here for several days, and for several days Margaret had been curious but had not asked. For years people had been wondering when the new big painting from Curtis Newns would make its appearance, the first truly grand painting since the monumental *Skyscape* of nearly twenty years before. She had hoped that this time, after so long, Curtis had begun something.

The starling in its cage made an electric, startling whistle. Margaret said hello to the bird, aware as always of its alert presence. Curtis was in the kitchen making coffee, and Margaret had a few moments to herself in this large room.

She found the cube of art gum eraser, and turned to go when something caught her eye, tucked into a blank tablet of drawing paper. She reached out to touch it, but withdrew her hand as the object rotated on the flat white surface of the drafting table.

It was a straight razor, old-fashioned, pearl-handled, and she had never seen it before. Curtis shaved with an electric razor, and when he had something that needed to be cut with a knife he had his old, favorite blade. This razor was new. It closed up with a snap, and when she held it in her hand it felt warm.

It was with a straight razor like this that Curtis had tried to slash his wrists at that party in North Beach years before. Five men had struggled with Curtis, getting the razor away from him.

But surely there was some other reason for Curtis to have an instrument like this, she tried to reassure herself. She was silly to be in such a panic.

Margaret moved quietly, carrying the razor to her dresser, hiding it in the bottom drawer among thick winter socks she kept there, rarely used and rolled into balls. Even there the razor did not look innocent, the glittering handle clasping its secret.

"I didn't know you had a bird," said Margaret's mother.

"For the time being," said Curtis.

"Is it sick?" asked her mother, looking sideways at Curtis.

"I certainly hope not," said Curtis with a laugh. "It's just that we have a little dispute over whether to let the bird go or not."

"We found it," said Margaret. "Well, rescued it, actually."

"From what?" her mother asked.

"From life," said Curtis. "From death."

"It was growing its first feathers," said Margaret.

"Aren't they ugly when they're young?" said her mother. "But I don't think I like them when they get old, either. It's their feet."

Margaret knew what her mother was saying—it was her way to say three or four things at once, none of which you particularly wanted to hear. Her mother was not simply expressing her opinion about the bird. She was saying that she had paid an uninvited visit to the studio down the hall.

It was an hour after the discovery of the razor, and Margaret told herself that she was acting calm. It wasn't easy. She was terrible at hiding her feelings.

Curtis must have asked something about their feet, because his mother-in-law went on. "They're so naked, and they have those icky little digits."

"Yes, they do," agreed Curtis.

"If it's happy, leave it the way it is, that's what I always think." Her mother looked good in her new tan, although the eye shadow she wore was too blue, pool-bottom blue.

"We call him Mr. Beakman," said Curtis.

"How cute," said Margaret's mother.

"The trouble is you don't know what the bird's thinking," said Curtis. "You wonder if it's happy or not."

"But you could say that about anything. About people," said her mother.

"That's right," said Curtis. "We are mysteries, aren't we?"

Margaret wanted to protect Curtis from everything, even from her own mother. Curtis needed her, and this fact filled her as her own blood and warmth filled her. She was in love.

They all were drinking Bloody Marys, and Margaret stuck celery stalks in the drinks because her mother always made them that way. Margaret used extra Tabasco in her own, a lot of it. The visit was going beautifully. They looked out at the view of the Golden Gate and admired it. Curtis sat at the baby grand and splashed out music.

Margaret's mother was making an effort. Being around Curtis made her nervous. But Curtis was solicitous, called her by her first name, Andrea, and asked her what sort of music she liked. And her mother, who was dropping by on the way back from a trip to Hawaii, said that she didn't really have any particular favorites, lying, because she assumed Curtis would not know anything she liked.

Margaret's mother had a new boyfriend, a smiling, relaxed-looking man named Hal Webber. "Everyone calls me Webber." He was more fit and quick to laugh than most of her mother's men, although it might have been the after-effect of a week at Napili Bay. He was something in cable television, her mother said. He wore a Rolex and a ring with a very large emerald.

Curtis played beautifully, a Gershwin medley. He remembered that Margaret had said that "Summertime" was a particular favorite of her mother's, and then when it was lunch everyone was so polite and relaxed it was exciting. It was the way it was supposed to be, the way it so rarely was.

They should have had help, someone to serve and wait for the guests' needs to make themselves known, but there was always trouble keeping household help. Curtis was having a good day, but these were rare.

Margaret didn't mind having to serve the gazpacho herself—it gave her something to do, and this was important ever since, some ten years before, she had heaved a porcelain Buddha at her mother and smashed it to pieces. Granted, seventeen-year-olds do things like that sometimes, and granted, further, that the Buddha had been gaudy shlock, the gift of a lobbyist representing the canned food industry. Her mother was old-Sacramento, and her family still had some political weight.

Still, the event lingered in Margaret's mind as a defining episode.

She was much nicer to her mother now, but she felt both apologetic and fervent in her dislike of what Curtis called Andrea's "Betty Boop crossed with Vampira" mannerisms.

Webber told a story about seeing a manta ray off the shore, and swimming along with it for awhile, and Andrea batted her eyelashes and made her wide-with-awe expression, a look she assumed was a man-killer. "Weren't you afraid?" she said.

Webber made a little shrug with his hands: afraid of what. But Margaret could tell he was flattered.

"I lived in Hilo for awhile," said Curtis. "It rained a lot. I remember toads. Hundreds of toads. And flowers. Beautiful flowers. And cockroaches. You wouldn't believe these roaches—the size of Chevies."

"Oh my," said Andrea.

"What am I doing—what a thing to talk about." said Curtis.

"But the toads would help out with those," said Webber.

"Oh, yuck," said Andrea, enjoying herself.

"Curtis used to eat bugs, didn't you, Curtis?" said Margaret. She couldn't help it. Her mother made being nice seem criminal.

"I didn't," protested Curtis, looking at Margaret for help.

"Larva," said Margaret.

"We're going to have to move in that direction," said Webber.

"In the direction of larva," said Margaret.

"As a source of protein for the world's hungry," said Webber.

Instantly Margaret decided that Webber was someone she could like. A strong person who could still enjoy himself. The sort of man who could fire three people in the morning and then make a big contribution to Save the Children and feel fine. He was, perhaps, not a noble person, but he wanted to be. He had that comfortable way of talking, someone who said things just as he had read them or heard them on the news.

"I act like this because my mother was so nice I knew I couldn't possibly compete with her," said Margaret. She took her mother's hand, surprising even herself. She felt gracious. Her mother dimpled, looking at Margaret with something like happiness.

"I love your goat," said Webber.

"You astonish me," said Margaret.

"He has such a smart expression," Webber said.

"I'm impressed that you're so widely read," Margaret replied, unable to hide her pleasure. Webber was referring to a character

Margaret had created for a series of children's books. Her stories were about a goat detective, Starr of the Yard.

Webber smiled. "Your goat's famous. Your mother said something about a TV series."

"I'm sure Starr would like you," said Margaret.

She wasn't sure, exactly. She was being polite. It was easy to be polite to Webber. She was fairly certain, however, that none of her characters in any of her books would have been able to stand her mother for half a minute.

It was enough to make things just a little uncomfortable in a pleasant way. Webber was almost flirting with Margaret.

So it was hardly a surprise when Andrea said, looking right into Margaret's eyes, "What have you been painting, Curtis?"

"I've been busy with all kinds of things," said Curtis.

If you didn't know him it sounded like the truth.

"That's great," said Webber.

Andrea knew how empty the studio was. "What sort of things are you painting now? More oils, or maybe acrylics. Or maybe watercolors, or drawings."

"Yep," said Curtis, so cheerfully noncommittal that they all laughed.

"I think you're not painting at all," said Andrea. "I think you can't paint with Margaret's help any more than you could paint without her."

Curtis smiled. It was not a nice smile.

"Listen to me," said Andrea. "Good heavens! As though I knew what I was talking about."

Curtis told her that he didn't mind.

"I really look forward to seeing some new work," said Andrea. "Not that I understand much about art—"

"I have a print of yours," said Webber. "One of the few things I kept after the divorce. A really wonderful print I wouldn't part with for the world."

Margaret put her hand over his, and gave him a look she knew he must have understood, a look that expressed thanks and, at the same time, just hinted at a question: what on earth is a decent man like you doing with my mother?

Except she didn't just hint at it. She came right out and said it, to her surprise. Webber laughed, and Andrea laughed, too, careful not to crinkle her eyes and give herself more wrinkles, but Curtis did not laugh.

Margaret felt now that it had been wrong to smash an image of Buddha. Such an image was sacred. It would not be so wrong to smash one of these Italian plates over her mother's head, although she refrained from doing so.

"Because it's true," said Curtis.

They were alone. The afternoon was late. Curtis had paced, helped with the dishes, sat at the piano. He had changed out of his broadcloth dress shirt and worsted slacks into jeans and a gray T-shirt. It was what he used to wear when he was painting. He dressed like this often, but it did not mean that he was about to begin work again.

She wanted only for him to be happy. And she was afraid this was going to end. The way she felt about Curtis had nothing to do with the facile, easy relationships she had enjoyed with men in the past. She felt rooted to Curtis, bound to him. She had wondered, as a girl, what love would be like. She had believed, in a half-considered way, that there would be one person, one man, and she would know when she had found him.

Now it frightened her. She could please him, but she couldn't help him—she knew this. And yet, he had allowed her to pretend. She had allowed herself to pretend. Someday he would be happy again.

Months ago she had begun dropping hints in public, implying that Curtis had stopped going to parties and galleries because he was working on something new. She had allowed herself to believe that the innocent lie would cause Curtis to begin painting again, as though a wish could be so easily fulfilled. She had wanted to help Curtis. Now Margaret wished she had kept silent. She felt the weight of public curiosity, people wondering what Curtis was painting, and when it would be finished.

Curtis played a tape of some of his music, languid, moody piano, discordant leaps, interludes. Margaret was fond of the pieces, but she understood that they were a replacement for the one thing that really mattered—the art he could no longer create.

"It doesn't matter if you paint," she said, hating the words as she spoke them.

He punched the tape player and the machine fell silent.

They were quiet for a moment, and then she said. "Sometimes I wish she really knew what I thought of her."

"Don't."

"I can't help it. She doesn't know anything about art. You threaten her."

"She's smart," said Curtis softly.

There were a dozen things Margaret could have said to that. He was looking at her as she stood there, before the sliding glass door, before the view of the bay.

"I found it, Curtis. I found the razor. I was getting an eraser—"

He looked at her, his eyes uncertain, sad. Then he looked away. "It doesn't mean anything."

She had trouble controlling her voice. "I'm afraid."

He gave a tired laugh. "I finally gave up, for about the thousandth time. I think about my art on greeting cards and T-shirts, and how people print it on napkins, throw it away. I just can't paint. I can't do it."

"Please don't think like that, Curtis—"

"I was out yesterday, walking, and I passed that shop on Columbus, the one that sells cologne for men, fancy brushes . . . and my hand fell on the razor. I couldn't help it."

"I took it, Curtis. I put it away."

What troubled her now was the way he nodded. "Sometimes I'm afraid, too," he said after a long pause.

She formed the question, but she could not ask him what she could do. She was afraid of the answer: nothing.

He wasn't facing her, and for a moment she wondered if she had misunderstood him. "Take off your clothes," he said.

It didn't take much of that sort of thing to encourage her. She was out of her linen blouse, and was shrugging out of the brassiere before she realized that with that look in his eyes she would feel so bare, so naked. Almost as naked as the small, unclad feet of a starling.

She hesitated. Sometimes she realized she did not know Curtis well. Not yet.

"Go ahead," he said.

3

For the first time in an age he was working, the sound of his pencil on the paper the slight rustle of a thing that was alive, alive and gathering, creating.

The sunlight was heavy, warming her skin, her body. The light was more than radiance—it nearly had a sound, a throbbing bass chord. Her nakedness was a part of this sound.

He was her husband and lover, but she felt herself aware of how stripped she was, how bare before his eye.

Lie down, he had said, on that quilt. Spread it over the pillows.

They were in the studio. The starling in its cage made its liquid, metallic sounds, enjoying their company. She was aware of her body, the rolling weight of the sunlight on her hips, her shoulders. Don't do anything, she told herself. Do nothing to break this spell.

"We ought to let him go," Curtis was saying, after a long silence.

It took a moment for her to follow his thought. It was essential that she say the right thing. "He couldn't survive," she responded.

There was another long silence. He caught her eye and smiled, a look that made a wonderful emotion sweep her, a mix of feelings— gratitude for her good fortune, love for this dark-haired, quiet man who had been so troubled for so long.

He did not speak for awhile. Then he said, "He might, though."

"But that's the problem," said Margaret. "He might meet a cat. He might not. We don't know."

The pencil made its sound, intent, cutting through the blank of the page. She was still, kept unmoving by the thought—*he's drawing*.

15

And he was drawing her.

She could never get used to the fact. The most famous artist of his time had married her.

She tingled with this: his eye over her thigh, her pubic islet, her breasts. She was strangely aroused. She felt herself moisten, soften under his gaze.

She warned herself, like a woman in the presence of barely tame deer: don't stir.

"We knew we couldn't keep him," Curtis said.

"We can. As long as we want."

He kept plying the pencil. What a deeply pleasing whisper it made, she thought. "It isn't natural," said Curtis.

"Nature isn't always good," she said. It wasn't really an argument. They had said the same words before, and had grown to love the quiet difference of views.

The starling fluttered its wings, a flash of black in the corner. The bird broke into one of its cries, and Margaret didn't have to turn her head to know that Mr. Beakman's bright black eye was seeing her here in this pond of light.

"You thought he would die," said Curtis, in a mock chiding tone.

No, she wanted to say. I knew that if any hand could save this creature it would be yours. She let herself continue the gentle, bantering. "How would I know a bird like that would eat anything we fed it?"

They had found the starling on the penthouse balcony, its feathers spiky, new. At first, its beak still had that exaggerated clown-mouth look of a nestling. The bird was on the point of starving, and the two of them hand nursed it on bread soaked in milk.

Weeks later, it was hyperactive, much more athletic than the parakeets of Margaret's girlhood. Mr. Beakman fought the cage cheerfully, made its warbling shrieks, and cried out with a fragment of song that Margaret knew meant: let me out.

"Did you hear that?" said Curtis. His pencil stopped.

It couldn't be the telephone. She had turned off the ringer, and turned down the volume on the answering machine in the library.

But it did sound like the telephone—the impulsive electronic trill. Like the telephone, but somehow wrong.

"I told you!" said Curtis, gleefully. "The bird imitates things."

Margaret listened again, with disbelief and delight. "How can it do that?"

Curtis laughed. "I think I heard Mr. Beakman imitating the garbage disposal the other day."

Mr. Beakman repeated the sound of the telephone. Curtis could not stop laughing.

It was spooky, though, this fellow creature not only sharing their lives but *hearing*.

And then Curtis was at her side. He was kissing her, spreading out the quilt so it was a soft countryside, farmland seen from the air.

She had wondered about this as a girl. Did artists and their models sometimes, alone in the studio, find themselves unable to continue working?

He made love with the same intent sureness with which he drew. He was in no hurry, knowing her and knowing himself well, knowing that there would be no interruption, no distraction.

She felt herself open, a book spread to the page on which a flower has been pressed. But this flower was firm-stemmed, moist.

Long afterward she kept him there, her legs, her arms around him. She rocked very gently, one way, then another. She was a boat, she thought. She was a boat, and Curtis was in the vessel, and he was safe.

They drowsed. The quilt was handmade, stitched decades ago, and stitched carefully so that the blanket had a pursed, gently furrowed surface that pleased the body, the stroking hand, as well as the eye.

A few days passed. Curtis was working again. Margaret knew that the world at large would be disappointed to know that he was not painting. Drawings were fine, the magazines would say, but when will he paint another masterpiece? But slowly, quietly, Curtis traced out the shape of Margaret's body, and she believed that this subtle art was cause for secret celebration.

There was no more mention of the razor, and the fear that its presence implied. She peeked into the bottom drawer sometimes and there, among her dark blue and coffee brown wool socks, was the luminous slither of the handle.

One afternoon after Curtis had posed Margaret once again on the blanket, and after they had made love, Margaret felt herself dissolve into a dream. In this dream there was no sense of danger. There were two people in the dream, on a blanket together in a sunny room.

Curtis startled her awake when he sat up. "We forgot all about Mrs. Wye!" he said.

Margaret hurried into her clothes. She wondered with some amusement if Mrs. Wye would be able to tell what abandon had just occurred. Surely, thought Margaret, there will be a look in my eye. Anybody with any sense at all will know.

Mr. Beakman cackled, springing from perch to cage-side to perch. "Don't tell anybody what you've been looking at," said Margaret.

Margaret had made raisin bread that morning, and she had promised the woman one floor down that there would be plenty for her. The elderly neighbor had suffered a very minor stroke a few months before, and Curtis often dropped by to see how she was feeling.

Margaret hurried into the elevator, and then down the corridor making up excuses. She could think of only the happy truth, which Mrs. Wye would be loving and wise enough to accept, if it came to that.

But the poor woman answered the door with a wide-eyed expression. "Oh, you shouldn't have bothered," said Mrs. Wye.

Margaret's first impression was that the woman had suffered another stroke, one of those flutterings that diminish and gradually dissolve the very old. "I promised you," said Margaret. "I used molasses this time."

"Oh, please don't worry about me," said Mrs. Wye, ringing her skirt in her hands.

Mrs. Wye was beautiful. She had appeared, under the name Diana Wynn, in a number of movies, usually playing the starring actress's girlfriend, the hat check girl, the woman at the office who does not land the leading man. There was a photograph on the Steinway of Mrs. Wye smiling at a handsomely intrigued Rex Harrison, and Mrs. Wye had been lucky and wise in her choice of lovers.

Mrs. Wye was white-haired and elegant. The stroke had made her more like a rare figurine than a woman, something easily broken.

Margaret's expression must have communicated mild confusion. "Then you don't know!" said Mrs. Wye, putting forth a trembling hand.

Margaret took the hand. "Mrs. Wye—you're cold!"

"It's so terrible," said Mrs. Wye. "I can't begin to tell you. I can't even say the words."

"It's going to be all right—"

"Poor Margaret, it can't possibly be all right. My dear, you will have to be strong."

Margaret did not understand, but a bad feeling settled over her. This was not something that concerned Mrs. Wye exclusively. Mrs. Wye was trying to warn Margaret to be prepared for a shock.

Margaret led Mrs. Wye over to the divan. The two women sat beneath a drawing by Curtis, a dancer sketched in pencil, an older drawing Curtis had given Mrs. Wye "to make her well." Mrs. Wye promised to give it back some day. She could barely afford to insure it.

"The news was on television," said Mrs. Wye.

Reflexively, Margaret glanced at the blank television in the corner.

"I was sure you knew," Mrs. Wye continued.

Margaret realized that Mrs. Wye was gathering her nerve. "Do tell me what has happened," said Margaret.

"It's so terrible," said her elderly neighbor, near tears.

Afterward, Margaret took the elevator one flight up and let herself into the penthouse, moving in a daze.

In the library the answering machine was alight, its tiny pulsing red light indicating the urgent messages.

She sat, wondering how she could begin to tell Curtis.

She switched on the television in the bookcase, hoping that some new, late-breaking bulletin would correct the devastating news.

Surely there's been a mistake of some kind. It can't be true.

She considered calling Bruno Kraft. He would know.

She watched the assorted news stories, waiting for the only one that mattered. It's a mistake, she thought. It's one of those things that get confused and garbled and you wake up to the truth and everything is okay after all.

But the news marched a series of disasters, diplomats, weather maps across the screen and then there it was. It was a scene of swirling crowds in a London street, the police holding out their arms, walking people back away from a fire brigade, a gray canvas hose dragged slack across the pavement.

It was night there, but the blaze of lights made every detail bright—too bright, the black paint on the fence rails gleaming. There was smoke lifting from a window, but it was only a small drift of white, surely not enough smoke to issue from such a disaster.

But the report was definite. She could not pretend that she misunderstood, or that the news services might have it wrong. There were interviews with various people, including a telephoned commentary by Bruno Kraft. The famous art critic's voice crackled, accompanied by a still photograph of the well-known feline smile, and the words, "Bruno Kraft, Rome," as though the somber tone of the voice represented not only one expert's view but the view of Rome, and, by implication, all of western culture.

"I can't imagine a worse loss for the world of art," he said.

Terrorists were possible but considered unlikely at this point, the reporter said. An electrical problem "in an adjacent building is one of several possibilities."

Margaret stood and snapped off the flow of words and images. The room was desolate, the furniture, the books, meaningless. She hated the sight of the dumb, unfeeling objects around her. She did not know how she could tell him.

Margaret did not understand where the fire had taken place. The painting was supposed to be in the Tate, and yet the television had depicted a square in London that Margaret could not recall. Margaret knew well where the painting traveled, keeping a mental note of its sojourn in Tokyo, its visit at the Pompidou, this famous painting on its seemingly endless tour of the world. The television had shown a place that was certainly *not* the Tate, tall brick Georgian buildings.

Mrs. Wye had told her to be strong for Curtis. "He will need you."

She had always considered herself resourceful. But this was something she could not do.

She stepped into the studio. *It isn't true. It can't be true.* It wasn't the Tate, so it couldn't be the right painting, it was all a mistake.

Curtis was bending over the pad of drawing paper.

His eyes were bright, but when he saw her he straightened, setting the tablet and pencil to one side. "Is it Mrs. Wye?" he asked. "Is she all right?"

She steeled herself. "I have some very bad news, Curtis," she said.

His eyes went hard. His lips were tight. He lifted his chin for an instant to say: what is it? He did not move otherwise, or speak.

She had never seen his anger, not the real anger, the rage that was so famous.

"Oh, Curtis," she said. "I'm so sorry."

4

Patterson stood where he could see just a little bit of desert through the window. It was out there through the palms and the aloes, a big pale empty place.

"There's another death threat," said Loretta Lee.

The desert shivered. It did this sometimes—mirage making it all shudder like so much ocean. Patterson didn't bother responding.

"Called in to KCBS," she said.

"We have to leave as soon as Bishop gets back," said Patterson, taking a certain pleasure in not responding to the news.

"It was Angie at the mayor's office." She held the cordless phone in her hand and wiggled it as though to remind him that she—and the world—existed. "She wanted to know if you wanted any special precautions."

Patterson was trying to paint a watercolor. It wasn't bad. He wasn't an artist, to his deepest regret. He had, though, a certain touch, he had to admit. "And you told her no."

"They're making a big deal about it."

Patterson made a show of faking a yawn.

"You're going to have to change the way you live, Red," said Loretta Lee.

He gave her a kind smile. It was fairly common: the post-therapeutic patient began to want to help the doctor.

She added, "We should stay here."

She actually sounded frightened, as though this was the first time. Poor Loretta Lee Arno wasn't quite ready to see him killed. That

21

was certainly sweet of her. "No special precautions. People need to see me and touch me."

"I'll call them and say you're sick."

"I'm never sick." Patterson didn't want to die. The thought of these death threats made him nervous. That's why he had moved the show from LA to San Francisco, back where it had originated all those years ago. San Francisco was smaller, calmer, with a more modest pool of homicidal maniacs to draw from. Even so, there were still enough deranged, hopeless, broken individuals in the City by the Bay.

At this moment Red Patterson was in the middle of the desert, in the safest place imaginable. The perimeter of the estate was comprised of electric fences and computer-monitored sensors, installed at a staggering price by a technology giant for "promotional consideration." This meant that their logo floated down the TV screen at the end of every show. There were occasional rumors of people who set forth to take a peek at Owl Springs and were never heard from again.

"You get sick," she said. "I've seen it."

"That's hay fever," he said. "I get it maybe two days a year. I don't have it now."

"You want people to think you're perfect."

I am, thought Patterson. Perfect enough. I should do the show from here, he thought. Live from Owl Springs. Live from Red Patterson's Desert Hideaway. It almost made sense, but then he wouldn't be able to see and touch the crowd. People needed him.

"I think you like it," said Loretta Lee.

"Like being afraid?"

"You know what I mean." Then when it was obvious Patterson was going to stand there picking out a new brush and not saying anything, she continued, "Where did Bishop take you yesterday?"

It was easy to make something up. "He found a piece of an airplane. Big old wing." He gave this some thought. "Off a B-29," he said.

"It seemed like more of an emergency."

"Bishop gets excited about stuff like that."

"It was an old plane that crashed," said Loretta Lee, not really that interested, just worrying the subject to death.

"Maybe a wing fell off. You know how well a plane can fly on one wing."

"You can trust me, Red. You and Bishop have all these secrets just between the two of you."

Patterson heard it coming, the whine of the airplane. It was Bishop flying back from Victorville where the Vega was serviced and certified. Bishop got to do all the flying these days because Patterson only had time to jet down here for a day or two once or twice a year. Television was consuming him. It felt good, though, this much success.

"There are people out there who are afraid of you," Loretta Lee continued. She was the most striking woman he had ever known, and he had known many. She was his personal assistant and nighttime companion. She was also a former patient, and so blindly loyal that at times like this she was a problem. Looking at her made him happy, though, and sometimes he thought he was in love.

"I don't want to get shot," he said, not looking up. For one thing, he was trying to keep his hand steady so he could finish this desert scene.

Owl Springs had been designed for a movie producer just before the Second World War. It could be reached only by air. It was an oasis. Sinatra had played stud poker on the patio, and JFK had enjoyed a tryst or two in one of the guest suites. Its glamour was a faded one, however, its charm hidden from the world, and Patterson liked it that way.

Patterson touched the saturated brush to the paper, and the blush of watercolor—pink, his least favorite color under most circumstances—was absorbed into the surface. You needed a sure hand—the paint dried in an instant in this low humidity. He stirred the brush in the water, the tinkle like the swirl of an old-fashioned glass thermometer in a tumbler of alcohol.

"I think you do," she said.

Do what? he wanted to ask, having lost the thread of their talk entirely. Christ, she could be persistent. "You think I want to get murdered?"

"Maybe. Unconsciously."

The watercolor was starting to look stupid. He threw down the brush. "You think an awful lot these days, don't you, Loretta?" He tried to make it sound like it was just a carefree disagreement, but he was irritated.

She looked down. Jesus, now her feelings were hurt.

He kissed her. He liked sex when he was pissed off. That gave it that extra edge. She had a printout of the calls she had just made, a callback list that hung from breast to knee.

He didn't even have time for a decent lustful interlude. The show's guests for the next month were in the computer. He accepted the list from her hand, and took the long walk down the corridor, across the dining room with its lead crystal wine glasses almost invisible, the drapes shut against the sun and heat.

There was one room Patterson really liked, the mirrored bedroom, the one with the adjoining viewing room. Voyeurism had been accepted by designers of the place as natural, necessary, even. Sometimes Patterson liked to step across the face of all those mirrors just to watch the sudden population of receding Pattersons. He wasn't complicated. The truth was simple—he liked himself. No time for that now, though. He continued, until he paused, let the last lave of air conditioning pamper him for a moment, and stepped into the heat.

The heat stopped him.

It was a wall, a solid substance. The plane was so far away all you could see was the light spark off it.

Loretta Lee had followed him. "People like you want to die. It proves something."

"You mean us messiah types," he said, jokingly.

"That's what I mean."

Was Loretta Lee getting too pushy? Was it about time to let her go back to Woodland Hills, to that condo beside an artificial waterfall, with that view through the khaki air of Warner Park? She'd like that, wouldn't she. Maybe she could find her agent, if he was out of jail.

"You're too important, Red," Loretta Lee was saying, massaging the back of his neck.

It was probably too late. Loretta Lee had become his perversion of choice. "I have to keep doing the show," said Patterson. "It's the way I do good in the world."

"You've done enough," she said.

She was a former soap opera actress whose character had been killed off when Loretta Lee had a little trouble with cocaine. She had worked as a discreet and expensive prostitute, until she was cured of her contempt for men before an audience of millions. Now she took care of details for the man who had saved her.

She retained something of an actress's flatness of affect, and a prostitute's bluntness. Sometimes just hearing her voice gave him an erection.

He laughed. "You want me all to yourself," he said.

"Of course I do."

The great preserver, the anhydrous air, made him wish he had worn his sunglasses. Dry heat keeps. Just stay out of the sun, that's all. It was the best place for the art, too, if the sun didn't fall on it, because the sun here flash-burned anything it touched. Christ, that Picasso, that really lovely crayon mother and child, bit gentle sweeps of black line. That thing was already yellow. Get a couple day's sun on it and the paper would be right out of *The Mummy's Curse,* crumbling away to nothing. And the work was only fifty years old.

He should sell the marvelous but aging drawing and throw in the Degas hound, the dog looking up, out of the picture so you couldn't see the snout. That was oil pastel on Fin di Siecle cardboard, and the thing was going to disintegrate despite the vacuum cabinet. Stick with those hardy Flemish landscapes, drunks screwing pigs, or thinking about it. Art of that vintage had staying power.

The temperature was about one hundred and twenty, he estimated. The mirage ripped up the view, rocks trembling up in the air like driftwood floating on a lake and the mountains with big slices of sky cut out of them.

"There was some other news," Loretta Lee said. "On CNN." She knew when to change the subject. She knew Patterson won every argument.

The plane, when it landed, was so beautiful Patterson just stood there in awe.

Then he asked her what the news was, in that polite but distracted way he could not help but use with her at times, and she said, "That famous painting got burned up."

Patterson turned to face her.

"That one you like. The sky painting."

Patterson stared for a moment. "*Skyscape?*"

Loretta Lee shrugged, looking troubled. "That famous one."

"The Curtis Newns! Burned!"

Her eyes showed sympathy, uncertainty. "That's what they said."

Sick. The world was sick. That was what was finally getting to him, how impossible it all was.

He felt the way he had when the Pieta had been attacked and damaged. He felt the way he had when he heard that Dubrovnik was being shelled, the medieval stonework pounded.

"How did it happen?" he tried to ask, but he was too shocked to say anything for the moment. This kind of thing was more and more common. A beautiful thing is asking to be destroyed. That's the way life worked.

"It was in London. They don't know—maybe it was terrorists," said Loretta Lee, troubled to see the way the news was hitting Patterson. "I have to think maybe someone burned it for the insurance."

Patterson shook his head in disbelief. "Nobody would do a thing like that. For one thing, you couldn't get away with it." And Patterson knew a little bit about getting away with things. "We live in a terrible world."

Jesus, what if something like that happened to his collection of airplanes? Like the one cutting its engine right in front of them. The plane was exactly like the one Amelia Earhart had flown.

He wanted to fly. He could feel it—the need to pilot the craft. But there wasn't time.

Bishop gave his report. The plane had passed certification and was in great shape. Bishop had once killed a man in self-defense, a brief struggle in a bar near Edward's Air Force Base. Patterson remembered the tearful session well, broadcast live, the once-tough pilot freed of his guilt, his stammer, his depression, in one confession under the hot lights.

But Don Bishop was not a creative individual. Aside from his guilt, now long forgotten, Bishop preferred the rational world of altimeters and cockpit logbooks. He was a man who didn't like to meet your eyes when he talked, a man with deft hands and a strong, square build.

Bishop was interested in the new death threat. "You gotta watch that stuff," said Bishop.

"They want me to be afraid," said Patterson.

He stood beside the glorious silver fuselage, and touched it. The fabric was hot. Patterson liked silver for a plane like this, the same color as the Ryan. For some people it was thoroughbreds, classic cars. For him it was the Ryan, the Stearman, the Lockheed Vega, the Stinson 105, each aircraft restored to what Bishop called cherry shape.

"We couldn't make it without you," said Bishop, sincerity making his voice rough.

Patterson very nearly had tears in his eyes. These two people would do anything to help him. Dedication—that was the only way to describe it.

Just a few steps would take them to the shade of the hangar, but there was something wonderful about such heat. Patterson swept both of them into his arms in a big, awkward, hearty embrace.

"I'm going to be all right," he said. He had a great laugh he saved for times like this.

The look in their eyes silenced him for a moment. They believed in him so much that he felt the responsibility, the weight of their love.

"Fear is for little people. People with no faith in anything," Patterson said with a smile. And for a moment it was true. He could do anything he wanted. He was bigger than what was called life.

"What kind of airplane was it?" asked Loretta Lee. "That one you guys went out to look at?"

Bishop took a split second. His voice was closed-in, noncommittal. "I can't remember what it was exactly—"

"Just like the *Enola Gay*," said Patterson. "The plane that dropped the bomb on Hiroshima."

Sometimes Bishop liked talking to Loretta Lee, once he got started. "One day I found a corset out there—a complete, whalebone corset. It was out east of the Providence Mountains—"

He got quiet when Patterson gave him a look. Bishop was wearing a short-sleeved aviator shirt, a military twill with button-down epaulets. His pants were permanent press, hard-creased. Bishop carried a small container of Mace clipped to a belt loop. One of the planes being flown to San Bernardino for service had been rushed by fans thinking the aircraft was piloted by Red Patterson. To protect the plane Bishop had been forced to bruise some ribs, bloody a nose, and he hadn't enjoyed it.

"Don't get mad," said Loretta Lee.

"About what?" asked Patterson. He was about to turn and walk into the shade, a canyon of cool so deep you couldn't see the details, the gate, the trees, only a vault of black.

"I've been keeping a secret from you," said Loretta Lee.

Patterson didn't like that. Sometimes she kept her voice so flat he didn't know when she was being sultry and when she was telling him the hard disk had just crashed. His voice was hard. "Have you?" he asked.

He knew before she showed it to him. It was one of his talents. Sometimes he knew what an assistant producer was going to say from the second he opened his mouth. For a moment he didn't really want to get a close look at what Loretta Lee had in her hand.

It was a small thing, glittering, pearl handled—a thirty-two automatic, a presentation-issue Walther by the look of it. She held it out to him flat, in the palm of her hand. "In case you need it," she said.

He had to love her. In a world where famous paintings burned up and famous people got blown to so much goop, such a pretty weapon was little reassurance. On the other hand, if anyone would be able to use a handgun like that to good effect it would be Loretta Lee.

The truth was, he thought, she looked good with a gun in her hand. Unbutton the blouse a little bit more and you had a perfect picture, the kind that makes your pants tight. "Put it back wherever you've been keeping it," said Patterson, and watched with interest as Loretta Lee tucked it back inside her clothes.

5

Despite his confidence, a very troubling thought hit him as he approached the executive jet. It was a Gulfstream V, a sweet thing to look at. It caught the sun, keen and metallic, an elegant shape in the pool of its own shadow.

The bad thought was: I'll never see this place again.

A premonition, maybe. He didn't know. It made him stop, and Loretta Lee, right behind him carrying a briefcase, held him for a moment, a half-accidental embrace.

As soon as he climbed into the cute little executive jet he knew he should have shot himself up with one of his mood-helpers, his own blend of phenelzine and just a whisper of phenobarbital, a combination of drugs that any aviation medical examiner could attest would be a sure disqualifier for piloting, but Patterson was always drug-free when he flew. Always. But now he was just a passenger flying back to a city full of firearms and madmen.

No one would blame him. Just one little skin-pop. That's all it would take.

Can you imagine a picture like that, worth millions, consumed by fire, Patterson thought. That wasn't helping his mood at all. It was depressing. It was not the thing he needed to be thinking about right now.

He had been feeling fine. A death threat. Big deal. But now all he could think about was the famous painting burning, and the transitory nature of reality bit into him.

"Angie's going to meet us at the airport," Loretta Lee was saying.

"They see this as a real threat and they want everyone to see how nice they are to you."

"They ought to be," said Patterson. And he had been in such a good mood just an hour before.

The aircraft taxied. In the absence of any air traffic there was no hesitation, no wait for a chain of jumbos to get sorted out. It was quick. The craft picked up a little speed, and then the jet was off the runway. The acceleration pushed Patterson back into the cordovan-upholstered seat.

Some people grew casual about flying, adopting a form of executive macho, never fastening a seat belt. Patterson always fastened his, as bored as he sometimes was with this sort of plane. A pilot has certain habits, a way of looking at machinery, the sky. To fly you learned to follow procedure. You kept records. A good physician was often a good pilot.

Loretta Lee sat beside him looking at the printout of former clients who had at one point or another killed someone. Patterson thought it was a sensible idea, but at the same time he felt the search was hopeless.

Patterson had worked with killers. He had shown the videotape of a man gunning down his wife at a barbecue just a couple of weeks before. He had interviewed the man. The overweight, sweating killer had provided a voice-over as his image was doing the shooting, bending down over the heap of bloody clothing that had been his wife. The man had wanted to explain. He had wanted to tell his story. He had wanted to be free of the "terrible guilt." The police had put cuffs on the man, right there in the studio, while the end credits rolled.

That was the point: if you appeared on Patterson's show you were healed, you accepted your future, you didn't have problems anymore.

Usually.

Bishop piloted the jet, a gift from a securities exchange broker doing time in federal prison. Patterson didn't mind the plane, finding it a quick way to switch from point A to point B, but the aircraft was too functional, devoid of romance. The jet gained altitude too fast for Patterson's taste, nose-up at an angle that would stall any of the *real* aircraft.

Bishop knew what Patterson wanted without being told. He circled Owl Springs once, wing down hard so Patterson could get a good look.

The oasis was an astounding green against the ashen-gray of the desert. Nothing grew on the alluvial waste that stretched down the hillsides. The verdure surrounded the Spanish-style villa, a style of architecture Patterson thought of as Seville married to Hollywood.

He had to plan the recorded message for his 900 number. People called it from everywhere. It only cost them a couple of dollars for a three-minute burst of Patterson on Life. Loretta Lee reported that the phone service was turning a profit of what she called "one-hundred proof dollars."

He switched on the little black Sony recorder, but he saw that it didn't have a tape in it. Loretta Lee nudged him and handed him a microcassette without being asked. She had a recorder just like his, and sat there with the black strap dangling, telling the recorder things she would have to do when she was back on the ground. She kept a taped diary sometimes. She was one of those people who would rather talk than write.

He wanted to work in the phrase from Jung, the one about the "uncontrollability of real things," and that other dusty psychological concept, Freud's Reality Principle. But it happened so often these days—he couldn't apply what he now knew to any of the famous theories in the field. Traditional psychiatry was a failure. It had no way of helping eighty percent of the people who desperately needed help. Of course real events were uncontrollable. Of course the physical facts of the world intruded on the psyche. Patterson found himself wondering if either Freud or Jung had ever bought car insurance.

So by the time they were in San Francisco, Patterson had a few thoughts on tape, but they weren't the big thoughts he had hoped for. He talked about death and violence, and how he felt when he made love with Loretta Lee, because that was his approach in his 900-number calls, intimate and frank. Patterson was someone you could believe in. People needed that.

Even that little buzz fear can provide had worn off. He felt wary and tense, a bad way to feel, although it made him realize that he was human. Nothing like feeling human.

The San Francisco airport was cold after the desert. There were dim figures, plainclothes cops, even a police dog. Patterson liked dogs, but this one didn't even wag its tail.

"Don't worry about a thing," said Angie.

"We don't worry," said Loretta Lee.

In the limo on the way from the airport, Angie sat across from him, the lights flowing over her. She looked pert and wide-eyed, a blonde emissary from the City of San Francisco to one of its famous residents. "We think it's just a threat," said Angie, "but we also think it's time to change the way we handle things."

"People come from all over the world to see Dr. Patterson. We go in the same way as always, we come out the same way," said Loretta Lee.

Patterson liked the *we*. Loretta Lee watched the show on remote, if she went to the studio at all. She was usually too busy with the calls and the mail, although she kept a tape of every show ever broadcast.

"I like things the way they are," said Patterson with a smile.

"It's not that simple anymore," said Angie.

"It was never 'simple,' " said Patterson.

"We're getting a lot of pressure." Angie touched her hair. "From segments of the medical community, among others."

"San Francisco must be the only city in America where anyone listens to those fools," said Loretta Lee. She had been in therapy for years before coming to Patterson.

"After the city government," said Angie, smart enough to smile slightly here, as though to say: the people who sent you me, "the university medical center is the city's biggest employer."

"Those guys are scared," said Loretta Lee. "Psychiatrists can't stand what Red's doing. He cures people. It drives the doctors crazy."

Patterson laughed, but quickly stopped himself. What was he laughing at? He was a physician himself, trained at UCLA, his skills polished in a ghetto emergency room. He had reached the point that he thought of the medicos as people far away, hostile and very unlike himself. But he was one of them—a trained professional. There was a smell of cadavers in his nose to this day. They used Formalin on the "bodies left to science," and medical students risked passing out and even worse, kidney damage from months of inhaling cadavers pickled in formaldehyde.

Even at a well-funded school like UCLA the air conditioners were not efficient enough to suck off that kind of indoor toxicity. He had found anatomy fascinating, but the thought of having to go to medical school again made him sick.

"I want you to know I support you, Dr. Patterson," said Angie. "I want to do everything I can to help you. More and more people are criticizing you. I'm not one of them."

There must be something about being around politicians all the time, thought Patterson. It teaches you to give little speeches wherever you go.

Loretta Lee stirred, shaking open a briefcase. "What you need to do is find out who wants to assassinate such a good man."

"We'd prefer it," Angie said, "if you let us keep the crowds on Van Ness behind a barrier."

"If the City of San Francisco doesn't cooperate, we can do the show somewhere else," said Loretta Lee.

"We don't want that. Besides, I personally believe in the work Dr. Patterson is doing. He proves that television can cure."

People talked in a stark, bluntly lyrical way around Patterson. He wasn't sure why. They used phrases like "doing good" and "terrible guilt," bare, emotional clichés without a trace of irony. Patterson brought out something earnest in people, something sincere and innocent and even a little stupid. Maybe, he thought, that was the secret to his power. People weren't complicated. They only wanted to believe.

People needed to see him, to be close. He owed people that. Still, if Loretta Lee hadn't been beside him in the car Patterson might have let himself be talked into a police barrier, or an increased bodyguard, or maybe a brace of German shepherds to keep the needful at bay. He wasn't proud of being nervous—but he was.

Still, he believed it when he said, "All I want to do is help people. They need me so badly."

He meant it. Here he was, anxious, worrying about being shot, and he was saying, basically, "Suffer ye the little crazy people to come unto me." And he meant it. He absolutely meant it.

Loretta Lee's eyes were bright, and Angie's, too, both of these experienced women hushed by what they thought they saw in him.

He tried to make it sound like a take-off of a hundred dumb war movies. "There isn't a bullet made that can hurt me," he intoned.

It didn't come out like a joke. It sounded brave. It sounded like faith. Sometimes he wondered what he really believed.

"But we think that the opposition to Red Patterson is getting organized," said Angie. "And legitimized, ever since that AMA statement."

It was normal to hear himself referred to in the third person. But it was creepy, too, as though his name and his picture belonged to history and not to a breathing man.

"I tell people," said Angie, "that you're a real doctor, a real psychiatrist. Some people don't believe it."

"He was in therapy for years," said Loretta Lee. "He studied with Dr. Penrose."

"Penrose was a respected psychiatrist," said Angie, and Patterson knew at that moment that Angie herself was an unbeliever, that this emissary from the City was half-convinced that it would be just as well if the Red Patterson show was erased from cultural memory.

She said *respected* as if the term didn't apply to him. She smiled as she said it, attracted to Patterson and maybe hating him at the same time. Sometimes Patterson wished he didn't understand people so well.

"Dr. Patterson explained all that in his book," Loretta Lee was saying. "Think of Patricia Freed, the anthropologist. He helped her with depression, so she could finish her big study of Micronesia. You must have read about that. And Allen More, the playwright. He was manic, a big drinker, stabbed his wife during a party. He was one of the first guests on Dr. Patterson's show. Allen More swears Dr. Patterson revitalized his writing."

Loretta Lee was impressive tonight, thought Patterson. And he found himself remembering Dr. Penrose fondly, a moody, white-haired gnome who warned Patterson continually against "empty wishful thinking." The wise doctor had drowned in a snorkling accident off Kauai.

"I just bought Dr. Patterson's book on tape," said Angie, the passing street lights gleaming off her teeth.

"You should carry around one of those Walkmen," said Loretta Lee. "That way you can listen to it any place, like when it's time to shut up."

6

It was the next day, after a great taping.

It was not just a great taping. It was a fantastic taping.

The show had been about danger, how it made life more vivid. He didn't know where the words came from sometimes. He just stood there, and the little white flame burned in his head. There was no script for moments like this. Even the floor director, cameramen, assistants to assistants, people who went out of their way to seem efficient and bored, had been stunned.

People just beyond the lights had looked at him with rapt expressions as he had said, "It's morning in our lives. Why are we still afraid? We can awaken from our fear now. We are all that we dreamed we would be." And, with a little more than half a minute left, he continued, "We don't need to ask when will I be whole, when will I be happy. The stranger we waited for is here, wearing our face, inhabiting our bodies, speaking in our voice."

Patterson had to stop and consider. Maybe there really was a Holy Spirit, and It really did feed you lines when you stood there looking into camera four.

It was time to head for the street. Something trailed from his arm, and glancing down he realized it was the bulletproof vest an assistant had pressed upon him. "You aren't going out without protection," said the assistant, a little guy with a bald spot. The network usually offered him handsome men and gorgeous women. Who was this little twerp?

"I've been here a month," said the little balding man. "You see

35

me every day. Steve Poole, with an *e*. I'm here to make sure you wear a vest when you're supposed to."

"I would remember you," said Patterson.

"I've been taking care of you, sir," said the little assistant.

"You're reminding me how bad my memory is."

"Wouldn't dream of that, sir."

"You and I share the same first name."

"Steven with a *V,* sir."

"Tell me, Poole, why is it that being called *sir* is so irritating?"

"We can't go out that way," said Poole.

"It's all right," Patterson said. "All these people want to be there when it happens." He had that tone in his voice that always amazed him. It was the sound of a man who lived in another world, the voice of a man at peace with life and with death. He let the bulletproof vest drop.

"It's my ass on the line, Dr. Patterson," said Poole.

Patterson gave him a smile. "No, it's not."

"At least let us drive the crowd up to the end of the block."

"With sticks, you mean," said Patterson. "And firehoses and maybe big dogs."

Poole gave him a level look. Patterson realized this was exactly the sort of little guy who could kill with his bare hands. "Thanks for trying to help," said Patterson.

The people around him were waiting for him to decide, but he had already made up his mind; there had never been any doubt. He wasn't going to sit around the studio while the cops beat people over the head trying to drive them back half a block. Patterson liked the feeling, a bunch of tough men waiting for his order.

"Let's go," Patterson said, and they all shouldered forward.

This was his reward for all his good work. Maybe they deserved to see him die, if that was what happened. Maybe his brains would splatter on somebody. They'd love that. He followed security down the corridor, a wedge of big men and a few big women.

There was still some makeup on his neck. He ran a finger under his color and it came out with hypoallergenic foundation-moisturizer, a dawn-pink stuff a Japanese manufacturer gave him gratis ever since he had taped three shows in Tokyo, three shows in five hours. They sent it over airfreight and Patterson had to give it away; he couldn't use the stuff fast enough.

A death threat made it so you didn't want to sit at the mirror, all those little light bulbs around your reflection. A death threat made things simple.

The big door boomed open, and there was the squeal, the gasp, the rush he always felt when people saw him and *knew*.

There was a tight, dead feeling inside. There were too many people.

He was out, under the sky, surrounded, alive. "Good show," said a perfect stranger. They were all perfect, faces, voices, his multitude.

"Thank you, Dr. Patterson," called another perfect stranger, female, slim, with a figure Patterson allowed himself to look upon with a moment's appreciation.

"You helped me quit eating!" cried a wild-eyed, wild-haired young woman whose mascara had run. Patterson thought she looked horrible, right out of Auschwitz, death-thin. "Thank you, Dr. Patterson! Please!"

Please because the security people, brave, farsighted, always people you could count on to muscle aside the innocent, step on the toes of the halt and the lame, were man-handling the bleary-eyed young woman, forcing her back. *Red Patterson Live* was the biggest show on in the late afternoon. There was a big surge in hand-carried televisions among office workers, and the gross national product was said to sag during Red Patterson's segment of the day. Love affairs were interrupted, pizzas got delivered late. The bars jammed with pre-supper drinkers, but booze sales stayed low until after the show. And kids were a surprise target. The brighter kids loved the show.

The young woman was still reaching out her hand, her eyes beseeching Patterson: *Please*.

"Dead man," said Patterson to himself, turning, laying a hand on the security guard's shoulder. "I'm a dead man." He knew what they saw, saw as though through their eyes, all of their eyes, the way it was every afternoon after he taped the show.

"We're never going to get out of here!" cried a voice, a security guard acting as an ad hoc Greek chorus.

It was a tourist event now—a brochure they gave out at Fisherman's Wharf had a star beside the paragraph, a red star. It was a must-see. The taping of Dr. Red Patterson's show, or "If you can't beg, borrow, or steal one of these premium tickets, cop a look for free when he exits the stage door on Van Ness. He shouldn't, but he still does."

He slipped by the guard, worming, fighting, and stretched forth his hand, and the woman's eyes widened in hope so keen it was like pain. She couldn't quite reach him. The crowd tossed, cameras were flashing, and Patterson reached out as far as he could over shoulders, through the crowd.

And touched her hand.

He hated this when it happened. It never failed to drive him crazy: the woman fainted.

It was a hysterical swoon, one of those rock-star syncopes, something that always embarrassed Patterson and annoyed him. What if someone swallowed her tongue when she passed out like that, or fell down and broke something, if she wasn't so squished by the bodies of the people around her that she *had* to remain upright? What if she cracked a skull on the sidewalk? Think of the lawsuits.

But it wasn't just that. Patterson cared about these people. He almost hated to admit it, but he did. He was exasperated and tired, but he couldn't stand to see these poor people suffer. It was the last thing this woman needed to fall down and get trampled to death outside a television studio in San Francisco.

The producer had begun making suggestions: tape the show in LA like you used to, or use one of those independent video bunkers in Marin or Berkeley, where the musicians lipsynched and people spent all night making close-ups of model space ships.

He made sure the woman was okay, made sure she was conscious and smiling—weakly, but it was a smile. It was a brave smile— emotion had swept her. She thought she was happy.

Patterson felt the familiar inner refrain: got to do something different.

Can't go on like this.

He shook hands, wrestled his arm back out of one frenzied grasp after another, smiled all the while. He couldn't believe himself. Here he was, smiling, waving, and he knew the risk.

He snaked his way to the limo, tangled with the CBS security like a running back shoving his own blockers ahead of him. People everywhere. This was tight security? This was a slow, steady riot.

Jesus, it was starting to hurt, that rictus he kept for all comers. He had made it to the automobile, but the car door was blocked by photographers, squinting up at him, cameras whining.

"Get that door open!" someone was bellowing. "Open the door!"

This was controlled hysteria, the forces of order barely more coherent than the citizens themselves. The station had beefed up its complement of uniforms, but the result was that the usual mob was simply increased in size, in weight.

The door was open at last, and Patterson was pushed inside, someone's hand pressed down on the top of his head, to protect it from the top of the doorframe, a gesture both solicitous and commanding: you go here now.

Patterson was on the seat, arm on an armrest, and now the door wasn't closing, slammed against an ankle or a briefcase. The engine started, but there were cries of "Hold it! Hold it!" People were in the way, tangled around the car, in the door handle, the bumpers, the street a mass of people shouting and taking pictures.

Patterson had wanted to be a doctor. What did he mean *wanted to be*. He *was* a doctor. An M.D. His drawings of the bones of the hand had been sold and framed. He had published articles on the spleen when he was only a resident at Oakland's Highland Hospital, probing gunshot wounds for the pumper, the trauma-severed artery that was spurting life.

He knew quite enough about bullets, soft-nosed, high-velocity, every sort of projectile. He had been continually amazed and horrified at the power of guns, the abrupt, unnatural navel of the entry wound giving way to the blossom-burst of the bullet's exit. He had contemplated a career of research or clinical, hands-on medicine before drifting into psychiatry because, if the truth were told, he was afraid of having patients who might die.

Disease terrified him—not that he was entirely squeamish. He admired the graceful, thread-thin vine of the lymphatic system, the lovely, burgundy lobes of the liver, the busy brain-gray plumbing of the guts. As an intern he saw people dying, and he felt abashed in the face of pain, in the face of the grief-stunned family, and had hoped for living patients, people who were likely to survive.

"Please move so we can shut the door please," a voice was calling. It was Poole.

Patterson could have chosen urology, with its reservoirs and ducts, or podiatry with its faith in bone to heal, like living wood, chalk fusing with chalk. But he believed in hope, an invisible, airy presence in the body. He wanted to be a physician. He wanted to be a living doctor, with living patients. He wanted to be a therapist.

The door would not shut. Someone was trying to thrust something in through the half-closed space, a bunch of color, reds, yellows—flowers. Patterson reached for the bouquet, and called out that it was all right, but security guards had the woman—if it was a woman—and the flowers were snatched away, scattered.

People responded to the logic of the times. It made sense. It was what happened when you became famous: people wanted you dead.

Everything comes to an end: the door was slammed. The limo parted people, guards, cops, photographers, figures helping each other out of the way, a Laocoön of traffic police, uniformed figures yelling into transmitters, stocky women holding back tourist's aiming what could have been pistols but which were, from the lack of effect, mere cameras, the latest in miniaturization, magnetic tape or Kodachrome capturing what would turn out to be an enigmatic shot, one that would require a voice-over in a living room down the years: "There's Dr. Patterson, you can sort of see him. Look at all the security; someone was going to shoot him."

"We're out of here," said the driver cheerfully, another stranger, a large, dark man. But he wasn't a stranger. He was a driver Patterson knew, someone provided by the city or the station or the network. But even he could be the assassin, driving off with his victim.

They weren't out of there. They were going nowhere. Patterson closed his eyes. He wanted to practice medicine. That was all. He wanted to help someone, just one person, in the way he had been trained. He was a healer. In his intellect, his heart, his scheme of the future, he was still just that—a physician.

They were moving at last. This was where the sniper would have a clear shot.

He couldn't go on like this, eyeing the rooftops as they glided past. He wondered which billboard, which gable, which parked car, hid the rifleman. Or the pedestrians at the curb—the windows, although high-impact, were not bulletproof, not at this angle, so close.

You won't even hear it, thought Patterson. The burst that blows all this away will be the single most important thing that ever happens to you.

And you'll never know it.

They whisked through an intersection. Another clear shot, if someone wanted to take it. Any of those blurred figures could be cradling a gun.

The only man who had understood Patterson was Paul Angevin, and Paul was dead, lost four or five years ago. They had found his fishing boat floating empty in the Pacific. Paul had been a TV producer mildly famous for his shows on the heart, the brain.

Patterson got Loretta Lee on the limo phone. "I take it you're not dead yet," said Loretta Lee.

"What I want to know is, why would a prospective killer call up and tell a radio station what they were going to do?" said Patterson.

"An extrovert," said Loretta Lee.

Patterson wanted to argue the point, but he couldn't. There were people who liked to operate in secret, and people who didn't. They were living in an age of people who couldn't stop talking. "Maybe he'll blow me up on the show."

"We'll schedule it if you want."

"Who is this little jerk? Poole."

"The network loves him. He's an expert."

"Let me guess. He teaches the FBI how to keep people from copying videotapes."

"He's been complaining. He says you want to get killed."

There was nothing like changing subjects. "Do you think Angie is trying to seduce me?" asked Patterson.

"I thought you didn't take much seducing," said Loretta Lee.

If I were a killer, smiled Patterson to himself, enjoying the sound of Loretta Lee's voice, I would be there, behind that approaching chimney, up on that roof. I would be chambering a shell and taking a deep breath.

Ready to squeeze.

7

Margaret's mother called. "We're both absolutely sick," she said. "When this kind of thing happens it just makes you wonder."

Margaret considered this. Then she had to ask. She kept her voice calm, even indifferent. "What does it make you wonder?" asked Margaret.

Andrea did not answer, except, perhaps, in an oblique way. "How is Curtis taking it?"

"You can imagine," said Margaret. But this didn't sound quite right. So she added, "He'll be okay."

Andrea let a pause enter the conversation, a way of indicating that Curtis must not be entirely okay. "I would so much like to talk to him," she said.

"He's resting," said Margaret. It was true enough.

"I was so hoping I could say something to him, offer our condolences—"

"Not right now," said Margaret.

There was another, careful little pause. "Do give him our love," said Andrea. "And if you need to talk to me, about anything . . ."

Her mother's use of *our* was something new. As she communicated polite concern, with an underlying, natural fascination with bad news, she was also letting Margaret know something about the future.

Mrs. Wye brought a plate of peanut butter cookies. The white-haired woman was stronger, now, perhaps because there was misfortune to be shared—a misfortune not her own.

"You shouldn't have come up all this way," said Margaret.

42

"I just wanted to do anything I could do," said Mrs. Wye.

Margaret thanked her, and tasted one of the still-warm cookies. It was delicious, and Margaret said so.

"I was hoping I could see the poor man," said Mrs. Wye.

"He needs some time to himself," said Margaret.

"Of course he does. He must be devastated."

"It's hard," said Margaret.

"And you look tired, too, dear Margaret."

"Not really."

Mrs. Wye stood there, one hand gripping an aluminum walking stick, the white rubber tip of the stick punched into the carpet. The carpet puckered there, slightly, as though Mrs. Wye was a much stronger, heavier person who had arrived to stand rooted on the spot. "I think I know what's happening."

There were eleven cookies left, petite pats of dough that had been indented by the tines of a fork before baking. They rested on a bone-white Spode plate. Behind the cookies, on the pattern of the plate, Margaret could make out a hunting scene. A woman on a horse was barely making it over a rail fence.

Maybe I am tired, thought Margaret. Too tired for conversation, anyway.

"How is he, in fact?" asked Mrs. Wye. She emphasized *in fact*.

"You don't need to worry," said Margaret.

Mrs. Wye gave the slightest smile—she knew. "I know how he must feel. Art is the way we expand out of ourselves, and into the future." Mrs. Wye shivered with the intensity of her feeling. "I hope he won't suffer a relapse, Margaret."

Margaret felt a kinship with Mrs. Wye. It was a sudden rush of gratitude, affection. "You know how fond he is of you."

Mrs. Wye's voice was strong. She lifted the aluminum stick. "If you need my help . . ."

Margaret thanked her.

"People expect everything of us," said Mrs. Wye.

"Maybe they should," said Margaret, knowing that Mrs. Wye did not mean simply *people*. "Maybe we're stronger than they are."

Mrs. Wye was gone before Margaret remembered the photo album. Margaret wanted to share these images with Mrs. Wye, but instead she sat alone holding the big, hand-bound book, leafing through the pages herself. Here was Curtis smiling, hands on his hips, Stinson Beach stretching behind him. Here was Margaret on the same beach, her turn now, smiling back at Curtis. It was painful to see how happy they were.

And here was a picture taken at Santa Cruz. Curtis had swept her along in a sudden desire to drive down Highway 1, and Margaret had left the radio playing in her apartment, her drafting table lamp on, forgetting everything but Curtis. He had been like that in those days, impetuous, joyful.

Here was a photo taken by a stranger, a man happy to oblige. Two people stood smiling, windblown, just a little sunburned. Curtis had his arm around her. That night they had made love, the lights of the boardwalk spinning, the twirling necklace of the ferris wheel far beyond the motel window. She could see the light in her mind's eye, the way Curtis had looked, the subtle, shifting colors.

It was the first night they had spent together, and Margaret had awakened in the early hours. She did not know where she was for a moment, but she knew who was beside her, and what was happening to her life. She had been too excited to sleep again, awake until dawn.

And here was another picture, the two of them at a table in one of those South of Market clubs, his hand stretched across the table to take hers. It didn't seem possible to her that they used to go out like this nearly every night.

The first impression she always had, entering the room, was that it was entirely empty. The emptiness was complete, unbroken, as was the silence.

Curtis said nothing, lying there in the bad light.

"This isn't like being alive," she said. "It's like pretending you're dead."

He did not respond. A single strip of daylight fell across the bed, and across one of his legs.

Through a part in the curtain was the blue sky. The sky was not yet obscured by the afternoon clouds that always arrived over San Francisco Bay in June.

It was difficult to say what she had to say. "Nobody is watching you," she said. "Nobody is trying to listen in on your conversation." She couldn't help it—her voice trembled.

He wasn't listening.

Earlier she had folded a washcloth across his eyes. She had read of people doing this in former days, when it was thought darkness and a damp cloth might be a cure for headaches. The washcloth had been cold. Now it was warm.

After awhile you could see fairly well in light like this. The eye adjusted. The single slant of light was nearly too bright to look at. She continued, "People aren't tapping your phone. It isn't real—the way you think." She didn't want to say the words. Talking about it made it sound worse. Phrasing it made her think: could he really be this disturbed?

There was a mirror across the room. She could see the reflection of a woman in a dark skirt, with long, dark hair, staring into the looking glass with an expression of calm. No one could have guessed what she was feeling.

"It's not even a matter of opinion," she said. "Whether Caravaggio was a better painter than Rembrandt is a matter of opinion. This is a matter of what's real."

It was like talking to herself. All right, she reasoned. Maybe that's all I'm doing. She could think of no better place to be.

She continued to speak, in a voice so low he probably could not have heard it anyway. "I was hoping that when I married you I could make you stronger." Her mother had told her she was a fool. Curtis Newns would be nothing but trouble.

"I am not crying," she said. "Not enough to bother you, anyway. Bruno is going to be here in half an hour. I don't want to see Bruno alone."

There was a movement on the bed, the angle of elbow, the slant of knee changing slightly. She read the meaning: I don't blame you.

But he did not speak.

The nude drawings, the ones of me, she thought. "He'll want to buy something—whatever you have. And then he'll want to see what else you're doing—what big thing you're working on."

His eyes were open. He was gazing at the ceiling.

"You want me to show him the drawings," she said. "But he can't have them. He can't even take a photo of them. I'll just let him look."

He continued his silence, but she did not feel so alone anymore. He was aware of every word. "You want him to think you're painting."

She knew him. She savored his silence, and continued, "Curtis, I would do anything for you. But you care what people think."

Curtis shifted one of his feet, slightly.

"And what people are going to think," she said, "is that you're as bad as ever—too sick to see your old friend Bruno."

She paused. She knew what Curtis would say: He's not a friend. She continued, "What will I tell him?"

She could sense the tension in him. She sat on the bed beside him, and ran a hand along his arm. "I'm afraid of what's going to happen to you."

Sometimes he reminded her of a leopard, a mustang, a captured creature who could communicate alertness, acceptance, tension with every angle of his posture, the way he breathed. Just now he was saying: there is nothing you can do for me.

She said, "I'm losing you."

8

The security guard in the lobby called to report that Mr. Kraft was here.

Margaret said that Mr. Kraft should come up, sounding just as natural as though Mr. Kraft was a regular visitor, or maybe someone arriving to measure the place for new curtains.

Maybe I should greet him at the door, she thought. Or maybe let him ring the doorbell, once.

He did not ring the doorbell. He knocked, and he arrived more quickly than Margaret had expected, so that she was far across the room, arranging a dry bouquet on the piano. This made her a little breathless when she reached the threshold.

Margaret opened the door, and he did not move or make a sound for a second or two. He looked at her, and she was aware of how much he could surmise at a glance. He seemed to know her at once.

He was bigger than his photographs, and better looking. The famous critic's hand captured hers. She was aware of the moment, having rehearsed it mentally so many times. She held forth her hand, and he took it, and she told him how pleased she was to meet him at last.

"Margaret Darcy," said Bruno Kraft, and the way he said her name made it sound lovely. "I have looked forward to this moment for a long time. Someone should have given me fair warning—you are absolutely beautiful."

Margaret gave a little laugh. "You're famous for your charm," she said.

"I am famous for my taste," he said. "And for my honesty."

But he had called her by her maiden name, the name she used on her books. Perhaps this was a way of separating her from Curtis, an imaginary, momentary divorce.

"Honesty is important. And sincerity." She was chattering, talking without bothering to think. She had warned herself against this. But it was such a relief to actually have him here, to have the anticipation over with, and she was giddy—the feeling surprised her. She was excited by something she had not expected.

She had anticipated his eyes, his searching, ironic glance. But she had not realized that she would find him immediately likable. True, he was impressive, accepting a coffee, making amiable chat about taxi cabs and traffic, but he looked so at ease with himself that Margaret found herself wanting to tell him everything.

Bruno Kraft held the cup and saucer in one hand, gracefully. "Andy Warhol said that Curtis was the best thing since the invention of the tape recorder. He said Curtis could fill up empty space better than Capote could fill up paper."

"I hate the portrait Warhol did," said Margaret.

"*Curtis in Black Leather.* It's really quite lovely."

"It makes Curtis look so angry."

"You mean Curtis isn't angry anymore? Tsk Tsk." He said this *tisk tisk*, archly, pretending, it seemed, to be someone in a comic strip.

"When we were married I knew we might appear to be an unusual couple to some people. A person with a quiet career married to—to *him*." Margaret reminded herself that Curtis was upstairs, listening.

"He's not here, is he?" said Bruno.

He was letting her lie. She could read his eyes. She shook her head, not allowing herself to speak.

He seemed to enjoy this. "Curtis used to vanish for months at a time," said Bruno. "Go underground. Actually, he was just hiding here. Or, rarely, up by the Eel river, fishing and drinking beer."

Margaret decided to be just a little bold. "Actually, I thought I wouldn't like you."

Bruno, head tilted back, eyes slitted in an exaggerated study, affecting surprise, but Margaret sensed real surprise, and some amusement. "Good Lord—an honest woman."

"I wish you could stay here in San Francisco. Curtis and I could use an ally."

He thought this over, and let her see him enjoying what she had said. "Strange that you say 'ally,' not friend."

She felt a flash of embarrassment. I am chattering, she told herself. "Both."

"Some people simply can't understand what makes so many American women so odd. They are odd, you know. Most American women speak in these brittle voices. Imitation male voices, compensating for the deficiencies of nature. But you, my dear, are a perfect example of American womanly charm. If we had world enough and time we would be fast friends. Or, I almost said, fat friends, in reference to my being out of training recently. You, on the other hand, must never eat."

"I love desserts," she said. "I have a wonderful recipe for bourbon truffles." She told herself that she sounded stupid.

"Then you have a fortunate metabolism. I admire that. I think that human beings blessed with one sort of talent, also have others. The talented so often are at least fairly good-looking."

"I'm better at more than losing weight." God—I have never sounded more like a complete ninny.

"I have one of your books," he said. "*Starr of the Yard*. I gave *Starr of the Yard in Paris* to children of good friends. When you can convince Curtis to come to Italy again you must sign my copy for me. Curtis didn't like Italy much, you know. He tried to be polite about it."

Starr of the Yard had various adventures, and worked with Scotland Yard in solving crimes. The crimes were mild, missing cows and stolen wheelbarrows, and, in the adventure taking place in Paris, a stolen tray of croissants. Starr's intelligent expression now adorned coffee mugs and T-shirts. He had the white splash of a star on his forehead, and an alertly cheerful frown a little like the look Bruno gave her now.

Bruno stirred his coffee, and then got up to step through the dining room to admire the view. "I like the fact that Curtis is still living in a high-security penthouse. An artist has to take care of himself."

"Why was the painting there, in Bedford Square," she said, "and not in the museum?"

"It was being restored." He closed his eyes for a moment. "You remember sometime ago a Basque terrorist, I believe it was, attacked it with what used to be called an ice pick."

She remembered well.

"There was a lab that was expert at sealing holes. Like a human celebrity, it paid a visit, was repaired. And was lost."

It was hard to ask. "It is actually destroyed, then?"

"Completely."

"Without knowing it," she said, her voice breaking, "I held out some hope."

"That's understandable. I'm so sorry."

He had an accent that was hard to place, American with the precise *t*'s of a British news reader, an accent she took to be a pan-Atlantic, international brand of English. When she had dried her tears, she agreed with him that the Marin headlands he could see across the Golden Gate were beautiful. The tide was going, the black-blue water muscling outward.

He had asked the question, and Margaret was not answering him.

He asked it again. "What has he been painting," but this time he did not inflect the words as a question. The words were nearly a subject heading. "Because I know you've been able to help him paint," he continued. "I believe that."

He turned to look at her. "You broke a thousand hearts when you married Curtis. Ten thousand women and roughly triple the number of men actually contemplated suicide."

"You don't have to be kind to me," she said.

"We adore you, Margaret."

"He's not here," she said. "Honestly."

"Of course not. He's out in the woods, somewhere, I imagine up in Muir Woods. Or in Guerneville, canoeing. Fishing. That's what he's doing, I just know it."

"That's right," she said. "He's up there stream fishing with a Mepps double-zero. He orders them by the dozen—he keeps losing them on the rocks."

Bruno chuckled.

"He isn't here," she said. "He's not hiding from you."

"He's hiding, Margaret, but I believe you, for the moment."

She was impressed by this, as though belief were a style of thought one could adopt or not, as one chose. "He's up at the Yuba River," said Margaret. "He needed to get away after—"

"After the news," said Bruno. He was silent for a moment. "I was stunned. I still am. It's an outrage. They've ruled out terrorism, by the way. That entire part of Bloomsbury is gradually being reno- vated. It seems a welder's torch set off a minor blaze. They thought the fire was out, but that night it returned to life."

His voice was sorrowful. "The art world has gone insane. Every Curtis Newns in existence has exploded in value. The trouble is that this was his only true masterpiece, the only work that the world simply had to possess. Of course, he may never paint another quite like it."

He was quiet for a moment. Perhaps he expected her to respond. But she was suddenly filled with hope, so full of feeling that she could not speak.

He continued, "That's really why I'm here, as perhaps you know." He turned to look at her. "We need him to try, Margaret."

She said, softly, "Curtis may surprise you."

Bruno dabbed at his graying mustache with the napkin and gave her a steady look. "I want to see what he's been doing."

"There's nothing really." She had a feeling that surprised her: she did not want Bruno to see the drawings, the images of her body.

"I can hardly wait."

Bruno no longer looked avuncular and amusing. His eyes were glittering.

She said, in a way that had to sound teasing, "I don't think you'd really be interested." She wanted to protect herself and Curtis, their life together.

"The talent flowers again," said Bruno, with a slightly threatening air behind his gentleness. "We knew you could do it."

9

They paused just outside the studio.

There was always a feeling of trespass about entering the studio, especially when Curtis was not there.

Mr. Beakman, the starling, jounced from food dish to perch to leather toy in his cage. He made a watery cackle, and then offered a strange, faraway sounding murmur, a noise that hinted at motion and power. Distant traffic, thought Margaret. He's imitating traffic, or perhaps the rumble of a jet. She had known this before, but it stopped her thoughts: animals are alive to the world.

Through the window there was an expanse of water, cliffs, green hills, a view that gave Margaret the feeling of being at the end of something. It was the end of a continent, of course, but also the end of what it was possible for humans to accomplish. To the east, the view seemed to tell her, lies all that people can do. To the west is everything else, the ocean, the wind.

"The work is over here," she said. She knew how to control herself, make her voice steady. She wasn't a weak person.

But Bruno was quiet in a way that told her how unkind he could be, a large cat of a man.

"His studios were always so spacious," said Bruno. "He was afraid of chaos, among other things. He was always neat." Bruno was one of those people who seemed to live everywhere, and who get tired only when faced with the ordinary. His one admission of age was the fact that he put on a pair of half-lens reading glasses.

Against a far wall were canvases Curtis had bought long before she had known him, framed, stretched empty canvases, as big in size and promise as his now lost masterpiece but untouched by a brush.

Bruno's eyes told her that he recognized this assembly of blank canvas. "All that empty canvas," he said. "It makes a room look endless."

She slid open a drawer, and withdrew a small kid-leather portfolio. She unzipped it, and withdrew a tidy pile of drawing paper.

Bruno held forth his hand. She let him take the drawings and step away, into the afternoon light.

What Bruno said was law. If he said the drawings were Newns at his best, then Curtis was reborn, his career alive once more.

The studio was chilly. Curtis liked it that way, and said that he worked well when he was a little cold and a little hungry. The paper made a dry, brittle whisper as Bruno looked though the small collection. Bruno paused, held one up for a moment, and then let the drawing slip back.

Bruno was in no hurry.

They were pencil on white paper, not the explosive canvases of the past. She loved Curtis for his courage, and when Curtis knew big work was beyond him, he took up the simple, the new. For an instant she could not suppress a sensation of pride. Me. He was drawing me.

She clasped her hands. As a girl she had bitten her nails, and her mother had painted them with a solution that tasted of soap to rid her of the habit. Why was Bruno taking so long? If they were good, and if they weren't—surely it didn't have to take all this time. But she had always been impatient. She had always wanted more out of life than most people. She made herself be still.

Bruno had large hands, the hands of someone who worked at something that took care, a violin maker. His nails were carefully and almost certainly professionally done.

She had a glimpse over her shoulder. A breast, a pubic triangle, an arm stretching out until the fingers became the space into which they extended.

She felt cold. He held up the drawings, turning each one aside to let the afternoon light play upon it. Margaret looked away. It was another sketch of her in the nude, sitting with her hands folded, looking out from the surface of paper with what you would have to call an expression of concern, the way she so often looked at Curtis.

Bruno thought that Margaret Darcy Newns was a perfect little woman, delightful, and he wished that she would go away for just a moment and leave him alone. It wasn't too much to ask, after all, but he didn't want to be discourteous. The poor child had been through so much.

Bruno did not want to show her what he was thinking. He thought: don't let her see how excited you are.

He gazed at her. "This can't be all," he said.

Don't say anything rash, Margaret cautioned herself. Help Curtis. He needs you. And his career needs you. "I think they're remarkable, don't you?"

"Curtis doesn't like them," said Bruno, sifting through them once again, and then tenderly putting them back into a neat pile. "He wouldn't keep them like this, in secret, if he was proud of them."

But she could tell. There was that trace of excitement in the famous critic's voice. She said, "He's not ashamed of them."

"Don't be afraid of me, Margaret."

"I know you like them."

"I *like* roasted garlic. I *like* Frascati, for that matter. I don't use *like* for something as important as art."

She was waiting.

"They aren't bad," he said, the the tone of someone being very kind, someone saying *see how nice I'm being?*

"But not what you hoped for."

"Not what I expected," he said, putting emphasis on the last word. "You know that what people want from Curtis are paintings. They want color, scope. They want him to be the Curtis Newns of years ago. Some people will say that unless he produces another giant oil he's finished, a spent force."

Maybe he really did feel they were inferior, she thought. "You knew he was having problems."

"Definitely." He reflected and then chuckled. "He's always had problems."

"He's changed," she said. "He goes out more now."

"I hear he's the same as ever."

"That's not true."

"And he's become even more of a recluse," said Bruno, "or perhaps you would have me believe that two years of married bliss has him seeking his own, private paradise. He's hiding."

He certainly knew Curtis, thought Margaret.

"You are loyal to him, Margaret, and that's sweet, but you can't think that marriage can turn Curtis Newns into someone boring and reliable. Has he attempted suicide again? Or has he attempted to kill anyone else lately?''

Maybe the big critic was jealous. ''I've been good for him. I help him.'' She found herself close to tears, feeling love for Curtis, and seeing how little she had been able to do for him.

''I don't like being too frank. It leads to a lack of manners. But I think he can and will do much better than this.''

In his mind was the single, flashing thought: you can sell every single one of these drawings tomorrow. They weren't *Skyscape*, but they were brilliant.

She said, as though she read his thoughts, ''They aren't for sale.''

His eyes narrowed. He made himself smile. ''They would help prove to everyone that Curtis is still recovering.''

It was even colder here now, she found herself thinking.

Bruno added, ''They prove how much he loves you. But, aside from that, they have charm. Or because of it. They are the work of a man in love.''

Inwardly, Bruno could hardly keep himself from shivering with pleasure—sheer, white-light happiness. He had to spar a little, toy a bit with this lovely girl, but the fact was that he could not leave the room without these drawings. It would be madness to leave them here. The problem was that he liked this young woman.

He had not expected to, really. She reminded him of a ballerina, someone small and strong at once, one of those people who seem all grace and compliance but who endure. If Bruno had been interested in women, this was the sort of person who might have captured him. As it was, he wanted to return to Andy as soon as possible.

If he waited, held off, banked his enthusiasm just a little, maybe Curtis would paint another big canvas. He had to. He had to paint something big. On the other hand, if he couldn't, perhaps these would do.

If he showed his enthusiasm, this girl would want big money and a splash in the media. *New Newns Nudes*. What woman wouldn't want her cute little behind in all the papers, sketched by the famous man?

We don't want to encourage Curtis in this vein, however exciting it might be, thought Bruno. We want him to get back to the large canvas, the giant view of the truth which Curtis had long ago mastered.

Still, it hurt him to see the drawings go back into the pretty kidskin portfolio. What a final sound a zipper made when it was closing up after a splendid offering.

"They aren't for sale," she said, and she sounded like a woman who would not enjoy further argument.

When they were in the living room again Bruno called Yellow Cab.

"I really believe that you've helped him," he said, and he took her hand.

It was easy to say because it was the truth: "I love him."

"Those drawings show real promise. But don't worry—they will be our little secret," he said. "By refusing to see me he's making himself all the more attractive. He knows me."

"He'll be so disappointed."

"I have business in New York that it would be absolutely criminal to neglect. Besides, do you think I should see him as he is now? Don't you think I should wait for him to get stronger before we talk?"

She began to speak, and he smiled and shook his head against her protest.

"Does he hurt you?" he asked.

She said that, of course, he had never hurt her.

"He always hurts women," said Bruno, knotting the sash of a handsome camel-hair overcoat. He said, with what sounded like sincerity, "It used to make me sick."

"He's never done anything like that to me."

"We all live a kind of fiction, don't we?"

The coat was something out of the Via Condotti, manly and well-cut. She wanted to be distracted by such details, the cloth of his tie, the soft-leather black shoes, how they made almost no sound across the hardwood floor.

Bruno took a stance at the foot of the stairs and called upward, "Goodbye, Curtis."

At the door, he said, "If I thought he would never paint again. . . ." But he did not complete the thought, looking, for an instant, sad.

He gave her a smile, thoughtful, measuring, and kissed her politely. "But why a goat, if I may ask?" he said.

"People ask, from time to time."

"Because it was a brilliant choice," he said.

"Starr just happens to be a brilliant goat."

"You don't know why, do you? One day it seemed that a detective goat was a good idea. Because it's a secret," he said. "Something even the artist doesn't understand."

"I don't think Starr of the Yard is art, exactly."

"I'm going to take a risk in New York," he said. "I'm having dinner tomorrow night with Renata San Pablo and I'm going to take a chance. I'm going to tell Renata that Curtis is back at work."

"I lied for you," she said.

Curtis lay in the darkened bedroom. His arm was across his eyes because he said the light hurt them, the slim slip of sun between the curtains.

"What did he say?"

"He liked them," she said.

"He didn't." His voice was very quiet, but even when it was a virtual whisper there was something crisp, perfectly audible about it. "He wanted something wonderful."

"They are wonderful," she protested. "He said they were very good, but then when I wouldn't let him have them, he tried to pretend he thought they were only okay. I could tell what he really thought."

Curtis was silent.

"Curtis, we have to go out. We have to let people see you. We want people to believe that you're going to be all right." It was her usual way of thinking—if you wished hard enough, and took some action to bring the wish to fruition, then there could be no question—the hoped-for happiness would come true.

He turned his head away, slightly.

"Tonight," she said.

She could do this—she could surprise herself. She could turn from someone quiet and yielding to someone sure of what she had to do. People who didn't know her thought of her as nice, pretty, inconsequential. Curtis Newns's other women had been glamorous, colorful, the stuff of gossip and story.

Two of her earrings were on the dresser, like the twin wings of an insect that had molted and vanished. They were made of lapis lazuli, her favorite stone. Painters in the early Renaissance had mixed lapis with oil to give their skies that solemn blue. Margaret believed that the best artists painted what the eye could not see.

She knew now what had to be done. They were running out of time. "We need to begin living the way we used to. Besides, Bruno's going to talk."

Curtis sat up, his eyes fierce.

She could not help it—she took a step back. "I lied for you. But he didn't believe me."

He sank back. For a long time he lay, his arms outstretched. "I heard him calling up to me."

When she did not say anything, he continued, "Why would he talk? If he keeps my condition a secret it makes people think that I'm still going to paint another masterpiece."

"He'll talk," she said. "Because Bruno needs to talk. His currency is telling stories about people." She wanted to explain that if a hope acted upon could become real, so could misfortune. Bruno was likely to say that while Curtis might be painting, he was still a psychological ruin. What people heard, and what people believed, had a way of coming true.

"You don't know him," Curtis said after a silence.

"I know enough." She turned away.

He said her name, and she knew she would wait there for hours if that was what it took to hear him speak again. "I trust you," he said.

"I know," she whispered.

"I know you, Margaret," he said. "But the trouble is—you don't know me."

As she shut the door she could not lie to herself. It was true. Something in Curtis was defeating her.

They had lost their last housekeeper two weeks before. Curtis had seen her rifling the garbage. The stout, warmhearted woman had contended that she was recycling plastic. Curtis said that he knew better.

Margaret jammed a cup over the rack in the dishwasher, the rubberized grill that was supposed to support and protect, and the translucent china broke. Fragments scattered into the well of the washer.

A company in Nancy, France, sent him cups, saucers, gravy boats, finger bowls. They hoped, she supposed, that some day Curtis would realize how much gratitude he felt toward them and decide to design a set of dinnerware.

Every day new gifts arrived for Curtis Newns: clothes, books, packets of slides artists sent, and strikingly immodest Polaroids of women who sought Curtis's attention. There were manuscripts from Ph.D. candidates, cases of liquor provided by people he had never met. Much of it never got opened.

Her mother, Curtis's old girlfriends—they would all be proven right. And none of them would hesitate to say so. The former model arm-in-arm with mobsters on the news, and that actress who had put on all that weight and then lost it, and that singer with the scorpion tattoo—each of them would come right out and say it. *Margaret was never going to keep Curtis.*

It made a pretty noise—another cup broke as she stuck it over the spindles in the washer. She shouldn't try to do the dishes when she felt like this.

She had never thought of herself as someone who was afraid. In high school, her friends had learned to talk about what they hated— what television shows, what kinds of food. But Margaret had felt like the citizen of another sort of republic, and knew better what she loved than what she disliked.

She had always been so sure of herself. She leaned against the sink. She was trembling.

10

It was a surprise when Curtis appeared in his slacks and a shirt he had just gotten out of its laundry box. It still had the folds and contours of the box, and the front pocket was stuck together from the light starch.

She asked him what he was doing.

"We're going out," he said.

It was what she had wanted. It had seemed like a good idea. But now she wasn't so sure.

"Let's go," he said. He had shaved and smelled of lotion. It was wonderful to see him up and looking so good, just a little puffy like someone who had had a long nap.

"Are you sure?" she said.

He buttoned the sleeves. "You're right," he said. "Bruno's going to talk. But what he's going to say is that I am in really wonderful shape, swimming laps every day and never having time to touch the piano because I'm busy making art."

"We don't have to go out to prove Bruno right, or wrong."

His eyes were the color of black coffee. She could barely discern the pupil, that point of deeper dark. "We're going out," he said, "because I want you to be happy."

She began to feel just a little bit encouraged. Why not? They'd have some fun. They'd be fine.

"What's that in your hand?" he asked.

"I broke a cup. I'm so sorry."

He smiled. It was a great smile. It might even be true, she

thought—that he was back to himself again. But Curtis was too
cheerful, too impatient to leave, an actor who knew his lines but had
not completely mastered his character.

She felt nervous as she put on something she felt would look good
in a newspaper photo, "Artist on the town after masterpiece loss."

They opened the front door, and locked it behind them. Each stage
of their departure was framed in her mind, like one of those serious
comic strips about people who live in apartment buildings and have
complicated, tense lives.

They were outside the apartment. They were in the hall. She
walked slightly ahead of him, as though to say *Hey, Curtis—walking's not so hard.*

She was trying to prove something to herself, too. She remembered
reading that sled dogs on the Amundsen expedition to the South Pole
needed to have a human figure walking ahead, where they could see
it. Otherwise, the dogs would realize they were heading off the edge
of the world and refuse to continue.

That's all Curtis needed—just someone encouraging him, striding
off ahead of him. She told Curtis that she felt like a comic strip
character, like *Mary Worth.*

"Or *Apartment 3G*," said Curtis. "Or *Rex Morgan, M.D.*"

The elevator slid open. Was there anyone in it? If so, Curtis
would wait.

The elevator was empty and stayed empty, all the way down.

A security guard said, "Good evening."

Yes, Margaret agreed, it was.

They stood in the garden amid the night-darkened impatiens and
nasturtiums. Curtis was looking, crouching. He wandered briefly
among the garden furniture, sprinkler heads leaking glittering water.

"I don't think he likes the cold," he said.

Curtis was looking for a desert tortoise that he had bought a week
after their wedding. They had released it into the garden of the condominium, reasoning that the reptile would be happier there in the
occasional sunlight and the green grass. They looked for awhile, but
did not see the tortoise.

It was good, though, to be doing something like this. See, Margaret
told herself. We're doing all right. Just going out for awhile. Just a
quiet evening, like people in an especially pleasing article in the
Sunday supplement.

*   *   *

They went to The Blond Spike on California Street, the one place in town where she was absolutely certain they would be noticed.

It was a good plan. They would drop by, eat a Sonoma-field-greens salad, say hi to the right people, and then slip out past the bouncers. Curtis often had lunch there, when he was in one of his public moods.

From the beginning, however, things did not work out.

For one thing, it was *too* crowded. She had wanted the sort of place they had frequented during the early weeks of their marriage. The more people who saw you the better. But a very famous television star had died in the men's room a month before, and after a lull in business people decided that this was a place where almost anything could happen. Now they turned people away at the door, which had never happened so routinely before.

And they still attempted to serve main courses, although no one really came there to eat. The portions were small, decorative nuggets of veal or Mendocino County filets. The tables were packed together, and one night recently the bodyguards of a basketball player had drawn their weapons on a game show host. Margaret hated the violence the place now seemed to attract, but she could understand the allure.

Which made it, she came to realize when it was far too late, a mistake to be there.

"At least five people are here just to watch me," Curtis said.

She thought about this for a couple of seconds. "Who?"

"The waiter with the bow tie with the blinking lights on it. Those two guys at the bar. The two guys with mustaches. And this guy here."

"People like to look at you. They recognize your face."

"No, I mean these people are here to watch me."

She felt cold inside, but at the same time asked herself: what did you expect? "I don't believe it."

"Take a look." He knocked over the vase with its single pink rose, swatting it to one side. "Pick the rose off the floor and look around."

She picked up the rose. Please, she prayed, let us get through the next half hour.

"He's the kind of guy I hate," Curtis said, bunching his fists, leaning forward on his elbows. He was trying—she could tell. Curtis was trying to keep his temper, but he was failing.

"Please try to ignore him," she said. She worked to control her voice. Maybe she could steer him out of the place in time. Where were the waiters?

"If he says one more time what a killing he's going to make tomorrow I'm going to break his neck. They hire people to sit next to me and act like an asshole just to humiliate me."

"Please, Curtis."

"Listen to him."

It struck her just then that one part of her mind had always refused to take his mental illness seriously. It seemed like such a willful game, a fantasy, like pretending to believe in a soap opera. Another aspect of Curtis was his abnormally acute hearing and vision. He really did see more when he looked at things. She could barely make out two heavyset men who might have had mustaches or not, she couldn't tell.

"Please try," said Margaret. The waiters here were famously temperamental. Imperious, deferential, solicitous, absent. She couldn't see one anywhere from her seat in what the headwaiter had described as the table "perfect for a man like Mr. Newns." Which meant, it turned out, where the other customers could see the famous profile.

She wouldn't let herself look worried. She was her father's daughter: never let them see you sweat. She made sure the crystal vase with the baby-pink rose was well over on her side of the table. It would have been a decent table under other circumstances—Curtis was always treated well. People liked him. It was a fact of nature—people respected him instantly, ungrudgingly, sensing that he was of star-quality even when they could not place the face.

But the man at the table to her left had one of those carrying voices, one of those conceited droning monotones that she had to admit was impossible to ignore.

The people at the table were having the kind of date typical in restaurants like this. The man felt entitled—obligated—to tell glorious stories about himself, and the woman felt equally obligated to sit there wide-eyed drinking it in, artichoke hearts barely sampled.

The man would not shut up. He was bragging about his power as a loan broker. "Must of these guys don't have what it takes," he was saying. "Women can't hack it, either. Do you know how few women there are in the field?"

Margaret couldn't make out his date's answer, but it was easy to imagine her "No, gosh, please tell me."

"Tenants are jerks," the broker was saying. "I used to own buildings on upper Broadway. Had to fire the management company because they were crooks. Even these rich old ladies would sit on their money every month until five days after the first. Two guys tried to rob me once. I mean literally.''

The trouble was you could tell the woman was suffering, enduring what was probably a first and last date, basically just hoping this, too, would pass.

You sat on the margins of other people's seductions, political miscomprehensions, and general lack of conversational grace, and that was okay, because you have your own life to live, and it's important to be tolerant and have a sense of humor.

The loan broker ordered another bottle to replace the empty in the ice bucket and made a point of looking their way.

She closed her eyes for a moment. Jesus, all she wanted to do was leave. That's all. God, just get us out of here without a scene.

Curtis sensed the man's stare, and he was staring back.

She had ordered sparkling water, a big bottle of Pellegrino, and had practically held her breath while Curtis ran his eye over the wine list. What had it been—several months without a drink? Curtis had looked at her, and offered one of his smiles—one of his wonderful smiles. "Just one glass," he had said to the waiter, "of the Orvietto."

But the Orvietto didn't come by the glass—big surprise—so he had ordered a bottle. It wasn't all that much, really, and Margaret had asked for a second glass.

The loan broker could tell that something was wrong, that the dark-haired man was getting angry, and the loan broker was one of those blandly good-looking men who like to show off before a young woman as long as it doesn't put him in any real danger.

The loan broker was making a show of looking over their way, now, actually giving Curtis long, even stares. This was even worse than usual. Most people in bars and restaurants, airport lounges, and hotel lobbies either backed off out of common sense, or they recognized Curtis as the famous ill-tempered genius and laughed, said how great it was to meet him, and let it go at that.

But this man was bridling. He muttered something. The man's date sensed the trouble, and stretched forth a hand to soothe the loan broker's nerves.

God, how stupid men could be. Margaret told herself to get up and leave now. Drag Curtis out of here.

"She's probably used to men like him," Margaret said, offering conversation against what she knew was an unstoppable force. And it wasn't true. It was pretty obvious. The woman's response was instinctive—the man was seductive the way a gangster is, all power and dollars. She wasn't having fun.

Curtis himself had a way of getting angry that attracted women. He had a way of looking both furious and emotionally bruised.

"I'm leaving," said Margaret.

"I'm not going to let him ruin your evening, Margaret. That's what he's there for. Sit still."

She stood.

"I swear to God, Margaret, if you leave I'm going to tear this place apart."

She allowed herself a wry thought: she liked a man who didn't exaggerate. He had demolished that bar in Carmel one afternoon.

But then it looked like everything was going to be all right. The staring contest seemed to dwindle away to nothing. Curtis was taking a bite of sourdough and chewing, trying.

The headwaiter floated by, but it was a deliberate, nervous sort of drifting. Margaret caught his eyes. "Right away," he said, meaning: we'll be glad to see Curtis Newns take a nice long walk in the fresh air. Since the TV star had overdosed the headwaiter had lost weight. He looked tired. She slipped the headwaiter the Amex card and knew it would be only another few minutes.

It was going to be okay. They were going to leave the restaurant, and get Curtis home, and there would be no problem.

You see? she told herself. He's not as bad as he used to be.

Curtis was a man who cared about what happened. If he saw the reports of a storm on television, children drowned, a village destitute, he would send a check to the Red Cross and spend a night tossing, getting up, wandering the semidark.

A hitch was developing. The headwaiter was not coming back. He was nowhere.

She couldn't believe it. Everything had stopped but the voice of the loan broker, a relentless, asinine drone.

There it was, the white jacket, the hand holding the tray, the check in its leather folder. Margaret signed the slip, her signature legible even now, snapped up the card, and all was well.

Then the loan broker made his mistake. He didn't make it quickly. He made it worse by taking so long. He eased himself up out of his chair, tossed down his napkin, and stepped over to their table.

The broker was tall, and had a pudgy, careless face, the face of someone who knew the computer screen better than the human gaze.

He had probably read a book or two. His eyes were intelligent, but lit with the overconfidence of booze. He had a square jaw, muscular shoulders—bulk. He had the thick neck of an ex-athlete gone only moderately to seed, the sort of man who had always been attracted to Margaret, thinking her "a whole lot of fun," the sort of man Margaret had always loathed.

"Is there some kind of problem here?" asked the broker.

Curtis took his time. He folded his napkin easily, carelessly, but in no hurry. He stood, and while Curtis was a good six feet, he was not much compared with the broker.

The broker let his gaze fall upon Margaret. He looked at as much of her as he could see, and when she stood he gave her a smile that said he liked what he beheld. "You having any trouble here?" the broker asked her.

Men were idiots.

The headwaiter put out his hands, and parted his lips, looking like a statue dedicated to maintaining calm, good sense, manners.

Margaret gave what must have been a weary smile, a look the broker misunderstood. What Margaret had meant to communicate was: please go away.

What the broker read was: I wish fate had brought us together before now.

Margaret saw what the waiters, what all the dazzled diners, did not: Curtis made the first move, a subtle, definite move as crisp as a white pawn's opening.

He stepped on the broker's foot. He put his shoe on the broker's and let all his weight press down, until the broker's eyes narrowed in nasty disbelief, squinted in that universal masculine expression of unintelligent ferocity.

The broker took a swing. He swept his fist back, and brought it forward. He had done this before in his life, the big ex-jock, and knew how to economize the punch, calculating where the head would be when the head saw the fist on its way.

Curtis stepped forward, and embraced the broker, the punch ending up nowhere. Curtis began digging his left fist into the broker's mid-section. It looked like Curtis was thumbing the big man in the ribs, prodding him affectionately.

But the broker made a windy, coughing bark, and staggered. Curtis stayed with him, walking the man back toward his table, working, now, with both fists. It looked playful, the heel of Curtis's hand flattening the big man's nose.

Blood blossomed, and the broker swung back, missing. Two white-jacketed bouncers were there, and it was going to be over soon. Except that now it did not look playful, not at all.

Margaret tried to give the broker's date a reassuring smile, but the woman looked bewildered, hand to her lips. And Curtis was really hurting the man, now. It had nothing to do with the man's manner, anymore, his conversation or his bearing or his attitude toward women. Margaret understood this much: Curtis wasn't fighting a human being.

He was fighting something in Curtis, something he thought was standing in front of him, ducking, bleeding, getting hurt.

Margaret readied a lie. It was not a complete and total lie. It was an artful fiction, one she knew the waiters would support. The big man had started it—offered unwanted and unrequested attention and had thrown the first punch. After all, being a celebrity these days wasn't easy.

Strangers joined in the struggle to separate the two. One of the diners had a police transmitter in his fist. He was one of the senior police bureaucrats Margaret had met over tea at the Museum of Modern Art, something in press liaison. More police were coming as Margaret whispered premature thanks into the ear of the graying cop.

Curtis was looking around as one of the burliest bouncers put his arm around the artist and said something in a joking tone. Curtis's eyes took in the scene without seeing very much. He was panting, a half-smile on his lips.

When Margaret was sure that the episode had spun itself out, that everything was finished, she began to experience a tiny bit of relief.

The broker touched his fingertips to his mangled nose. He examined the blood. He looked lost in a reverie, a philosophical consideration of clotting factors, of hemoglobin. The big man shook himself, and the bouncer who had his arm dropped it.

Then, like a man reaching into his hip pocket for a wallet, the broker worked at getting something out of his belt, or his pants, something back there, something snagging and not coming out as easily as it was supposed to.

It took awhile, but he finally got it out.

The pistol was black—a dead, carbon black. It made the man's fist look pale and freckled. The people in the restaurant had stirred, surprised, disturbed, and, Margaret sensed, perhaps even a little pleased at the tussle they had witnessed.

Now chairs toppled, bodies fell to the floor, there was a general gasp, a cringe throughout the room, as the revolver, dull and chunky with its snub-barrel, searched up, away from the floor, up toward Curtis's knee, his groin, upward.

The fist was trembling, the pistol unsteady as the fingers worked to unfasten a safety or a catch, thumb and fingers hesitating as Margaret forgot every promise, every sorrow.

11

Her father had known it: the moment is everything.

The feel of the felt on the bottom of a chess piece, the subtle absence of sound as the piece slides across the chess board.

She did not know what allowed her to act. Later, she would understand. At that moment she knew only this room, this tableau. Just a step was all it took.

She put her hand over the pistol, over his fist. She said, in a whisper, "Thank you so much for doing everything you could to help."

What an absurd thing to say. She sounded like a demented stewardess, or lethally sarcastic—or both. She had no idea what else to do.

But then, just that simply, she did.

His hand was cold. Her heartbeat was so strong she could feel it in her fingers, feel her pulse against the man's knuckles, against the gun, each heartbeat moving the man's arm minutely but urgently as his eyes met hers with an expression of anger fading to shock: what am I doing?

Then the room flung itself into motion. There were hands, faces, voices. Two uniformed police were there, grappling the big man easily and kneeling on him, fastening the handcuffs on him as though they were a well-practiced team, the two cops and the arrested man all a part of a crew of stunt men.

Margaret found herself sitting, gazing at the unwrinkled white table linen. Someone thrust a glass of water into her hand. It was the police bureaucrat, and he was saying, "Don't worry about a thing."

*	*	*

There was nothing like his painting. She had run across it in the local library as a girl, the big volume of contemporary art, much of it already boring and out of date.

The Sacramento summers were hot, the sun broken by elms and oaks. The winters were, to a girl, long and ceaselessly wet, the lawns bleached white by frost. The art she could find, needed to find, found herself thinking of the first thing in the morning, always eventually left her dissatisfied.

But not Curtis Newns. His work did not have "sparkle and magic," as the notes in the book expressed it. Magic, Margaret knew, was what her own art relied on. Even in high school she had earned awards, savings-and-loan-sponsored art contests, county competitions, harbingers of the success she would be enjoying ten years later. Her drawings had always been, in the phrase of an early catalog, "deft, delightful," deer rendered in colored pencils, the inevitable grazing horses in watercolor. Magic was charm. Magic pleased. Curtis's work had something better—it had power.

The local bookstore had carried books about railroads, paperback mysteries, cookbooks, the books that her neighbors found diverting, helpful. She had ordered the catalog of his "Burn Heaven" show and called up every other day until it arrived. She sent away for posters of his shows, and her father took pains to say that he found Curtis Newns's work "very interesting," trying to establish a link with a daughter he knew he had lost.

But her father had chess, and the articles about chess, the problems he created, over the years of her mother's increasing bitterness with a husband who was "a hopeless adolescent." He had chess, and he had fishing. Her mother had called him, with pained affection, "the man who flunked adulthood."

Only in the end did Margaret see that her father was not a dreamer at all, that her mother was wrong. But by then the chess tournaments, in which her father would play twenty nervous, brilliant people at a time, and the chess problems he wrote, and the computer firms he consulted with, beating every piece of software anyone sent him, were all in the past.

On the wall of her bedroom as a high school student she had hung the glossy, bright print of *Skyscape*. Someone somewhere believes in life, the painting told her, believes in the sun that is traveling toward you across the empty morning. A *New Yorker* article Margaret clipped and saved said Curtis brought the power of Monet into a "post-industrial feel for the last wilderness, the sky." Margaret knew this was true, but she also knew what humanity the great painting implied, what faith.

She had dreamed once that she was lying in bed naked, holding an art book copy of *Skyscape* to her breasts, the cold resin-slick page on her nipples as she rocked, eyes closed, to peak after peak of pleasure.

They left The Blond Spike. There were a few photographers, an Eyewitness News van. People wished them good night.

Curtis said nothing. Margaret drove. It was good to have the driving to make her concentrate. There was a truce between them for awhile. They would be silent because it had all been said before. Because words of any sort reminded both of them of promises, and promises had once again failed.

I could just say: it's all right, Curtis. Forget about it. And for awhile it *had* been all right. Curtis was moody, fiery. She had known that.

They had moved to this high-security building in Pacific Heights because it was safe. No fans could stalk Curtis to his doorway, no striving fellow-artists could waylay him for a kind word or a loan. The police took special care to watch the politicians and fellow celebrities who lived nearby, and the building had security guards. They were on the fifteenth floor, and the penthouse apartment was so big she felt that she lived in a house perched, somehow, on the edge of a cliff.

The apartment was decorated with paintings, his own work, things he had done before he met her at one of his openings. She had been just another one of many, she knew, just another smile uttering compliments.

Then they were home.

You couldn't see the beautiful paintings in this light. They were maps of night sky, glints of bad light off the acrylics, the oils. When he was like this she knew he hated light. They sat in the dark.

Well Margaret, she asked herself like an interviewer, that withered little man from the *Chronicle*. How did the evening go?

Exactly as planned. Hey, don't look surprised. I planned this.

Our little way of having fun.

Curtis did not move. She poured him some cherry-flavored Calistoga water, the refrigerator light illuminating the kitchen, the light reaching him where he gazed down, like someone trying to recall something that would change everything.

She put the glass on one of the coasters her mother had given them for Christmas, enameled copper rings backed with cork. Margaret felt a little sorry for her mother. The woman never knew what to give them, never sure who her daughter was, what she liked, what she loved.

He left it untouched. The sparkling water made the faintest fizz, a happy sound. If only he could speak. That would begin their lives again. But he didn't talk. He sat, but it was not the posture of a person at rest. She wondered if she had ever really understood him. Maybe, she thought, she wasn't the right companion for him. Maybe she had no idea what it was like to be him, to exist inside his body.

Margaret found the telephone. She pushed the memory button at the top of the row, over the police and the fire department, and the button Curtis never pressed, Bruno's number in Rome.

The lawyer's voice was sleepy, but as soon as she heard Margaret's "hello," Teresa asked, "Is anyone hurt?"

"Well, not hurt. Not the way you mean it."

"Good Lord," said Teresa, and Margaret could hear the woman fumbling for a lighter, snapping it, inhaling. "What happened?"

Margaret told the story. She told it well, and even made it sound a little bit funny. Another breezy evening with Curtis Newns and his wife, the former Margaret Darcy, the Bay Area's artistic Fun Couple. "I thought it was okay when it was over. Like it was almost a joke." She gave a little laugh, inviting Teresa to find this all amusing.

Teresa did not laugh. "Are you okay now?"

"I was always okay."

"How is he?"

Margaret glanced at him. Curtis did not move.

"Calm," said Margaret.

"Really—what's he doing?" She had known Curtis for years, and Margaret was still a relative newcomer, and ten years younger than Curtis.

"He's okay." Meaning: I can't talk now; he's sitting right here.

"They didn't take him into custody." It wasn't a question, more of a statement to be confirmed.

"They were more concerned that we could drive safely."

Curtis was rarely arrested. It was a part of his power—the law did not dislike him any more than women and critics.

Margaret continued, "I was ready to tell everyone that the other person started it, which was a little true. Or else mention your favorite phrase, 'mutual combat.' And the restaurant loves him, they'll probably put up a plaque."

"This man took a concealed weapon to a restaurant?"

Margaret spoke through her tears, "He collects rents. He had a gun permit." He wasn't even a loan broker. He worked for an absentee landlord, renting out apartments in the Mission. And it turned out he wasn't even a real estate agent. His broker had fired him.

"You know what I'm going to tell you," said Teresa.

"I know exactly, and I know you're right."

Teresa said that now it was time to forget about the police and think about other issues. Maybe it was time to think about Curtis. Maybe it was time to think about her own future. She meant: someday he'll hurt you.

And Margaret was listening, but she wasn't listening with her complete attention. Curtis was on his feet.

He walked to the sliding glass door, and undid the latch. The door slid with a low, pleasant sound, and then Curtis stepped out onto the balcony.

She had always been afraid of this. She had hesitated to buy one of these penthouses, fifteen stories up. She herself suffered just the slightest bit of vertigo. Nothing really dramatic—just that spark of anxiety when she approached the edge of a great height and that realization that it would be so easy.

She had not been afraid for herself. She had been afraid that Curtis would do this: step out, stand there, and then throw one leg over the retaining wall, balance himself.

And be gone.

He wasn't over the railing—not yet. But he was leaning on it, looking out at the bay, the cool night wind streaming along the half-opened drapes, making the pleated fabric billow and float.

It hit her: she could not trust him. She had never been able to trust him. She could not help him, either. He was beyond her.

It was as though the love was an extra organ in her body, a gland with ducts and veins. When they drew the symbol of love as a stylized heart maybe they had an idea, after all, maybe it was something like that, secreted somewhere near the liver, or behind the real heart, the one that beat out life. Curtis was a part of her.

Teresa's voice was a tiny squawk. Margaret lifted the phone to her ear. "I don't know what he's going to do."

The telephone cast light, a pale glow from its buttons where they lit up. When Margaret hung up the phone, cutting off whatever Teresa was saying, the room was too dark. She hurried onto the balcony.

Curtis stared down at the city glow of the clouds reflected in the wrinkled bay. He turned to face her, and put a hand out; a gesture of acceptance, benediction, but also a way of warding her off. She could not see his expression, only a faint gleam from his eyes, but she relaxed inside, knowing—sensing—that he was not going to hurt himself.

"It's cold out here," she said, a way of telling him that she would be happier when he was back inside.

He nodded. He stepped back into the apartment, and she fastened the door behind the two of them and drew the drapes shut, as though that barrier would make a difference, as though that was all it would take to save his life.

She fumbled, and found a light.

She blinked. Curtis sat on the sofa. His head was in his hands.

She wouldn't talk to him now. She would wait.

But the feeling now wasn't one of being powerless. Her feeling was something else. Now that she knew he wasn't going to do anything terrible, a new feeling was free to sweep her and she felt herself breathing hard.

He did not make a sound.

She said, when she could not keep quiet any longer, "We have to change the way we live."

He looked up at her with a tired smile, a smile of such elaborate world-weariness that she wanted to slap it.

People who didn't know her very well thought she was nice. She could manage. But she had grown up around nice people, people who lived on elm-lined streets and went to church and followed baseball, and she had sworn away all of that for this.

For what? This was his first marriage, but at thirty-eight Curtis had worked his way through one relationship after another. More than one of his ex-lovers had moved far away, to New York, London, to avoid risking seeing him again.

"I want to help you," she heard herself say, her voice remarkably firm, as though she knew exactly what to do.

He was laughing, quietly, his shoulders shaking. There were tears in his eyes. Because they both knew that there had been so many therapists in the past, long stays in health resorts in Mexico, vitamin B injections, Jungian analysis, earnest months of drug and booze-free living only to end in the legendary and even publically approved spinouts.

The phone had been ringing. It was a phone they had bought recently, and it made a peculiar warbling sound Margaret did not at once associate with incoming calls.

It was Teresa. "I'm coming over."

Margaret reassured her.

"You don't realize that he is really a textbook case," said Teresa. "It's not drinking, and it's not temper."

Margaret insisted that Curtis was going to be all right.

"You've been the picture of patience," said Teresa.

Margaret heard a strange sound, a noise that wrenched her vitals, because she knew exactly what it had to be.

She let the phone drop. She was wrong, she tried to reassure herself. She had to be mistaken.

He had gone into the studio for a moment and brought out a knife. It was an ugly, paint-crusted blade he had used for everything from sharpening pencils to applying paint to canvas when brush and pallet knife seemed somehow pallid alternatives.

The multicolored steel was in Curtis' hand, ripping through the canvas of one of his most brilliant paintings. What van Gogh could do with a field of wheat, Curtis did with the energy and color, the sweep and vitality, of lanes of freeway. A painting like this transformed the mundane landscape into a place of passion.

The blade was sharp. It tore through the glistening artwork, the line dangling in shreds. It was hard to force the blade through the canvas. The old knife was something primitive, something shamanistic and brutal, weapon as primal art. She almost thought—wanted to hope—that was what it was for an instant. He was doing something impromptu and sudden, something good.

But the feeling in her stomach told her the truth. She had her arms around him, but he was muscular and seemed rooted where he stood. She fought for the blade, but he tossed her away with a single chop of his arm.

The canvas was white, slashed through.

12

He could have explained to her if he'd wanted to, but he didn't feel like talking.

This old knife was having trouble. It was stained and ugly, although it did have a decent edge to it. He had a whet stone and an oil cloth and kept the blade keen.

"Please stop it," she was saying. He had started back to work again. He really loved this old knife, but he had to face it: it didn't cut canvas like this worth shit.

If he did not destroy the painting, they would just come and take it.

The cop from the press liaison office said that the man was going to be charged with something, not to worry, go home and take it easy. That man had been there with a mission. He had been working for someone. The deal was: get Curtis to act crazy so we can sue him and sell his paintings to the highest bidder.

So we can burn them.

It was brilliant the way the world worked. You had to be careful. Margaret, for all of her intelligence and all of her goodness, didn't understand that. She didn't understand that what you made, you could unmake. So he was cutting these really pretty good oils, strong paintings, but they were his. It was okay.

Her eyes were wild. She was actually afraid. That stopped him. He didn't want to frighten her. He didn't want to do anything but have her calm down and let him finish cutting up this stuff so then he could carry it out to the garden and have a good fire. Then he could take a shower and go to bed. It had been a horrible evening.

It was starting to be a horrible night. My God, couldn't he just take care of a little personal business for awhile? Cut up his own work and throw it away and then go to bed. Couldn't he do that?

You painted something and it evolved into a thing that wasn't yours. He painted in his head, now, started with a blank space and filled it with juicy pigment, in his mind. The only work he had done in an age was in pencil, putting her image on paper. She fascinated him.

He turned again and showed her the knife, like: I'm busy here, can't you see that? And she backed away, with her eyes all big and practically sticking out of her head. She put her hand to her throat.

Jesus, she was such a sweet girl. What, twenty-eight? That's right—they had her birthday about a month ago. No, two weeks. She had brunette hair that was streaming down her shoulders, and she had that dark-eyed look that made him think of early movies. She looked like a silent movie heroine, all pale and big-eyed. In silent movies if you didn't overact you were not really coming out of the projector and onto the screen.

"You think I'm going to cut you with the knife," he said, making his voice sound nice.

"Don't cut up those pictures, Curtis, please," she said, trying to hang onto him.

"They *are* mine," he said.

"They're beautiful!"

They were, in their way. That was a part of the problem—it made them all the more valuable. It was a matter of logic. He tried to explain. "Sooner or later someone will get a lien on my property. Teresa can't work miracles. It will happen, and I won't let my paintings fall into the hands of people like that. He wasn't there by accident."

"You aren't right, Curtis, you don't have any judgment."

Now *this* made him just a little bit angry. Just a little bit pissed off. Because he *was* an experienced artist, and a professional. And he knew what was real.

Somebody told him that Monet had once owed money to the French government. The tax collectors were closing in. He destroyed over one hundred of his paintings.

"Look," Curtis said, really forcing himself to sound calm. He impressed himself. He sounded wonderfully calm, completely in control. "Look," he said again. "I told you I was sorry."

"Please stop it, Curtis."

"I'm sorry about the restaurant. I'm not sorry about this. This is okay. I'm rational. Relax."

His friends said she was just a wispy, soft girl, a woman from the Central Valley. Just another of those earnest, beautiful women you can pick up every day on the way home, six pack in one hand, woman under the other arm, your daily minimum requirement set for another night. They might be smart and they might have talent of their own but they are lightweights. Pretty. Soft-voiced. A dove.

But he'd taken her to Reno, and they'd stood there in the Chapel of the Chimes and the minister was even nice about it, shaking his hand and saying the old, dumb, serious things and the art world had not been amazed so much as amused. Curtis Newns had gone and *married* one. Why? Why go to all the extra trouble?

But they were wrong. Not gloriously wrong. They had a point. She was quiet. She looked good in tight pants. She had one of those figures you associate with angels, pink-nippled and innocent but with that other-worldly ability to shock. Margaret was complicated, and it was Curtis himself who was the human cartoon, the caricature, the man you could just put a label on and know all there was to know: Curtis Newns, whose signature on a canvas was money in the bank. Curtis Newns, world's oldest *enfant terrible*.

He loved her. There were some basic truths. He had skin, he had hair, he had bones, and he loved Margaret.

He got the paintings cut up, all three, and stomped the frames, and it was a pretty good job. You really couldn't tell what the paintings were supposed to be anymore. He rolled up the flapping canvas. A good night's work.

"It's all right," he said. "I'm done." It was a lie. He planned to go into the bedroom and finish the job.

"I won't let you touch the paintings in the bedroom."

He showed his teeth. Showing a woman his teeth was usually a pretty good method to get them to shut up for a second or so.

"I won't let you hurt them," she said, her back against the bedroom door.

He liked the way she put it: *hurt them*. To her the paintings were alive. They were alive to him, too, but in the way that cattle is alive to the rancher. It walks, breathes, and dies.

He was going to take each work and slash it, and then take it down to the freeway, 101 south of Van Ness, and let the wheels finish the job, the endless traffic, the trucks and the cars, the rolling stock of the entire country.

He had painted many pictures of freeways, the search for happiness transformed into a blitz of color and speed. Hockney had said Curtis was the "Turner of traffic." Curtis enjoyed depicting the freeways at dawn, the russet lanes already filling with the points of light that implied destinations, responsibilities, dreams.

Some people envision themselves diving into rivers. Curtis dreamed of plunging into eight lanes.

He wanted it all back. After years of having people following him, eagerly awaiting his next painting, he would like to roll it all up and lose it.

Where had she learned this kind of courage? Margaret wasn't afraid of much. Look at her, now. She was going to do something terrible if he tore up any more art.

He used his Jack-the-Ripper-speaking-very-sweetly tone. "Let me into the bedroom."

She didn't move. "You're going to sit down in the living room where I can keep my eyes on you."

He gave her one of the looks that scared the shit out of women if you turned it on them on a first date, made them wet their pants and go dumb. Avedon said Kodak wouldn't print looks that bad.

And she gave him a bad look back. It was pretty impressive. The girl was still there, looking back.

And he laughed.

They both were laughing. Her laugh was a little brittle, a little hysterical, but it was a laugh. It was funny, this ongoing battle that had just now culminated in a staring contest and then it was just too much and they had to laugh. She thought it was all okay.

He could hurt now. Really hurt her.

Because she was trusting, had her arms around him. And he still had the knife.

This thought made him wrench away from her. He threw the knife, hard. It struck a doorjamb, and trembled there, splitting the wood.

It was himself he didn't understand. It was his own mind he didn't know any more.

"I'm going to go sit down," he said.

"That's right." She was leading him by the hand, guiding him, trusting him. "Sit down here," she said gently, with a caring tone in her voice.

All he could think was: don't let me.

Don't let me hurt her.

A knock sounded at the door at the same instant the doorbell jangled. Someone heavy-handed was there. There were steps on the hardwood, and softer ones on the carpet.

I'm trapped, he thought.

Have to get out of here.

Teresa Madison stood beside the coffee table, a tall woman, refined in appearance, her black hair with a single splash of white. She was regal. She looked like the Statue of Liberty come to life to kick some legal butt. There was a security guard behind her, looking over her shoulder.

"I don't know how you put up with it," Teresa was telling Margaret.

"I don't know what's he's going to do," said Margaret, her voice broken.

Jesus, maybe Teresa was in league with the bad guys somehow. You can't tell with lawyers. Maybe Margaret was too. Look at this: he was surrounded.

Trapped.

If you're really surrounded, there's only one way out. Even Custer carried a derringer so he wouldn't be taken alive. The phrase had a nice ring: only one way out.

Taken alive. You don't want that to happen. Fifteen floors ought to about do the job. Let them see what kind of art they could get out of him after that.

He stood, and then he stopped himself. He couldn't understand the look in their eyes. Teresa was a friend, wasn't she? And Margaret—he trusted her, didn't he?

He put his hands to his eyes. His hands were trembling.

He just wanted a few moments alone so he could rethink a couple of things.

He knew he was right. He knew he made sense. But there was just a little bit of doubt. Just a little.

He was afraid.

13

It was day three of the death threat.

Another day in the thrill-packed life of Red Patterson. He had to think of it that way, right out of a boyhood television series. He was a fighter for truth, justice, and the American psyche.

There had been another call to a local radio station. A man's voice, according to what Angie had chirped over the phone: Red Patterson was going to have his brains blown out.

The stage had a cooling system. Nice, cool air blew from a grill in the floor. It was usually very refreshing to stand there and feel glacial air up his pant legs. Today the cooling system was paralyzed. Twice during "right back after this" one of the powder puff experts had to dust his face so he wouldn't gleam under the lights.

The taping wasn't going well. Two mathematical geniuses, twins who were joined at the head, turned out to be irritable. When one member of the audience asked how they "managed toilet stuff" the twins replied that they were interested in nonlocality related to the pilot-wave theory, and weren't interested in talking about going to the bathroom.

Only Patterson's best efforts saved the show, moving the audience near tears as he asked the kind of questions that would make the irascible twins appear courageous, which, of course, they were. At the end of the show there was applause, genuine, loud. The human spirit was wonderful.

He was on the phone to Loretta Lee as soon as he was in the dressing room. "The twins were awful," he said.

"I told you they would be," she said.

"Don't they realize they're lucky to be on TV? If people want to know about how they get sucked off they should tell us."

"The burn victims next week are going to be great," said Loretta Lee.

"How great?" said Patterson.

"Lots of scar tissue. Survivor guilt. Suicidal depression."

He sat in the dressing room listening to Loretta tell him about the upcoming guests. No secrets, there was a guarantee on that. These future guests wanted to talk. The taped show played silently on the monitor.

Something wonderful was happening to the world. There were no secrets anymore. Child molesters and rapists had confessed their crimes on his show. If you wanted to kill someone you broadcasted it. And it made sense that some people wanted him dead. There were people who did not admire his work. They had a point. Paul Angevin had said his show would end up a "freak circus," without the dignity of at least being honest about itself.

He took a slug of Diet Coke. He tossed down the towel he was using to rub his face clean.

Loretta Lee had a wonderful telephone voice, calming, sexy. Patterson watched his image on the monitor. I'm good, he thought. I can't help it.

Too good to quit.

"They were joined at the head, right?" Loretta Lee was asking.

"At the head. Like two ice cream cones stuck together," said Patterson.

"It makes you stop and think," she said.

Patterson said that he guessed it did.

The limo pulled into the large, virtually empty garage, and they waited while the garage door thumped gently shut behind them.

The house in the Marina had always been a tasteful fortress, a clean-lined, rectangular building with few windows and a wall, low profile, and easy to guard.

But he couldn't find solitude, even now. He paused in the atrium beside a potted palm. He heard the murmur of voices, and the trill of the telephone. His house was, essentially, the muted, dignified campaign headquarters of a man who never lost. It was always like this, but tonight there were more people than usual.

His life was an entrance from one stage to another. He checked his reflection in a hall mirror, and only really registered what he saw after he had stepped away from the looking glass.

He was a handsome man, better looking than ever. He couldn't help it. He didn't, in a way, even think it had anything to do with him—not the real him, the actual, sentient being. At the age of forty-seven his hair was just beginning to darken, less the sunset-red of his younger days, an autumn brown untouched by gray.

The name on his birth certificate was Stephen Boyd Patterson. It was not clear why his parents had chosen the first name. He suspected some religious inclination had made his mother anchor her son to the first Christian martyr, the spelling old-fashioned. The middle name was easy to understand. William Boyd, movies' Hopalong Cassidy, had once loaned the married couple enough money to satisfy a collection service.

Patterson had a wrinkle above one eyebrow, and his mouth had a determined set to it. Otherwise, he was the virtually the same man, in appearance, who had stepped from a local newspaper column, offering advice on bed-wetting and premature ejaculation, to syndicated radio to television, the man who had turned the talk show format into a forum for what one television critic called the "hyping of American angst."

What he needed was a neck massage from Loretta Lee. She was downstairs in her office, on the phone, no doubt.

He shook hands, asked if everyone was comfortable, and he knew that, as always, he made that golden impression on people. The living room was populated with CBS security advisers, two plainclothes detectives, and that striking, well-dressed blonde, Angie. She was the representative from the mayor's office, and was the power here.

He paused at a side mirror. And then he reentered the theater of his life, made sure everyone there had the various diet colas and flavored sparkling waters of their choice, and had Jeff, the man who could make every drink in the book, make him a predictable and hammer-simple martini, with a single olive, straight up.

The cocktail went down fast, and tasted clean, sharp. The attractive young lady from the mayor's office was at his side. He knew that she was going to run down the list of "everything we can do," reassure him, confide in him how much she had liked a recent show.

Loretta Lee joked about this kind of thing, but she would be very pissed off if he actually did engage in a little corporeal dalliance with this city official. He was not at all surprised when the mayor's representative said, "I'll get rid of these people."

"They're here to make sure I don't drop dead," he said.

"You won't."

Patterson thought that he'd like to be a little more certain about that. "The person who calls the radio station is male, right?"

"We think so."

"You mean it might be a woman with a very deep voice. Or maybe it's a transsexual, halfway through hormone therapy—"

"Like one of the people you get on your show."

"Why don't they do voice prints?" asked Patterson.

"They're working on it. But what if they do a print and it's no one anyone has ever heard of? Just a voice."

"Just a voice that calls up and says it's going to kill me."

"We think it's the same voice every time."

"Isn't science wonderful. You narrowed it down that much." There weren't really that many people here, it just seemed that way. Everyone was reluctant to go. They wanted to be with Red Patterson in his moment of danger, share his trials with him. It wasn't just professional duty. They wanted to be here if and when it happened.

It was almost a party, except for the tension. Someone knocked over a half-empty cola, and salted peanuts spilled from someone else's grasp. It didn't matter. The carpet was due to be cleaned to-morrow. Jeff made him another martini, and, when all the other visitors had departed, or at least retired to their squad cars and look-outs, Patterson offered the young woman a drink.

"Angie," she said, telling him her name, as though he might have already forgotten. "No thanks."

There was a courtesy involved even in such relationships, and Patterson had always stressed the importance of gentle behavior. He had always tried to be civilized in his relationship with women, even courtly. He was about to sip his drink, but stopped himself. "Angie Turner."

She smiled. "I was watching your video on memory just the other day. You called your trouble with names your own personal mne-monic banana peel."

"I have a theory about you," said Patterson. "My theory is that you're trying to be seductive, but that you actually hate me and halfway think it would be a good idea if I was dead."

She kept smiling. It shut her up for a moment, though.

He paused, eyeing the drink in his hand. "I don't have a private life," he said. The way he put it made it sound like no problem at all. "All my fears, all my weaknesses, have been on the show at one time or another."

"There's no reason why you should so much as look at me," she said. Maybe her feelings had been hurt. He couldn't tell. Maybe he should apologize. "And, on the other hand, why should I want to go to bed with you?"

He was right—she thought that being slightly obnoxious made her more attractive. Maybe it did. "I'm tired," he said. "I want to get away from all of this." He stopped himself. He had not been prepared to be so honest.

She said, "You can, can't you? You can afford to do anything you want."

"Anything."

"I finished your book. I think anyone as smart as you are ought to be free to do anything he chooses."

Patterson nearly laughed, but did not want to appear insulting. He knew that liberty was the one basic ingredient he most lacked at the moment. He did enjoy certain comforts, it was true. He did own some prize pieces of art. That was so important to him. The glorious Jackson Pollock, the de Kooning, even—and this was reason enough for security—an early van Gogh, from the period in which he was so heavily influenced by Japanese prints. And, the prize of the collection, on the far wall, the Curtis Newns, a vision of the San Diego Freeway the way few people ever saw such a highway, a study in freedom and desire.

He invited her to follow him to his private office. As she walked with him down the corridor, she said, "We think it's an organized group," she said.

"A Kill Patterson club."

"Probably not very many people. It wouldn't take all that many."

No, thought Patterson. It only takes one.

They entered his office and Angie handed him a cassette. "Go ahead and listen to it. See if you recognize the voice."

She was one of those blonde women who have decided that red is their color. She was right. Her lipstick, her skirt, were dazzling, arterial red, but it had the effect of making her look somehow generic, another striking woman in a town full of female professionals on the make.

"I'm not sure I want to," he said.

"It could help. And you want to help, don't you?" she said with what she must have thought was a seductive smile.

"If it's someone I know I'm supposed to be able to tell you." Her smile *was* fairly seductive, he thought. "I have to warn you— I'm terrible at stuff like that."

The door opened and Loretta Lee took one look at her, at both of them. "I'll take it from here," said Loretta Lee.

Angie said that she was consulting with Dr. Patterson on security.

"He's safe with me," said Loretta Lee.

The tape was a voice, but Patterson could see why there was a little confusion as to sex, identity—anything specific at all. If a garbage disposal could speak it would sound much like the voice on the tape. "Dr. Red Patterson is going to die."

"I thought it said something about my brains," said Patterson.

"It's not funny," said Loretta Lee.

"Angie told me it said something about my brains getting blown out." Actually, Patterson was feeling just a little sick.

"It's some kind of voice filter," she said. "So you won't know who it is."

"It's very effective." He considered ringing the kitchen and asking for a tray of something easy on the stomach. He was like a guest in a hotel, living as though this was another man's home, another person's life.

Maybe Paul Angevin had foreseen this, too.

That night, Patterson stared at the black nozzle of the firesprinkler in the ceiling.

How *did* the twins manage it? Did they take turns on the toilet? And sex. What a scene *that* must be.

But the early shows had been wonderful. People with problems sat before an audience. They talked about their lives. They found themselves stronger afterward. The show had evolved into something brittle, hard-hitting, and just sometimes a little mean. But it was still beautiful, when the magic worked.

Paul had said that he would do everything in his power to keep the show from ever being broadcast. It might start out with focus and dignity, he had predicted, but all that would decay.

Maybe tomorrow, Patterson thought, I will be killed. It certainly would solve a few problems, and it would guarantee the keeping of a few secrets, although Patterson knew he was absolutely innocent.

There was no question about that at all.

14

"You poor dear," said Renata. "Is that what you ordered?"

Bruno had really terrible things he would like to say to Renata San Pablo. She had delayed him, made him stay away from Andy a few more precious hours.

Instead he gave her a smile. He had a simple policy in dealing with people like her: utter insincerity. "They look lovely," said Bruno.

Bruno gazed at what had been set before him as a "Continental breakfast." Two little pastries flavored with fruit preserve were abandoned on his plate.

"I have one cup of decaf every morning," said Renata, "and then nothing at all until after four."

He had hated leaving the drawings with Margaret. He should have done something to keep his hands on them. But Margaret herself had stymied him. She was sweet, surefooted, like one of those nimble mountain goats one reads about, well-balanced in oxygen-poor air. Margaret of the Yard. Why be cruel to her?

He had decided it was wrong to lie about Curtis to Renata. Telling her that Curtis was working on something grand would be a way of putting pressure on himself and on Margaret. After all, in the weeks ahead he was the one who would have to call or visit Margaret and ask how the great new work was coming along.

On his arrival at the Plaza Hotel, the young man at the desk had said, brightly, "We have a message for you." And there it had been, a cute little computer printout that read: "Can't make tonight. Breakfast tomorrow?" By which Renata meant a meal well into the day, virtually a lunch. He had tried calling Margaret and the answering machine had been turned off.

"I can't eat sugar anymore," said Renata. "It gives me a headache."

"How awful," said Bruno.

"You didn't answer my question about Curtis Newns."

What I would like to do, Bruno thought, is reach right across the table and give her left tit a pinch. A hard one. A pinch and a twist.

It had been the question Bruno expected, the one he knew everyone would be asking him.

But answering it would be difficult. Bruno's words would be repeated, and Renata was always dangerous. If he was silent too long she would draw her own conclusions. Bruno decided to take that little risk, after all. It was not difficult. A little lie can be fun. "I came away from San Francisco with a very exciting secret."

"You devil."

He would make her wait.

"Don't torture me, Bruno. You'll regret it."

"I would have thought that's exactly what you deserve."

"You're so sweet." She was both bovine and fanged, an ungodly combination. He could handle her easily, but she had that animal persistence. You couldn't ignore her for a second—that was her charm.

"My lips," he said, "are sealed."

Renata leaned back in her chair. Bruno suspected that she had practiced this look over her five decades, the way she looked at her appointment secretaries and ex-husbands. "I heard he's back to his old ways."

"They seem perfectly happy."

"You saw them both?"

The potted palms that surrounded them were graceful, even adding a touch of elegance to what was really a place of terrible service and worse food. "Naturally."

"I'm so glad," she said, crinkling her eyes. She meant: if you're lying I'll kill you.

He said nothing. He enjoyed Renata. She bought art from museums in need of a new sculpture wing or that pricey new director, sat on the art until it was even more valuable, and then donated the inflated art to other museums, taking a huge write-off. She had created a foundation, named after herself, to actually own her paintings. *Skyscape* had been on "traveling loan" when it was burned. The insurance money from the loss of *Skyscape* would be put to good use, and might even end up funding that dream of hers, a museum dedicated to her own—admittedly excellent—taste.

He enjoyed the thought of teasing her. He sampled his cherry danish. He was accustomed to the tasteless bread and delicious caffé latte of Rome, but he had recalled, from his youth, an America of wonderful breakfasts—crisp hash browns, and fluffy scrambled eggs, and if you ordered breakfast pastries they arrived huge and hot, shot through with raisins and confectioner's glaze.

"I saw that thing about a fight in a restaurant," said Renata. "On the news this morning."

"Yes, wasn't that amusing?"

"Good old Curtis, you mean."

Maybe, thought Bruno, that's what I mean. Curtis did act like that, in past years, when he was a very productive artist. A scuffle or two might be a good sign.

"I was wondering, in an idle way, if he'd been working," she said.

What she meant was that she did not necessarily want a new and impressive Newns on the market unless she got a chance to buy it first. Renata did not like things to be complicated for her. She liked to make difficulties, not suffer them.

Perhaps it was partly out of spite for last night that he took the risk. Perhaps he was for a moment inattentive, but later he would consider that it had felt and sounded like a blunder without actually being one. It would, there was no question, cause her some unease.

"He's working on something very fine," he said.

Her nostrils flared, just slightly. The wildebeest scents water, thought Bruno.

"How wonderful," she said.

There was a spell of quiet. Then Renata could not feign indifference any longer. She had never been much good at feigning anything. "What's it like?"

Why not go all the way, he thought. "It's a painting, naturally."

"I don't believe it." Did she hear how she sounded? "Bruno, you're teasing me."

"This painting," said Bruno, "is going to be exquisite."

"Of course it is. It's wonderful. Tell me what it looks like."

"I'm not prepared to describe it in detail."

"Is it something fine and sweeping, like—" She had trouble finishing the thought. Even Renata had feelings.

"It is."

"No!" Renata widened her eyes, considered, then let doubt cloud her eyes. "He can't."

Bruno knew how to play silence out, so much line after the shafted whale.

After awhile, Renata offered, "People would kill."

"This will be worth killing for," he said.

Renata had that look Bruno particularly hated in women, that hunger. It did, though, make her look impressive. "I want to see a photo."

He shrugged. "It's barely begun."

She looked at him with an expression that was not friendly in the least.

"I'm telling you the truth. It will take time," he said.

"I made him a wealthy man," said Renata.

"I know how important you are to Curtis."

Some gallery owners were mere dealers, businesspeople, sometime investors. Renata was of another league entirely, and she knew it. "Who else knows your 'secret?' "

Bruno felt himself becoming circumspect, now that he had something Renata wanted, even though it was not something that actually existed. "You are always first with any news I have about Curtis," he said. Then he almost wished he could be frank with Renata. This surprised him as a sign of possible weakness in himself. "Curtis is still Curtis."

"Tell me about his wife."

"She's refreshing."

"Not our sort of person," said Renata.

"She's intelligent, maybe a little innocent." Why was he being truthful with this woman? he asked himself.

"But she inspires him," Renata added.

Like many otherwise worldly people, Renata believed in "inspiration."

"I think she does."

Before Margaret, Curtis Newns's art had ceased, unless you call one botched start after another a kind of experimental creativity. The question was: what was Curtis about to do? He might resume his career—or continue to fade.

"Her father was something interesting," Renata said, sipping her decaf.

"He wrote books about chess."

She absorbed this, wrinkling her nose. "You're fond of her," said Renata, exaggerating *fond*.

But he *was* fond of Margaret. A likable, direct girl, in a world of people like Renata. And himself.

"We're monsters, aren't we?" said Renata.

It was the sort of thing that made Bruno realize why, years ago, she had been the first person to know. He remembered sitting in the airport so intent that a kind woman next to him told him how breathing exercises could help with fear of flying. He had not been afraid. He had been rapt. He had seen an artist who would change his world. Renata, a woman for whom art was a form of nuclear weapon, had believed him, made a few calls, and made Curtis Newns a name.

Why have I told her such a lie? Bruno asked himself. When Renata finds out that Curtis is not working on a new painting she will destroy me. She will whisk through my hard-built fame like a wrecking ball, because forgiveness was not one of Renata's characteristics.

Tomorrow he would be in Rome, with Andy, and they would have nothing to do with any of this. Bruno was very good about forgetting unpleasantness.

But Renata was saying, "You must let me see a slide of this painting, Bruno. You can't keep it secret from me," and to his own horror he was was saying that yes, maybe he could manage to send her a slide some time before long, a statement which made Renata smile.

Because Bruno knew that as long as Curtis Newns was important, Bruno Kraft was a man whose future lay before him, whose comments would be solicited, whose face would appear in magazines.

As soon as Curtis was known as a relic, Bruno would begin to be just a little bit dated, his life one of those pleasant reruns screened at three in the morning when all the more lively and youthful have long since been broadcast.

And surely, Bruno reassured himself, Curtis would be painting something wonderful soon. It had been a long time.

It was not like Bruno to pray. But just now he couldn't help it.

15

"You'll see a doctor," said Margaret.

The bedroom was quiet. It reminded her of that day in Sacramento when her father lay unable to move, unable to speak. The room had been cool, the light like this, muted to the point of total absence. But she had been able to see enough to know that he still heard, still knew.

She soothed Curtis, gently brushed the hair from his forehead. It was a pallid euphemism, to say *doctor* when she meant *psychiatrist*.

He seemed about to say something, taking in a breath of air, lips forming a word. But he subsided.

"If you don't . . ." But she couldn't say that. She just couldn't bring herself to say it—it wasn't true.

"I'm not going to hurt you," said Curtis.

"Of course not," she whispered. Of course you won't hurt me, Margaret thought.

He closed his eyes, then opened them. She could read his question: what's happening to me?

"If you don't change, Curtis. If you don't get help somehow." Go ahead, she commanded herself. Maybe it's true, maybe it isn't.

He struggled through the effects of the drug. "I promise."

"You'll see someone," she said.

His voice came as though from far away. "Someone who can help me."

Curtis was asleep. The Thorazine was working. That, and the fatigue. She had given him the shot herself. She had felt terrible, the needle slipping into him, the plastic wrapping that had protected the disposable syringe rustling beside him on the bed.

What was it like, she wondered, to be so afraid. She gazed at him from the bedroom door, and then shut it, careful not to make a sound.

Congratulations, she told herself dryly. You just made it through another colorful night with the man you love.

Another night like that and one of us will be dead.

Teresa was waiting in the living room. The imposing woman was gazing out at the colors dawn cast onto the Golden Gate and the headlands beyond. Curiously, Curtis had never painted this view, had never done any painting at all during their marriage. Margaret felt that if she herself started painting again, the first thing she would attempt would be the wheat-bright color of the cliffs.

The television was on, the sound barely audible. Margaret did not want to hear what Teresa was about to say. She busied herself in the kitchen for a moment, pouring coffee. She filled only one cup, her own remained empty.

There was something else she was trying to avoid. The new bare spaces in the wall were disturbing. Art restorers could work miracles, she told herself. Surely the paintings could be repaired. Still, the sight of the empty spaces before her and the memory of the knife ripping through the canvases made her cringe.

There had been other bad nights, many of them, but it had never come to this. Margaret did not even want to talk. "He's all right, now," she heard herself say.

Teresa took the cup and saucer Margaret offered her. "He's never going to be 'all right.' "

"He's gradually getting better," said Margaret.

"He's not—he's as sick as ever."

"I'm helping him."

"You're lying to yourself. We all admire you for your efforts," said Teresa. The attorney turned to admire the view once more. "But you should be realistic."

"You want to help arrange a divorce," said Margaret.

Teresa half turned, as though to hear something far away. The heat from her coffee licked at the window. Teresa had a classic profile and an imposing presence. She had rescued Curtis from lawsuits and jail, and at one time, briefly, Curtis and Teresa had been lovers. "That, and a few years in a sanitarium. I still feel the same way. You shouldn't be surprised.'' She left the window, putting the coffee untouched on the table.

Over the last two years, Teresa had been loyal, sure, patient. There had been no one else to turn to. "I believe in him," said Margaret.

Margaret was surprised at Teresa's response. The glamorous attorney put her arms around Margaret. "We all know you did the best you could."

It was a legacy from her father. Her father had been cheerfully frank about the way he viewed the world. There were people on the inside, in power, he had believed, and then there were the people on the outside. Peter Darcy, author of articles on the Catalan Opening Strategy and the little-known Hegland Defense had seen himself as one of life's outsiders.

"Leave him to me. Let me make the decisions if you can't. He's beyond what anyone can deal with," Teresa was saying. "You can't pretend that you can control him."

Margaret was an outsider. She was not one of those people accustomed to having their way. She felt, as her father had, that this gave her an advantage. She had fewer preconceptions, fewer debts, slimmer expectations. She could live on faith. "He does what I ask him to do."

Teresa gave her a short, intense look: does he? "You can set up a trust for yourself, with my help. Make yourself financially secure before he starts—"

"Before he starts costing me too much money," said Margaret, completing Teresa's thought.

"How much do you think it'll cost to repair those paintings?"

"It doesn't matter," said Margaret quietly.

"I don't think the insurance companies will cooperate when they know what happened to them. Maybe that doesn't bother you. You can pay for the repairs. This time." Teresa waited, and then continued. "Women can't afford to be fools, Margaret. But maybe you don't have to worry about money. You're doing brilliantly. Someone was telling me we're going to see Starr of the Yard on the cartoons every Saturday."

"They have people working on it, in Manila. That's where they can afford to have people ink in all the pictures." But it was a pilot, an hour-long version of her first book, and not, thank heavens, one of those rigid, aimless animated series she thought must aggravate children rather than entertain them. She had helped with the script, and while the work had not been easy she had enjoyed it. It was silly, though, to even think of her slim career at a time like this. "They had trouble with Earl."

"Earl?"

"He's Starr's companion. The duck."

"Yes, of course." When Margaret was quiet for awhile, Teresa added, "What's the matter with the duck?" Somehow it was important to keep talking about something reassuring.

"He has so many feathers," said Margaret.

"Naturally."

"It's hard to ink them. He's semi-naturalistic. And he has so little personality. I even took him out of some of the later stories."

"You should have picked some other sort of animal," said the lawyer. "Ducks are overdone. But it doesn't matter—the goat is the one who matters. I saw a pack of Kool-aid with Starr on it. Business must be good."

"I'm sorry about the Kool-aid," said Margaret. "I don't think Starr would care for that."

"You're a success. Enjoy it."

Margaret turned on the remote and watched as the television picture clarified itself. It was the early morning news.

Margaret had always declined to learn chess. It was her father's game, and she knew that she could never approach mastery. She did enjoy fishing with him, though, the boat chugging down the Sacramento River, catfish fighting in the plastic bucket. And sometimes all the way out under the Golden Gate Bridge, donkey engine silent, the sail bellying, the tide running out. She had not enjoyed the fishing so much as the way the boat sliced the swells, her father squinting up from the helm.

She did not let herself think about the heat, the record-breaking temperatures of his last day. Her mother had been permanently changed by the fact that her charm, her allure, could not keep her husband alive. Margaret did not let herself think about many things, and yet she could not say that she had forgotten or suppressed them, banished them from her mind. She carried the past with her, half-known, like the feel of her tongue against her teeth.

"I'm not leaving until you've made a decision," Teresa was saying.

"Curtis must have been terrible to you," said Margaret.

Teresa's eyes were darker for a moment.

Margaret put her hand on Teresa's arm; the woman was stiff, proud.

Margaret had become pregnant after their marriage. Not before—after, she was sure of that. Curtis had not believed it possible, and his reaction had been so emotional that Margaret had been certain, at first, that he didn't want the baby. But then she had understood. He was amazed that he, Curtis Newns, could be a father, as though fatherhood were something for other, dull, unimaginative men, commuters and consumers. Those men, she knew, faceless and boring, but they had something that Curtis felt he lacked, some essential root in life.

This had been her gift to Curtis, this voice in her womb, this sweetness that woke her with the feeling of being ill, and feverish, so feverish that the illness was a source of insight, strength.

There had been weeks of happiness. Then one afternoon she did something uncharacteristic for her—she took a nap. And as she dozed she had a dream, one of those half-aware, heavy afternoon dreams when one is still certain that sleep has not arrived.

In the dream there were steps, distant steps growing louder. Steps rasped on a front porch, the front porch of her family home. It was warm in the dream, summer, but still early in the season, the summer still rising, not yet harsh. There had been a knock at the door in her dream, an insistent but not unfriendly rapping.

And the door opened, and her feeling in the dream had been mild shock, bemused concern: how can I open the door from here? I'm on the bed, there's no way I could reach the knob from here.

Then she woke, and there was blood.

Teresa was saying that she remained true to Curtis, but a man like that belonged in a hospital. "I would manage things for Curtis, and for you," Teresa said. "The estate would prosper. You would never regret it."

Then they both were quiet, watching the television. The news was covering the further violence at The Blond Spike.

"I told them," said Teresa, her voice taut, "if they ever put Curtis into a story like that again I'd skin them alive."

Curtis looked good in the splash of light as he exited.

The story described a gun, the heroic well-known artist, and further evidence that a San Francisco night spot was attracting trouble.

Teresa was on the phone. She punched numbers, and then hung up, hard. She said quietly. "Do you see how hard it is to get anything done?"

"I know you've worked hard."

"You don't know what work is." Teresa punched more numbers.

"I can't keep doing this. That story looks okay. He looks like a hero. But you and I know the truth."

"Curtis *is* a hero."

"You're pathetic," said Teresa, slamming down the phone. She gathered up her handbag. "I'm not going to keep doing this."

Margaret said nothing. The television news had reached the top of the hour. They were recounting the morning's top stories.

"Or maybe," Margaret said, watching what unfolded on the screen, "there's a better idea."

16

Patterson would never get used to feeling this way: this is the day I will die.

And then again, maybe it wasn't. It gave a sort of zen-like flatness to things, not at all the battlefield zest he had once studied as a young doctor, interviewing shattered veterans. Maybe dying was as disordered as living.

Loretta Lee was mouthing something at him. She had applied a new shade of lipstick to her full lips, a color he would have called butterscotch, a look that made her appear exotic and edible. This made her impatient kiss of the air, attempting to get his attention, all the more hard to ignore.

"You have to hang up," said Loretta Lee in a whip-crack whisper. "You have two calls waiting and—"

He waggled his fingers at her. He was sitting in his office wasting his time: he was explaining things to an assistant producer, one of those faceless successors to Paul Angevin. These people always sounded young and sure of themselves, and they always liked the way they sounded, the inflection you hear in radio ads for banks with free checking.

The television was on, mute, in one corner. Lucy was talking to Ethel. Ethel was nodding in agreement. Lucy looked way too excited about something, classically manic. Funny how black-and-white looked so much more authoritative. Maybe if the Archangel Michael showed up on the *CBS Evening News* he'd be colorless.

"I realize that Mr. Poole is highly regarded as an expert in studio

98

security," Patterson was saying. "And he's a nice, nonabrasive presence in his way." Patterson could have said that small, nervous little men were not what he needed around his studio, but that wouldn't sound right.

"We want to take every precaution," said the young voice on the phone.

"Maybe I don't like Mr. Poole because we more or less share the same first name. Maybe he reminds me of one of those little animals you read about in story books, mice who wear cute little blue jackets. I don't want to get into all kinds of psychological explanations for why I feel the way I do."

"No need. Not at all. We understand. You want to take a second, though, and look at this the way we see it. Not so you'd change your mind, but so you'd have some sympathy."

Patterson couldn't believe this. This was beginning to sound an awful lot like an argument. *Sympathy.* Loretta Lee was putting one hand on her hip, and throwing the hip out and heaving a huge sigh.

The conciliatory voice mistook Patterson's silence for encouragement. "You are what matters. You know that. We only wanted to make sure you have the absolute, best we could possibly find—"

Sometimes Loretta Lee thought she was the most important person in the solar system, in addition to being about the most seductive. Patterson did not take his eyes off her when he said, "If I have to look at Steven Poole again I will personally strangle him." He hung up.

"The cops are on line three," said Loretta Lee. "But before—"

Patterson jabbed a finger into the button on the telephone. Loretta Lee was right. It was the police. They had a list of hundreds of possible hit men, former guests on his show. They had a list of dozens of former girlfriends, jealous husbands, ex-secretaries, former household help. Patterson was much-loved, and had a way of forgiving his enemies. Still, there were a few dry rocks above the surface of his forgiveness, people who despite their faith in Patterson might wish him harm. The police had a list so long it was a work of epic literature. The voice on the phone actually began to read this list.

Wonderful, thought Patterson, dropping the phone into its cradle.

Jeff's coffee was magic. It was always just the right temperature, and it was delicious, flavored with Kern County cream.

"There is one more phone call I think you really have to take," Loretta Lee was saying. "You should've taken it before you wasted your time with the cops."

"It's a good thing you're beautiful, Loretta Lee."

"I'm not the one acting like a jerk."

"Unless it's Dr. Penrose come back from the dead, I am not talking to anybody else on the telephone," said Patterson, fumbling for the remote so he could turn off the television.

"This isn't your usual telephone call," said Loretta Lee. And the way she said it made Patterson cease examining his own face on the front page of the newspaper, and look up.

There was the blinking light on the telephone, insistent. Loretta Lee told him who it was.

He didn't say anything for a moment. He tried to read her eyes. "It's got to be a hoax," he said.

"I recognized her voice." His look was skeptical, and she added, "from interviews."

"She's on the line now?"

"She was."

"Jesus, you made her wait?"

"I can fit him in today, I think," said Patterson, after a pause, as though riffling through an appointment book.

"He's afraid of being seen," she said. "If you could talk to him in private."

"Don't worry, Mrs. Newns. You'll never regret this."

"In absolute confidence," said the artist's wife. "You don't know how afraid he is."

"Absolute confidence," he said.

"In secret," she said, her voice so low it had trouble finding its way through the receiver. "Please."

When he was off the phone Loretta was watching from the doorway. Her eyes were wide, questioning. Patterson couldn't even make a sound.

He didn't show up.

Patterson had his consulting room open, had adjusted the curtains because he had heard that the talented man did not like too much light. The room was spacious, adjoining his house but secure from it, as consulting rooms often were in the days when doctors held their surgeries in the same buildings in which they lived. The stage was set—and the great man was late.

It was early afternoon. Patterson was pacing his consulting room, fuming. He knew what was happening. He could tell. Jesus, he'd been a total idiot. This was a hoax, just as he'd suspected from the very start.

It was like the time someone called up pretending to be Elizabeth Taylor. He had spent twenty minutes talking to this breathy voice on the phone about the dangers of diet pills. This was too much. He was not such a fool that some strange voice on the phone could talk him into delaying his entire day.

Curtis Newns could see anybody in the world—why would he bother consulting Red Patterson?

In the beginning he had felt that a psychiatrist was the child of an especially potent god. Dr. Penrose himself had exemplified a moody, benevolent divinity. That a forgetful, grumpy, lively troll had the power to enlighten—this was proof of Heaven's arbitrary bounty. Forces of nature stood with the psychiatrist, strapped invisibly like the gunslinger's bone-handled firepower. Yet, year by year, Patterson had squandered this gift.

He had delayed the taping of today's show. Something important had come up, he had explained, no explanation necessary, really. Patterson had something important to do: nothing more need be said.

Someone was making a fool of him. Maybe the assassination committee had decided to shift tactics. Don't shoot the man, just irritate him to death.

He stiffened.

There was a murmur beyond, somewhere in the house. There were muffled steps. there was someone in the hallway, and he could hear Loretta Lee's voice saying something polite and inaudible at this distance.

There was the carpet-whisper of someone's approach.

The figure in the doorway did not appear eager to enter. The man was dark-haired, with a cool glance that did not look unsettled. It looked measuring, calm, doubtful.

It's him, Patterson thought.

It's really him.

Patterson made the usual gesture of welcome, one hand out indicating that the man could step this way, through the open door. Patients appreciated a quietly welcoming gesture like this.

The artist stayed in the doorway. He looked back to smile at Loretta Lee, ran his fingers along the walnut doorjamb, scuffed his shoes over the carpet as though testing its quality. And only then did he slip into the room. He stood there, as though an assailant hid, waiting to do him harm.

Patterson shut the door carefully, as quietly as possible. There were only the two of them, he thought. The two men.

Patterson found this thought somewhat funny. Why shouldn't there be just the two of them? He was a psychiatrist, and here, after years of public ministry, was a client.

Newns did not sit. He stood with his hands thrust into his pants, eyeing the place, tilting his head as though to listen to this room's special variety of silence. His dark brown hair was uncombed, and he wore a loose, casual sweater. The artist regarded a watercolor on the wall. Patterson had painted it himself, a hummingbird pausing before a geranium.

My God, thought Patterson. I should have taken that old thing down. I had no idea he was going to stand there like this and look at everything.

Newns took a few more steps to examine a print on the wall, an old etching of the O'Connell Bridge, not really much of a work of art, more of a souvenir. Of all the art works I own, thought Patterson, he has to look at these.

The River Liffey had been gray-green and the day had been misty, although when Patterson had commented in a nearby pub that it was a damp day there had been a cheerful argument. No, this wasn't mist. This wasn't even fog. This was a fine day. Encouraged by stout, Patterson had selected this print in a local shop.

This was the culmination of his dreams—to be able to work with a man like Newns—to help someone grand, someone who gave so much to the civilized world. Patterson supposed there was an element of vanity about his excitement. Newns was a famously mercurial individual, a man whose temper was widely accepted as the serrated edge to his genius. To be the doctor who at last helped steady this artist, helped anchor him—that would be an accomplishment indeed.

Perhaps the world at large would never know about this illustrious client. Patterson would accept that. He had a high enough public profile as it was. It was enough to be here with the man who at the age of nineteen had mounted a one-man show at the Whitney.

At last the artist spoke. "You painted the hummingbird?"

Patterson considered his response. The work on the wall was unsigned. Patterson could say that he found it somewhere. Hummingbirds were an important symbol. There was no telling who had painted it. He coughed. "Yes, that's one of mine."

"It's good. The flower, too."

Patterson was embarrassed. He began to say that he should have taken the trifling thing off the wall, but the artist interrupted him.

"Tell me where I should sit."

"Anywhere you like," said Patterson.

The artist sat in the obvious chair, the one with its back to the hummingbird.

17

Patterson had been meeting celebrities since his childhood. He knew how it is with famous people. They are always shorter or older or fatter than you expect, or they smell like garlic. The guy who plays Tarzan is dressed for golf and laughs too much. The guy who plays Superman has hair sprouting out of his ears.

But sometimes a famous person looks and acts like someone who deserves to be famous. It's like being at the zoo, and walking around the corner to the lion enclosure—and there is a lion, as advertised, ignoring the blackbirds.

Curtis was a lion. It was something the artist was probably not aware of, the way a muscular man, or a beautiful woman, might wear their vitality without knowing it. Patterson had wondered, as a boy, what it would be like to have the circus cage clang shut and have a lion sitting there, blinking the way cats do, yawning the way they do, just a few feet away.

Patterson sat across from Curtis. He knitted his fingers together, and realized that, unthinkingly, he was trying to imitate Dr. Penrose. This was irritating. Patterson had long ago outrun the insights of his early therapy, if not his respect for the distinguished physician who had provided it.

It was a strange feeling, this excitement, like stage fright, a sensation he had not known in years.

Newns leaned forward, and clasped his hands. Patterson could not help thinking: those famous hands. He had watched that film about Newns several times, the famous one that won the award at Cannes

fifteen years before. An interviewer had asked Newns to draw something. The request had sounded irritating, a bright, I-bet-you-can't
tone. Newns had borrowed the reporter's Bic and executed a sketch
of the interviewer that was reminiscent of Rembrandt, a quick portrait
that would have been unflattering if it had not lifted the smart, shallow reporter to the level of universal humanity.

Silence. This was not ordinary silence. This was the quiet of a
man who would have great trouble speaking.

"What was it that made you take your wife's advice?" asked
Patterson when it was plain that Newns was prepared to sit there for
a long time, his hands clasped.

Newns looked at Patterson, his lips shifting from thoughtful pout
to a warm, surprisingly delightful—smile. "Gratitude."

Patterson smiled in return. This was going to be difficult—and
exciting.

"Gratitude for her," said Newns. "And I was thankful that you
agreed to see me," said Newns. He had a pleasant expression, watch-
ful, encouraging.

It had been some years since Patterson had practiced his first-
interview technique, but he remembered what to do. "The patient
may not even wish to claim his own agony," Dr. Penrose had said.
"He may wish to adopt the strategy that it is you, in your inability
to understand at once what brought him here, who suffer the
greater problem."

"She asked for my help," said Patterson, "and I am glad to give
it. But I wonder—what made her call me?"

There was no immediate verbal response. But the question did win
from Newns an acknowledgment. The smile faded. The artist looked
away, at the walls, at the expanse of a room, which was almost
entirely unused space.

If that was what the artist saw when he looked at the room around
him. Patterson knew what enigmas people are to each other. More
than once he had read newspaper accounts of people on trial for
murder receiving their life sentence "without emotion," and marveled at the simple-minded arrogance of the reporters.

In therapy there is nothing more insistent than a question. A statement can be refuted. "You came here for help," can be refuted in
many ways: help wasn't what I wanted. I was forced to come. This
isn't what I expected. I have changed my mind.

But: "Why are you here?" is more difficult to rebut. I don't know why. I'm not really here. I'm here physically, but not mentally. Why do you need to know?

Newns stirred at last. To speak was apparently an effort. "I've had other doctors. Everyone knows about me." He left it like that for awhile, a simple statement.

Patterson did not respond. He was fumbling for the most honest but at the same time most diplomatic answer when Newns added, "Don't you know what I did last night?"

Patients know by instinct the power of the question. The question steals the truth, huddles the fire from the cave, and brings it home.

"No," said Patterson. "Tell me."

There was a pause. Then, "I don't believe you."

That's interesting, thought Patterson. He's calling me a liar. "What is it I should know?"

"It was on the news."

Patterson could not recall having heard specifically anything that might have caused the artist to seek therapy today. Patterson felt like rejoining that a death threat acted as a considerable distraction. "Perhaps you could tell me."

There was no answer for a long time.

When Patterson had almost decided that the artist was never going to make another sound, Newns said, "I hate this. Jesus, what a disappointment."

"You're not comfortable here." It was Rogerian half question, wimpy understatement. That kind of therapist sat around waiting for the client to teach himself to jump through the hoop.

"People shake your hand," said the artist, "and they feel like they can go on living, don't they?"

Patterson decided to stay Rogerian for the time being. It was boring, but it didn't risk anything. "You feel as though you won't be able to go on living."

Newns seemed to be answering another question, the earlier one about the office. "I'm comfortable enough," said the artist after a silence.

Patterson could sense the absent audience. They were getting up to get a beer, go to the bathroom. They were reaching for the remote on the coffee table. "What is it about the office you find most troublesome?"

"I didn't say there was trouble."

Dr. Penrose had always stressed the importance of the patient's defensiveness. "They know what is wounded, and how to avoid being hurt. Watch them, listen, and you will discern the injury."

"But you did indicate that there was something about this place you didn't like," said Patterson. As he spoke he had an uncomfortable thought: I'm rusty. I'm really terrible. I've been out of the therapeutic arena too long.

But Newns was not being merely defensive. This was more like ritualized combat: gentle, quietly tense, but a chess game nonetheless. And the man was testing Patterson: how bright are you? What can you do for me?

Can you help me?

Patterson could not suppress his anxiety. Ten years ago I would have been confident, sure. I've lost something.

It was a surprise when the artist said, "I need help."

You can't do what you've been doing. You can't trade your life for years in front of the cameras, America's favorite shrink, and then expect to be anything but a fake. I want to help you. But I can't.

Curtis's speech was slow, each syllable a weight. "I wouldn't be here at all," said the artist. The words did not come easily. "But I'm afraid."

Where's the old Dr. Patterson, the young man who knew exactly what to say?

"I'm afraid, too," said Patterson.

"Of what?"

"Someone's trying to kill me."

That was good, thought Patterson. Inject a little reality into the interview. Tell the client that we all have problems. But that wasn't why Patterson had made the statement. Not at all. For a moment Patterson had not been a therapist. He wanted to dispense with all pretense.

Patterson needed Curtis Newns. It was that simple.

There was a long pause. Then, "I thought someone like you would be used to that kind of thing," said the artist.

"Would you be used to it?"

Curtis considered. "I'm not like you."

"What sort of person do you think I am?"

"Someone who has gotten used to danger."

"Someone who doesn't feel fear?"

Newns considered. "Not like a normal person."

"If I can't feel fear maybe I can't feel other emotions either."

"Maybe."

"Feelings like compassion."

Newns gave a slight smile. He was a remarkably handsome man, a friendly lion. "Possibly."

There was something a therapist had to determine during the first session. It was integral to the therapist's role in the community, as well as his responsibility to the patient. "Are you afraid that you might hurt yourself?"

There was no answer.

"Are you afraid that you might hurt someone else?"

"I love her."

Patterson waited, listening to the room, to the vaguest fibrillation of the traffic somewhere far away.

"I'm afraid," said the artist. "I'm afraid of what I might do."

Patterson knew all about the power of movies, and television, even that less magnified venue, the stage. People who have been on television carry with them, no matter how slight or colorless their off-screen appearance, a residual glow, a power.

This power was real, and it was earned, no matter how spurious its source. Most men and women setting forth to "tape before a live audience," as the nearly quaint phrase put it, would look stiff, or wobbly, unsure. They were right to be unsure.

Patterson knew how to ignite his guests and make them, for a moment, as full of hope as he was himself. He knew how to use that moment, the stage fright, the unreal weight of the lights, to capture life. He was not indulging in empty vanity when he told himself that he awakened his guests, as he awakened people far away, people he would never know, to hope.

I've been wasting time sitting here, doubting myself, he thought. The guest scheduled for today, the singer who had been arrested twice for shoplifting, could be artfully rescheduled. Loretta Lee was deft at knitting and reknitting the guest list.

Patterson knew exactly how to help Curtis. This was the day. Let another night fall, and another morning arrive, and who could say when such a chance would come again?

18

I look good, thought Patterson.

The bare light bulbs illuminated his face. Patterson regarded what he saw in the mirror as a navigator might regard a map, a very familiar map, one he didn't even have to look at anymore except as a reassuring habit.

"I can't," said Curtis.

Patterson turned away from the source of heat and light, his own reflection. It was a few hours after their first meeting. Patterson believed in moving fast. In life, as in flight, speed was all-important. You slow down and you start to sink.

He gave Curtis a smile, stepped over and put his hand on Curtis's shoulder and gave it a squeeze. This was the way a director, with professional cheer, helped an actor shaken out of character by a minor accident—a crashing chandelier, a kicking horse.

They were in Patterson's dressing room. Most guests for the show primped and paced in the green room used only for guests on Patterson's show, their nerves steadied by the presence of soothing assistants. Patterson was happy to share his own dressing room with Curtis. Patterson had stayed with Curtis all afternoon, easing the artist toward the moments that would change his life.

They were only a few minutes away. The two hundred men and women lucky enough to have reserved tickets for today's taping would already be in their seats, hushed, excited. The event had already been delayed, and delayed again.

This was big, thought Patterson. This was bigger than when the U.S.

Senator confessed that he was an addict. This was bigger than when that famous singer brought snapshots of the boys he'd molested.

Curtis sat on the desk in the dressing room with his arms folded. He was still wearing the sweater, and his hair was uncombed. Patterson knew how Curtis would look on the screen, intense, quietly tormented, the sort of talking head the camera adored.

Patterson selected a tie. He liked this one—little scribbled flowers, something he'd wear to a wedding. He was excited. "Leave everything to me," said Patterson.

Patterson had seen hundreds of people like this, maybe thousands. When it came time, they didn't want to step out onto the sea, that tossing water, and walk.

There was a quick, pro forma knock, and the makeup artist showed uncommon sense. She stepped in, took one look at the two of them, and stepped right back out again.

"I realize that in some ways this is exactly what you're afraid of," said Patterson, using the same resonant, soothing tone he would use on a nervous mare.

Curtis would not meet the doctor's eyes.

"You're afraid of becoming a new man. This is understandable."

Curtis gazed at the floor. Patterson had a troubling thought: what if Curtis refused to go on? What if he wouldn't leave the dressing room?

But he would, Patterson knew. This always worked. The earth rolled, the sun burst over the horizon. The miracle always came again.

"You know that ninety minutes from now you will be transformed. That's how it is with me. You sit under the lights with me, Curtis, and when you walk away you will be new—changed—ready to live."

Curtis did not speak, but his eyes were bright, eager to believe. But he couldn't—not yet.

At this point, it didn't matter what words Patterson used. It was all in the tone, the cadence. "You've seen it work," said Patterson. "You know it works, and you don't really doubt it."

"You once made a blind man see," said the artist, his voice quiet.

More than once, Patterson wanted to say. No big deal. Hysterical symptoms were easy to flush down the psychic toilet. "You owe it to Margaret."

The artist took a deep breath, nodded. But he looked away, into the mirror.

"You're going on, Curtis, because I promised Margaret that I would help you." I don't know how I do it, marveled Patterson. My voice changes, I feel myself grow taller, and here I am—telling this illustrious man what to do.

Curtis looked away from his reflection and shook his head. "I just can't believe—"

Patterson smiled. "Don't believe. Don't. Just take what happens as a gift."

"Narcissus will never wake from his faith," Dr. Penrose had written. "His empty faith in his own image will always both satisfy and fail him." Patterson knew better. What we wake to is always morning, and if an artist can be shaken into confidence by the stage, the camera, a kiss of public love, then who can say that it is an empty future that lies ahead?

Paul Angevin had called it an evil thing. To share confidence with a doctor or a priest, a lover, a group of friends, that was one thing, Paul had argued. But to play to the voyeuristic hunger of millions— that was not medicine.

Too bad Paul isn't here now, thought Patterson.

They were late. They were going to broadcast live on the East Coast, and local programming in the Bay Area was being interrupted. It had been a while since Patterson had taken such a risk before the Big Audience.

It might not work—but if it were a sure thing, there would be no thrill. There has to be a moment during which Lazarus is still, stone-silent, deaf to the command to come out.

The makeup artist was there again, and Patterson indicated that she could stay. She was a butterfly, her touch sure, professional. A voice called out the dwindling seconds. Curtis did not flinch when he was burnished, just slightly, by the makeup, anointed, sent into that other level of reality, the fiction that illuminates.

It was time.

Curtis gazed out at the glints of color beyond this fierce, blank heave of light.

Feeling paralyzed him. Above, beyond the lights, was a black void and a suggestion of girders, cables. Red Patterson's desk was a polished expanse of oak. The furniture was well-made, not the cheap stuff of many television sets. The carpet in view of the audience was boardroom thick, a luxuriant cobalt blue. Behind the desk there was no carpet at all, just an expanse of black tiles on which Patterson's chair could turn silently on its casters.

All those people, thought Curtis. All those eyes. But he could not concentrate on that virtually invisible audience. The doctor's presence tugged at him. If only there were some way to break through to the doctor. If only there were some way to really show him what it was like to feel this way.

They talked for a long time about Curtis's career, his early success, his travels. There was a break, and Curtis sipped water from a paper cup, and then it was time to talk again. At last the chat twisted, got hard. "What is it you're afraid of?" asked the psychiatrist.

As though fear was something you could trace with a pencil, like the outline of the hand. As though talk could accomplish anything. There had to be a way.

Curtis couldn't talk.

During the breaks Patterson did not take his eyes off Curtis, telling him how wonderful Curtis was doing, how fortunate they all were. And then they were back again, the four cameras out there somewhere, still, hulking shapes that Curtis gradually was able to forget. They didn't matter any more.

What was it like, the famous psychiatrist should be asking, to have a life like yours? People asking him to sign cocktail napkins, women sticking out their bare arms and, from time to time, other parts of their anatomies, for him to draw a "cute little boat like the one in the museum." This had gotten to be a party tradition. "Cute little boat" referred to the galleon in *Spanish Main*, a pastiche of images he had intended, in his wily twenty-year-old mind, to depict nothing much. But because of the title, people saw one of the squiggles as a "caravel out of a luminous summer," as one really urpy critic put it. So there it was, even on notecards, the "Spanish Main: Detail" that did, he supposed, look a little like a ship if you wanted it to.

The lights sucked up the air. The glaze of hair on the backs of his hands were irradiated by these lights, pulled upward, the tug of an electric current. Well-designed air conditioning kept Curtis from feeling hot, and Curtis had to admire the lighting, the light used as paint, giving the two men shape and hue.

After awhile the audience was gone, the dim figures of technicians beyond the cameras faded. He felt strangely alone with Red Patterson, but better than alone, the air rich with the attention of unseen companions. Suddenly it was like prayer, but prayer you were sure was being heard. "I can't paint," Curtis said.

"What happens when you try?"

Curtis liked this man. Patterson had presence, and one thing Curtis knew: the beautiful has life.

"I can't begin to tell you," Curtis said. And he almost had to laugh at the way the words came out of him. Even prayer falters. There was no way he could communicate with a living soul.

The psychiatrist was sitting there. Curtis was sitting there, and they were both helpless for a moment. It was absurd to think that therapy would help.

Dr. Patterson sat there waiting, his eyes saying: go right ahead.

"I trust you. But," Curtis continued, "it doesn't do any good to talk. I've never had any faith. . . ."

"In words." Patterson completed the thought for him. But maybe that wasn't the way he was going to complete the thought. Maybe he had been going to say: in people. In my feelings.

There had been other therapists, drug counselors, vitamin injections, that were supposed to heal the liver and the neurons both, a brown syrup the body had somehow used up and couldn't self-manufacture.

The famous Dr. Patterson should be asking him what it was like to have a life like that. What it was like to have a life that was all electricity and color up to the age of thirty-five, and then dried up.

What it was like to stop painting, except in your own mind.

He wanted to tell the doctor—show him, let him see with his own eyes—how Margaret had stepped out of the blur of art-opening plastic wine cups and sodden potato chips.

He was sitting too long, spending too much time in silence.

"I can't," said Curtis. "I can't tell you."

"What is it you're afraid you might do?"

Oh, yes, that, prime question—the question he really had to answer. A painting was an act, a possible crime, a new life that had not existed before. *Because they want to buy or steal my work as soon as I finish it. Because they want to own me.*

Before he could stop himself, he had said just that. He had said that people were out to take his work away, wrest it from him while it was still fresh, newborn.

"Who are these people?" asked Red Patterson.

If he was dangerous, Curtis recalled, then steps would have to be taken. That was what the doctor had said in London after a blackout, the morning light bright by the time he had awakened curled around a broken bottle on Neal Street. There had been blood on the bottle, old, dried-up and port-black. Curtis had gone to the medical school on Gower Street and they had been delighted to let him talk to one of their brightest, a heavy man with black, pointed eyebrows.

"I pick up a brush, and there isn't any hope in it any more. No joy. No feeling at all. When I squeeze paint onto the knife, I stop."

Has he really said it? Had he really confessed the truth? Or had his own thoughts become so vivid, and so painful, that they were louder than speech?

"Are you saying that when you leave us this afternoon," said the famous doctor at last, "walk out that door, you will never be able to paint again?"

Curtis looked into the doctor's eyes. The doctor vanished as tears welled.

"I'm a sick man," said Curtis.

Jesus, this was going better than he had dreamed.

It was all taking too much time, Patterson thought, that was the only trouble. People were getting a priceless look into the emotional state of this artist, but television was time, containers of time filled with light. You filled up seconds, and then minutes, and when your time was full you were done. I'm doing beautifully, Patterson thought. But there was a clock in the distance, beyond the artist's head, the red digits displaying the time remaining.

And it wasn't enough. Once again, Curtis fell silent. When Curtis stopped talking, the audience shared his anguish. The audience here—and the other, immense audience—was rapt, trapped by Curtis's look, the way he tried to talk and failed, the way his eyes asked Patterson for help.

Patterson kept it gentle, so it sounded like a request. "Tell me about the knife."

"It's just a knife." But his manner told Patterson something quite different. The knife was remarkable in some way. "One of my foster mothers gave it to me. It was a present—she made some extra money selling Christmas cards. I was too young for a gun, and she hated guns anyway. So she gave me the knife. She warned me to be very, very careful with it."

Patterson gripped the arms of his chair. Of course, he thought. *That* knife. The knife Newns used in the films of the artist at work, applying the daubs of color, earth, sky, with the edge of a knife so that the paint appeared to have been sliced onto the canvas, diagonal jagged wedges of pigment.

"But I can't talk about the things I have inside me," said Newns, and Patterson saw before him a gifted man, even an articulate one, made nearly mute by his own emotions.

"But that is exactly what you're doing," said the psychiatrist. This was all so wonderful. They should be able to go on for another hour. But the red digits kept changing, the time left dwindling. In the tradition of private practice, the fifty-minute hour was always running out, but when it was time to leave the patient could say something, a last bit of anguish to build on during the next visit. Television was inflexible. The clock was a god.

The artist's voice was broken. "I can't do it any more."

Patterson waited, listening, sensing that to speak now would be a mistake. The audience was frozen. As jaded as people were, they could tell when someone was naked before them. People could tell when someone was desperate.

But all that angst-laden silence ate up seconds. They were running out of time, and there was nothing Patterson could do. During the last break you could see the floor director smiling encouragingly, and the four cameras stayed where they were while Patterson told Curtis how great everything was going.

It was the truth. And yet, the red numbers were insistent. There was a little more time for Curtis to share his doubt, for the audience to feel what he was feeling.

There was something else that bothered Patterson, a thought he barely allowed himself to consider. The famous miracle wasn't happening. This was fantastic television, but the magic moment, the cure, wasn't taking place. People were loving every minute of this— but Curtis was faltering, searching. The big, closing release wasn't about to happen. Patterson couldn't deceive himself. When the show was over, and the image of Curtis no longer captured people, some would ask what Patterson had actually accomplished.

There were sixty-eight seconds left.

"All my best work is done," the artist was saying. "I still try sometimes. But—" He made a gesture, tossing something away.

Patterson stood. He had to do something, and it had to be quick. He looked directly into camera three. "I'm taking you under my care, from this moment, Curtis. From now on I promise you—no one will hurt you."

The crowd was still, afraid to make a sound. "You will be in torment no more," said Patterson. "I am changing my life—for you."

And then, the audience realizing what Patterson was saying, there was a rush of applause.

Patterson flicked his hand, and the applause stopped. Patterson raised his voice. He spoke quickly, but distinctly. "You can have my estate in the desert, Owl Springs, miles from anything, perfect security, perfect peace. It's yours, Curtis—for as long as you want it."

The applause was loud, continuing. Patterson could sense tears in the eyes of viewers, tightened throats.

Forty-five seconds left. Again, he silenced the applause with a gesture. "I promise you, Curtis—I promise the world," Patterson was saying. The sound engineers would just have to jack up my voice, he thought, so it can be heard over the applause. "You will find there in the California desert healing like you have never known before. Your paintings will flower. You will recover your soul." He said the next words with special emphasis. "There will be a new masterpiece."

The applause then went on too long, and it was too loud. There was more that Patterson was ready to say.

"*Skyscape* is gone," said the doctor. "Destroyed."

Curtis opened his hands: it was the truth.

Patterson was feeling a little breathless, keeping the words fast. "We'll make them forget all about *Skyscape*, Curtis. We'll do something even more magnificent."

When he turned to gaze upon Curtis Newns the look in the artist's eyes silenced him. Patterson could not disguise the impulse from himself. He coveted Curtis, and all that Curtis represented. There was another feeling, too, shattering, all-healing: he loved Curtis.

Curtis was alight with hope.

Patterson was careful to keep his best profile to the camera that was panning from psychiatrist to patient.

Twelve seconds left. Barely time to help the artist out of the chair, walk him to stage front, to embrace him, the way the director liked to end the show, a nice floor shot, Patterson and his guest, credits, applause.

All she could think about was: where is Curtis? He should be home by now. She should have known, she would realize later. She should have guessed.

But she kept herself busy to help control her anxiety. She was answering correspondence. She had a series of computer files, each letter answerable by using one of several formats. The intelligent, courteous fan got one sort of letter, the gushy female fan got a letter equally polite but more reserved in tone.

A few galleries sent expensive catalogs, hoping, perhaps, for a comment from Curtis that they could use in promoting an upcoming show. Margaret entered the *thank.ltr* file and made the appropriate alterations in each case. When she was finished she printed out a letter and signed it *CN/MD*. Before they were married she had decided to keep her maiden name, feeling that Margaret Darcy was both her professional name and a name that kept alive her loyalty to her father.

The phone made its noise. She snatched at it eagerly.

It was Teresa. There was a thrill in the lawyer's voice as she asked, "Are you watching television?"

The television was turned to the all-weather station, and it took a few moments to find the right one.

Margaret dropped the remote.

She felt disbelief. She had hoped Patterson would help Curtis. She had imagined private consultations, the two men agreeing on a schedule of visits. But she had not expected Patterson to put Curtis on the show.

Then she told herself that this was what she should have expected all along. Of course, Curtis was on television. That was how Red Patterson worked. It was probably even a good idea, she tried to convince herself.

She heard what Red Patterson was saying, but it made no sense. Except that it did make sense. The meaning was quite clear.

Curtis was sitting there. He looked happy. Patterson was acknowledging applause, waving to Curtis to join him at the edge of the stage.

Curtis rose, and put his arm around Patterson. The men were hugging. Curtis was laughing, joyful. She hardly recognized him.

Margaret was only vaguely aware of the phone on the coffee table. Her voice was strange and weak when she spoke at last, asking if Teresa was still there.

"It's wonderful," said Teresa. "I'm sitting here with tears running down my cheeks. The most beautiful thing I've ever seen."

Margaret couldn't speak.

"Red Patterson will do for Curtis what he did for Cal Ackman, the designer, the one who went on to win all those awards. And Jessica Adams," Teresa was saying, "the woman who wrote those books about life among the chimpanzees. She dedicated her autobiography to Red Patterson."

All Margaret could think was: Curtis—what have they done?

19

Margaret put on a shawl because she felt cold. It was black cotton, a Mexican cloth with delightful highlights, a present from Curtis one evening, for no particular reason. He gave her things, shared jokes with her, told her his dreams, even the nightmares. She was over-reacting. Her confidence had always been dappled with foolish imper-fection. There was no reason to worry.

Curtis would be home soon.

There was a long wait. The starling squeaked, trilled, imitating nothing, Margaret was sure, simply making its own, energetic noises. Margaret told the bird that everything would be fine, that Curtis was on his way home.

The apartment was a strange place, she thought, wandering from the studio, to the bedroom, to the living room, huddled in the shawl. This rooms were empty and unkind when Curtis was absent.

No reason to worry.

Mrs. Wye called. Wasn't it wonderful, she said, to see Curtis so happy. It was so smart of Margaret to think of Red Patterson. This was such a breakthrough, and it would help so many people to see joy return to Curtis Newns.

The sun began to swell and dim, slipping into the Pacific. The early evening clouds, typical of summer, were slow tonight, clawing their way toward land.

She picked up the telephone, put it down. Jesus, where was he?

She turned on the answering machine, but she could hear her mother's phone call. "Do give us a call, Margaret, when you have

a chance.'' There was one of her mother's long pauses. ''I know
you're busy.''

Why would her mother sound so triumphant? There were other
calls, one after another. Margaret turned down the volume on the
machine so she couldn't hear them.

In an instant it all changed.

He was in the room, calling her name.

Curtis swept her off her feet, up into his arms and spun her around.

It was so sudden. He was through the door, slamming it behind
him, picking her up. She had never seen him like this.

The shawl fluttered, wafted in the air, and fell, draped over the
arm of a chair. She was breathless. She laughed, confused. ''Curtis,''
she said. ''I was so surprised when I turned it on—''

He put her down. She staggered, giggling dizzily, and fell onto
the couch.

''I was on the show!'' said Curtis.

Her voice sounded weak. ''I know.''

''I was on his television show, and do you know what happened?''

Why, she wondered, was it so hard to say it? ''You were happy.''

''Exactly. Happy! For the first time in years I believed in myself.
The man isn't like any other psychiatrist I've ever met. He makes
things happen. At first I didn't know it would work. Even during the
show it was hard to explain how I felt. But then, by the end—''

''I was so surprised,'' she said.

He gave her a look of wonder. ''It was your idea.''

''I didn't know.''

''What didn't you know?''

''That you would be on television. I thought you'd have a consultation—''

'' 'Consultation,' '' He laughed. ''People don't 'consult.' People
don't just stew in their own misery anymore. They change—all at
once.'' He roamed the room, exultant. ''It was wonderful!''

She followed him down the hall, into the bedroom. ''What are
you doing?''

He hauled a big, portfolio-sized black canvas bag from the closet.
He flung it onto the bed, and tugged a black leather carryon from
the closet, too, the sort of bag he took when they flew to Kauai for
the weekend, in those days when they were first married and the
marriage itself had given him happiness.

She had made him happy. She knew that.

She asked him again: what was he doing?

"You saw the show," he said.

Her eyes must have expressed her confusion. He stuffed a wad of underwear into the black bag and said, "I'm leaving tonight."

She stared, feeling stupid.

He glanced up at her, folding a shirt. "I'm going to his place in the desert."

Ever since the miscarriage bad news had felt like this. A bronze bell struck in her, soundless, reverberating, the resounding of her womb. She wanted to sit, but she remained upright.

A dozen questions silenced her, choked her. She was losing him. She kept herself to the easiest, most practical question. "How will you get there?"

"I'm going over to his house in the Marina. He'll get me to the airport. He has a jet." His tone implied that it was all logical.

The statement sounded so naked: "I want to go with you."

"That's not the point."

"What is the point?" she asked, in someone else's voice, the voice of another woman, someone who was still rational.

He adopted that tone men use when they have made up their minds. It was hard and self-satisfied. "I'll be there alone. Maybe I'll see him when he flies down on weekends. I'm going to paint again, Margaret. And I'm going to be away from all this."

All what? she thought. Or did she actually ask the question aloud?

Because he answered it. "All of this fear. It's safe out there in the desert."

There is a way to keep him, she thought. I just have to think more clearly.

"He promised me," he continued. "Everything is simpler and quieter there."

Curtis would never come back to her. Somehow she knew that.

"It's what I need to do," he said, jamming a T-shirt into the bag. He was always terrible at packing, everything jumbled together. Even now, she wanted to help him, help untangle his socks, help him order his life.

"Don't go," she whispered.

He didn't hear, or perhaps he ignored her. His tone was kind, patient, a man explaining the obvious. "Dr. Patterson will fly down every now and then, and we'll talk, and then when I feel strong enough I'll come back. Don't be so sad. I'm doing it for you. You can come down and visit sometimes."

She put out a hand, to touch him, remind him that she was here, that she loved him.

He laughed. He looked so wonderful, she thought—dashing, eyes bright. "Look at how sad you are! This is a wonderful opportunity, for Christ's sake. You should be thankful to Dr. Patterson. Do you realize what he's done for me?"

"You aren't going."

He gave her a look of puzzled amazement, pretending that he hadn't quite understood her.

She persisted. "I won't let you go."

She had always had an ability to tell him what he should do, and because he trusted her—and because she had good judgment—he had always followed her advice. But now he zipped up the leather bag. "I'll be in the studio," he said, "packing a few things."

It didn't happen so quickly. A person did not change like this. She knew better.

Teresa's answering machine responded to the call. Margaret hung up and tried Teresa's car phone.

"I'm stuck in the middle of a traffic jam," said Teresa. "I had to leave for Oakland right after the show." She drawled something about the "approach to the Bay Bridge," "jackknifed truck," deliberately sounding like a traffic report.

Margaret described Curtis, his mood, his destination.

"That's wonderful!" said Teresa.

"I don't like it."

"It's been a long time since I earned a fee in court. I help chiropractors set up corporations these days. You don't need a legal mind for that, you need a secretary. But let's see if I can state my case for you: he's going to paint again."

"I don't believe it."

"Don't be so selfish, Margaret."

"There's something wrong."

"You told Curtis to see Red Patterson, right?"

"I don't like this."

"You're jealous."

Maybe she was. Margaret closed her eyes.

"I don't like to be critical," said Teresa, "but I think you have a tendency to sulk when you don't get your way."

Maybe, thought Margaret. Maybe not.

"You're twenty-eight," said Teresa. "Not so young any more."

Teresa was eight or nine years older, but was one of those women who seemed to neither age in any important way, nor to doubt themselves. Even that splash of silver in her hair might well be a hairdresser's whim, thought Margaret.

When Margaret did not speak, Teresa continued, "Vanity is a natural weakness. Take a good look at yourself—maybe you're not enough for Curtis any more."

"He loves me," Margaret said, feeling her voice fade out to a whisper.

"Why shouldn't he? You're still a very attractive woman. But you didn't really expect Curtis to be happy with you until the next ice age, did you?" There was the sound of a car engine. "I don't think you want Curtis to paint again. I think you want him all for yourself."

"That's not true," said Margaret, anger strengthening her voice.

"Then what are you afraid of?" said Teresa.

Curtis closed his large black portfolio, and tossed the overnight bag beside it. He picked up the phone and called a cab. Then he stood gazing outward, his hands on his hips.

"Light like this is what kills you," he said, looking out at the low clouds blotting the view. "Try to paint this and you'll end up with nothing."

Begging wouldn't work. A tone of command would not work. Perhaps understatement would succeed. "I wish you would stay," said Margaret.

Her mother had told her that she could do whatever she wanted with her life, but she had no business marrying a man like Curtis Newns.

Her friends had envied her. "You aren't *really*," they had said. Her sister, married to a jovial, lazy man who wrote software, had said, "Why couldn't you do something normal for a change?"

Because I'm not normal. I wanted something wonderful from life, and I got it. For two years.

"If I hadn't had the miscarriage," she said, her voice hoarse, "you would stay with me."

She had put up a print of *Skyscape* on the wall. It was a stunning painting, even reduced and given the prosaic, flat finish of paper. She still kept that article from the London *Times*, the one that said that the painting demonstrated "that the horizon itself becomes human under the touch of a master like Curtis Newns." This was the same article that escaped the usually tentative confines of British journalistic prose and said that *Skyscape* was "the most important painting of our time."

Curtis saw her folder of articles once and found it amusing, all the clippings she had kept, folded carefully. Some people collected autographs, butterflies.

He put his arms around her. He told her that he would come back, that he wasn't walking off the end of the world, that he wasn't going to vanish.

And then the security guard called and said a cab was here.

And Curtis was gone.

Don't ever feel sorry for yourself, her father had said. Letting yourself feel self-pity is to give in to a form of intoxication. It is worse than even self-congratulation.

When you play a gymnasium full of chess opponents, each player keenly alert, sitting at the long, meeting-room tables, fingering their own, familiar chess pieces, you don't have time to even think, not in any usual sense. You move from player to player, perceive the move they have just made, stretch forth your hand, make a move of your own. Your will doesn't act. Your ego doesn't. Your talent does.

There might be twenty or thirty strangers there, young and eager, and they will all lose, because they don't have the talent.

Margaret knew her next move. She picked up the telephone and used the number the famous doctor had given her very early that morning, the number he had said was his private line.

20

On the way home in the limo, in the middle of feeling so good, Patterson began to think about the tape, the voice that had sounded like a talking garbage disposal. There was just a little doubt, just a tiny question: didn't he recognize that voice?

"That's what I say in my book," Patterson was saying to the voice on the phone. He couldn't remember exactly *which* book. "You make it public before a huge audience and it dies. You know who understood this? The Greeks did. No question. You purge it and you go on living. You keep it inside and you're sick—it's that simple."

"Really impressed," the assistant producer was saying. "You wouldn't believe the calls."

Yes I would, thought Patterson. He was home safe, feeling good. "People are actually progressing, evolving. They don't think the way they used to," he said, aware that this made his reference to Greek tragedies slightly irrelevant. "We don't have to be like human beings of the past. We're different."

It felt great to be able to preen a little—why not? Still, he was glad when he was off the phone. Jeff, reliable, timely, slipped a martini onto the desk. Patterson smiled his thanks. It had been a wonderful day.

He was home, in his office, watching as an old movie of his father's played soundlessly on the television screen. Finding it had been an accident. He had wanted to watch the news, because his publicist had guaranteed this would make CBS national, at the very least. And there on the American Movie Classics Channel was his dad carrying a shotgun, gesturing with the double-barreled weapon, a gun that Patterson himself had fired as a boy in the desert, blasting sun-faded Burgie cans. The old twelve-gauge was now in the Movie-land Wax Museum, beside the unlifelike image of his father.

The phone rang, his private line. "I just got off the phone with the wife," said Loretta Lee.

"She must be pretty happy."

"You want to be careful of the wife," Loretta Lee said.

"She sounded charming when I talked to her before."

"She could have Curtis examined by other doctors if she gets suspicious."

"Suspicious of what?"

"You and I both know that you are running just a little bit of a risk."

"What on earth are you talking about?" On the television screen Buck Patterson had just climbed into the saddle.

"Don't be mad when I tell you what I think. I think Curtis Newns belongs in a mental hospital."

Patterson bristled. "You forget who I am." This sounded just a little megalomaniacal, so he added, "Besides, now I'm going to start to get *real* clients."

"I wonder if maybe even you might be out of your depth, Red. And when he can't paint after all you've said, you'll look like a failure. Or maybe that's not quite the word. Maybe you'll look really bad, Red."

Patterson stirred in his chair. His hand curled around what he imagined was Loretta Lee's sexy throat. "I'll talk to her again. What's her name, Margaret. Convince her everything's all right."

"If she gets the idea that her husband should be in other hands, there might be legal means at her disposal—unless you persuade her."

On the screen, Buck Patterson was riding hard, a pace that would kill a horse. "Why don't you have any faith in me?" said Patterson, making his voice sound happy, at ease with life. "Everything'll be fine."

"I don't think she's convinced of that," said Loretta Lee. "She's not dumb. She's thinking what I'm thinking: what are you going to do with your prize, now that he's in your cage? I want to help you, Red. I'm your friend."

"What you are, Loretta, is a former patient, a woman who used to be into fellatio with assistant directors for a shot at a screen test. I know what I'm doing.''

"If you have to say so, it isn't true."

Patterson laughed, a karate-chop chortle. "You're quoting me, aren't you?"

"Who else? 'Some statements of belief are weakened by being said out loud, like a man announcing he isn't lying.' "

"That's on one of my tapes—"

"It's in your book."

"Loretta Lee, you're smart, and I love you, but sometimes I don't know."

"I'm trying to protect you, Red," she was saying as he took the receiver away from his ear.

Patterson put the receiver into its cradle. He was happy, and grateful to Loretta Lee. She was sassy and needed a vacation, that's all. Red Patterson was a man with an open mind. Everything was great, but he wanted another drink.

He had better plan some time away from that woman, he thought. She was wonderful, but she lacked a certain sophistication.

It was early evening, but the carpet cleaners were still not done. The cleaning machine was in the hall just outside the door, a sucking sound, like a wind machine, one of those big canvas belts they rotate off-camera to simulate the noise of a storm.

Later, he would remember that moment, and remember thinking about his father's Colt, how it would be easier if the Colt was here in the desk, loaded. Patterson did not own a gun, but he knew how to use one. A firearm was what he needed now. Then there wouldn't have to be people in the living room, drinking his coffee, and Angie, the woman from the mayor's office, would not be tapping on the door to the study, stepping over the carpet-cleaning machine as she came toward him.

Angie was good looking, blonde, willing, thought Patterson. She would do, considering that Loretta Lee was so busy. On the screen, Buck Patterson had just fired about the fifteenth shot in a row from his big Colt.

His son had the oddest realization. His father's image on the screen was that of a man years younger than his son was now. Patterson jabbed at the remote with his forefinger and the screen went dead.

"Leave it on," said Angie. "I like your dad's movies."

"Somehow, you don't seem the type," smiled Patterson, knowing how out of fashion most westerns had become.

"You look like him," Angie was saying.

"Do you know what I need more than anything in the world?" said Buck Patterson's son. What he needed was another drink. What he needed was for the carpet cleaner to finish and leave. "For a start, I need someone to massage my neck, right here."

"What was he like?" asked Angie, stepping behind him, her hands wise, soothing, finding the tendons in his neck.

"Just like what you see on the screen," said Patterson.

What was it like to have Buck Patterson as your old man, a friend would ask Red on the way back from a class in anatomy of the neurosystem or the toxicology of the human brain.

By the time he had fathered his only son, Buck was already a film veteran, one of those men who are called "ageless" only because their age is hard to guess, not because of any preternatural youth-fulness. Buck was described as the poor man's John Wayne in one of those every-movie-ever-made video books. What was it like to be the son of one of the world's last cowboys? What was it like to have an actor dad?

For one thing, it wasn't an act—not entirely. Buck Patterson was authentically of the West, hated barbed wire, and could ride. He had that trailer out in the high desert near Victorville. He had a crescent divot in his skull where a mare had kicked him during his childhood in a place that was never defined—Arizona or Nevada or perhaps even ordinary rural California before the subdivisions.

Buck Patterson wore Levis and a romantic, sweeping dust-gray Stetson. He had a string of live-in ladies who made his coffee and shared his bed until the day came for every one of them when they remembered something that was demanding their speedy return. Buck Patterson had a saddle and he had a six gun, a forty-five that was not exactly authentic in the strictest sense, being a Depression-era copy of the real thing. It did shoot after a fashion, although you had to aim well to the right of anything you wanted to blow up, and stand pretty close.

And during the TV series there was that ranch on Catalina Island, if you could call a stand of cactus and a pair of geldings a ranch. It was a big house, though, and you could watch the water taxi out of San Pedro roll in every day, and the big white ship, too, and the plane that skimmed in and landed on the water near the casino, which by then was a museum of stuffed wild boar and old photographs.

His dad had never liked to watch himself on television, and on the rare moments when his father saw the tight-lipped marshals he so often portrayed, he would swear and turn the channel. And by such actions Red Patterson had learned that his father was not an aging idol, he was a part of a tradition, a phony tradition, but an honorable one. When he heard his father play the clarinet or the piano, or tap dance by himself in the kitchen waiting for the coffee to perk, Red Patterson sensed a tradition of cowboy showbiz that stretched from Annie Oakley and Wild Bill Hickok, people indistinguishable from the real thing because they *were* the real thing.

Or real enough. As an adolescent, Red Patterson had always found his father embarrassing. For a man who made millions, the actor was often amazingly short of money. They lived a splashy, casual life, a new car, new clothes, hamburgers for dinner. It was hard to bring friends around to visit a man who liked to play a steel guitar and yodel. But once there was a king snake on the front steps and Red Patterson was about to chop it up with a hoe, the way boys will, thinking, innocently enough, that killing something was the equivalent of popping a balloon. And his dad had plucked the glorious red and black reptile off the concrete and held it writhing and told his son, in a gentle voice, "This snake looks pretty so you can tell it won't hurt you."

And then there was the time when the German-accented actress dropped by the duplex in Studio City. Patterson had been sure the woman had made a mistake. Nobody like that would be interested in his dad. But his father played an improvised suite from *Carmen* on the piano, and entertained the actress with some Texas swing, and then sang every single song the actress could think of. Buck knew them all, although in retrospect Red figured she must have been slow-pitching his dad, feeding Buck songs she figured he would know.

It was impressive, though, and when the boy had been sent off to bed with a bourbon-scented kiss from the blonde and a wink from his dad, he could hear them out there, romantically grown-up, their laughter out of another country, not so much in the past, but parallel to the one Buck Patterson's son was likely to know, a better, smokier, softer-lit world.

His father had not lived to see his son's career in full-flower. Buck Patterson had made a western or two in Italy, made a series of ads for "range-rugged, quarter-ton pickups," which by themselves generated a trickle of unlikely sales in Japan. And then, as easily as a man falling asleep before television, his father had died, beside yet another new female friend in an apartment in Sherman Oaks.

Patterson had loved his father, and understood his impatience, as well as the romance his father felt for both the desert and for show business. To know how to soothe a skittish mount was as fine a skill as knowing how to act on no notice at all, called up because the man scheduled to play the wagon master had mumps.

Angie's hands were intelligent, knowing. "You're good at a lot of things, I bet," said Patterson.

"I thought I got on your nerves," said Angie.

"Then I certainly gave you the wrong impression," he said.

Her lips tasted of sunlight—allspice, cloves. Christ, when was that carpet cleaner going to be done? He was right in front of the desk, now, the machine making a terrible racket. And of course you had to remember, Patterson reminded himself, that Loretta Lee was just downstairs and could walk in at any moment. Angie actually *did* get on his nerves, but nerves were complicated.

The man cleaning the carpet was familiar. The carpet machine he steered was a large disc that buffed the woolen rug. It wasn't much like the sound of a distant wind now. The noise was too loud, and Patterson was about to say something when he stopped himself. How could he complain when the man was doing exactly what he was supposed to be doing?

Patterson had never quite gotten used to servants, cooks, house-keepers, guards, gardeners. He had been raised around wealthy people who had been dishwashers, actors who found themselves playing Roman senators after years of cadging drinks in the sort of taverns that feature pink flamingo wallpaper. Patterson told himself that he should not let this black-haired, blue-eyed carpet specialist disturb the mood.

But, once again, Patterson *knew* this man from somewhere.

He was just a little too good-looking for such a menial job. He was foraging ahead with the carpet cleaner, and at his hip, pistol-fashion, the worker wore a portable vacuum cleaner, a Hoover Wet & Dry. There was eye contact.

It was the eye contact that started it, that glance, that mutual moment—this man resembled someone who had been on the show, but Patterson, with his inability to remember names, found himself fumbling mentally.

Angie had awakened to the fact that there was something wrong. It was not trouble, and certainly not danger. But Angie's job here was to make sure that Patterson was happy, and the psychiatrist was puzzled, concerned, trying to remember.

Patterson would remember this moment, too, how from the beginning the man had made one clumsy move after another.

The blue-eyed man unhitched the portable cleaner at his belt. It would not come free. When it did, he held the portable machine like a handgun, which is exactly what it resembled at the moment—a futuristic pistol, a ray gun from some old science fiction movie.

The blue-eyed man stepped away from the carpet cleaner, the big saucer of the machine continuing its blind buffing of the carpet, filling the air with the pleasing smell of artificial lemon.

The carpet machine bumped a wall, skittered with a certain dignity toward a bookcase. The machine plowed forward, like a carnival bumper car, and struck the bookcase. Books toppled to the floor.

Things happened slowly—the blue-eyed man could not get the device in his hands to work the way he wanted it to.

Angie put out her hands, took a step toward the man who by now had the Wet & Dry in both fists. Patterson played such games himself, even as an adult, pretending that a hair dryer was a death ray.

But he knew—in his gut he knew.

The front of the portable cleaner blew off. The sound killed all other noise. Patterson could hear nothing. Or, almost nothing. There was one blast, and then another.

Angie toppled back, flung farther backward by the force of each shot, as Patterson stumbled, holding Angie upright. He couldn't help it—it was an impulse. He was holding her as a shield, cowering, as her head burst.

Patterson was down, Angie sprawled on top of him, his face hot with something molten, a substance that flowed into his eyes, into his nostrils. He gagged.

They sounded like doors being slammed. Gunshots. He had a mental sense of what was happening, the carpet-cleaning man nailed against a wall by bullets, plaster and blood, things falling.

All of it falling, the entire room disintegrating, the match-head stink of gunfire suffocating. Patterson couldn't take a breath. He was drowning.

Hurt, he thought.

I can't feel it, but I'm hurt.

Loretta Lee was in the room, out of nowhere, standing in the middle of everything, emptying her gun into something on the floor.

Patterson turned his head to one side and vomited, or was it something worse—a convulsion? He retched, agonized, clearing his mouth, his throat, his being of the taste in his mouth, the stuff from the head of the dead woman in his arms.

21

There was a knock at the door, soft. Margaret wasn't even sure she heard it, a little tapping, persistent and timid.

Then, the doorbell, a set of chimes out of the bronze age, resounding and impossible to mistake.

It was Mrs. Wye. "I tried to call you, Margaret—"

Margaret put out her hand. "You'll wear yourself out," she said, "running around like this—"

"Don't worry about me," said Mrs. Wye, and the way she said it made Margaret unsteady.

"You should be resting," said Margaret weakly. "Look at the time."

The elderly neighbor was dressed in a flowing dressing gown, whispering satin and a hastily knotted sash. Mrs. Wye looked years younger, flushed and wide awake.

"Haven't you heard?" said Mrs. Wye.

The words were delivered with care, years of cinematic diction making each consonant count. The walking stick gleamed, white rubber tip lifted into the air. "It's terrible to be the first with bad news again," said Mrs. Wye.

Margaret heard the news through a sudden haze. Her own body detached itself from her will. Her arms hung heavy, lifeless. Her brain told her that she must have misunderstood.

Margaret rejected the message as impossible: Dr. Patterson had been shot. Other people were shot, too.

Mrs. Wye's voice had a steady, lapping quality, impervious to

Margaret's need to deny what was being said. It was a terrible scene, on Channel Five and Two, and possibly others, Mrs. Wye wasn't sure. She hoped Curtis was at home, and safe. "Because I worry so much about him," said Mrs. Wye.

Curtis was running.

It was dark. He had been running for a long time, but he was not tired.

He had long ago shed his black leather overnight bag, and the cumbersome portfolio so he could make his way more easily through the streets.

As a boy he had marveled at the glow of brakelights, the way they gleamed, the essence of Christmas, of Independence Day fireworks, and not hidden away for a once-a-year festival—they were on display each night, every night of the year. Sometimes colors broke upon Curtis with an inner sweetness, a spice: headlights would dissolve on the tongue, powdered sugar, brakelights would be like red-hots, cinnamon and fire, and the proud green lights would chime in like lime sherbet, dignified and profound. Curtis had thought it was a pity Goya never had a chance to see the blaze of emergency vehicles around the metallic carnage of a crash.

Art is an afterthought, one of life's sweet by-products. It was time to do something that mattered.

What a grand, bitter joke it was. He had thought that the famous psychiatrist was the answer. He had been there when the shooting started, actually within the walls of the house.

There had been a long moment when none of it made sense. The sounds from the distant rooms had sounded like rude merriment. Then the men in suits, lounging about the living room, had stumbled over each other. Pistols had been tugged from recesses in clothing. The coffee table, the chairs on the margins of the room, had been knocked over in the haste.

My God, a voice had cried, *they got the doctor.*

It was a male voice, one of the security men, the sound of his cry all the more searing because of its anguish, the men fighting each other unthinkingly in the corridor. And somehow, when he was aware of where he was and what he was doing, he was running. Someone had called out *stop him*, thinking, perhaps, that the artist was a part of the conspiracy. And he was, but an innocent part.

Curtis ran. The pace was starting to hurt. There was a stitch in his side. He told himself to think of pleasant thoughts, to drive the pain from his mind.

The first box of crayons—how well Curtis remembered, the waxy smell had been so promising. His days had been ladled, his childhood a series of caring homes, nourishment provided without much love but without much harm, older men and women motivated by unthinking kindness, as trees cast their shade in the heat without considering any alternative. Curtis did not hate life.

Was someone following him? He glanced back as he ran. Cars were low, sullen shapes. A bus was a source of tinny light, the passengers a few silhouettes of heads looking away, looking out, turning to look back at him—surely at least one, lifting a hand to speak into a transmitter.

He ran faster. Sweat made him blink. The night sky was clouded over, the low overcast lit by the city below it. The damp made his hair and clothing wet as he ran, the very slight mist darkening the sidewalk in the muddle of light under the streetlamps.

He could sense the command: *stop him.*

He was running past parked cars, his strides carrying him down-slope, toward the freeway, 101, the lanes of traffic he had re-created on canvas so many times.

He stumbled and fell against a curb, and slumped against a big metal tub corrupted with rust, an ancient mailbox. He was on his feet again at once.

Not far, he told himself.

Almost there.

He wanted to call out: *hey—look at this.*

He was about to do something they couldn't take away from him.

Curtis didn't know when he had begun to understand the way reality worked. There had not been a single moment. Gradually, over the years, he had begin to realize that his mail had been opened before he got it, and that his telephone conversations were accompanied by the slightest hiss of static, the result of an extra shunt fed into the line so that his calls could be recorded.

As he ran he became gradually aware that there was too much similarity in the anonymous men and women he saw on the street. These were, most of them, ordinary people out to buy beer and Band-Aids. But some of them, those turning away so you couldn't see them talking into their collar mikes, were Watchers.

If only he had known this all along. He had done all the right things, following what he interpreted as the correct format throughout his teenage years. He had believed, in those distant days, that the world was a meritocracy, that you achieved success in big things by first mastering the small, the academic, the local. He had gone to school, San Francisco State, earnestly taking classes for a semester or two in art history and watercolor, because he knew that to follow the prescribed procedure was to find success.

And it was success that he wanted, after a youth that was a string of foster homes, homes in Oakland, Berkeley, San Leandro. He had heard of artists hindered by uncaring parents, narrow-minded stepfathers, unloving guardians, but most adults in Curtis's life had responded with kindness. One foster father let Curtis have half the space in the garage of the San Leandro tract house, and most adults had encouraged the youth, seeing in him something uncommon.

He had worked hard on his art, drawing, painting, staying up all night, aided occasionally by amphetamines he bought from other students, and by filterless cigarettes he later grew to loathe, but usually kept awake only by his desire to finish one work of art and begin another.

He had talent as a youth, and he stood in line with his registration packet, with his application for the scholarships. His life as a very young man had been a matter of standing in line, knowing how to queue, how to wait one's turn for space in the classroom, room at the gallery, knowing how to show up to the drawing class on time, in a prominent place so the teacher could see the thin, dark-haired student with so much talent.

Until Bruno Kraft had stepped before him at his first opening, one of those white-wine and Doritos affairs. Bruno Kraft was widely published at the time, but still building his reputation. "Stop doing whatever else you're doing," the critic had said, "and paint."

The stitch in his side began to hurt badly. He couldn't tell his enemies from his friends—that had always been his problem.

The rush of the freeway traffic was loud, the ceaseless wheels of cars, of trucks, freight and lives sweeping everything to one side or the other on their way toward a thousand destinations.

Curtis stumbled again, and almost fell, but caught himself against a newspaper rack. The stitch in his side had become a steel bite. Jesus—he was tired. Sweat soaked his shirt. But he was there now—the eight lanes of Highway 101.

For a moment he saw what he had always seen in freeways, how much they promise, and how much they deliver. This is the way, the highway says. This is the way home, the way out.

He ran up the on-ramp, his knees wobbly, weak. A driver some-where leaned on his horn. There was another twisted blare as Doppler effect bent the sound of a car horn.

In an instant he was not tired. Not even a little bit. He could see it in his mind, the painting he would make of this, a brilliant, life-time-best painting, all light and movement.

The stitch didn't hurt anymore. The car exhaust was sharp in his lungs. He could taste the grit, the road grease, the fumes of brake lining and transmission fluid.

Margaret ran a red light. She didn't even see it, and then, seeing it, she was already across the intersection. She swerved to miss a woman cradling a dog in her arms. A car was double-parked in the lane ahead of her as someone heavyset and slow got out of the passenger's side.

She had always been impatient with people who complained about the traffic in San Francisco, feeling that the problem was not nearly as bad as people contended. She steered around a large, dark car trying to edge into a parking place Margaret could see with the briefest glance was way too small.

"Among the top stories we're following, there has been a shooting at the home of Red Patterson," a voice on the radio was saying.

A policewoman held out her arms, palms forward in the headlights, pale as the gloves of a mime. Margaret did not stop. The police-woman pounded the hood of the BMW as Margaret finally braked. The woman's face adopted the expressionless mask of authority as she tugged at a flashlight, her book of unwritten tickets, her radio.

Margaret left the car idling, door open in the middle of the street, and ran past the cop. The woman called after Margaret, but Marga-ret sprinted.

An ambulance made its way through the crowd, then gradually broke free of the knot of people and was free, siren running, lights hammering the dark.

Margaret tried to elbow through the crowd outside the fortress of Red Patterson's home, but there were too many people. Emergency lights flashed. Yet more police cars angled into place in the street. There was chaos, a hubbub of voices, weeping people, shocked, star-ing, blindly curious.

A path had been cleared when a body was taken out. The path closed in again as people explained to each other what they had seen, what they had heard on the radio, what someone said they saw on the news.

Maybe it was a massacre in there. Hey, it happened all the time. Someone said they had seen Patterson on a stretcher, but somebody else said this wasn't true. The crowd was stupid with excitement and someone else said the only thing that made logical sense: *They haven't brought Red Patterson out yet so he might be dead.*

Margaret climbed forward. *Let me through.*

There were too many guns out in the streets, someone said. The cops couldn't do anything. Cops made it worse. One voice rang out above the others, a man greeting his friends, who were just arriving at a run. "They shot the shit out of him!" cried the voice.

Margaret struggled, working her way toward the yellow ribbon marked *Police line—do not cross.* The yellow plastic band was twisted, the imprecation not to cross upside down, backward, all but impossible to read, and yet its message did not have to be read. Its presence bespoke crime, violence, the law hastily at work. Margaret elbowed her way further and called to the woman police officer on duty that she was looking for her husband.

The woman could not hear what Margaret was calling, and did not care to approach, but a plainclothes cop recognized Margaret and pulled up the glossy yellow ribbon for her to pass into the crime scene.

It was a house of dramatic paintings, the thick carpets, slightly damp, the still-moist nap already blotted with footprints. There was the perky fragrance of lemon-scented carpet shampoo. The rooms were quiet, but with the busy murmur of a bank, an insurance company. It did not seem like a crime scene. It seemed like a very busy place where everything had to be done perfectly.

Yes, Curtis had been here just when the shooting took place, said a cop in a blue sports jacket. "I think it was him. There's a checklist of visitors."

"But Curtis is all right?" she asked.

"I don't know. I don't even know where he is. Look around."

She looked, and she asked, but knew as she gazed at one person after another, that Curtis had vanished. When the checklist was produced, Curtis was the only name at the top of a clean sheet, although his name was misspelled *Noons.*

The crowd was stirring outside. People gathered in small groups up and down the darkened street of neat lawns and careful hedges.

The policewoman made a gesture of exasperation when she saw Margaret. "This is your car," said the woman, confirming, not asking.

"I need to find my husband," said Margaret.

The woman made a gesture, one hand out, someone waving away a very slow fly. "I just called a tow truck."

He's all right, though. Wherever he is, he had to be all right. He will come back to me, she told herself. Now he doesn't have any choice.

But that wasn't true, she chided herself. In life, as in chess, the trouble is so often that there are too many choices.

She had recorded an interview recently for KQED FM. "Curtis is about to enter a new stage in his career," Margaret had said. It was painful to remember the self-assurance in her voice.

Brilliant, she thought. Absolutely brilliant.

The policewoman was scribbling a ticket. Margaret put her hand over the hurrying pen. The woman looked up, a figure of authority interrupted, and too surprised to be displeased.

"I'm Margaret Darcy Newns," Margaret said. "My husband is lost."

The freeway gleamed where the headlights reflected on the swath of oil down each lane. It was loud, and it smelled of engine exhaust.

It wasn't going to be that easy. Cars barreled past him on either side, insensate, as oblivious as though driven by the blind.

Curtis danced toward the next pair of headlights to approach in his lane. The car grew huge, then, at the last, swept sideways, the driver fighting the wheel. The car, a big Detroit barge, screamed past, out of control.

None of these guys are going to hit me, thought Curtis. Absolutely none of them would do the predictable. How many had it been— five? Six? Each one saw him at the last moment, jammed on the brakes, fought into the next lane.

So Curtis stood still, in the middle of the fast lane, as a truck, a vague dreadnought in the dark, flicked its headlights from low to high beam and back again, bearing down ever closer, to the human body that was the only thing between its mass and the end of the world.

PART TWO

THE HOLE IN THE SKY

22

One step out of the apartment, into Via Cancello, and Bruno realized that he had forgotten the string bag.

He let himself back into the apartment. He tiptoed—Andy was still asleep upstairs. The string bag wasn't where it belonged, however, on its hook beside the stove. Bruno made his way as quietly as possible up the stairway. The steps were small, in the Continental fashion, and Bruno was not.

He could not find the bag of white netting anywhere, until at last he remembered one of Andy's silly little habits. The bag was stuffed into the mouth of a gargoyle on the dresser in the bedroom. Andy stirred in his sleep, made a half-word, and continued in his slumber. Beside the gargoyle was a pack of Marlboros, half-hidden under an empty camera case, and Bruno did not like this. Andy did not smoke.

I wish, thought Bruno to himself, that I had not seen that.

He was happy to be in the street again. There were things Bruno tended to forget about Rome, and rediscovered each time. The intensity of the traffic surprised him, even when he had been gone only a couple of weeks. That, and the onion-like scent of exhaust, and the *prrrp* tires made along the dark gray cubes of paving stones.

Maybe Andy had taken up smoking. He was still young enough to find the acquisition of a new vice something of an accomplishment.

Bruno had a flat near Holland Park in London, and a long-term understanding with the St. Francis Hotel in San Francisco, but spent as much time in Italy as he could. He had been born in Iowa, and raised in Colorado, his father designing bridges and flood-control waterways for the highway department, a careful, artistic man who liked the way a highway looked as it stretched ahead in the sun.

Bruno was not much interested in gradients and concrete. He was a man unlike anyone his father had ever known. He was like his long-dead father only in that he took an interest in the world of the real, and in the way he could not remain depressed about anything for very long.

A pack of cigarettes—hardly reason to stay unhappy on a glorious morning like this. The wash of details heartened him—the cheerfulness of the brush-shop owner as she opened for business, cranking the metal barrier upward until it settled into its recess with a metallic grumble, the bright sprinkle of sawdust over dog and cat soil in the street. Such sights allowed him to forget, for the moment, any doubts he had about Andy, about life.

The sun was warm. Fountains played, statues glistening with water, water splashing ceaselessly in the shade. Trash was set out in plastic bags, the handle loops knotted to forestall the cats, and street sweepers tossed the bundled garbage into the miniature—by Colorado standards—trash truck that followed. Romans were generally taller and more handsome than it was easy to remember, since one of the characteristics of this city was that the memory could only hold so much of it, there was so much that fled through the senses like water though the fingers. This was a place to see, not to recall.

Bruno smiled to himself as he remembered the one visit Curtis had spent here. Bruno had taken a room in the Hotel Raphael for Curtis, and introduced him to gallery owners, artists. Curtis had been polite, but late at night, after a fair amount of English gin, had confided that Europe was okay, but no improvement over the U.S. "I don't see the point," he had said. "Nothing really happens here. We built a culture in a few decades. Here everything is talk, or war."

Curtis was innocent of that sense of being excluded that made many people look beyond their native countries for intellectual nourishment. Curtis was, in a harmless sense, patriotic, preferring basketball to soccer, mashed potatoes to polenta. The visit had been years ago, but Curtis had probably changed little in that regard.

In the Campo di Fiori Bruno haggled briefly over tomatoes and zucchini, accepted a free bunch of basil from the woman who believed this rewarded her customers and brought them back to her. She was right, he reasoned as he thanked her, and then moved on to admire the fish staring upward from the ice. The ice was melting, already a stream of it across the cobblestones, and Bruno knew that soon all of this, the stalls, the shoppers, the white signs proclaiming the prices of pears, onions, potted flowers, would be gone, swept away to reappear again the following day.

Bruno walked briskly through the early morning blaze, bought a copy of *USA Today* at the Piazza Navona, and tucked the newspaper under his arm.

And he felt suddenly uneasy.

He strolled back toward the apartment, out of the piazza, past Passetto, the restaurant with the excellent carbonara, and when he was well within the shade of the street, he let himself think about what he *thought* he had seen on the front page.

He stopped walking. He felt an inward quiver. He hadn't been wearing his glasses. Surely, he thought, it didn't say *that*.

He leaned against a wall to let a Vespa clatter past and then shook out the newspaper. He held it at arm's length and read for a moment. Then he folded the paper again, folded it hard.

Bruno needed to sit down.

He found himself in Ristorante dell' Orso, out of the flow of motorscooters and hurrying pedestrians. He sat at a table. He let the bag of white netting half-tumble at his feet with its load of vegetables.

He took his time, feeling, as he sometimes did, that little movements could change everything. It was an attitude easy to maintain in Rome, where the way one tossed off a cup of espresso, or slipped off one's sunglasses, bespoke so much about one's life.

He slipped his glasses out of their case, and when he had read enough, he put his glasses back into their case and closed his eyes.

His favorite waiter, the blond from Lucca, smiled down at him, asking if he needed anything.

Bruno thanked him, and explained, in his fairly decent Italian, that the heat was too much for him suddenly. He asked for a cup of espresso, and when it arrived he absentmindedly fed two cubes of sugar into the cup.

This situation was difficult, but not impossible. He told himself that he would have to contrive something very clever to tell Renata. She knows I was, at the very least, exaggerating when I described Curtis Newns's work-in-progress. After all, there was Curtis, in the article about Red Patterson, announcing to the universe that he was not painting anything at all, had stopped painting completely.

True, the famous psychiatrist had announced that Curtis was going to paint with Patterson's help. That was good news. Except that now

Red Patterson had been stricken with "undetermined injuries," and the would-be assassin and two other people were dead.

And what of the wonderful new masterpiece, Renata would be thinking. Bruno drank down the coffee, left four thousand lira on the table, and reentered the heat.

Curtis would just have to find himself a new miracle worker, thought Bruno. The situation was slightly embarrassing—nothing more. Bruno found his way out into the Via dell' Orso, wondering what in the world he was going to tell Andy.

Andy was a devout follower of Red Patterson. He had videotapes of Red Patterson on Depression, Red Patterson on Dreams, Red Patterson on How to Steal and Get Away with It. Well, maybe Bruno had the title of that last tape slightly wrong.

Imagine—violence like that. It was the sort of thing one expected about the Home of the Brave. And people asked him why he preferred to keep his visits to the United States fairly short. America was not the country one remembered, reliable, optimistic.

He had just flown in last night. He had spent several hours in London, gazing upon the remains of the famous painting, commiserating with technicians, solemnizing art's great loss still further in an interview with the Sunday *Times*. He had not realized how thoroughly linen and oil gives itself to flame when the opportunity presents itself. He had been happy to leave London, and was feeling wonderful about being here, in his favorite city.

It would be a miracle if Renata were not on the phone this very minute. Bruno would have to devise another lie—it would be fairly easy, really. He would say that Curtis was exaggerating—that he had a perfectly excellent work in progress, and that Curtis was keeping it secret.

Later, Bruno would wonder if he hadn't had just the slightest inkling that something further had gone wrong.

Andy opened the door to the apartment, breathless. "Did you see what happened to Curtis Newns?"

"You mean, what has happened to my career, don't you?" said Bruno.

He could joke about it now. A few minutes reflection had convinced him that his life was not scattered about in ruin. It was one of those durable monuments, like the Pantheon, powerful, although lacking a certain superficial perfection.

Bruno had seated himself, and now, standing up again, was sure that he had misheard what Andy had just gone on to say.

"I saw it on CNN," said Andy.

As though to refute Andy's words, there was no news on at all, only the usual hash of American and Italian comedies. Bruno turned the set off again, and stepped toward the phone, which he knew was waiting to ring.

Andy was better at finding what he wanted on the television. When important events took place in the United States, American news was carried on Channel Four. Today the reception was poor. The news was about the U.S. economy, U.S. politics, U.S. pollution, the usual run of self-involvement that made the land of his birth seem both energetic and adolescent.

There, Bruno was beginning to think. I know all about this. Andy's wrong.

The two of them were on the screen, the psychiatrist and the artist. Red Patterson and Curtis Newns were hugging, there was applause, and then there was a jerky, wobbly picture that the voice-over explained was Red Patterson's house besieged by onlookers. And then a still photo of Curtis Newns as the voice intoned that he was listed in grave condition after an apparent suicide attempt on "a busy San Francisco freeway, after learning of what was initially thought to be the murder of—"

Bruno used the remote to snap off the sound.

Good Lord.

"What is it about television? A person tells you something, you don't believe it," said Andy. "You see it on the tube and it's the truth."

Bruno put a finger to his lips to hush Andy. Bruno needed to think for a minute. Curtis was one of those people you found yourself believing would never die. Despite his dynamic behavior, or because of it, he had seemed too vital to end up a mere corpse.

"You think I'm not shocked. I think it's a terrible thing," Andy was saying.

Before Curtis dies, someone should get their hands on the drawings his wife has there in the studio—the last work of Curtis Newns. It might be too late. Curtis might already be dead.

Bruno was not one to dwell on unpleasantness, but he did not feel confident at all. He hurried upstairs, grabbed the bag that he had not troubled to unpack, and looked at the print of *Skyscape* on the wall.

The timing was terrible. Andy was a photographer, collecting atmospheric views of the Jewish Quarter, the hidden fountains, the sleepy, furtive cats of Trastevere. Andy was attractive and bright, but he had that impressionable quality Bruno had recognized in so many young people. They were lively, but filled with easy fantasies of what tomorrow was going to be like. Facile, cheerful, Andy was one for whom the world was a map easy to master, greater distance meaning only a moderate increase in the price of a first-class ticket. Their relationship was loving but indescribably ephemeral. Andy would be gone, Bruno was certain, on his return.

"You're going again, aren't you?" said Andy.

"This is an emergency."

"What good can you possibly do?"

"I'll be back as soon as I can."

"We were going on a picnic to Ostia Antica." Andy was allowing himself a minimal sulk, but Bruno could hear a touch of relief.

Bruno felt terrible for a moment. Dear boy, he thought—dear, shallow boy. Who was it who smoked the American-brand cigarettes? The waiter from Lucca, perhaps, or the broad-shouldered young teller at the *cambio* window at the Banco d'Italia.

Bruno eyed the flat gray telephone. He could pick it up, make a few calls. Maybe he could stay here, and Andy would have a deepening understand of things, of Bruno himself, as a result. People had so little understanding of each other. Television, instant travel, the revolving door of lovers had made life both exciting and easy, even in these days when so many good people were dying, or gone. Even the cloak and jewel of one's sexual identity had become less a matter of discretion, of silence, and little more than another option in life's boutique.

Perhaps Andy would never know what it was like to build a career, a persona, a view of the world stone by stone, a bridge from uncomprehending past to a future of passion, of beauty. Bruno loved life. He had courted it and won.

Bruno punched Curtis's phone number into the telephone. He let it ring nine, ten times. He hesitated, then punched in Renata's phone number.

She was, of course, the last person in the world he wanted to talk to, but Bruno did not let squeamishness or the time difference slow him down. Renata's line was busy. Or perhaps she had left a telephone off the hook; Renata was often careless about details like that, preferring to live in the bigger picture of hired people who opened mail and answered phones.

When the phone rang Bruno did not want to answer it, but it was that sweet girl at the BBC, the one who did all the obits, asking for a statement from Bruno "just in case we learn the worst." Bruno ran through the usual bio, the artist orphaned, his parents killed in a landslide in the Santa Cruz Mountains. Very early promise, astounding success while he was still in his teens. If he died a great loss to art world, to the world of thinking people.

That sounds so *archaic*, he told himself. There are no *thinking* people anymore. The sweet BBC voice thanked him, and rang off.

Bruno realized how badly he was trembling. It was the truth: he loved Curtis.

Margaret Darcy Newns, thought Bruno, will not necessarily have the good judgment to let me and me alone dispose of the latest, marvelous drawings of Curtis Newns. Besides, bereaved family members had been known to destroy valuable manuscripts, precious works, in the blind throes of sorrow. And maybe there *was* a grand work-in-progress, a new painting half-done but exciting enough so that Bruno could point to it before selected journalists and say: I knew he was working on something exquisite, and here it is, a bare inkling of what it could have been, of course . . .

There almost *had* to be something like that tucked away somewhere.

"It's so sad," said Andy.

Was it possible that Andy wanted him to stay?

Trembling, giddy, almost believing that if he arrived in San Francisco in time all would be well, he took a moment to reflect upon Andy's words. Like so many of the young, Andy was preoccupied with his own reactions, discovering in sorrow something new about himself.

But Bruno did not believe in lingering over sadness. He believed, above all else, in the preemptive strike.

"After all the things Red Patterson tried to do for him, too," said Andy, putting the espresso maker on the stove.

That stopped Bruno. "Patterson is personally responsible for this."

"He was just," said Andy, airily, "trying to save Curtis Newns from himself."

Bruno saw actual spots before his eyes, flashing. "Patterson is a fake."

"He has revolutionized psychotherapy," said Andy, in the tone of someone explaining the profound to the dim-witted.

"I am going to expose Patterson for what he is," said Bruno, glancing through his wallet, aware that while the San Pablo Foundation would pay for all of his expenses there were tips, snacks, the occasional liquid refreshment.

"Do you realize the thousands of people he's helped, worldwide?" asked Andy. "There's a network of people devoted to him."

Bruno smiled. "He's going to need them."

"Red Patterson might not even be alive," said Andy, with that talent for the dramatic that Bruno had so recently found refreshing.

When the phone rang again it was Renata San Pablo. The connection was crisp. Satellite lag was a phenomenon of the past. "I don't know where to begin," she said.

"I know exactly how you feel," said Bruno.

"I am wondering how to make you suffer," said Renata, with something like good humor. She was no doubt enjoying this, thought Bruno. So much of her life was a game. Although it was a contest she felt she needed to win, it was a pleasure, too. Just now she felt she had Bruno at a disadvantage, and this made her perversely kind, despite her choice of words.

"How nice of you to call and ask for suggestions," said Bruno.

"Do you know that old phrase, 'shooting fish in a barrel'?" said Renata cheerfully.

Meaning: I'm the fish, thought Bruno. Already he could tell that Renata would not stay angry. After all, Bruno was too useful to her, and had been too amusing for too many years. "Yes, but I've always wondered about that," Bruno was saying. "Does it mean fish in a barrel full of water, or just flopping around at the bottom. Because, if there's water, the bullet might be deflected or slowed down."

"Not slow enough," said Renata soothingly.

23

People outside the bathroom door were making a real fuss. All he wanted was to be left alone. That was not too much to ask.

There was another knock on the door. "Dr. Patterson—are you okay?"

Quite a bit of time had passed but he still needed to pull himself together. He was tired of rushing through everything, day after day. He deserved some quiet. The truth was, he had felt very shaky, and he was just now starting to feel okay. Not really wonderful, but not bad, considering.

He sat before a mirror in the bathroom. The chamber was as big as some of the living rooms of his childhood, a spacious atrium with asparagus ferns and limestone tile. The shower stall was a niche, and the bath itself sunken, surrounded by fronds. The commode was discreet, parenthetical. There were little pockets in the tile, like acne scars, and if you looked closely they were the impressions of shells. You could pad around in your bare feet across a fossil record.

Beyond the door, out there, people were very annoyed. They stood, like parents barricaded by a teenager, trying to be patient, failing, perfectly able to break the door down. At least, they *thought* they could. Patterson knew it would not be so easy. Besides, they were kept from battering it down by the feeling that Red Patterson had a right to lock himself in his own bathroom after everything he had been through not even two hours before.

"Dr. Patterson, we just want to examine you," said a male voice, one of the paramedics, or maybe even one of the neurologists from the university hospital. "We just want to verify your condition."

Unlike most residential lavatories, this door had a real lock, and a substantial frame. Patterson had explained to the designer that he did, after all, keep drugs in his home, and the door was equal to the average attempt to storm the room.

Patterson had commanded the medics in the corridor to give him a little solitude, and since it was evident he was in no danger of dying they agreed, especially since a quick visit to the shower was what he needed more than anything.

The light was very good. He had arranged for that, too, stipulating that he needed a Broadway-quality makeup glass in the bathroom. He could see his face very well.

"He can't hear us," a voice out there was saying. "He's passed out."

"I'm perfectly all right," Patterson sang out. "There's nothing wrong with me." This was, Patterson had to admit to himself, somewhat contradicted by the situation. Perfectly all right people did not sit before a mirror as the hours dragged past. "I'm feeling fine."

He rubbed some alcohol on his forearm, primed another hypodermic, and skin-popped just a little cocktail of his own creation, one he would sell to a drug company someday if he ever got around to it, just the right balance of morphine and a brace of uppers. It cleared the head.

His face was a mask of scarlet that had dried into a dramatic shade of cherry-cola brown. His hair was matted and spiked, stiff with gray matter. He smiled, and his teeth were white in the flaking visage.

There was a familiar voice at the door. "Red, let me in."

No doubt they were all sure that this person would be able to get Patterson to open the door. "I'm not really receiving visitors at this point," said Patterson coyly, rolling down his sleeve.

"People are pretty much losing their sense of humor out here," said Loretta Lee.

"I am so sorry to disappoint them."

"You don't sound good," she said.

"I am the picture of calm."

"You sound really strange, Red."

Patterson offered a stage sigh. He strode to the door and said, like a man holding hostages, actually making a joke of it, roughing-up his voice, mobster-style. "Okay, but you're the only one who can come in."

Loretta Lee slipped in, and Patterson locked the door behind her.

"Good God!" she gasped, and she backed up, all the way to the marble column. She clung to it.

"My new look," he offered.

"Jesus, are you all right?"

"This is the residue of an anatomy not my own," he said.

She was pale, and he really thought she might crumple to the floor. "No, stay away from me." She made herself smile. "Please."

"I understand perfectly," he said. "I offend the fair lady." It was really a fair knockoff of some sort of British actor, or maybe it was that upper-crust accent Tony Curtis used in *Some Like It Hot* when he was pretending to be the rich guy with the yacht.

Loretta Lee, ever practical, gathered up the hypodermics and found a place for them in her purse. She seemed reassured, now that she understood the chemical inspiration for his mood. "Take off your clothes," she said.

"An interesting request," he said.

She looked off-green as she unpeeled the stiffened clothing from his body, but he had to admire the fact that if she did puke it was while he was in the shower.

But the sight of all of it reconstituted by the stream of hot water was too much to look at without feeling the mind curdle. Stuff clotted on the drain. Too much to have really happen without losing some sort of grip.

Angie had suffered several gunshot wounds, among them a wound to the side of her face. The force of the bullet had caused her front teeth and most of the mastoid process to burst into shrapnel. This assorted package of projectiles, blown backward, had struck Patterson with sufficient force to cause a mild concussion. Further, the failure of her cerebral assembly, the young woman's frontal and parietal lobes had nearly caused Patterson to suffocate.

Even now, calm as he was, he couldn't help it. He retched, hard, dry heaves, nothing in his stomach at all.

He shivered. Loretta Lee handed him a towel. "I have bad news, all kinds of it."

"You sound upset," said Patterson.

"Maybe I might as well tell you while you're in this mood."

"I distinctly remember you—tell me if I'm wrong—I distinctly remember you shooting that cute little gun of yours. Am I right?"

She did not respond.

There was a bruise in his forehead, a burst of shade. Even the powder puff as it dashed lightly over the bruise caused some small pain. There was a distinct pattern to the bruise, if one examined it closely. It was the shape of a triangle, caused by a piece of Angie.

"You can tell by looking at me something very bad has happened," said Patterson thoughtfully.

"I don't know if you're ready," she said.

"I feel all right. Actually, I feel wonderful. Tell me anything you want."

"Are you sure?"

"Talk."

"Jeff was in on it," said Loretta Lee.

Jeff of the perfect martinis and the excellent coffee. Jeff, the perfect servant. This hurt. This would take some getting used to. Patterson squared his shoulders, looked hard into his reflection. "The Jeffs of the world are always in on everything," said Patterson, trying to convince himself, and succeeding. "He was too smooth."

Loretta continued, "You remember the record company guy, the one who talked about the Man Boy Love Association."

"The one with those interesting videotapes?"

"The one who died in a single car accident last December. That one."

"I remember him. Fairly well." Actually, Patterson had only the vaguest impression. Freckles? Hairy nostrils?

"Jeff was his cousin." She dried his back. "Helped build a vacuum cleaner around a Smith and Wesson so another cousin could do the job."

Patterson groped for the column, the neoclassical excess of real Canadian marble, and took a moment to focus his mind. "What a marvelous accomplishment."

"Jeff saw things weren't working out, tried to come to his cousin's assistance, and took a bullet. He confessed on the stretcher, just before he died. Arranged for his cousin to dress up like a fake carpet cleaner, made the fake appointment, saw him through the security."

"The guy was doing a pretty good job on the carpets, too, wasn't he?"

Loretta took too long to respond. "I guess."

"Jeff is dead?"

"They tried but there was too much bleeding and he didn't have any blood pressure."

"It's hard without any blood pressure. I'll miss him. How about the carpet cleaner with the special gun?"

"Dead. *Really* dead. You'll have to replaster and everything."

It made no sense. But, at the same time, through his numbness, it did. "Christ, it proves we don't know anything about anybody."

"Yeah, it proves that. Are you feeling okay?"

"I realize that Angie is dead."

"I'm sorry, Red. There's even more bad news."

Patterson was pulling a purple dressing gown over his shoulders. He couldn't help it—he started to laugh.

He couldn't stop laughing.

Loretta Lee looked troubled.

"I'm sorry, Loretta Lee. Go ahead—hit me with the worst news you have left."

"Curtis Newns is dying."

"Loretta Lee, you have the worst sense of humor of anyone in the world. You could have it removed, you know, surgically repaired."

"Maybe I should have waited and told you all of this later on."

He stopped laughing.

"It's true," she said.

"How did *that* happen?"

Loretta Lee told a tale of a freeway, a truck, a glancing but skull-shattering blow, the artist tangled in the chain link of the center divide.

He needed another shot. He needed a drink—but not gin.

At last he could talk. "I tried to do good, Loretta Lee. I wanted to be a doctor."

"It's not your fault," said Loretta Lee.

"How could it be my fault?"

"I said it wasn't."

"Curtis Newns is suffering from acute anxiety, delusions, and years of psychological neglect." He stopped himself. At least I sound like a doctor, he thought.

"So no one will blame you."

"How could they *blame* me?" he said, keeping his voice steady, stepping toward her so fiercely that she stepped back.

"They can't."

"I feel great. They tried to kill me, and it didn't work. Talk about surviving—it's sweet, you know that? It has a flavor all its own."

It was true—he felt wonderful. He was fresh-washed, clean. He sat before the mirror again, and went to work. He looked like life. He would walk out to the steps of the house where, in the dark, videocams were awaiting his statement. The dawn-pink Japanese makeup was not working well enough to disguise a dramatic, if temporary, disfigurement in his forehead.

I have escaped death, he thought. And I will bring life to Curtis Newns. No one will be able to stop me. I can do whatever I want to do.

"Curtis isn't going to die," he said.

"No one knows—"

"I know. Look at me, Loretta. We're going to the bedside of Curtis Newns."

He instructed Loretta Lee to bring him clothes, and stipulated which slacks and which shirt, and decided that he would not wear a tie. He would sport a manly careless appearance, suitable in a man who had been nearly assassinated that very evening.

But Loretta Lee was not moving. She was just standing there. "I don't think I can face Margaret," she said.

He puzzled over this for an instant. "His wife? Why not?"

"I think, in a way, we're responsible," she said.

"Responsible for opening up Curtis's career for him? You should feel really good."

"Are you sure you're feeling all right?" asked Loretta Lee.

And then, there he was, sitting with his back to the marble pillar, which didn't feel very good, digging into his spine.

"You fainted," said Loretta Lee.

Patterson said that he might have fainted a little bit, but it was nothing to get excited about.

Loretta was worried. Her eyes were big. "You have to be realistic, Red," she said. "You're going to need a long rest."

"Do you think we can go back and make things the way they used to be?" said Patterson.

"Of course we can," said Loretta Lee.

As if she knew anything about it.

24

When Margaret first arrived at the hospital, Curtis was dying.

Dr. Beal managed to be both elliptical and blunt. "He's fighting, but in a case like this. . . ."

"I want to be with him."

"He tolerated the procedures well," said Dr. Beal. He gave her a tired smile. He looked older when he smiled, as though trying to inspire hope drained him.

"Take me to him now. Why are we waiting out here? I belong with him."

"I just want to caution you."

"Curtis wants to live," she said. "He doesn't want to die." It sounded so stark. It frightened her to say this sort of thing. People only speak for the dead, or the nearly dead. *Father would never have wanted this to happen.* It was also something like a lie. Curtis had apparently wanted to die when he set foot upon the freeway.

"We can only do what we can do," he said. He was a well-known surgeon, a man with hair so close-cropped he looked monkish, like someone who had forsaken pleasure and adornment so that he could endure times like this.

"I want to see him," she said.

"Of course," said Dr. Beal. But the man made no move to escort her, only let her stand there for a moment, as though hoping she would change her mind. He was like someone who had learned to act in a gentle manner, without feeling much real sympathy.

They let her into the recovery room. She spoke to Curtis. He was unconscious. His breathing made a sucking sound, like the hooked tube a dentist uses to suck up saliva, blood.

Later, Dr. Beal said that he had heard of a baby who had drowned, and was found after twenty minutes at the bottom of the pool. The baby was taken out of the pool, and an uncle held her upside down, shaking her. She lived.

Margaret was not sure why Dr. Beal felt the need to tell this story. Perhaps he wanted her to be reassured. The baby miraculously survived. So would Curtis. The story troubled Margaret. Curtis was not an infant. He had not been drowning. Margaret wished the doctor had kept the story to himself, or shared it with someone else, someone who could have found the story a source of hope.

Perhaps her feelings distorted the experience. Perhaps the hospital's tyranny was as sweet-tempered as possible. But Margaret felt the place dismissed her, seeing her as an appendix soon to be excised. Word came to her through a string of doctors who said less and less. "Maintaining," said one surgeon. "Hanging on," said another. "Clot-free," said yet another. Adding, "so far."

After twenty-four hours, crisis became the norm. There had always been this state of war, thought Margaret, this state of deep panic that bleached out to a death-march weariness. The battle never faded in a place like this. People simply forgot, and went on with their lives.

Even though the word she received was always couched in the terminology of gravest injury, it was evident that some hope was discerned in the blood chemistry, in the dilation of his pupils, in the determination of Curtis's body to reassert its hold on the future.

Margaret realized that her life, as it had been, was finished. The mailgrams, the faxed messages were not merely messages of encouragement. They were evidence that Curtis was leaving her. If he lived, or if he died, Curtis Newns belonged to the world from which she had borrowed him.

A stunningly beautiful woman from KPIX interviewed Margaret, and the hospital provided a publicity consultant, a woman with large hoop earrings who had once visited Arles "to see what van Gogh saw in his last days." The problem was that the woman with the earrings had emphasized *his,* implying that these were Curtis's own, self-tailored last hours, and that it was a solemn and exciting experience to be so close to history.

Margaret ended the interview abruptly, saying that she wanted to be alone.

Her mother joined her at the hospital, and watched the television in the other waiting room. She would return to Margaret's room to report what the world was learning.

Margaret sat in a private waiting room, one reserved for families of people like Curtis. The room had more tasteful venetian blinds on the windows and fresh flowers; instead of tattered magazines there were newspapers, and instead of a television a bookshelf sat in the corner, apparently just installed. It smelled of glue and varnish, and its shelves were empty.

"Curtis is still critical," said her mother. "But I can tell his condition is improving."

Margaret felt hope. "How can you tell?"

"The spokesman for the hospital is calmer. He doesn't have that haggard look he did yesterday. He even smiled, a little."

"So you can tell how Curtis is doing by how a spokesperson acts." This was not a question. Her mother's attitude made a kind of sense.

"You can tell how things are going by reading between lines," said Andrea. Margaret had the briefest conflict with the metaphor, the lines in a televised face being, as far as Margaret could imagine, generally enigmatic.

But it might be true. It *was* true. Margaret was sure of it. A spokesperson was a human being, and you could often tell what a person was thinking.

"Red Patterson is taking a break from his show," said her mother. "He needs a different focus."

"No doubt," said Margaret, prepared to feel sympathy for the man because he had nearly been shot.

"Red Patterson is going to dedicate himself to Curtis," said her mother.

Margaret was dazed by this news. "He is?"

Her mother's voice had an edge. "You should be thankful."

Margaret tried to consider this.

"It was your idea, Margaret—and it was brilliant. You encouraged Curtis to see Patterson. You knew exactly what you were doing."

"It was a mistake," said Margaret. "I didn't want Curtis on the show."

"Curtis and Patterson belong together, don't you think? They're both out of some different sort of universe than our ordinary one."

It must have caused her mother some special sensation to express herself so fervently. She had to take out her compact and apply fresh lipstick.

The compact snapped shut with the clean sound that brought Margaret back to her childhood. She had loved her mother so much. "Patterson says that his entire career will be Curtis now," said Andrea.

After thirty-six hours, everything changed.

Margaret tried to see Curtis more often, but it was futile. Guards shook their heads sympathetically. Nurses smiled and said that she couldn't, not now. Dr. Patterson had given orders.

"Red Patterson's taking care of Curtis," said Dr. Beal. "That's all I can tell you."

Her first thought was that she no longer trusted Red Patterson. After all, she told herself, she was Curtis's wife, and she had the legal authority to decide her husband's medical fate. But she realized at once how wrong she was. She was being selfishly possessive. Of course Red Patterson would make the right decisions. Of course if anyone could save Curtis it would be the famous doctor.

Dr. Beal must have recognized Margaret's initial doubt. "Curtis is considered, in a special way, Red Patterson's patient. You're lucky. Curtis is lucky."

"I have to make sure that Curtis is still alive," said Margaret, feeling chastened.

"Good heavens, you must feel pretty far out of the loop to even worry about such a thing," said Dr. Beal. "You have to trust us, Margaret. Do you realize what's happening? Right now, while we're talking?"

The doctor described the campaign to save Curtis. Surgeons were being flown in from around the country, kayaking expeditions, golf games, routine surgeries in far-off cities, all interrupted by Patterson's call.

Margaret accepted all of this, while disliking it for a reason she could not quite understand. Not only was the well-known artist in need of help, but the aura of Red Patterson had settled around the hospital.

Dr. Beal had changed. He had always seemed reserved. Now he thought for a moment longer before he made any remark. "Can I be frank with you, Margaret?"

She braced herself for bad news. "Please."

"Patterson is controversial. Some medical people aren't exactly wild about him, others admire him a lot. Ordinarily, Patterson would have nothing to say in a case like this—he could offer some advice, but nothing more. Right now Patterson is so important that whatever he says goes. If he wanted to have Curtis moved from this hospital we would have to go along with him. Hospitals are a part of the real world, too. If he says we're doing a good job, our funding blossoms. If he says we stink—we do. The ordinary surgeons in this case are just that—ordinary surgeons. Patterson can do whatever he wants."

Margaret recalled the deathwatch for her father, the afternoon outside glorious summer, willows and dry heat. Her mother had maintained a stoicism that caused Margaret to mistrust her, but now Margaret realized that her mother's manner disguised her own variety of deep feeling.

"You miss father," said Margaret.

Her mother examined her nails, and laughed sadly. "Do you know what he would do if he were here?" said her mother.

"He would disguise himself as a doctor, go in and see how Curtis was doing, and if he didn't like what he saw, he would kidnap Curtis, right out of here."

"He wouldn't do it, but he would talk about it," said her mother.

Andrea was right. The chess genius's active mind had sometimes balked at physical danger, the barking dog, the skunk in the garage. Margaret wondered if, by arguing with her daughter, Andrea kept alive a deep conflict she had enjoyed with her husband, a conflict composed of love and exasperation.

Her mother added, "He would agree with you about Patterson. And he'd be wrong."

"I am so glad to see you again," said Bruno Kraft, kissing Margaret on the cheek. He was wearing a gray silk suit, and his dark glasses hid his eyes.

Margaret did not wait for him to ask. "He's still alive. But they use the phrase 'in danger.' Stable, but still. . . ."

"In danger," said Bruno thoughtfully, completing Margaret's sentence.

"He's going to be fine," said Margaret's mother.

Margaret introduced the two to each other, relieved by the simple courtesy of the process, so that when Bruno turned back to her she was able to ask, "What is the press saying?"

Bruno smiled sadly, ironicly, to discount what he was about to say. "Bad news, but I have to confess that I've made a career of mistrusting what I'm told." He folded his dark glasses and slipped them into the breast pocket of his jacket.

"We certainly don't need any pessimists here," said Margaret's mother, smiling slightly to offset her words. Margaret thought her mother's response less than rational. The presence of the famous critic both impressed and antagonized her, as though now Andrea could not be the wisest figure in the forum.

"I understand that Red Patterson is looking after Curtis's needs," said Bruno.

"With Dr. Beal's permission," said Margaret.

"And yours, too, of course," said Bruno.

"I haven't had the opportunity to meet with Dr. Patterson," said Margaret.

"That doesn't sound right," said Bruno.

Even in this moment of crisis, when Margaret and her mother were bound together by the past, and by the present, Margaret could sense her mother's impatience with, as her father used to put it, "Everything that sounded like the truth."

"We certainly have no reason to object," said Andrea.

Bruno smiled, perhaps slightly uncomfortable at stepping into a script written for mother and daughter. "I have to believe he'll be all right with such an illustrious physician looking after him."

Margaret hesitated. "You're not here just to help Curtis."

"Of course I am, my dear. And to help you. If there's anything I can do."

"You thought he wouldn't survive," said Margaret. "You want to know what happened to the drawings."

Bruno looked at her as though discovering something of interest. "I was curious, it's true."

"The drawings are lost."

He seemed to grow taller. There was a short silence before he spoke. "They can't be 'lost.' I saw what good care you took of them."

"Curtis took them with him when he left, zipped into his portfolio. Maybe he was going to work on them some more, out in the desert. The drawings are gone."

Bruno took the dark glasses out of his pocket, like someone who cannot wait to resume a disguise. He did not put them on. His eyes had that glint, that hard look she remembered from before. "They can't *all* be gone."

Margaret looked away. "I've had to make some painful decisions about the future."

"You should go home and get some sleep," said Bruno.

"If Curtis lives—" The words stopped her. She felt grief stifle her. When she could speak again, she continued, "I have to realize that I haven't been able to help him. I have to face the truth. The question is: do I love him enough to let him go?"

"You're tired," said Bruno.

"I've been telling her that for ages," said her mother. "Poor Margaret."

"Don't hate me because I let the drawings get lost," said Margaret.

"Don't be absurd," said Bruno. "It would be impossible for me to hate you." It was true. He wanted to hold this poor creature in his arms.

Although the pictures simply could not be gone. The thought was an outrage.

"I kept Curtis in trust," said Margaret. "So many other people could have been in my position. Maybe other women would have done a better job." She looked hard at Bruno. "If I can't help him— I'll let him go."

"I'm so glad," said her mother. "It's for the best."

Bruno gave Margaret's mother a long glance. Then, to Margaret, he said, "You and I must have a nice, long talk before too long."

Dr. Beal had such an intense look that Margaret caught her breath, and waited for the news to be the worst possible. Bruno sensed it, too. She felt him stiffen beside her, and her mother stood up.

"You might as well go home and rest," said Dr. Beal, displaying one of his joyless smiles. "Curtis is out of danger."

25

It was nearly dawn. Andrea, Margaret, and Bruno shared a taxi, Bruno in the front seat beside the driver's clipboard.

What a sleepy little town San Francisco was, thought Bruno. The cable car tracks on Powell gleamed, long shiny strips, like scars where a wound has healed. A sole figure hunched along a curb, pausing at a trash bin to extricate a squashed aluminum can. It was too early for pigeons.

The taxi driver was a broad-shouldered woman, her hair gray stubble all over her head. It seemed to Bruno that he remembered a time when women went out of their way to look pretty. He remembered white gloves, cashmere, mock pearls.

"It's so thoughtful of you to drop me off," said Andrea Darcy, batting her eyelids at him.

"We certainly wouldn't want you to come to harm," said Bruno. He held the taxi door for her, and then sat where she had been sitting, in the back seat beside Margaret.

Bruno was aware that Margaret and her mother were involved in an armed truce. Bruno himself had few relatives left. He had one sister, a woman with florid handwriting, which appeared at Christmas, wishing him well from "Bea, Mike, Pepper and Honey." The last two were animals, dogs, and inevitably the names of the final pair changed over the years. Mike was a biochemist at the University of Hawaii, and Bea was a high school principal. There were occasional pleasant visits to Honolulu. Bruno liked his sister, and enjoyed playing brother-in-law with Mike, a cordial, squat man addicted to plastic-tipped cigars. When Bruno had realized, long ago, that he would father no children of his own, the entire concept of family began to dim in his estimation.

A taxi can be a pleasant interior, momentarily one's own enclosed space. Bruno had, more than once, fallen in love in the back seat of a taxi. "You're doing wonderfully," said Bruno.

"I have the feeling you're watching me," said Margaret. "Through binoculars, from a great distance. To see what sort of stuff I'm made of."

"You look so tired. We'll have our little talk some other time."

"I know what you want," she said, not unkindly.

"Curtis will survive," said Bruno, hoping he believed this.

Margaret did not answer.

"I used to read your father's chess articles," said Bruno. He was exaggerating; he had never played chess in his life. "He must have been a charming man."

"My father loved his life, but my mother wanted something more simple, something a lot safer. They had real estate in Sacramento, vacations in Paris. My mother was proud to see her parties mentioned in the society pages, and Dad didn't mind it. He liked to go barefoot all day in the back garden."

"Does your mother like Curtis?"

"She's afraid of him."

"That's hard to imagine," said Bruno, meaning that it was not.

Margaret gave him a smile Bruno found beautiful—calm, accepting. "I know you want to kill me," said Margaret.

"That's being a little crude, don't you think?"

"Right here in the taxi. You wish I were dead."

Bruno made himself sound coy. "Not exactly."

"I did the worst thing I could have done. I let some of Curtis's art get away."

"The drawings were lovely," said Bruno. And, he did not add, worth an incredible amount of money. "I should have taken them away with me. Stolen them out from under you. So it's my fault, too, you see."

"I'm too tired to lie, Bruno. And I'm so happy that Curtis is officially Out of Danger—" She said the words with a certain snap, so that they appeared as on a sign, in capitals. "You pretend to be above things like anger, but I'm not fooled."

"I wouldn't dream of deceiving you."

"You weren't just joking about stealing the drawings, were you?

You would steal them, and get away with it.'' She surprised herself. The combination of exhaustion and joy made her feel cunningly lucid. She could go without sleep forever. It gave her an advantage over Bruno. It was a strange feeling, and a powerful one. ''You would be delighted if I vanished and you could have Curtis all to yourself.''

''You'll feel better after a little sleep.''

''So will you. Let's have our talk now, Bruno.''

Honesty was a poor foundation on which to build a friendship, Bruno had found. A cheerful pretense was so much more reliable. He was about to say something to that effect, but he saw the look in Margaret's eye and silenced himself.

Loss came in all sizes, thought Bruno, and all shapes. How did a decent person like Margaret get so tangled up in the machinery of life?

Margaret knew that she should eat something, but she could not.

The waiter brought a plate of hash brown potatoes and two sunny-side-up eggs. Bruno did not begin eating for a moment. He took a taste of his coffee.

''If Patterson can help him—'' She opened a hand, and let it fall to the table, a woman surrendering to the inevitable. ''It hurts me. But I love Curtis.''

''Let's stop pretending to be nice, for a moment. I think Patterson is a dangerous man.''

She said, ''People believe in him.''

''Do you?''

''You're afraid that you'll lose control over Curtis yourself,'' said Margaret. ''His next painting will be thanks to Red Patterson.''

''At least we're being cynical now. That's an improvement. And it agrees with you—you get the sweetest blush in your cheeks when you look at me that way. But it's not just that. Let's pretend for a moment that it's all right if Curtis doesn't paint anymore, if that's what's best for his mental health. After all, the world still has prints of *Skyscape,* if not the original.''

''Is that what you really think?''

''I'm glad that you're suspicious, Margaret. I have to tell you something very frank. I want you and Curtis to be happy. But I can't afford to sacrifice for his mental health, or your happiness.''

''His happiness doesn't matter.''

''You really should have something to eat,'' said Bruno.

"You don't care what Curtis does, as long as he makes art again, preferably soon."

"Of course I care." Bruno broke the yolks carefully with his fork, one after another. "You and I could fight Patterson together, if we decided to. But let's try to be realistic. It's unpleasant, I know. But let's force ourselves. It may be necessary for us to let Curtis go with Red Patterson."

"Necessary," she said, making the word sound nasty.

His voice was a purr. "It's something you already know. You and I both need Curtis to go out into the desert with this wonderful doctor. I need Curtis to paint, and so do you. After all, it doesn't make your marriage look like a success the way things stand now."

"Why do I like you, Bruno? You go out of your way to be unpleasant."

"Have you ever met Red Patterson?" asked Bruno.

"No."

"You're going to let Curtis go off into the desert with a man you don't even know, aren't you?"

"He's the sort of person you feel that you know, you see him so often." She said this like someone trying to convince herself, and almost succeeding.

"Were you upset when Curtis was on the show?" Bruno asked, "or had you expected it?"

She did not answer him directly. "Red Patterson must have thought it was the right thing to do."

"Do you think it was?"

"I've never seen Curtis as happy as he was at the end of the show, when they were arm-in-arm and all the credits went racing past, so fast you couldn't really read them."

"We both need to take a risk or two. I want a new painting. I want a new masterpiece," said Bruno, correcting himself by emphasizing the last word.

It took an effort for her not to cry. "I know he'll come back to me."

He gave her a thoughtful smile. "You don't know how tired you are, Margaret." Bruno recognized this sort of fatigue. It was like a drug, liberating as it consumed.

Margaret gazed at the surface of her coffee. It was furred lightly with vapor that did not rise, pooling there on the surface. "I wish I had known Curtis a long time ago. I wish I could somehow magically join him in some wonderful period of his life. Like the months he spent in Hawaii. He talks about it sometimes. I wish I could be there with him.''

Bruno had always assumed that Margaret felt that Curtis the artist was more important than Curtis the man. Now he saw something he should have anticipated more fully, but had not. Margaret wanted to hear about the days when Curtis had finished with school, and with a few early sales in his checking account, was able to enjoy the green hillsides of the Big Island. She wanted to hear about Curtis relaxed, untroubled. She wanted to hear about Curtis being happy.

Margaret was earnest, vulnerable. For a moment Bruno missed the friendly insincerity of Renata San Pablo. ''Hilo's a beautiful town,'' said Bruno. Actually, he had passed through it once and found it squat, dull. ''It rains a lot, so it's very lush.''

''I can imagine it,'' said Margaret.

Bruno was always forgetting how much people could love each other. He could almost resent her freedom to consider nothing, for the moment, but the thought of Curtis sketching a hibiscus. ''I didn't visit Hilo when Curtis was there,'' Bruno said. ''I was living in London in those days. Besides, I prefer the Kona side of the island.'' Bruno had the impression that Curtis had bought a motorcycle, drank a good deal of beer, and had been glad to leave Hawaii after a month. Curtis had done very little work there.

You can trust nothing, Bruno wanted to tell her. Faith was composed almost entirely of self-deception. ''Let's imagine the future,'' he said. ''Let's imagine that things work out the way people believe they will. Let's imagine you and Curtis together again, and a wonderful painting drying in the desert air.''

''I want to believe it,'' said Margaret.

''But you don't.''

''I don't think I do.''

The potatoes were delicious. Crisp, just the right amount of salt. He could feel her doubt, and her weariness.

Bruno reached across the table and patted her hand. She liked that, found it reassuring.

26

Curtis was awake. Margaret did not need any sign. She could tell—he was a presence in the room.

His eyes were alight, and when she spoke he turned his head to see her, moving it in little jerks until his eyes were on hers. It was like early, stop-motion animation, weeks of effort condensed into a single movement. She was about to tell Curtis to lie still and not try to do anything.

"Don't touch him," boomed a male nurse in a slightly foreign accent. "You can see but you cannot touch."

"You break it, it's yours," said another nurse. Everyone was in high spirits.

"I made it," said Curtis.

It was like a badly dubbed film. His lips moved. Then, quietly, there was his voice.

It was hard to speak—she felt such happiness. She wanted so badly to touch him, to take him in her arms. The bustling in and out of nurses and orderlies were all a part of what was, in her eyes, a general celebration. "I'm so happy," she said. The words were so puny.

His voice was a cough. "I bet everything's mashed. Arms, legs, butt."

"Not everything. I saw a chart. Your private parts are in pretty good shape."

"The crowd goes wild," said Curtis, imitating a sports announcer, and coming out with what sounded like a radio so far away she almost could not hear it.

She kept her tone bantering, offhand, but she could not keep her voice from trembling. "I think one of your finger bones is still intact, too."

Curtis parted his lips in a silent laugh. "I was run over, right?"

He sounded proud of it. "They found you on the center divide," she said.

"Lying down? Standing up? What was I doing?"

Dr. Beal had said that Red Patterson did not want anything upsetting his patient, including Mrs. Newns. She kept her tone light, with difficulty. "I get the impression you were more or less not doing anything."

Medical personnel ran in, ran out. How could they have a moment together in a place like this? She told herself not to cry. Whatever happened, she had to keep his morale high. It was easy enough, really. She was happy.

"I know the pain is bad," she said.

He managed a smile. "Not when I'm looking at you," he croaked. "All that talk about how terrible pain is. It's completely exaggerated. Pain is not so bad, when you really start feeling it."

"Maybe you're just tough."

"I always wondered what it was like to almost die," he said. Then he swallowed and said, "Red Patterson was in here." It was hard for him to talk further, his voice dwindling.

Margaret had heard all about it. The man had come up the back elevator, normally reserved for "freight"—bodies descending en route to the mortuaries. "He wore a cowboy hat and a big long coat," the nurse had said, "so nobody would recognize him, but you could tell in a second who it was."

Normal speech was not possible. Every phrase had to be translated from feeling, into words, then into a simplified, hospital-appropriate English. She said, "I saw it on the news again. Red Patterson's still going to help you."

Margaret was surprised to see Curtis's tears.

"I love you, Curtis," she said.

He lifted a finger as though to say: of course you do. You can't help it.

"You want to go," said Margaret. She was not asking—she was prompting him. "Don't you. You want to stay out there in the desert for awhile." Because my love isn't enough.

But he had closed his eyes.

*   *   *

Margaret was ready. She was perfectly ready, wearing a pleated skirt, and that blouse Curtis had bought her, the one with what looked like starbursts all over it. She figured she needed something with a lot of color to get Red Patterson's attention.

She had not expected to be nervous, not *this* nervous. She found herself wishing she had brought Bruno along for the companionship. She felt like someone in a fairy tale, farm girl off to visit the king. Or even worse—the giant.

There were still police vehicles on the street, supervising the steady traffic that snaked past, tourists gawking, childishly gaping. People with cameras were courteous to each other, discussing the best angle, getting snaps of the house where Red Patterson was almost killed.

Because public impression had become confused. Patterson was okay, but he was not okay enough. Patterson had taken on the mantle of a man who had survived assassination. It was not mere attempted murder. Patterson was a Caesar who had taken the dagger's thrust and lived.

Even outside the house she could feel the tension. The San Francisco afternoon was chilly, fluffy clouds rolling in from the ocean. Cops sat in unmarked cars, watching. It wasn't just her—everybody there was nervous, all the security people tight-lipped. A woman examined Margaret's driver's license. A man found her name on a clipboard. Another man spoke her name into a transmitter, *Margaret Darcy Newns,* and she felt herself enter the giant's hall, where the shadows were cold.

She was led into a side room where a man waved a security wand over her, the sort of device used at airports when your change purse sets off an alarm. The room was bare, except for a roll of black cable on the floor and a video camera, recording her image.

A woman introduced herself as Loretta Lee Arno, and led her into an office. "All this security is a big pain in the butt."

"I wonder how Dr. Patterson is feeling," said Margaret.

"Nothing really bothers Red," said Loretta Lee. But then her tone became more truthful. "It was a hard experience for such a sensitive man to go through. And he can hardly wait to get out of here."

"Out to the desert, you mean?"

This question did not seem to merit an answer.

Loretta Lee sat on the front edge of a desk. Margaret sat in front of her, on the edge of a chair, wishing that she had remained standing. "I run things," said Loretta Lee. "If it gets done, I do it."

Loretta Lee looked hard, beautiful but tough to shake. She looked at Margaret and did not look away. It was a staring contest for a moment. "Red needs Curtis," said Loretta Lee.

"Curtis and I are grateful."

"You're here to say no, aren't you."

Margaret felt surprise. "Can I say no?" she said, too eagerly. "Or is it too late?"

There was sadness for an instant in Loretta Lee's eyes. "The world has to have Red Patterson back again. Working with Curtis Newns is what Red Patterson needs."

"I think it's a matter of trust," said Margaret. She hated herself for softening the statement with *I think.*

"If I thought Red Patterson was doing harm, to anyone, I would feel responsible. And I wouldn't let him do it. I'd stop him."

It was a staring contest again, but for some reason Margaret felt that she was winning. Something passed between the two women. Loretta Lee's look softened. "You're not just trusting Dr. Patterson. You're trusting me."

The room was spacious, and oddly under-furnished. There was a smell of fresh latex paint in the air, and the carpet underfoot was new. A television was on, the sound off. There was a commercial; you could buy an album of country songs sung by a group of men who were supposed to be brothers. They did not particularly resemble each other.

The man was as far away as he could get, leaning against a far wall with a slouch she associated with Westerns, the gunslinger who would not turn his back to the rest of the room.

He watched her for a moment before he moved.

His smile was welcoming. He was tall, and he stepped toward her confidently. She offered her hand. His grip was strong, and he kept her hand just a little bit too long, holding her hand, actually, as though they were lovers, or intimate friends.

What struck Margaret most, however, was her awareness of all of this—that he was a man acting welcoming, behaving in a confident manner, a good actor in rehearsal.

"You're a beautiful woman," said Red Patterson.

The brightest source of light was the television screen. Shadows jumped, jittered.

She said that she didn't want coffee or a drink, and she sat. He sat across from her, looking relaxed, and Margaret told herself that the meeting was going well so far.

"I know Curtis believes in you." She picked her words with care. "But you don't."

The carpet had a strong, chemical smell, the scent of factory-fresh fibers, adhesive. "I want to. But I was shocked to see him on television."

Patterson said nothing, but he looked at her with kind, thoughtful eyes.

"Maybe I should have expected it," she said. "Maybe I was naive."

"It would have worked. If the shooting—"

There was a moment of awareness. Margaret knew that this must be the very room, this new carpet, this fresh paint, so much cosmetic to cover the signs of violent death.

"I felt betrayed," she said.

"I'm so sorry," he said.

His apology had weight. "I spoke with Bruno Kraft," she said.

"I knew he was in town. I've always wanted to meet him."

What motivated her to lie just then? "He has persuaded me that Curtis should just stay here in the City with me for a while." She was almost certain that this modest lie would be detected by the famous doctor. But she continued. "Maybe it's best that he forget about painting. Maybe he should just be a human being."

He was quiet for so long she began to think that now she had really blundered.

At last he spoke again. "You've been listening to a lot of advice," said Patterson.

"What difference does it make," she said, "if we take a few months—"

"It makes no difference. You're right."

"Curtis is grateful to you—"

"Whatever you decide. Curtis, and you, and Bruno—just put your heads together and decide what to do. My life belongs to Curtis now. He's all that matters."

These words made Margaret uneasy. "That's a very generous statement."

"I love Curtis." His features appeared carefully drawn, eyebrow well-delineated, skin smooth, a portrait rather than a living face. There was a quality of earnestness about his eyes, a seeming sincerity that was disarming.

No wonder people opened up to him, she thought. "Curtis's recovery has been faster than the doctors expected."

"My patients always do well," said Patterson, smiling agreeably. "And you're doing well," he added, like a fellow performer complimenting her reading of a script. "I'm very impressed with you. You're a strong woman."

His compliment stirred her, won her over, as she knew it was intended to win her. But the man had power.

He continued. "I want what's best for Curtis."

Margaret was dazzled by this man—and puzzled. "Everyone acknowledges the good you can do."

"Some people don't believe." He shook his head, smiling sadly. "I think my critics dismiss me. They think I'm a creature of television, a monster. They want to keep me from doing good in the world. Curtis Newns is a client out of my dreams, a man I care about deeply, a man I can help return to his full creativity."

The man *might* be sincere, Margaret knew. He certainly sounded earnest. His speech was slightly too measured, like someone reading from a script he had almost fully memorized. This same quality made his words seem thoughtful, someone who would rather listen than talk. Or perhaps he had been taking some sort of medication. He had that odd, a-beat-late quality she recalled experiencing herself, when she took pills once for a cracked molar.

He continued, "I know you don't want to be separated from Curtis. You must love him far more than I do. I can understand why you might be concerned."

"Let me come with him," she said.

He took a moment before responding. "I've considered this. I would certainly enjoy your company. But I have to wonder—is that such a good idea?"

"It would reassure me."

He gave her what he must have known was a handsome smile, the sort of interested look that is hard to resist. His gaze was both intelligent and erotic, so that a conversation like this did not seem far from an act more carnal.

"Owl Springs would be wonderful for both of you," he said. "I have a staff there, and all the comforts you might dream of. It's far away, out in the desert, inaccessible by car. We do have aircraft—"

She had read about the place, but felt it was necessary, for some reason, to make conversation, to fill the silence. "You fly? I mean, you have your own plane—"

"I have a license. And I have a small collection of aircraft. I fly, when I get a chance. But I do think Curtis needs time to himself, time to be alone, quiet. Don't you realize what a wonderful opportunity this is?"

She did—that was the trouble. Curtis would thrive in a place she had heard described as "an oasis safe from the daily riot."

"Owl Springs is everything you can imagine," said Patterson with a smile. "And more. Few people know this, but unauthorized aircraft are forbidden to fly over the estate. My land is next to a military preserve, and was declared off-limits as a legal courtesy to me. That makes the place especially peaceful."

"Curtis would love it."

"He would, very much. But wait," he added, reading her expression. "You don't have to decide now. There's plenty of time."

She felt grateful to him, impressed with his warmth, the kind look in his eyes. But she still doubted him. She felt the suspicion lingering, a residue, nearly sinful. She lacked faith. Red Patterson was elusive.

"Out there in the desert," he was saying, "anything is possible."

"I came to tell you that I wouldn't stand in the way," she said. "I wanted to be sure."

He did not show surprise or gratitude. He had the ability to seem interested only in her. "Are you sure?"

"Of course I am," she responded, wanting to be more confident than she was.

When she was about to leave, she followed him to the door. He was close to her, and as she looked up at him she saw what might have been, intuitively, the source of her lingering doubt.

The man was wearing makeup, as though about to step before cameras. But Margaret understood that he was not doing his show these days. The look in his eye told her that he knew that she perceived this, and he shook his head, as though to say: this is our little secret.

Margaret was so close to Red that she could feel the heat of his body. "It was horrible," she said. "What happened here."

He kissed her—a diplomatic touch on the lips. She told herself that it was not romantic or erotic. It was even a little formal.

She would put her fingers to her lips in the days to come and try to tell herself that she had been given a blessing.

When it happened it was very quick.

Loretta Lee called her just before the surprise maneuver took place.

"Everything is going to be just wonderful," said Loretta Lee. "Curtis couldn't be in better hands."

Margaret was able to careen through the traffic in the BMW just in time to give Curtis a kiss on his cheek, another on his mouth, and then for the cameras, a last kiss slightly off target, just below his nose.

It was going to be all right, they both agreed. The event seemed whimsical, not serious at all, in that way that good-byes often manage to blend pathos with prosaic comedy, delays, wind doing awkward things with clothes and hair.

It was very windy, and neither of them could hear the other very well. A team of doctors and nurses wheeled Curtis into a special van. Later, Margaret would watch this on the news. There was footage of Curtis smiling and waving, an unfocused, public benediction that made it appear that he was bidding farewell in a more general way, saying good-bye to all that smacked of illness and confusion. As he waved the plastic tubes tugged at plastic bags suspended above him, and the sacks of clear fluid swayed, festive and rhythmic.

The automatic lift of the van failed to carry him upward. A mechanic fiddled with something. Curtis looked like a man healthy enough, if a director had called *cut!*, to climb out of the chair and stride off into the afternoon sunlight.

When the van was gone there was a perfunctory flurry of attention around Margaret. There were a few questions, a few photos taken, but only one question stayed in her memory, nagging her afterward: were you surprised that Curtis was taken away so soon?

When she was home that evening she let the starling go. She did it with the same abrupt decision with which she would have killed it to keep it from suffering, or cut off an injured leg—the sort of speed required when one acts with uncertainty, hope, and ultimate doubt that one is doing right.

She told herself that she acted out of mercy. She was aware of the act as partly symbolic, but afterward she would find the symbol frustrating, elusive.

She believed that Curtis had won his argument, and that she agreed with him at last: a cage is an evil thing. The glossy black bird was out of the cage quickly, hopping along the rail of the balcony. It released one of its squeaky calls.

It flew very badly. There was a flutter, black feathers flung down into the late afternoon, like the fan of a storybook senorita tossed down into the growing dark.

27

Her mother called that night to say, "Thank heavens it's over."

There was a rustle and thump outside, on the balcony. Margaret looked up from the telephone, but then told herself that she was hearing things. "I'm so glad that Curtis is in such good hands," said Margaret, realizing how bright and insincere her voice sounded.

"Webber and I were just watching it on the news. Curtis certainly looks like he's lost a lot of weight."

Surely, she tortured herself, there *was* something out there, a set of wings in flight against the glass door. "I thought he looked fine," Margaret said.

"You must come and see us soon, Margaret. You were looking tired yourself, you know. You get those little shadows under your eyes, the same as I do."

Tear yourself away from the phone, she told herself. Rush out to the balcony—the bird has come back. "I feel perfectly wonderful," she said.

"You have such a bright future, Margaret. And Webber was saying how good you look on television, despite everything."

She told herself to drop the phone and spring to the sliding glass door. But the phone had a mastery over her, and she knew the starling could not have returned. She guessed that he was already lost, finished after only an hour or two of freedom.

So she plunged on in what seemed like pointless conversation, the give-and-take she had indulged in on rocky flights as the *fasten seat belt* sign winked on, chatter as tranquilizer. "I didn't have a chance to plan any special clothes. I just wore whatever I had on—"

175

"And he was suddenly whisked out of your life."

Margaret's mood turned from familial patience, a remnant of the desire to please her mother that had so adorned her girlhood, to something quite different. "You love doing this, don't you?"

Her mother sounded almost pleased. "I want only to help you, Margaret."

"You feel that you absolutely *have* to call me up and needle me."

"Perhaps it's the truth that causes you pain, Margaret."

"You're always so sure of yourself." This was all useless, Margaret knew, a slipping back into old domestic politics, Margaret playing adolescent, rebel peasant to her mother's duchess.

Her mother adopted a forgiving tone. "This has been such a strain, hasn't it?"

Margaret felt like a child, reduced to knocking the chess pieces onto the floor. She concluded the call politely, and hung up.

Outside, there was no sign of the starling, only the continuing wind hissing in the cypresses below.

Bruno called to say that he was heading back to Rome. He had met with the San Francisco police, and found them perfectly cooperative, but the wonderful drawings were gone. "We can hope that some ignorant child with accidental good taste found them in the gutter and now has some remarkable pictures to enjoy. Maybe some morning he'll suddenly realize that right next to his basketball posters is one of those famous lost—"

"We have to be realistic," said Margaret.

"Not unnecessarily so," said Bruno. "Not if it's terribly depressing. With any luck, we'll have some wonderful new Curtis Newns' work to champion. Are you all right?"

"No, I'm not. I'm doing very badly," she said, in a burst of feeling that surprised both of them.

"I won't abandon you," said Bruno. "But I really do need to get back to Rome—"

"I wouldn't ask you to stay here," said Margaret, close to tears.

"You would be right to ask, Margaret. But I'm afraid my own life is just a little bit of a mess these days."

"Everything is ruined, isn't it?"

"You can't possibly believe that, Margaret. Give it a few weeks, a few months. Let Curtis do his work. It's really what we need, isn't it?"

"You're a wise man, Bruno," she said.

Bruno responded teasingly, "You're trying to think of a way to blame me if everything fails, aren't you, dear Margaret?"

She slept fitfully, except towards dawn. As she made toast there was a knock at the door.

Mrs. Wye was at the threshold. "There is a curious something that has just happened."

Recent events had made Margaret wary of this neighbor, a person she ordinarily liked very much. Mrs. Wye had put on some weight and did not carry a walking stick. Margaret could hardly bring herself to frame a question.

"I do believe your bird is on my balcony," said the white-haired neighbor.

"I was sure he was dead," Margaret said.

"Such an odd bird," said Mrs. Wye. "Tame, but he doesn't seem to want to be touched."

Margaret brought the cage out of the studio. The cedar chips at the bottom were still fresh, and there was still water sloshing in the drinking dish wired to the rungs.

Downstairs, the starling sat on the carpet near Mrs. Wye's television, its wings outstretched. Margaret caught her breath, thinking that the bird had broken a wing, or was in a trance state that might occur in starlings in the seconds before heart failure.

The bird was warm in her hand. The creature made a stream of metallic cackles at the sight of the cage, climbed up the steel bars, and fell inside, alive.

Margaret tried to lose herself in her work.

There was much to do. There was the troublesome duck, Earl, to distract her. Earl played Watson to Starr of the Yard's Holmes, but generally the role he played was to squawk loudly when danger was approaching. A runaway hay wagon. Starr of the Yard would be examining the fresh prints of a mysterious creature, wondering *musk ox? water buffalo?* and Earl would squawk and warn Starr, who, with a degree of aplomb and humor, would dodge the hay wagon with the grace befitting a goat detective.

The trouble with Earl was that he had been an afterthought. Starr was bright-eyed, loved marshmallows, read the financial page, and despised horses, which Starr felt were entirely overrated as useful animals. "A goat race would be much more exciting," was the sort of thing Starr would say.

Earl had too little personality. His eyes were two tiny dots, and his feathers were hard to draw. In one tale after another, Earl was a sidekick, company to the quick-witted Starr, but adding little to the story. One of her most successful stories had excluded Earl altogether. *Starr of the Yard in the Mayan Temple* had been a very ambitious tale—treasure hunters captured Starr, and he ate his bonds.

This episode had been so exciting that a film company—not simply a television production company, but something promising fluid animation and a musical soundtrack—had taken an option on the work. The company now was casting about for animators.

It was Margaret's favorite book, at least partly because she was able to draw jungles and huge Olmec heads. No one had complained that she had blurred Mayan with other cultural traditions. But librarians, bookstore clerks, and young readers had asked time and again: where was Earl?

Margaret usually wanted to reply that Earl was nowhere. Earl didn't exist, and he didn't matter. But she had failed to anticipate that what we accept on faith comes, in its small way, alive. There is a logic to loss, and a mandatory accounting of a lapse in what we have agreed to pretend. Earl's absence was a gap, a place in her tapestry that no longer resembled itself.

So, in the weeks of Curtis's absence, Margaret tried to absorb herself in her work, and *Starr of the Yard Comes Home* was a reuniting of the two main characters in a way she knew was a grace note to her own hopes. This time, she promised herself, Earl would have more of a role to play.

Furthermore, there was the design of a Starr of the Yard doll to oversee. The prototype sent to her from the factory in Williamsport, Pennsylvania, was a cheerful creature stuffed so full and firmly that he was hard-muscled rather than cuddly, and his horns were too short. The intelligent, cheerful frown was there, but the entire impression was that of an imposter.

She contributed drawings to an auction to support the local public television station, and sat in on luncheons and panels, ignoring the stares and the sympathetic smiles. She kept busy.

But Curtis was still gone.

His absence hovered over her life, her days a play devolving into earlier and earlier rehearsals, until the comments she made at the children's literature convention sounded like someone who could hardly concentrate on matters at hand. She was forced to have questions repeated, and when she tried to describe the book she was working on currently her mind went blank. Only later did she realize that the title, with its promise that Starr was coming home, amounted to a confession everyone understood more clearly than she could herself.

Margaret and Mrs. Wye spent more and more time together, sharing egg salad lunches and vegetable lasagna suppers. Mrs. Wye took an interest in Mr. Beakman, and checked out books on the care and feeding of caged birds, failing, however, to find starlings in any of the volumes.

Sometimes Margaret called Owl Springs, and Loretta Lee answered, when she got anything other than an answering machine. Everything was just fine, Loretta Lee would say.

Just fine. The two words would turn themselves over and over in Margaret's mind. *Just fine.* Meaning, she supposed, exactly excellent, perfectly splendid. In truth, the words communicated nothing.

Loretta Lee had an intriguing voice, and there was a trace of friendliness behind her few words. "Curtis and Dr. Patterson are working hard," said Loretta Lee once when pressed.

"Working at what?" Margaret had asked, excited.

"Nobody tells me," said Loretta Lee, letting the word *nobody* sound so elongated and mournful both of them had to laugh.

One afternoon Margaret was having lunch with Mrs. Wye, in Mrs. Wye's apartment, big glossy photos of leading men and child stars piled neatly on a corner of the table. They had just finished delicate sandwiches, vinegary cucumber and butter. "You don't like any of it at all, do you?" asked Mrs. Wye.

Margaret allowed herself to misunderstand, for a moment, imagining that Mrs. Wye could be referring to the sheet music she had just spread on Margaret's lap, or, perhaps, the frail, crustless sandwiches they had just eaten. "Curtis is already working on something new," said Margaret, feeling over-rehearsed.

"But you feel abandoned," said Mrs. Wye. "Or maybe that isn't quite what you feel. You feel that you have abandoned Curtis."

Margaret was quick to say that she knew Curtis was doing fine. "It's intuitive," she said.

"If something were wrong you would know it?" asked Mrs. Wye.

Margaret stopped herself on the point of saying: of course I would.

"I certainly wish my mind worked like that," said Mrs. Wye, with a laugh that was silvery, certainly much-practiced, and which Margaret could not echo.

"But when you stop and think," said Mrs. Wye, "there really isn't very much you and I could do if something went wrong, is there?"

28

Margaret wondered why Curtis did not call, and why she never had a chance to speak to him when she called Owl Springs.

"Dr. Patterson and Curtis are like this," Loretta Lee said, and Margaret visualized the woman holding up two fingers held close together, or two fingers pinched tightly together to cling to something gossamer, easy to lose. Although Loretta Lee was friendly, it was easy for Margaret to understand that her phone calls were a slight nuisance, a hindrance to the success Patterson was sure to be having with Curtis.

Margaret taped the show every day now, in case there was a chance to learn about Curtis, or to see the work she was certain must have begun.

The show had changed. Red Patterson's television slot had been taken over by a suave, tanned man with blue eyes named Marvin Kelvin. Marvin Kelvin entertained guests who were troubled, individuals who had been raped, molested, battered, people who had been injured by events or genes, citizens who had been cheated of something essential.

But without Red Patterson the show lacked that final mastery over fear. There was no surprise awakening, and no sense of having been forgiven. There were no miracles, few tears, and many of the guests slipped into a mild form of belligerence. The world was unjust, they said, and the studio audience, and the viewers, were doing nothing to help. The tone of the show had become common and anecdotal, but there were no complaints from the psychiatric community.

A columnist or two called the show "ordinary trash." Without Red Patterson there was little hope, and little scandal. The show's ratings dipped, but only slightly, and Marvin Kelvin was on the cover of the Sunday paper's television supplement, and then on *TV Guide,* and was asked to testify, in Red Patterson's place, before a Senate Hearing on abused children. In several weeks Red Patterson had become a historical figure, imposing, potent, but no longer a part of the daily spin.

The day before Margaret was to visit her mother, Marvin Kelvin concluded his show with, "And tomorrow we'll have some long-awaited word on Red Patterson and how he's doing at Owl Springs with celebrated artist Curtis Newns."

There was applause. The long, pauseless sentence had slipped out as Margaret reached for the remote, and only when she rewound the tape and watched it again did Margaret feel certain that there was going to be news at last.

Margaret did not want to be late. Traffic was hectic, big rigs gunning engines, switching lanes. Buses to Reno, billboards for Harrah's, dominated the road. There was a caravan of these chartered buses, as though a small nation had decided to go gambling. After Vacaville, and all the way east, it was hot, and the car's air conditioner was a relief.

There was none of that bay-softened air here, none of that ever-presence of the Pacific. The pasture land and rice-growing country spread on either side of the freeway. The horizon all around was tarnished with a vague agricultural smog, the haze from so much vegetation lying green and fertile under the hot sun.

Her mother lived in a house surrounded by oak trees. Roses lined the walkway to the front door, and the plants had been trimmed to resemble lollipops, long thin trunks with a tight, brambly bouquet of pink or white.

"I've been admiring your books," Webber said. As if to prove this, he had several of Starr's adventures laid out on the coffee table. *Starr of the Yard in Egypt* was open to a rendering of the Sphinx. "I want you to sign these. I'm giving this set to my grandchildren."

"Webber owns cable all over Northern California," her mother said. "If you watch CNN, you're probably watching it on Webber's system."

"Maybe, maybe not," said Webber.

"Are you being modest—or truthful?" asked Margaret.

He laughed, as though to admit that he was neither. "You ought to paint again," said Webber. "I mean, in addition to your books. You have real talent."

"Do you paint?" asked Margaret.

He enjoyed being asked. "I'm only an art lover," he said. He emphasized the last word, perhaps to imply that he felt passionate toward more than art. Margaret could see the stone of his ring, the mint-candy gleam of emerald.

Margaret had a strange, uneasy thought: my mother's boyfriend is coming on to me.

"We're going to miss the show," said Andrea, ostentatiously drying her hands, not to demonstrate that she was laboring hard to prepare supper so much as to say: I can wipe my hands on anything here.

Today's program featured people with no arms or legs. This was a pretty cheerful bunch, even when Marvin tried to goad them into complaining about their condition. It was possible that the guests were anticipating the "latest from Owl Springs with Dr. Patterson."

Andrea hovered, sitting, then standing to shift the plate of salted nuts in Margaret's direction. There was a parade of commercials, childhood photos of the guests, one of whom had published an autobiography. The spouses joined the guests, and the show settled into a remarkable display of good feeling.

Margaret asked "What is it that you do, exactly, at your cable service? I picture a desk, lots of desks, secretaries, window envelopes coming in with checks from subscribers, and every now and then someone calls up because they can't get the Playboy channel. You have a satellite dish on the roof and you spend a lot of time on the phone. You have some pictures of grown children on your desk, even though they resemble your ex more than you."

"You've been spying on me," laughed Webber.

The show would be right back, after this.

They all had Bloody Marys now. Margaret was tense, and not in the mood for one of these celery-laced cocktails. "Are you going to marry Mother?" she asked.

Webber was still smiling. But his eyes flicked to where Andrea was sitting and he took a moment before he said, "You are so much like each other, you and your mother."

"I think that comes as a surprise to both of us," said Margaret.

"Webber wants to tell you something important," said her mother.

"Are you guys going to gang up on me?" said Margaret.

"Margaret has always talked like this," said her mother. "She thinks manners are a throwback to the age of gaslight."

"I like manners," said Margaret, and she was about to add, "what I hate is hypocrisy." She stopped herself. This so often happened around her mother. She regressed to a snotty adolescent, belligerent, defensive. "I'm sorry," she said.

"You have a lot on your mind these days," her mother said, sounding gentle, accepting.

The commercials were over, and the guests were enjoying a joke Marvin had made. Margaret could barely sit still. Everyone on the show was long-winded, with the grinning carelessness Margaret associated with sportscasters when the local teams were doing well.

Andrea and Webber had fresh drinks, the dish of salted nuts was nudged in Margaret's direction again, and once again declined.

With every minute Margaret felt more desperate, more depressed. The show was going to be over soon.

And then, when there was no time left on the show at all, when it was time for the credits and the name of the airline that had provided travel arrangements, Red Patterson appeared.

His image on the screen caused tremendous applause, more than the normal studio-prompted celebration. This applause erupted into cheers, and the camera scanning the audience joggled a little, everyone surprised at the excitement.

So when Red Patterson began to speak the first few words were lost. "Really enjoying the quiet out here," said Red Patterson. "And Curtis Newns—thriving. Absolutely thriving."

He looked relaxed, surrounded by aloe plants and the fronds of various palms. The sunlight might have been supplemented by artificial light, because where Patterson was sitting looked like some shady refuge from the heat. Margaret felt hope die, felt herself understand what she was looking at.

This tape might have been made weeks ago. It was plain that the questions being asked by Marvin were not being uttered before this particular live audience. Patterson thanked Marvin, wished him luck.

Over supper, a complex taco salad, Webber said, "You want to think about this, though."

Margaret dabbed guacamole from the corner of her mouth. She had not been paying attention.

"Good money after bad," said Webber. "We have to have realistic hopes."

She pieced together what he had been saying. I don't even know you, Margaret wanted to say. How can you possibly give me advice? Her mother had put him up to it. Maybe it was a way of courting her mother—showing how well he could advise her adult daughter. Her mother may have even scripted the advice, although her mother's style was not usually this ordinary.

"Webber's wife was mentally ill," said her mother. "So I thought you would listen."

"I'm sorry," said Margaret.

"Sometimes we have to let go," said Webber.

"Let go and do what?" asked Margaret.

Webber took his time in answering, a man who would rather discuss the bond market or his most recent vacation. "There's the temptation of denial. To tell ourselves that everything will really be all right, or that everything's our fault."

Was this man being wise, Margaret wondered, or simply intruding his opinions where they were not wanted? He had friendly eyes. He broke off a tortilla chip and fished the fragment out of the sour cream. Despite her resentment, she knew his statement might be the result of suffering. "You'll forgive my asking—what happened to your wife?"

"She's still living," said Webber. Observing the question in Margaret's eyes, he added, "We're divorced. She lives in San Jose, in a residential care center."

"What do you like about Curtis's art?" asked Margaret.

"Its vitality." Webber leaned on the table, elbows on the cloth the way her mother had always scolded her for doing as a girl. "Although, to be frank, it always seemed a little hectic for my tastes, a little strange."

Her mother had an air of cheerful indifference to the weight of the subjects at hand. It was like her mother, thought Margaret, to turn to a man as a mouthpiece. This near-stranger was speaking as an ambassador from mother to daughter, in the presence of both of them. Margaret felt sharp resentment: this was how her father had been used, smiling his hesitant smile, saying what the daughter knew were her mother's words.

"Do you play chess?" asked Margaret.

Webber understood the question, and knew it was more than casual. "Not very well."

"I never learned at all. I knew I would never be that good at it." She meant *that* good—as good as her father.

"Webber is buying a radio station."

"Television isn't enough?" asked Margaret.

"He has to invest the money, he says, or lose it." Her mother smiled at Webber.

"It's only money," said Webber. He was hesitating, ready to say something but holding back.

"Not many men wear emeralds," said Margaret.

He looked at the ring, gazing into the stone for a moment. "It belonged to my mother. I had it reset, and I wear it for—well, for peace of mind, I guess." He smiled, but Margaret could see sadness in his eyes just then.

"His father manufactured shatter-proof glass," said Andrea.

Something about this statement made Webber narrow his eyes and study the guacamole.

"Webber has something to tell you," said Andrea.

"I'm going to offer you a position," said Webber.

Margaret used a napkin to remove the few grains of salt on her fingertips.

"We are starting to originate some programming," he continued. "Some pretty good stuff. But we need someone with ability and a name to. . . ." He made a show of choosing an especially large tortilla chip. He gestured with it, pointing at her when he said, "Oversee things."

"He's planning programs for children," said her mother, in a tone of delighted wonderment.

"And he wants me," said Margaret, letting her voice stay flat.

Webber took in air through his teeth, making a short, tense whistling sound. "As program director. You'd have virtual control."

"You mean—if I abandon Curtis."

Webber had the grace to pause for a moment. "Money is not an issue."

Andrea looked on, smiling with half-closed eyes. She did not mind what Margaret had mistaken as Webber's flirtatious manners. Webber was a man used to being liked, and Andrea approved.

"I like you," said Margaret.

Webber looked on, cautious and relaxed at the same time, a man at ease with good and with evil because his encounters with both had been so brief. He did drop his gaze for an instant.

"Or, I did. I thought you were kind," said Margaret, disliking the way her voice broke.

"You have a future," said her mother.

Margaret took a long time in the bathroom, admiring the large porcelain mallard in the corner. The artist had known exactly how a large male duck would look if an uncaring god had transformed it into shiny, glazed clay.

"I learned something from my father," she said, standing on the front lawn, taking Webber's hand.

Webber knew he was supposed to ask, and he did.

"I learned never to play a game I thought I couldn't win."

The drive home was over a hundred miles, and she kept the needle well over the speed limit most of the way back.

Entering the penthouse she snapped on one light, just enough to see the telephone.

Margaret called Bruno's number in Rome. An intelligent-sounding young man answered, and she could hear the phone rustle into place somewhere thousands of miles away and the male voice call Bruno's name with a careless, upward lilt.

It was good to hear his voice.

"I've been worried, too," said Bruno.

29

At dawn and at dusk you could hear swallows, the squeals of birds like wood screws. When you looked up, little black knives were busy, carving the outline of an invisible city.

Bruno did not like worry. He saw it as one of life's minor illnesses, best defeated with medicine or, better yet, a brisk self-enforced change of attitude.

First there was the call from Renata San Pablo. "How is your darling Curtis really, Bruno?"

There was the pleasing thought that Bruno was secure in Italy, far from this woman. Bruno smiled into the sleek telephone, a compact, lunar-pale instrument, the color of several of his favorite suits. "It's so good to hear from you, Renata," said Bruno, and it was almost true.

"People are expecting something wonderful," said Renata. Then, in a tone that might have been sincere, "How long does something like that usually take?"

Then there was the call from Margaret, the poor girl sounding quite upset by something she had or had not seen on television.

"Don't worry," he said. "It's in my hands."

If only I believed it myself, he thought.

Living in Rome had taught him that work did not matter, knowledge did not matter, being brave or wise did not matter. Even faith—and sincerity, that virtue Americans so admired—did not matter much. What mattered was knowing what to do, and when. Afternoons were for rest, mornings for decision, evenings for friends, for love.

There was a brief screening process, each voice a little less unhelp-
ful, until by the fourth voice he was speaking to someone who knew
who he was.

It was that simple, after a delay making himself known: of course,
Dr. Kraft, we will be pleased and honored. Dr. Patterson has so been
looking forward to someday—

Doctor Kraft something of a mistake, although there were one or
two honorary excuses for styling himself so. Academic flourishes of
that sort seemed fatuous to Bruno. At the same time, Bruno was
happy enough to avoid talking to the famous psychiatrist.

Isn't it funny, he told himself. I'm a little afraid of the man.

There was some weight to the man's reputation, and it was best
to avoid a confrontation, Bruno thought, until Bruno was sure of his
own forces.

Bruno spoke at last to a sultry female voice, and when he said
that he had doubts, that he really did have to see with his own, et
cetera, there was no trouble at all arranging a meeting, a quick hello
in the desert. It would be an honor, said the woman, who identified
herself as Loretta Lee Arno, a name Andy would later claim to recall
from a soap opera, something about Hollywood and incest.

Then there was a call back to Margaret, all balm and reassurance.
Yes, I will definitely make sure that Curtis is quite well, said Bruno.

"I'm so worried," she said. She sounded close.

"Let's not be overly concerned," he said, allowing himself to
preen for a moment. "I did make a very modest threat. I told Loretta
Lee Arno that unless I was convinced that a new Curtis Newns was
in progress, I would be forced to go public with my doubts."

Bruno packed his bag. It did not take long.

Was Andy's excitement authentic? "How wonderful to be able to
meet Red Patterson!"

"It's actually not Patterson I'm interested in seeing."

"I know, you want to make sure Curtis Newns isn't a raving
lunatic."

"I don't really care what sort of lunatic, raving or not, Curtis has
become," said Bruno. "As long as he's been busy." This accompanied by a zip of the shaving kit, which was itself thrust into the large
bag. The piece of supple leather luggage was technically too big to be
classified as carryon, but Bruno allowed himself this modest liberty to
avoid having to claim baggage, and no steward had ever complained.

"I wish I could go."

"You love it here. You're just glad to be getting rid of me again," said Bruno.

Andy was helping, putting the strap of the bag over his shoulder, slouching along with it, lumbering down the stairs. "I think you're the one eager to go away."

" 'Eager' isn't the word."

"You're going to decide you have to drop by La Jolla to get drunk with some old friend or other," said Andy. He had been raised in New Jersey and had a mixture of faith in, and contempt for, the glamour spots of Southern California.

"I haven't been drunk in years," said Bruno. "I never liked it. You close your eyes and the earth swings out from under you, like a trap door."

"You'll want to see that hideous actor you have a crush on," said Andy.

"Water under the bridge."

"I was going to start working on you today."

This particular reminder pained Bruno. They were outside, now, making their way up the narrow street, pausing to let a motorcycle putter past. Andy had promised to create a series of portraits of Bruno, for which a new cape had been purchased, and a remarkable dark felt hat, and various locales searched for and discovered, including a corner in Trastevere where a particularly large white cat held court, drowsing on the hoods of cars. The series of photographs was going to evolve into a *Bruno Kraft's Rome*.

It was a minor miracle, in this city of great miracles, that Andy was still here. He did turn out to have a sincere cigarette habit now, and swore that he used to smoke all the time as a teenager. He had surrendered the habit, only to return to it now that his teenage years were so distant that any remembrance of them was a pleasure in itself. He had even developed a morning cough, and the smoker's habit of hunting up an ashtray upon entering a room. Although he was in his early thirties, Andy still might pass as a young man.

Don't go, Bruno told himself. Stay here.

The shade was cool, the sun heavy on Via Dell' Orso, and Bruno continued to let Andy carry the bag, as though this might be the last favor Bruno would ever accept from his friend. Andy would be left to his own devices, and Andy was, like the figure in an old song, an unconstant lover. Bruno could not have described how he knew— he knew.

Rome was abuzz with potential lovers. Bruno himself had been attracted to the occasional debonair native or sunburned tourist, and if his own lust had been less dissipated by Andy's attentions, Bruno might have fallen to unfaithfulness. Of course, so many of the really attractive young were crippled by a combination of ignorance and arrogance. Just the other afternoon, there was a striking individual in Tazza d'Oro where Bruno had stopped for a coffee. But a quick chat had revealed a fondness for pop musicals, dead actresses, and the fact that the last book the youth had read had been forced upon him as a junior in high school, "that novel with the retarded person who lives in the South."

Stay here. Let Curtis and Margaret and Red Patterson drift toward whatever crash awaited them.

There was a farewell embrace, and then a taxi—a fast taxi, a blurred, giddy careen, the wheels squealing sideways over the traffic-polished stones, through the Porta San Paolo, south toward the airport.

Nothing really mattered very much—that was the truth Bruno had learned over years of passing through to the first-class waiting lounge.

Under this gloss of indifference, however, Bruno was not amused or detached. He was nervous. He felt the wings of the jumbo jet describe the fluctuations of the air at thirty-six thousand feet and he was not comforted, as he had been so many times, by the technology that protected him.

He took some aspirin, four of them—Italian aspirin were too small to do much good. The headache remained. For the first time in his life he felt trapped by the fuselage. He slept, and he dreamed. In the dream he did not want to go where he was going, the destination toward which he seemed to plunge like a stunt diver from a distant perch towards a fatally tiny tub of water.

Los Angeles was a parking lot of buildings, TV antennas, and those metal crowns that sit on rooftops and rotate, ventilating, Bruno supposed. There were telephone poles and vacant lots of broken, glittering glass.

As the large jet approached the airport there was not as much smog as one might expect. The air was not clear, however. It looked as though the oxygen had been used up and replaced with something life-sustaining but degraded, a recycled sky.

Patterson's people met him, all smiles, strong handshakes. Yes, said Bruno, this is the only luggage I have.

He was the sole passenger in the executive jet's cabin.

The interior was luxurious, but it was a neutral sort of plush, high-backed leather seats and a boardroom ease. An attendant offered him a drink and "a bite to eat." Bruno expressed regrets that he was neither hungry nor thirsty. He asked for aspirin and was given three large Excedrin.

The smaller plane darted, so unlike the airborne whale Bruno had just escaped. This was almost fun, this spearing upward, this gliding along, this banking so Bruno could see. Even by jet it was a long trip over lunar emptiness.

Why am I apprehensive about meeting this TV personality, this exaggerated talent? he asked himself. Red Patterson is the one who should be apprehensive, and I should be coasting along over the desert feeling absolute ease.

Owl Springs lay below them.

From the air the oasis was a rich tangle of verdure. Bruno was reminded of his first lover, a youth so pale that his dark pubic hair was in breath-taking contrast to the lithe chalk of his limbs.

The aircraft did not approach with a grande dame's descent, like the jumbo jet. It paper-airplaned down, gliding, and Bruno found himself almost enjoying the sensation of having the entire pulse of his body located in his throat.

That's where they are, he told himself with a boy's wonderment. In that secret place—that's where Dr. Patterson and Curtis are hiding from the world.

Bruno felt his old confidence return. His headache was gone. I'll stay only a short while, he promised himself. Just a quick visit, just a look—an hour or two.

There can't possibly be any harm.

30

It was one of those days that go so far and then stop dead. The pool doesn't ripple. The wind doesn't stir. Visitors from New York or Boston make it out to the California desert and go wild about the weather, say how wonderful it is. Especially in winter—all that sun. A week later they hate it. Patterson knew: hate didn't carry much weight. The sun was stuck in the sky and nothing was ever going to happen.

"You used to tell me what you were thinking," said Loretta Lee.

He wanted to smile. He had never been so indiscreet. You gave Loretta Lee something that resembled the truth, the way a bat resembles a bird. "You can usually guess," he said.

"Bruno Kraft won't stay long," she said. "Maybe just an hour or two, right?"

Red Patterson sat very still because it was hot. He stayed very quiet and concentrated on the trouble that was on its way.

Loretta Lee was wearing the briefest imaginable swimsuit, a device that was all strap and the kind of pink you see in used-car lots. She did not have much of a tan, detesting what she called "cancer wrinkles." The telephone lay beside the tube of SPF 45 sunblock.

There had been a certain amount of uneasiness in Patterson's mind about the desert beyond the oasis, ever since Bishop had found those people, those lost campers. There were things out there, other things, and although they were lost to the world they had not vanished. It was just another reason to be where he was, in control.

The telephone trilled. Loretta Lee spoke into it briefly. She put the phone down and said, "The flight from Rome was six minutes late. They just left L.A."

"How do I look?" he asked.

"You look okay."

"I have to look better than okay."

"You do."

Bruno Kraft was one of those cunning predatory people without morals, Patterson believed. In Kraft's books, in his televised programs on art history, Patterson had discerned a man of cutting intellect and little feeling, the sort of man who makes an excellent hunter as long as it's out of season.

"You want to put on something else," said Patterson.

"You told me that an hour ago."

Patterson had been forced to invite the famous critic when Loretta Lee told him that Bruno Kraft was about to go public with his "doubts." Patterson's intentions were simple: get the man here, and then get him out, quickly. Other, corollary plans lingered in the wings, outside the light and heat, but those could wait.

The body knew that air could not be so hot. The flesh understood—this could not be real. But it was. The sun was all over them, the real sun, not filtered and buffered, but the naked radiation, rich with both visible and invisible spectra, sunlight that sang off the white stepping stones making a virtually audible hiss, as water dappling the poolside vanished, unpeeling and turning into air.

The scent of the air was sterile, blank purity soiled here and there by the musk of plant life in the eleven-acre oasis. If you made the mistake of tilting your head back it was there, the white hole in the sky.

He took a sip of iced tea. The ice chimed prettily. The sunlight off the pool was softened by his sunglasses, aviator-fashion made by hand in Milan.

Loretta Lee said, "I don't like what's happening."

"I don't like it either. I'll be glad when it's over. He's going to be a very unpleasant guest, but I've told you how we'll treat him." He put a hand to the frame of his glasses. Imagine, he thought, making glasses everyday, week after week. The result was an elegant piece of work, but imagine the monotony.

"That's not what I mean."

Patterson was amazed, not for the first time, at how inconsiderate Loretta Lee could be. "You have everything you want," he said.

"I don't like what's happening."

Patterson laughed softly. "Everything is going to be different now."

"You shouldn't have sent everyone away."

"You like arguing with me, don't you?"

When the video crew decamped, all the staff had left with them, the nurse, the extra cook, everyone packed into the plane, waving happily, all of them sure everything was going to be fine because Red Patterson said so.

"I want you alive and happy, Red."

"Things have gotten real simple. It's something that occurs to a man when he is almost killed."

That shut her up, he thought.

He added, "It's time to focus."

She took a moment to shape her argument. "Look at the pool, for just one example," said Loretta Lee. "Don't you remember the time it got a tarantula in it?"

One of the things he found fascinating about Loretta Lee was the way her mind worked. "It was a dead spider," said Patterson with quiet exasperation.

"A dead spider!" said Loretta Lee, as though that proved something incontestable.

"We don't need to keep a staff here just so we can fish out a drowned spider, should one appear."

"That's just an example, Red. Things go wrong. This is a big place."

The two of them sat in the shade beside the swimming pool. The dense palms and dark green grass gave the stunning impression of oasis. The edge of the pool was tiled with the same extravagant gold mosaic Hearst had used for his castle, except that this tile was unvisited by tourists and rarely so much as photographed. A leaf had fallen from one of the yuccas, a long spine like a stilletto without its hilt.

Patterson finished the iced tea and put the glass on the small table. The cubes had already melted. He stood and took a moment to get ready for the real heat. He stepped from the shade to the sun, blinking against the press of the light. He retrieved the pool rake from its hiding place.

He used the long implement to secure the leaf from the bottom of the pool. The leaf spun free, and it took a second or two to balance the spine in the rake, which was really more like an oversized hook. The bottom had been repainted twice in the eight years he had owned

Owl Springs. Legend was that Marilyn Monroe had belly flopped in
the nude off the sparkling, sandpapery diving board.

"I might put the cover over the pool," he said, setting down
the rake.

"And the cooking. You're not going to see me in the kitchen
making pancakes—"

"You will if I ask you to."

There was a long pause. "Sure. If that's what you need," she
said, softening her voice, and doing that thing with her eyes, making
them look both wide and unobservant at the same time.

They would be here any minute. He didn't have time for her.
"You forget that when we met you were just another stunning beauty
exploring that traditional plan B of the actress."

"I don't like this, Red."

"I need Bishop, and I need you. That's all."

Loretta Lee couldn't argue with that. She was quiet, observing
him, not simply looking at him, taking him in with a long silence.
Patterson let her look. He was right. They would all live a simpler
existence. They would be happy.

She said. "And Curtis. You need him, too."

"Yes, I need him."

"What's the matter with you, Red?"

"I have seen what they used to call the light," he said, sitting
down again, stretching out his legs. You could hardly breathe the
air, he thought. Lungs couldn't take this kind of dryness.

"I've heard you tell people to beware of sudden changes in behavior." She tried to say this cheerfully, so if he was offended she
could pretend it was a bad joke. "That they can be symptoms of
mental illness."

He wondered over the fact that you could love a woman and be
sick of her at the same time.

"And the policy stays the same," he said. "Don't go near Curtis's suite."

Inside, it was so cool the sweat on his arms and legs felt like
frost. The chill was refreshing, but it imparted something phony to
the taste of the air.

He padded down one corridor after another. He paused outside
Curtis's suite, selecting the key from his pants pocket.

He opened the door, and slipped inside. He was about to hurry
down the hallway, and into the studio, when he heard it.

There was no mistaking the sound of the small jet, the Gulfstream V, Bishop himself piloting it, taking a wide approach so the critic could have a good look at what lay below.

And so Patterson would have plenty of time to hear them and finish the preparations. Bishop was smart. Bishop knew things, and he did not make mistakes.

Loretta Lee had thrown on something shimmery, dazzling, and she looked perfect, although she appeared too nervous hesitating there in the dining room, like a hostess whose cook had just run off with the maid. Patterson was touched—she bitched about everything, but she was loyal.

He kissed her. "Give him the impression that I will be down very soon," said Patterson. "I'm preoccupied and can't tear myself away. We want Bruno to feel that he is a respected visitor, but that we really don't have the time to entertain even someone as important as he is."

The jet was on the airstrip. The thrust reversers made the compact engine rumble, and once again Patterson told himself that where he really wanted to be was in the air somewhere.

"I look okay, too, right?" she was asking.

"Delectable."

He waited in the library, the window open so the air-conditioned cool eddied in the heat from outside. He heard Loretta Lee sliding the glass door. He heard the tiny but distinct scrape of the pool rake as Loretta Lee hung it on the hooks where it belonged.

The jet whined, and there was the long pause, the long wait, as the man from the outside, the man who could alter everything with a few words, gathered himself to make his final, personal descent into the heat.

31

Bruno expected it to be hot. Heat didn't bother him. But he had not expected it to be like this.

The executive jet touched the ground, lifted slightly, then settled into a smooth roll. Its engines made that sweet, pleasing whistle of power ebbing. The steps extended to the pavement, but Bruno was still well within the cabin when the heat reached him.

An attractive woman who introduced herself as Loretta Lee Arno held her hand out to him as he paused under the full force of the afternoon sun. "You can call me Loretta Lee," she said.

"Bruno," he said, offering her his name with a little smile, as though it were a gift. We don't need last names, he thought. We are just old children, let loose in the tired, dissolute playground of life. "I hadn't realized it when we spoke, but I do recall you from *Hollywood Midnights*, I believe it was. It's your voice—it's so distinctive."

She did not respond to this. "Dr. Patterson is very excited that you're here," she said. "He asked me to tell you that he's trying to do something very difficult just now. He wanted me to ask you to please be patient."

"I couldn't be more willing to cooperate in any way I can." He made sure that his voice sounded slightly bored, a trick he had learned from English friends of his youth who, pretenders to elegance, spoke in a slow, careless drawl, as though half-asleep.

But it was all pretense. He was as nervous as he had ever been, but more than anything, at the moment, he was eager to get out of the sun. The Italian summers could be heavy-handed, but this was

197

punishing. Mirage began at one hundred feet away and quaked, mercury-bright, so dazzling that it reflected things almost perfectly, palms, the outline of the villa.

He was accustomed to the enclaves of the wealthy, the security-burdened Greek islet, the Montecito villa. But this place was different, more handsome and more remote than any place he had ever visited. His shadow pooled under his feet, an ugly shape.

They walked toward the shade, toward the big iron gates. The fringe of the oasis seemed to retreat before them, tantalizingly.

The shade, when they reached it at last, was cool. Loretta Lee led him to poolside, where a sparrow was taking a bath in a trickle of water. Bruno wondered if anyone had been swimming here just moments before. The thought was electric—perhaps Curtis himself.

She vanished for a moment, leaving Bruno in delicious shadow. She returned with Bruno's drink of choice, iced coffee, on a tray. She sipped a tall drink of her own, something clear and sparkling embellished with a wedge of lime, and they strolled for a moment with their drinks, enjoying the botanical cool.

Patterson was not to be seen. Bruno began to feel irritated. "What is this very difficult thing that Dr. Patterson is trying to do just now?" he asked.

"Did you see Dr. Patterson the other day? On TV? They had him sitting here for the video, right under this big aloe."

"I heard about it, but I'm afraid I missed it."

"You never in your life watched *Hollywood Midnights,* did you?"

"Of course I did," he said, and, to spur the subject in a new direction, Bruno remarked on the beauty of the garden. The plant life included the bright green tines of cycads, and dozens of varieties of cacti. A fountain played somewhere, or perhaps it was the spring itself, the source that gave its name to the acres of green.

"All your doubts would have been settled if you'd just seen Dr. Patterson explain how well everything's been going."

"I'm sure you're right." The coffee tasted good, although already the melting ice was starting to dilute it.

"The difficult thing Dr. Patterson is doing is this: it has to do with you. He's with Mr. Newns right now, trying to talk him into seeing you."

"I certainly hope he succeeds." Although, Bruno did not add, I am much more interested in what Curtis has been painting than complimenting him on how well he looks. "Is he recovering from his injuries?" he asked.

"Mr. Newns loves the solitude," she said. "He's a very private person. I hadn't realized that."

"I think that's the value of art, don't you?" said Bruno. "Artists bring out of themselves, in solitude, what can become the colors of our lives." Bruno regarded what he had just said. He liked *colors of our lives.*

The house itself was mock-Spanish, with wrought iron grilles over the deep-set windows. The walls were sand-pink, the pastel bleached in places where the sunlight coursed through the dense plant life.

They returned to poolside and sat, teak furniture creaking under their weight. Loretta Lee was one of those beauties common around the film and television world. She was not the product of education or good taste. Her presence was animal, all energy and good camera angles. You see men and women on the screen and you think: people like that don't exist.

"I used to like painting," she said. "I didn't try to do it myself— I mean, I used to like art books and museums."

"Really?" Bruno was being polite. Given the need he would be polite to Godzilla. But he wanted to get on with this meeting, and he was not prepared to engage in small talk with this healthy female mammal. He was thirsty for more iced coffee, and he wondered if the headache might be about to return. The thought that Patterson was this very moment in conference with Curtis made him eager and edgy. He was so close to the truth.

"I think Dr. Patterson looks at me and sees someone who has a lot to learn," she said.

"He couldn't possibly think of you as ignorant."

"I am, in a way, but I do okay. I take care of everything."

This claim of universal husbandry confused Bruno for an instant. Her gaze was too steady, her air of simplicity both genuine and practiced. She was one of those seemingly straightforward people Bruno had always found enigmatic.

"It must be interesting to work so closely with Dr. Patterson," said Bruno.

"If you had to pick one painting in the whole world as the most important, which would you pick?"

"You mean, if I was forced to pick—at gunpoint?"

They both laughed at the thought, but then Loretta Lee appeared to be sobered by some thought or memory.

"I thought that Curtis's painting of the sky was the finest single work painted by a living artist," said Bruno. The thought of the painting saddened him for a moment. "Some people would say the painting by Velázquez at the Met, the portrait of Juan de Pareja, is the single most important painting in the world, but the very thought of picking one painting is so indescribably limiting I can hardly stand the idea. Besides, portraits are a category of their own, aren't they?"

Bruno's voice had started out in the tones of a self-guided tour, but his comment had ended with Bruno gazing about himself in disbelief. No one kept him waiting this long.

"Dr. Patterson will be with you very soon," she said.

He must have betrayed his impatience with a twitch, a look in his eye. He didn't like that. He had learned long ago, bidding at Sotheby's, waiting for the display carousel to turn and expose a priceless dream: don't show the slightest anticipation. He had started out placing bids for people who could not be troubled to make their way to New Bond Street themselves. The experience had taught him much of what he knew. "I'm sorry. Please forgive me," said Bruno. "I could sit here forever, it's so lovely."

Loretta Lee knew better. "We have to cooperate with Dr. Patterson, Bruno. If he wants us to wait—then we wait."

How odd it was to have this woman, still years from her first chintuck, speaking to him so frankly. Maybe he would find it refreshing, if he got used to it. "Tell me—" He was about to ask: what is the new painting like? But that would loosen a tangle of questions—where is it? When can I see it? He could not keep from asking. He was just about to lean forward and whisper *tell me something—anything*.

Loretta Lee stood and flashed a smile across the pool, and Bruno stood to follow her gaze.

Bruno had hoped to see Curtis. There, across the shimmering surface of the swimming pool, was Red Patterson.

Patterson was deep-chested, dressed in something vaguely cowboyish and expensive, open collar shirt, denims, snakeskin boots. His face had the unmistakable, vital glow of a careful tan.

Patterson embraced Bruno, gave him a hearty, healthy hug, and then held Bruno at arm's length. "I am so happy to have you here," he said.

Bruno had expected to dislike Patterson. He was surprised at his own reaction. He liked Patterson at once, and wanted Patterson to like him in return.

Patterson was happy. Bruno felt himself relax. This exuberance was so impressive, so capable of rolling away all that lay before it, that it was only as they were about to enter the house that Bruno stopped, and looked back at the palms and cacti around them.

"I want to see Curtis," said Bruno.

But Patterson had already hurried away, into the villa. "Don't stand around down there. Come on," said the energetic psychiatrist.

Bruno felt light-headed. The two of them were striding through the chilly interior of the big house.

"I know how you feel about this," said Patterson, leading Bruno up another stairway. The famous man's boots clumped on the hardwood floors. "So why waste time?"

This was happening so quickly. "I realize what an intrusion my visit is," panted Bruno.

"I'm delighted that you're here," said Patterson over his shoulder. "I love your tape on Cézanne—pure brilliance."

Bruno was out of breath. The broad dark oak door had to be unlocked, and Patterson held the door open so that Bruno could enter. He was ready to call a greeting, but then his instincts told him that the artist was not in this room, that this room had been abandoned to the merely physical—walls, floor, vaults of light.

But there was a presence.

A work of art stood at the far end of the room under the folds of a cloth.

This was a large room, a ballroom or a banquet hall, with dark wooden beams in the ceiling. The room could be well lit, but it was partly shuttered, the sunlight spreading across the wooden floor in irregular shapes. Dust motes, fine, subtle, spun in the shafts of light.

There was the intoxicating smell of oil paint, and a large glass jar containing a sheaf of brushes. Bruno liked this—a jar of economy-sized peanut butter, say, or institutional pack pickle relish spending its long retirement serving art. A tarp was rolled up neatly against the wall, leaving the floor unspotted.

He was letting himself notice these little details because he was stalling. The longer he waited, the longer he would delay what would almost certainly be disappointment.

Patterson was poised like a showman, a stage magician. The painting was a broad rectangle covered with a sheet, completely disguised by the folds of muslin.

Bruno had traveled to see this—and now he could not bear to look. He gave a nod.

Patterson stood to one side, lifted a hand, and gave a tug.

The sheet gave way and spilled to the floor with a soft sound, a sound that altered the pressure in the room like the pulse of distant thunder. Bruno stepped back.

Patterson opened a pair of shutters, and then another. The sun was so bright that it took awhile to get used to the radiance, the great empty expansiveness of the canvas sending the afternoon sun right back into the room.

So I am disappointed, after all, thought Bruno.

The canvas was empty.

He put a finger to his lips.

Wait.

He took a step. He was wrong—the canvas wasn't empty. There they were—the skeletal lines, the reach of colors, the depth pin-pricked in with dabs, faint, deft, of azure.

There was a sweep of feeling in Bruno, unmistakable: this was it.

This was what he had been waiting for.

This canyon of blank space fell away from him, rolling to a horizon, a world only Curtis could envision, that other, newer world, keener than the one born every day.

Bruno slipped on his reading glasses. He stepped to the canvas, so close the weft and fiber of the surface was vivid before him. The smell of the oil was strong, and yet he wanted to see the cut and smear of the painting knife, and identify the touch, as sure as a signature, of the brush against the fabric.

Curtis had begun a masterpiece.

But the work was so lightly touched upon the canvas, and the canvas so big, that Bruno needed a few more moments to take it all in.

The shroud rose back into place.

32

Patterson locked the studio door behind them. "You will want to fly to San Francisco tonight," said Patterson. "To reassure Mrs. Newns."

"Of course," said Bruno.

"And then I suppose you'll return to Rome—what a wonderful city."

Bruno agreed that this was his plan.

"I'm afraid you may have to hurry just a bit. I arranged to have a few members of the media meet you at the airport in San Francisco."

"Why not?"

Patterson laughed. "You're good at this, aren't you?"

Bruno laughed, too. He made a sideways motion of his head, acknowledging the compliment.

"I'd ask you to dine with us," said Patterson, "but I think the world is eager to hear from you."

"Actually, I was reluctant to tell you that I wanted to leave right away," said Bruno. "I was afraid you'd be offended."

"There is no need to be afraid of anything," said Patterson. "Ever again."

After a sip of iced coffee, and a brief chat about Curtis's past, his foster families, his mistrust of anything European and fondness for everything American, Bruno rose to leave.

And to think, thought Bruno, that I had begun to consider myself a force that might be fading, someone with a interesting history and a dullish future. Bruno laughed at himself. How fresh everything looked, the spikes of the sego palms, the glorious saw-tooth edges of the aloes.

It was still afternoon, but shadows were lengthening. The desert beyond was golden. Patterson saw him to the edge of the airstrip, then walked back to remain at the very edge of the shade.

Bruno ducked inside, happy to seclude himself in the cool interior of the aircraft.

It was quick and easy, thought Bruno. This is how they do things in the New World. Easy in, easy out, and I have a future again. He waved at the figure at the edge of the oasis, the glowing man Bruno would have recognized anywhere, the way the famous have of weighing into us. You can close your eyes, Bruno thought, and there they are, the well-known celebrities living and dead, tattooed on the psyche.

This icon was waving at Bruno once again, and Bruno waved back, health and farewell, a true physician.

However, as the jet taxied, Bruno's delight began to fade. By the time they were airborne Bruno began to reconsider the image of Patterson. That tan, that exuberant, confident smile.

What sort of man was he, really?

But soon Bruno was lost in an optimistic reverie, and it was easy to forget Red Patterson altogether. The man was not important, really. He was a mere midwife, an attendant upon the creation of this new future.

Bruno had long been aware of a certain artificial quality in himself. He had learned how to sound arch and debonair by watching movies. The image of actors like George Sanders had influenced Bruno as strongly as any human being he had actually met. To have contact with a work of art, to be aware of a future stirring itself awake— this was what Bruno needed.

The flight north took perhaps an hour and a half—Bruno wasn't sure. It seemed like a long time. When Bruno at last looked down at the glittering freeways and streets in the darkness he felt that this living map, was somehow his.

He left the jet and a cool breeze buffeted him as he crossed the concrete. It was early evening, the sky dark, a typical San Francisco summer night. An aide guided him, whether a Red Patterson functionary or someone who worked for the airport Bruno could not tell.

There was a passage from cold and half-light to airport interior. Then there were people, many of them. So many times Bruno had arrived at an airport and seen the people waiting in the lobby. The people in these foreign airports were always expectant, anticipating the arrival of friends, family. And Bruno had felt at such moments how wonderful it would be if only one person in the throng of strangers would be there to give him a welcoming embrace.

So it was sweet to see so many glad to see him. For a moment Bruno was surprised. He had expected a few reporters, some video-cams, a microphone or two. But this was a crush of people behind a bank of lights. Bruno had underestimated the power of Red Patterson's name.

And, he thought, the power of my own name. It was the sort of sight Bruno relished. He recognized faces. He nodded, smiled. He was prepared to speak without notes. His own handwriting had a tendency to displease him, anyway, staggering across the page—especially when he was excited.

The crowd—there was no other word for such a large gathering—subsided into silence.

"I have a statement," he began.

Bruno had always admired the diva's power over her most distant balcony, her control over the standing-room-only. Bruno did not have song, or voice. But he did have this—his sliver of power.

"I have a statement regarding what I have learned in my meeting with Red Patterson in Owl Springs."

People stirred again, recorders ready, cameras in hand. If there had been any doubt regarding the importance of Bruno's message, it was now in full retreat.

It took a moment for this new stir to subside. The hour was not late—there was still time to make the eleven o'clock news. But Bruno would be wise, he knew, to speak simply, light a verbal fire-cracker or two, and then pass on out of this hall of working men and women, to return to his private joy.

It was only then, as the cameras and the microphones were ready to take him in, that he realized that he should have called Margaret. There was no question: she should be the first to know.

It was too late. The expectant faces awaited him.

"I am pleased to be able to announce news that will delight the art world, reassure the world of psychiatry, and be a source of satisfaction to all of us." He allowed himself a quiet laugh. "I am more than pleased. I am ecstatic."

33

Bruno called her, sounding brisk and happy, and she didn't have time to ask him anything. He said that he had just finished a news conference here in San Francisco, and that he was grabbing a cab and was on his way over.

She had been at work at her drafting table, doing a little more drawing before she went to bed, sipping a cup of warm nonfat milk and hoping to feel sleepy soon. She had been plowing ahead with an assortment of sketches of ducks and goats. Bruno's call came, and she was thankful.

She set out some cheese and bread, a melon and an avocado. Bruno might be hungry. She brought a bottle of white wine out, too, because she felt from the way he sounded that there was something to celebrate.

She was wrestling with the cork—which was crumbly, and the better bottle opener was lost—when the security guard rang to say that Mr. Kraft was on his way up.

He came through the door looking like someone who had run a tremendous distance. He fell into the sofa and accepted a glass of wine.

It did not take him long to assume his usual appearance, poised and sure of himself. He requested some aspirin, and she struggled with a childproof cap until several tablets spilled into his hand. He swallowed four with the wine, pocketing the rest.

"He's started something new," he said.

"That's wonderful!"

"Please forgive me, Margaret. I have just this minute realized that I'm starving."

"How did Curtis look?" asked Margaret as she served Bruno.

"There's a new major work underway." He looked up to see her expectant expression.

She waited, her expression saying *go on.*

"Don't you realize what this means?" he said.

He was out of the sofa now, folding his arms, gazing out beyond the balcony of the Newns's penthouse. The water of the bay was black, invisible, and there were only a few lights on the Marin headlands beyond.

"I don't know that it's quite accurate to call this painting a new *Skyscape*," he continued. "But that's what it is to me. Not a replacement, and certainly not a copy from memory. But something of great value. Something to let us know that the world is a place of promise, not just loss."

"Drawings?"

"No—a painting."

"What was it like?"

"Sketchy, to be frank. Barely begun. But magnificent."

"A big canvas?"

Bruno chewed, swallowed, applied a napkin to his mustache. "Huge. As big as anything he ever did. He hasn't begun anything like this in years."

"You took photographs of it?"

"It wasn't necessary. Besides, I'm not the sort of person to carry a camera around wherever I go."

"And how was Curtis?"

Bruno held forth an open hand: what difference does it make?

She kept her voice very calm and steady. "You did see Curtis, didn't you?"

"He didn't want to see me."

She said nothing for a moment. "You went all the way there and didn't even set eyes on Curtis?"

Bruno looked mildly outraged. "You know how Curtis is. He refused. What could I do?"

"We all know how helpless you are."

"I was a guest in the house of Red Patterson and I had no right to insist that I see someone who does, after all, have a recent history of avoiding me. You might say I actually respect Curtis for having a certain consistency of character."

"I wonder—did you actually see the painting, or was the painting somehow off-limits, too? Was it described to you, how wonderful it was—"

"The painting exists," he said in a tone of scorn. He frowned into his wine, dabbed a finger into the glass, and removed a speck of cork.

"You want it so badly you might think you saw something that wasn't quite real, maybe just a big blank canvas."

He adopted a mocking tone. "What is it you think, Margaret? Tell me what it is I saw down there in the desert."

"He could have shown you anything on canvas and you would have come away convinced because you needed something there, something that would rescue you and your career."

He set down his glass, pressed his lips into the napkin, and tossed it down. "I don't have to stand here and listen to this."

"You do," she said. "Because I am going to call a press conference of my own. I'm going to call a few friends and tell them I'm worried about the health of my husband. I'm going to tell them that I don't believe the new painting even exists."

"Don't be childish."

"It worries you though, doesn't it?"

"Absolutely not. You will not go before cameras and call Bruno Kraft a liar." Referring to himself in the third person empowered him to use his most disdainful accent. "People will think that you're confused and shrill. They will feel sorry for you. I will see to that. You won't stand a chance. You'll be a figure of amusement."

Margaret gazed ahead from where she sat on the sofa, focusing on nothing. "I thought you were a friend."

"You're jealous of Red Patterson. Jealousy's one of the deadly sins, Margaret. It's a destroyer of happiness. You resent Patterson's success in making Curtis happy where you failed."

Their eyes locked. At once Bruno felt himself falter. He was too good at invective, he thought, once he got going. It was a nasty habit.

"I'm sorry," he said. "Please forgive me."

"I'd let Curtis go if I believed it would make him happy," she said. "In a way, I've already lost him, haven't I?"

"I shouldn't have spoken to you like this."

"You may be right, Bruno. Don't worry. I forgive you. But you do owe me something, don't you?"

"You're a very unusual person, Margaret."

"Tell Patterson that you're disturbed at what I've told you. That I'm handpicking art critics of my own to fly to Owl Springs and examine the painting. That I'm consulting a new psychiatrist—several of them. That there is a growing number of people who don't believe in Red Patterson.''

"You're bluffing, dear Margaret.''

She did not answer, except to pick up a knife and cut the avocado into two neat halves.

Bruno wanted to sit down. He found himself wondering about the painting he had seen just a few hours before. What *had* it looked like? He wouldn't allow himself to think like this. Doubting himself made him feel anxious. He wanted to be alone, or with Andy. Andy—that was who he needed.

The strong, common sense of Andy, who was always changing his hairstyle, always criticizing Bruno's choice of necktie and his shoes, always looking forward to seeing the latest movie, enjoying the silliest pleasures. It was because he lived in the moment, in his relative youth, and in his freedom from ambition. Andy was daylight, and all of this confusion was darkness. Bruno was confused—he could not deny it. Maybe he was wrong. Maybe the painting was not by Curtis Newns. It looked authentic. But was it really?

It was a terrible thought, the sort of doubt that makes the high-wire artist waver and fall. Bruno put the question out of his mind.

"You aren't sure of anything, are you?'' said Margaret in a tone of gentle pity.

"Do you like jello?'' said Bruno. "It's been years since I had any. My mother used to make strawberry jello with bananas sliced up in it.''

"I'm fresh out,'' said Margaret.

"I don't want any. I was just realizing that it's been a long time.''

"You disappoint yourself.''

"Please shut up, Margaret.'' He said this gently, and put his hand on her head, a gesture of benediction. Her head was warm, her hair soft, delightful to the touch.

"I'm going out there to see Curtis,'' she said.

"I'll call Patterson. I'll tell him how dangerous you are.''

Her eyes stayed on his, and he guessed what she was about to ask. "I used to wonder what it would be like to be beautiful,'' said Bruno. "You see these photographs of beautiful young people, naked. There's such power in the human body. And I wonder sometimes what it must be like to know that a photograph of one's erection is out there in the world.''

"You're afraid,'' she said.

"Too many good people have died in recent years." For a moment he resented her for making him mention, even in passing, the subject of AIDS. "It's made me honest with myself. I have to stick with what I know and what I love. I love Curtis's art, Margaret. I love my prestige. That sounds smug, but I mean it honestly. I love Rome, and I love Andy. I'm not going back to Owl Springs."

"Tell Patterson I'm coming."

"You don't want to get tangled in whatever's going on down there, Margaret. Why can't you just accept it?"

"Because you can't. Because I love Curtis. You're not a bad person, Bruno. But I trusted you, and I shouldn't have."

Bruno made the phone call. His voice was quiet; she could not make out all the words.

When he was off the phone he stood there in the living room adjusting his cuffs, looking around for a mirror. He went to the mirror she had hung where one of the slashed paintings had commanded the wall.

Margaret watched him, and he made a pretense of ignoring her.

"That was it?" said Margaret. "That was the call? You hung up and everything's the same."

"Everything has changed," said Bruno. He seemed satisfied with his tie, patting the knot. "Dr. Patterson was unable to come to the telephone. I spoke with his assistant, Miss Arno. I repeated your threats. Is there anything else you want me to do?"

"You've had a busy evening. You must be tired."

"TWA has a 1:20 A.M. flight, stopping at Saint Louis. I'll be in Rome by the time I am once again in a good mood."

She felt herself lose something, further faith in him, in the way reality was ordered.

"But surely you need time to rest." It occurred to Margaret that a man who traveled all the time might be running from something.

"I'm going back to my own life. And Margaret, if you are wise, you will stay where you are."

"You can't abandon everything like this."

"You mean: I can't abandon *you.* Stay here, Margaret. Here you have a certain amount of power. You can call friends, reporters. You can even call a radio station and threaten to shoot someone. But out there. . . ." He gave her a smile. "Don't go to Owl Springs."

There was a folder of papers from an art restorer, pages describing in centimeters the rips in the canvas, and advising further consultation with experts in distant places, but assessing the damage as being, "well within the bounds of what can be made to resemble the pre-damaged state." As though to mock what they would seek to mend, the paintings were reproduced in black and white, the cuts in the paints marked with paste-on arrows, like the exhibits of the victim's clothing in old crime magazines.

There was the cage, and the starling, asleep under his nighttime hood of blue drapery. Mrs. Wye was especially fond of the bird, arriving daily with a piece of something new to see if its taste for food could be further expanded—cinnamon toast, strudel, spartan sheaves of millet, rinds of gouda. The bird so far had refused none of Mrs. Wye's gifts.

Bruno was gone, departed with a crisp kiss and a suave farewell, the sterling courtesy he would have shown to someone he loathed.

This, she told herself, was her life, this wicker holder in which she kept her colored pencils, this Rolodex of phone numbers, this pile of books, unopened jiffy bags of gifts, samples, catalogs, this apartment of hers that she no longer wanted, not without Curtis.

She did not really fall asleep. She slipped into something like a trance, however, very late in the night, because when the phone rang it startled her, more than awakened her—made her stay where she was for a few heartbeats, wondering what on earth that insistent sound could be.

It was a voice she recognized immediately. "I hope I didn't wake you."

"No, I wasn't really sleeping. I wasn't able to."

"I understand you want to spend some time with us," said the voice.

"That's exactly what I want," said Margaret, feeling herself stir to increasing wakefulness, feeling herself rise to something like happiness.

"Pack light clothes, shorts, a swimsuit," said Red Patterson. "I think the time has come for you to visit us in the desert."

PART THREE

SKYSCAPE

34

Loretta Lee stood at the foot of the stairs. There was no sun where she stood, and no sound.

She was worried. She was probably worried because that was her specialty, the one thing she was really good at, but there it was and she couldn't deny it.

She had always been lucky. This was what she told herself all the time. She had grown up in a landscape of shopping malls and duplexes. In the Southern California neighborhoods where Loretta Lee had learned to smoke cigarettes and drink tequila, a person wasn't really supposed to look at anything. You noticed the clothing styles in magazines, faces and bodies on television. No one bothered with the scenery. There were big rivers, empty and paved with cement.

She had been happy enough growing up, but it was a happiness that, in retrospect, was cut off from passion. There were hot afternoons, spent watching television while the lawn sprinkler outside made its steady whisper. There were prayer-silent foggy mornings, walking the way to school in a world no wider than a kitchen. Loretta Lee and her mother had a favorite restaurant, a smorgasbord behind the Mesa theater where they both liked the meatballs and the strangely sweet gravy.

But it was a life that settled steadily around her, like fine fragmenting ash that drifted down out of the sky during a brushfire. Patterson had awakened her. She reminded herself how much she owed Patterson as she stood there in the silence.

The doctor had just left the house, going out to the hangar as he

215

often did in the early morning. She told herself that there was nothing to prevent her from going up to the studio, up to the room where Patterson and Curtis did their work.

Go ahead. Tap on the door. Ask Curtis if there's anything you can get for him.

She even took a step up the stairs before she asked herself what she thought she was doing. She had always trusted Patterson, even though she prompted him, coaxed him. He needed her, and that knowledge made her feel more alive than she ever had in those vague, wasted days in L.A.

But she took yet another step, climbing the stairs. If Patterson asked, she would say that she was just making sure Curtis had everything he wanted. She had a fantasy conversation with Patterson, explaining that she felt that it was a part of her job to make sure that—.

The fantasy faltered. *Taking up psychiatry, are you?* Patterson would say. *Think you know how to help Curtis better than I do?* he would ask with a smile, one of those bad smiles, the kind that chilled her.

Patterson needed her. Sometimes he frightened her—he was so sure of himself. No human being could be that sure. People made mistakes.

Her girlhood had been spent telling herself that she could manage. Her father was a clear memory, but a simplistic one, muscular, healthy, cutting the crabgrass with a power mower. He vanished early on, before she was in kindergarten. Her mother was a buyer for a local department store, specializing in notions and yardage, pretty, in a thoughtful, introspective way. Someone had to make sure the lawn was raked and watered, light bulbs replaced when they burned out, kleenex brought to her mother's side when something on television made her cry.

Her mother made grocery lists, Loretta Lee did the shopping. Her mother made a list of books to bring her in the hospital, and Loretta Lee went to the library. Her mother left lists behind at her death, and Loretta Lee added her own little check beside each disposal of furniture, each donation, each table lamp carried away at the yard sale.

Loretta Lee had done what she could, and she missed her mother. She had grown up to be the sort of young woman who was impressed by very little.

Loretta Lee had ambition in her late teens and early twenties, suffered from ambition, had it like a disease. Her agent was always quick to answer her calls, but he was quick at everything, eating, talking. Sex with him was like something out of a National Geographic special, lightning copulation, instantaneous ejaculation—bug sex. He was one of the many people she knew who saw life as a matter of getting as much as possible in the shortest amount of time.

Sometimes she woke at night aching with envy. Other people had careers—she had a series of trashy poses she worked hard to get. By the time she saw herself on the cover of soap opera magazines, it was too late. She was depressed the way some people were obese. It was a hard problem to lose.

Patterson's office had been just off Santa Monica Boulevard, a building full of pricey financial consultants and title companies. A girlfriend, a fellow-actress who suffered migraines, had urged Loretta Lee to visit. "This guy is all you need," she had said.

One visit and Loretta Lee realized that no one had ever listened to her before. When she spoke the doctor understood her. He would lean forward, his eyes bright and caring, and she would feel herself unfold, change, open into a new, more loving person.

It had been a long time since she had found herself awake at night, too empty inside to sleep, too empty to get up. But lately she stared into the dark at night, worried. Red was changing. There was something about him that shook her. Maybe she was being ungrateful and foolish, standing on the stairs as though she knew what she was doing. She had to be wrong. Whatever Curtis and Patterson were up to, it had nothing to do with her.

She wasn't even surprised when she heard his step behind her, in the hall. Patterson was like this—he sensed things.

"You're up early again," said Patterson.

"I have trouble sleeping," she said, truthfully.

"That's the easiest problem in the world to fix," he said.

She knew that sometimes Red didn't have time for her. This was not because he had stopped caring for her, she knew. It was because he had so much else on his mind. "I'll be all right," she said, descending the stairs.

"You aren't worried, are you?" he asked.

"Like you used to tell me—just a little faith."

"That's all it takes," said Patterson, stroking her hair, looking into her eyes. Then he took a handful of her hair, very gently, and kissed her.

"You aren't going up there, are you?" he asked.

"No," she breathed.

No, of course not. She wouldn't dream of it.

*   *   *

At first there was life in the room. "Since you won't paint, I will," and there was the sound of turpentine splashing, a brush stirring. And the smell, the bright, biochemical charge that Patterson loved.

Curtis climbed. He worked his way upward, onto his feet. It was sudden. Patterson looked on. Curtis stood before the canvas, his healing injuries throbbing. He lifted his right hand and touched the canvas with a forefinger. It made a pleasing, gentle *pop,* a raindrop falling onto a sheet of paper.

Patterson parted the curtains, and let a steel probe of light fall into the room. He opened the curtains wide, and day was all over the room.

Curtis groaned as he bent over. He picked up the cardboard box, and tilted it. White tubes of paint scattered at his feet.

"If you need another shot I'll fix you one," said Patterson.

Curtis Newns was holding a tube of paint, unscrewing the cap. Curtis had the knife in his hand, the legendary blade he sometimes used in applying paint. There was the sound of paint being squeezed, gently, deliberately, onto the supple steel.

Then he stood before the canvas and saw the work his hands had done. Patterson knew what Curtis must be experiencing now. Curtis saw the white sky of the canvas as an enemy that had become an ally. It was the only ally he had left.

He did nothing, standing there as though unable to decide what to do next. He opened his hands and closed them, and let them drop to his sides.

"You don't believe in me, do you?" said Patterson in a tone of wonder.

Later Patterson would wonder if Curtis had ever lifted his hand to the canvas at all. Each day was like the one before it. It was a routine now. The doctor wheeled Curtis in the stainless steel chair to the place where the canvas was waiting.

Down in the heat there were nice, slate-gray plants and Patterson would look down at them and think how wonderful it was that everything was just the way he had dreamed it would be.

"Tell me if you want anything," said Patterson.

That's how it was—silence, and an all but empty canvas. They shared day after day like this. No doubt Curtis wanted a television, but Patterson thought this would not be a good idea; it would be a potential distraction. The doctor did not want anything to take Curtis's mind off what the doctor began to think of as the White Hole, although, naturally, it was a rectangle of cloth, waiting as canvas always did, winning in the end even when you smeared it with color.

After days of what Patterson considered defensive introjection, he changed tactics. Patterson closed the shutters, saying Curtis could look at the garden only if he began to paint. He said Curtis could even go outside if he began to paint a little bit, and the doctor gave him shots of head-clearing stimulants, drugs that Patterson knew made Curtis feel really wonderful, but did nothing to make him paint.

"I started to collect things when I realized that it was the best I could do," said the doctor. "I bought art, began to build my collection of aircraft. Some people love vintage cars, but cars seemed like such earthbound contraptions to me. I envied the artist. But I knew I could never be one."

Curtis was silent.

"I understood at last why people wanted to appear on my show. It wasn't so they could be healed. That was a part of it, but only a small part."

Curtis would not talk anymore.

"Sachs says that the impulse to creation was the search for companions in guilt," said Patterson, measuring the huge canvas with his eyes. "He was an important writer on psychoanalytic issues, and his phrase stayed with me. The view is built on the theory that creativity springs from the conflict between a man's longing for women and his dread of them. One chooses to paint as a refuge from the vagina. Out of a fear of that little cleft, that little entrance into the dark."

Curtis was stubborn, Patterson knew, but he was listening.

"Companions in guilt," said the doctor, speaking more to himself than to Curtis. "The viewer of the painting shares in the artist's plot against the void." The doctor sighed, picking up a brush, testing the pliant hairs against his fingertips. The brush left the slightest film of oil on the ball of his thumb and the doctor sniffed it as Curtis looked on.

"I used to think that I was like a god," said the doctor. "That I sat in the place of something divine when I was working with my patients. I believed that there was something not only sacred about sharing their secrets, but something more than human about my own role in their lives. But then when I discovered how dramatically television worked to cure my clients, I felt both exaulted and humbled. It wasn't my own powers doing the healing anymore, it was something else, the power of public confession, perhaps.''

Curtis listened but he did not speak.

"Faith," the doctor continued. "The faith we have in appearing in millions of replicated images. I gained greater power, and lost faith in myself as a physician at the same time. I want that faith back, Curtis. You can help me."

The artist was supreme in his silence. In the old days Patterson would have terminated the session. "I understand," said the doctor. "The act of painting has become dangerous, hasn't it?"

One evening after he wheeled Curtis back into his bedchamber, Patterson turned with the key in his hand. "Don't tell yourself for a moment that what you need is Margaret," he said. "Margaret was an adversary, someone trying to turn you into an ordinary man."

He stood at the door to the bedchamber and looked at Curtis, swept with love for the artist. "Soon there won't be a Curtis Newns or a Red Patterson. There will be only the painting."

Later, in the hall, Patterson stopped outside Loretta Lee's bedroom. She was in there talking, like someone talking on the telephone, but the tone wasn't right. There was something confessional about the tone, secretive. He listened, but could not make out what she was saying.

Patterson dismissed this, and it was only later, as he undressed in his own bedroom, that Patterson recognized what was happening. He usually draped his clothes casually over a chair as he got ready for bed, but this time he folded them carefully, thinking. He should have been aware of this before, but he had been oblivious to the obvious danger.

Loretta Lee was keeping secrets.

35

"Someone with *Good Morning America* was on the line," said Loretta Lee, "wanting to get footage of Margaret and Curtis hugging and kissing when she shows up. I chewed them out so bad they actually apologized."

"I'll get his ass fired, whoever it was," said Patterson, in a bored tone.

"It was a her."

"You faxed everybody and God that statement already, right?" said Patterson. "The one about Margaret joining her husband for a nice long visit, the need for the continuing therapeutic solitude. . . ."

"And the continuing quiet essential and curative. Sure. And everybody figures that you owe Margaret reassurance, and she'll get it and maybe have like a second honeymoon out here, with you helping them with the rough parts."

"Sounds kind of fun, doesn't it?"

"I don't see why you have to bring her all the way out here, Red, not really." She did have the sense to hesitate, unsure whether she should pursue the subject.

He did not encourage her.

She kept talking. "At least, her visit could be short. She could just fly in the way Bruno Kraft did, take a look, and leave, right?"

They were outside in the night, sitting beside the pool, sipping spearmint tea. The pool lights were pretty, Patterson thought, the ripples illuminated from within. You had to give those early Southern California designers credit. They had a good idea of how moguls and starlets ought to live. A person who could afford it could live in a California that was just as glamorous as it was supposed to be.

The surface of the pool was blemished by a small upwelling where the water from the filter surfaced. It was hours after Bruno's call from Margaret's apartment. Kraft's cultivated delivery, like the voice-over in an ad for expensive cars, had described Margaret's threats as though they were of mere interest. The press were already aware that by this time tomorrow night Margaret would be listening to the purling waters of Owl Springs.

"You didn't like Margaret?" said Patterson, examining his fingernails in the shivering light from the pool.

"I look forward to seeing her again," said Loretta Lee. She sounded okay, but something bothered her.

Maybe she hadn't been such a good actress after all, thought Patterson. "There's no reason," he said, "for you to feel threatened by Margaret."

"Of course there isn't."

"And there's no reason to feel threatened by me."

"Of course not, Red. I wouldn't feel threatened by you under any circumstance. What a thing to say. I just wonder why you're letting her visit."

"Kindness," said Patterson.

Loretta Lee said nothing.

But having used the word "threat" and "Margaret" in the same brief span of time exposed Patterson's anxieties, if only to himself.

"We'll take good care of Margaret," said Patterson. "She's a charming woman. We'll make her feel that she's a part of this place. She'll never want to leave."

"I'll be glad," said Loretta Lee, "when we can go back to the way things used to be."

"I thought you wanted me to rest."

"I don't call this rest."

Patterson guessed that it was three hours before dawn. He looked up at the stars, and there, timing it just right, was a meteor. Just a quick flash—you didn't see it and you saw it, all at once.

"I'm starting to have trouble again," she said. "Like in the old days." She was wearing very little in the way of clothing, something see-through and held with a bow at the neck. "I stop in the middle of doing something and wonder."

Bishop's bedroom light had been out a long time. The man kept a pilot's habits, brutality sublimated into the care he took with airplanes. A creature of some sort whispered through the air, a soft sound, a stocking tossed across a floor. Bats, thought Patterson, or one of the owls.

"You remember," said Patterson, "that stockbroker I had on the show last year, the man who never slept."

"What a dull man. Jesus. The only interesting thing about him was that he never put his head on a pillow."

"He said he didn't miss it."

"But you got him to admit that he did miss it. You got him to admit that he really did sleep, but while he was in the middle of doing other things, little tiny naps, and what he really wanted was to lie down in a big bed under a quilt with the rain on the roof."

"People never tell the truth," said Patterson. "At best, they tell a lie that resembles the truth, like an insect that looks like a twig."

"You've always underrated my intelligence, Red."

Sometimes he thought Loretta Lee would never shut up. "You're joking."

"At the same time you plugged it in and used it, like some sort of kitchen appliance."

He had known for a long time that some day Loretta Lee was going to be more trouble than she was worth, although if you ran a spreadsheet on her she still looked attractive enough.

When Patterson made no remark, she added, "Is Margaret going to help Curtis—help him paint the picture?"

"I am taking Mrs. Newns under my wing." He thought that image would be the sort of thing Loretta Lee would understand, obvious and simplistic. A big rooster protecting the little hen.

"But it will help Curtis, too, right?"

"I think you really should be going to bed, Loretta Lee. Your voice has that scratchy sound it gets when you're tired."

"Sometimes you talk to me in that fatherly way and it thrills me," she said. "Other times it just pisses me off."

"It's the adolescent in you, full of feeling, empty of understanding."

"Tell me what's happening here, Red. I trust you."

He could always just drown her here in the pool, he thought. Unthinkable, of course. Besides, she was as strong as a young moose. He kept his voice gentle. "Those two statements don't go together."

"Let me be a part of your plans."

"Are you really ready for that, do you think?"

"You know I only want to help you."

"But that was always your problem wasn't it?" he said. "You could have relaxed and made a little cigarette money, and retired by now married to—"

"To what? What was I going to do with my life?"

"You thought I was the answer. 'I know what I'll do. I can't manage my own life, but I sure can handle Red Patterson's.' "

"Do I really sound like that? One of those accents? I worked hard to get rid of it."

"Nothing wrong with a little twang."

She must have mistaken his tone. Or maybe she sensed that this was her last stand. Patterson knew that Loretta Lee would never have marched into the Little Bighorn with anything less than a machine gun. She put an arm around him.

She whispered, "Make me feel better."

They went inside. They tiptoed, as though afraid to wake a crowded household.

She led him by the hand into her bedroom, and he was surprised to see new prints on the wall, cinnamon-red prints of Cézanne hillsides. Patterson smiled. Loretta Lee was trying to learn something about art.

When they first met, her pubic hair had been shaved, in preparation for a starring role, under the name Beverly Pasadena, in a movie with a good deal of action but featuring one character after another with remarkably simplistic motivation.

Patterson had rescued her from so much sleaze, and here she was, naked, slipping into the satin sheets, perhaps a little disappointed when the only act of affection Patterson was prepared to offer was a glass of water from the spring and four beet-dark Seconals, the old, bad drug, the purple bombers that had taken so many movie careers into the permanent sweet night.

But she was like a picture, a pinup on the men's room wall, pink and brunette. Well, a little carnal play wouldn't do any harm. It might relieve a little tension in both of them.

"I've been good for you, haven't I, Red?" she whispered into his ear.

He did have a lingering fondness for Loretta Lee, thought Patterson, as he eased himself into her, letting himself take his time, waiting for her to ask him to *hurry, hurry, please hurry up,* just like she used to.

After all, Patterson thought, what was the act of love but the power to give pleasure, and to forestall it. Loretta Lee must realize this, and fear it: the difficulty was that love was not enough.

He knew how to work her body so it gave them both pleasure. Later, after he had made her gasp *please please* until it was nearly a scream, he lay there next to her in the dark. He could feel her stirring against the weight of the barbituate, working back up to him. "You'll tell me what you're going to do, won't you, Red?"

"Of course I will," he said.

Paul Angevin had warned him years ago. A psychiatrist sees himself as magic, but he tempers this sense of power with respect for his patients and knowledge of his own shortcomings.

Paul Angevin had gone to various medical experts, and collared network executives, trying to stir up opinion against the show. Paul had told everyone it was a bad idea, a sick plan, talk-show glitz coupled with the needs of real people to be healed. Paul had been a troubled man himself, a heavy smoker, a man afflicted with psychosomatic tics, rashes, illnesses. But Paul had been earnest, and people had listened to him.

A televised psychiatrist, Paul had written in his last memo, "cut off from the council of colleagues by their inevitable envy and his own vanity, trapped in the rich-oxygen of adulation, will fatten into a power he can use but not control." The show had begun by then, and Patterson had already experienced the confidence the show pumped into him.

She was asleep. Patterson was out of bed, back into his clothes. He listened to her slow breathing. He didn't have to search very hard. He opened the nightstand drawer. The light was not good, but he could see a box of suntan-shade panty hose, an electric razor. And several microcassettes, the kind Loretta Lee used in her tape recorder.

Patterson hurried quietly through the corridors. In his own bedroom Patterson popped a cassette into his little black Sony and sat listening.

Loretta Lee was saying it was so hot out by the pool that the lizards ran high up off the ground, as far as their legs would stretch. She went on to describe a dream about the lizards. "Someone's in this big house," Loretta Lee was saying. "And I know they're going to find me, so I try to hide, but all these lizards are in the way, all over the floor—"

Patterson worked the fast-forward. Loretta Lee's voice became a high-pitched scramble. He switched it back to normal speed, and

Loretta Lee was saying that sometimes she felt afraid. "Red doesn't look so good," she was saying. "He looks tired and tense and—"

Patterson worked the fast-forward again, whisking through what he gathered were more unflattering descriptions of himself, and more unremarkable dreams. Dreams, Patterson reflected, were considerably overemphasized as a source of psychological insight. There was a description of the house, how empty it felt. Loretta Lee talked about the locked silence of the studio.

"I've never seen Red like this," Loretta Lee's recorded voice said. "I look at him and I think—he needs help. I think maybe if things get worse here I might have to do something." There was a click. She had shut off the tape. When the tape was recording again she wasn't talking. "If things get worse," she said at last, "I might have to call in someone who can help." There was the sound of Loretta breathing. "Some kind of doctor. Some kind of authority—"

Patterson switched off the recorder.

He had hoped he would find out how innocent she was. Well, that was another pet illusion he wouldn't bother feeding any more. Loretta Lee had kept a diary off and on for a long time. He should have cured her of the habit.

Maybe she had been contacted by one of those tabloids. He could imagine the conversation. *Just keep a daily record of what goes on down there and sign right here at the bottom of this page.* Maybe someone from another television network took her out for a drink a few weeks ago, bought her dinner and showed her his checkbook.

It didn't matter who had bought her. Patterson had a lot to do.

He found his way to the studio, unlocked the door and when he was inside the big room he felt the wonder of the place, the presence of the painting. He switched on the light.

He locked the door behind him. He stepped toward the painting. It was draped with muslin, shrouded. Bruno Kraft had stood right here. Right here—and he had seen the truth.

Paul had been wrong, ultimately. Television was life. Bring all the people who have lost themselves back to the harbor. Back to life. It was not that difficult.

I have come to show you all how to leave the past. I will show you how to take one step after another upon the supple uneven surface, the sea. And you will walk. He had heard himself saying those very words on his first show, stimulated by the presence of the cameras, unsteady before a half-empty audience, most of whom were shills, there on free tickets pressed on them by the publicity department. Television had taught Patterson that anything was possible.

Patterson whisked away the sheet. The painting changed the light in the room. Television was life—but art was something more, something that out-lasted hope and doubt.

The painting was far from finished. There was so much emptiness here, so much left to be filled out, or captured, as if a painting was like one of Michelangelo's sculptures, already in existence and waiting to be freed.

And yet, Patterson was a doctor, a pilot, a man who knew the value of being. It would be a good idea to drive out into the desert and just make sure that everything was okay.

He replaced the shroud and left the studio, testing the lock. He paused before a door down the hall, stood before it, and actually had the key in the lock.

He had told Bishop that evening, just before he had called Margaret, to prepare to wake early and "be ready to deal with a problem," a phrase Bishop had recognized from long ago. "Anything you want," the pilot had said. But at that time Patterson hadn't been sure. He was just making contingency plans. You never knew what you might discover.

But now Patterson knew.

Patterson's bedroom window had a deep sill where one could sit and observe the pool. That is what he did, looking out upon the dark garden, the aloes and the papyrus silhouetted against the rippling pool.

He unzipped an old-fashioned doctor's bag, his own personal pharmacy. He loved the black leather, and imagined the sort of country doc who would have carried such a case in bygone days, all bedside manner and mustard plasters, in those years before it was understood that everything was chemistry, molecules linked to each other like so much playground equipment.

He selected a hypodermic, but hesitated on the choice for the work that had to be done. He gave it some thought. Sodium pentothal was the chemical he believed would be most reliable. It had worked before, and it would work again, although there was a nice sodium pentobarbital that would do almost as well. This, on top of the medication Loretta Lee had already swallowed, would keep her quiet for a long time.

Patterson had wanted more than to attend the dying, clip the tumor from its hold, stitch the shocking lips of the wound. He had wanted the spirit to exist and be free, he had wanted to ennoble what was left when illusion and pain and ignorance faded, and the self was left with so little covering.

Loretta Lee was a threat. He stood over her in the bedroom. She had that fallen, sweet look people so often take on when they sleep. He stroked her hip. When the needle went in she opened one eye, and opened her mouth like someone about to whisper an affectionate secret.

An hour before dawn Patterson left the big house. He hurried through the desert dark toward the garage. The stars above had weight, the moon so sharply cut out of the dark and its own unripened half, that Patterson had to pause and take it all in.

There was a large padlock on the garage. The lock would not release. The garage was one of those built to handle luxury cars of an earlier time, cars that never arrived, because this oasis was too far out into the Mojave. The road linking Owl Springs to state highway 127 was never built. The dream cost too much, the glamour not worth the very great trouble of having every cube of sugar and every loaf of bread flown in from Victorville.

When he finally got the lock off, the garage door was heavy. It had to be dragged, sliding, scraping. It made a squealing, animal sound as he pushed the heavy door all the way open.

God, it was quiet out here.

The door of the Range Rover opened, and then shut with a loud *chunk.* The ignition whined. The engine fired with a rumble. The air was so clean that the smell of the super-unleaded exhaust was enough to make him cough. He released the brake, nudged the accelerator.

He let the vehicle roll down across the apron of the landing strip, and did not turn on the headlights until he was well away from the house. There was no one to watch, no one to notice, but still he was careful.

It was cool enough this time of night for him to roll down the window and smell the dry air, the stone and empty atmosphere of desert. The big all-terrain tires popped and crunched over the stones, quartz geodes, agates, chunks that glittered in the moonlight.

He turned on the headlights and was immediately sorry. The stones ahead of him were too bright, and the rest of the desert too dark. He drove off across the rise and rubble of the land.

It was time to visit Paul Angevin.

36

It was a hard drive.

That didn't bother Patterson. In fact, it was reassuring.

You had to have a lot of sympathy for poor Paul. Bishop had flown him all the way out to Owl Springs for a discreet meeting. Patterson had hinted at compromise. It was the putative Golden Rule of the business: *Hey, we'll work something out.*

There was a predawn glow in the sky. Sometimes the tires slipped, slid to one side. Sometimes they bounded over a barrier of rock so rugged that Patterson was certain that the tires would be ripped to rags.

Patterson had always enjoyed a feel for machinery, the way some people have a rapport with animals. Engines had always been coaxed to life at his touch, and even the most stiff-handling Ford had proved adequate with his hand at the wheel. He had never been afraid to fly. An airplane was a machine, and machines were an extension of Patterson's body—of his will.

So he took a certain pleasure in the drive. The wheel fought him, and he had to hang on, downshifting, and manhandle the Range Rover, even with its power steering.

At last he reached the spill of yellow rock.

If he left the engine running it might overheat by the time he returned, he reasoned. It was a moment of intuitive assessment. An engine, like a human body, is a tiny universe of heat. He listened to the breathy power of the pistons and turned off the ignition.

The silence was a shock.

It always was. The senses knew such absolute quiet was impossible. The engine made cooling, ticking sounds. The sun was still below the horizon, but the pebbles and pores of the rock were gaining further definition, sharpening into a landscape, the light seeming to come from inside the land, not from the sky.

He took a swig from the canteen, and slung it over his shoulder. There was a landmark that guided him, a place in a cliff that looked torn and yellow, mustard-brown, a sharp, naked gash in the stone. This gnarled mineral spilled from the slope all the way to his feet, caramel, butterscotch, molten sulphur alternating as he hiked up the gradual slope.

Anything was possible. The trouble was: some of the things that were possible were bad. His father had once nearly killed a man on the set, a flat, hard-baked stretch of Death Valley being filmed as a backdrop to a scene in which Buck Patterson took a slug in one arm, reeled, and squeezed off a shot from the hip, the sort of aim that cinema skeptics all over the world knew was impossibly difficult.

But this Colt Peacemaker had a speck of lead residue from target practice. The wound had been tiny, but nearly mortal. The actor recovered, not due to ready medical help—there was none for miles. The fragment was small, the aorta wall just thick enough. Even so, recovery had taken six weeks.

The incident had impressed Buck Patterson into being sure that, no matter how heated the drama being portrayed, he never really took aim at anyone. He always fired wide, or into the air above the villain's head. And it had shaken his son to discover that play, the rowdy and sometimes tiresome theatrics of movie-making, could kill.

It was a long walk.

It wasn't hot yet, but so dry each breath made him feel parched. The ground was growing brighter, glowing from within. There was a wind, a light stirring from the east, and at times like this Patterson had the impression that the rising sun itself was compelling the atmosphere forward, driving it ahead of its approach.

Maybe he's not there.

Maybe something has come along to move him, a coyote, or the wind.

Permanence was a law here, more absolute than gravity. A can of Dinty Moore stew would lose its color, the paper label bleached ash-white where the sun fell on it, but the can itself would be a rustless star glittering in the grit for decades. Many times Patterson had seen a gleaming pinpoint become, on his approach, the metal butt of a shotgun shell, or the single staring lens of a broken pair of sunglasses.

This far out there was no sign of litter. In the predawn sky overhead there was a tatter of contrail, otherwise this was a world before any human deed, before the first tool had been chipped out of the first flint quarry. Lifeless as the Martian surface, the place was not even a *place*. It was timeless, as the years before a man's birth are timeless.

Patterson trudged through the emptiness, certain that something would be altered. Christ, he knew whole careers that had grown, flowered, withered in five years.

It had been nearly that long since he had visited the place. Bishop had been capable, knowing exactly where to leave him. Bishop had noted the distance on the odometer, marked the bearing on the compass, and memorized the site so that when Patterson asked him one night what it had looked like Bishop could tell him exactly, and give him the instructions it took to guide him there.

The fact was that Patterson had half-expected a man of Angevin's tenacity and stubbornness to walk out of the desert, all the way back to Owl Springs.

It could have happened. Patterson had never actually done any real, hands-on harm. It was Paul's own fault. Paul could have survived if only he had not panicked or suffered the sort of bad luck that seems inevitable only after it has actually fallen. The past is closed, locked-in, set. The future is open, airy, all-capable.

He can't still be there.

He was.

Paul's head and shoulders were silhouetted against the cheesy yellow of the rock. There was the shirt, the same ridiculous Hawaiian flowered shirt and the same khaki pants, a baggy style with many extra snap pockets, a fashion that had passed out of favor in the last couple of years. The same silly Converse high-tops, a fifty-five-year-old man dressed up like a teenager. One of the shoes was unlaced.

It was a relief to see that Paul was still in his place, and it was good to see how hard it was to find him, here in a cleft between two rocks.

"I just had to drop by," said Patterson. He hadn't meant it to sound so offhand. His education and general experience had not given him the vocabulary for an occasion like this. Patterson was accustomed to hearing seasoned executives respond to astounding news as though the entire society had learned English from Saturday morning cartoons.

Paul grinned, his eyes squinted shut.

Patterson remembered well the words Bishop used when he reported back. *I found the peckerwood about ten yards from where I left him.* There was the green plastic canteen, there was the backpack that had, at one time, held trail mix and Fig Newtons, all a man would need to eke out a few more hours in the desert, if only he had not sprained an ankle.

"You wouldn't have made it anyway, Paul. That little canteen would replace maybe an hour's worth of sweat. You were always going to end up like this."

It was touching. The love he still felt for Paul shut him up and made him want to do something to help this human driftwood.

Paul stayed where he was, a leather Buddha. And beautiful in a way, as Paul had not been in life, shriveled to purity.

You shoot a guy up with sodium pentothal and you pack him into the back of a Jeep and have your right-hand man find a nice little place in the Eastern Mojave, and this is just about a guarantee. Your guy will be a fossil in twenty-four hours. It was almost good to know, one of those iron laws—death, taxes, sunlight.

"You wouldn't believe it," said Patterson. "But I actually miss you. You were wrong, but you cared about things, and a lot of people don't care about very much."

Because, thought Patterson, I'm not a monster. You were the monster, trying to keep me from doing my good work. Just as now there were people getting in the way of the painting, the work that would be the absolute vindication of his career. Did Freud ever get a chance to work with Matisse? Did Jung ever work with Joyce? Did any other psychotherapist's work ever result in an unquestioned masterpiece?

"I wish you could see how wrong you were," said Patterson to his old friend.

This was still a good place. Still a secret place. There was plenty of room for another person, right here beside Paul.

37

Bishop was waiting for him by the Ryan S-T. The low-winged aircraft had open fore and aft cockpits, and streamlined wheel pants, and in the morning light the silver-doped wings were dazzling. Bishop had the log in his hands, noting the work he had just completed on the vintage plane.

The sun was bright. Both of them carried the weight of it into the shadow of the hangar.

Bishop took off his aviator sunglasses, his eyes steady, querying. *Tell me what you need me to do.*

"You know how much I depend on you," said Patterson.

You killed a friend in a bar, one punch, a cracked skull. The law forgave you because your opponent had been holding a Marine-surplus combat knife. But you could not forgive yourself. Only I could show you how to do that.

Patterson looked off toward the desert. He made a show of having so much that he could say.

"Who is it?" asked Bishop.

Patterson shook his head.

"Just tell me who it is and I'll take care of it."

Patterson put a hand on the pilot's shoulder. *Where would I be without you?*

"Anything," said Bishop.

Like before, when Bishop had even arranged for fishing gear to wash up at Punta Bandera, just south of Tijuana on the Baja coast. Paul had suffered from so many disorders it didn't take much imagination to see him having a heart spasm and turning into fish bait. That was what people said—*Not a surprise to me.*

Paul had waited too late to criticize the show, waited until it had begun, waited until Patterson had been changed by the power.

"Nobody's going to lay a hand on you," said Bishop.

It was a surprise to see Loretta Lee by the pool.

It was a surprise, and it was irritating. Her feet were dangling in the water, and she had twin smudges under each eye. She looked awful, hair lank, her tan yellow-green overnight.

"Up so early?" said Patterson.

"You shouldn't have done that," she said. "You should have trusted me. You think I can't keep my mouth shut."

"What a shame to see you feeling so bad."

She had that slack-jawed stare Patterson had seen in junkies. She could still talk; it would take a lot to keep Loretta Lee from talking. "I know what's wrong with me."

"Let me take your temperature."

She blinked, looked upward, in his direction, found him with her eyes. "How much did you give me?"

"You must have what we used to call Viral GOK—God Only Knows," said Patterson. "Christ, we can't make it without you, Loretta Lee."

She was rubbing her hip where he had given her the needle. She had the constitution of a buffalo. Almost frightening.

"That Seconal," he said, "doesn't agree with you at all, does it?"

"What room is she going to be staying in?"

"Margaret? I haven't thought about it."

The words came slowly, but the woman had a certain clarity of mind even now, pushing her thoughts ahead like heavy furniture. "Of course you have. You think about everything."

"You choose the room. After all, you're the hostess here."

"I feel like throwing up," she said, in a voice so quiet he might have mistaken the words, the spring splashing, the sparrows chirping. "When I look at you."

"We'll put her in the mirror room," said Patterson, as though just deciding, although he had always intended to put Margaret there.

"I guessed right," she said.

It made more sense when Loretta Lee stood, lost her balance, and fell into the pool. Patterson had a certain faith in his knowledge of pharmacology, and he did not like this faith shaken.

He waded in after her, his trousers instantly sodden and heavy, but the water feeling good in the rising heat. He dragged her from the pool, surprised at how heavy she was. That had been the root of the problem with Paul Angevin, that was the continuing physics lesson of his life. An inert body is very heavy.

He had her on the concrete, the surface so hot it hurt her where he stretched her flat. She was thrashing, one hand in his face.

Then Bishop was there—efficient, farsighted Bishop.

Patterson had a sudden, disagreeable thought. *Sometimes I don't really understand Bishop.* Compact, terse, Bishop strained to simplify himself, considered his words before he spoke, said what he believed Patterson wanted to hear. One night Patterson had heard clarinet music, not badly played and too bright-sounding to be a recording, drifting from Bishop's bedroom.

"Get my bag," said Patterson. Why, Patterson wondered, am I surprised when he obeyed just now, without a single question?

"I know all about you and Bishop," said Loretta, her wet hair spread about her on the concrete. She spoke like someone addressing the sky. "I've been lying to myself a long time."

"You are upset about something, aren't you Loretta Lee?"

He must have squeezed her shoulder a little hard, or bumped her hip where he had been just a little clumsy with the hypo, making sure she was out.

She swung at him, a furious, mile-wide slap, as she struggled to sit up. The open hand caught him in the face, a weak blow. It made one ear go deaf with a windy crash, and the point of one cheek tingled.

And it drew blood. He touched his lower lip. There it was, red salt water on his fingers.

She hurt your face, thought Patterson. He tugged his temporarily deaf ear. His hearing cleared. Already he could hear the tinkle of the spring again in perfect stereo.

He wanted to tell her: you shouldn't have done that. You shouldn't have hit my face. I was going to give you a chance, a nice chance to go on and have a secure, comfy future, and here you are, making a really stupid career move.

She was panting, on her feet, unsteady, trying to look confident, but failing, leaning on a poolside chair for support. "Tell me you didn't listen to my tapes last night. It was just a diary, something I was making because there wasn't anyone else I could talk to. I looked in the nightstand and they're gone. Tell me you didn't give me a shot last night while I was asleep.''

Poor Loretta Lee is near tears, he said to himself, and I'm just standing here watching. "Don't worry," he said. "I'll give you a chance.''

He held her in his arms. He forgave her. He was good at that. It was important to learn how to let go.

38

"A friend told me that gladiolas are out of fashion," said Mrs. Wye.

She had an armload of flowers, wrapped in green paper. The paper was worn where Mrs. Wye had clung to it, and made a crackling sound. One end of the paper cone was sodden where stem juice had soaked into it. Mrs. Wye looked very pleased, but pale, holding herself upright against an unyielding force. Margaret said that she should sit down, but Mrs. Wye gave her her look of amused irritation and stood there, cradling the flowers like a bundled baby.

"Imagine a flower going out of fashion," said Mrs. Wye. "It's like sunset going out of fashion. Can you imagine someone saying, 'I'm so terribly sorry, but standing and looking at sunsets isn't quite the thing these days'? But I thought about it, and I could see what she meant. There is something just not quite right about glads. Pretty, but cheap, the poor things. I felt sorry for these and I bought them."

Margaret made a gesture, offering to take the flowers, and Mrs. Wye half turned away. Margaret tried to remember the location of the nearest florist. "You went all the way by yourself?"

"I was perfectly fine, all the way there, all the way back. Slowly. I used to be able to walk there in fifteen minutes."

Margaret was aghast. "I wish you hadn't done that. I would be happy to take you anywhere."

Mrs. Wye remained standing, clinging to the flowers. "I will take care of myself."

"Please tell me you won't do that again."

"I will make no false promises, Margaret. I am willful and foolish."

Margaret insisted that she could not enjoy the flowers for long. She was about to leave for Owl Springs. It was a surprise to Margaret when she realized, looking into the bright eyes of Mrs. Wye, that Mrs. Wye had become something like a mother to her, the sort of mother Margaret had imagined herself wanting.

Chatty, accepting, Mrs. Wye was a delight. "Don't worry about the bird. The bird and I will be just fine. You just go and be with Curtis and have a wonderful time. And when the flowers wither, I'll replace them."

"You could have had—" Margaret couldn't bring herself to say *a stroke*. "You could have fallen down. There beside the golf course."

"Oh that nice green grass. They overwater it, you know. It's so squishy underfoot. I would rather die trying to live than getting ready to die. I've thought about it."

Mrs. Wye still held the green-paper cone, and the smell of the flowers filled the room now, an earthy perfume. This time when Margaret held out her arms, Mrs. Wye gave her the flowers.

There was a period of flower arranging, deciding where each flower should stand among its mates. Mrs. Wye sat, her hands in her lap with the peaceful disorder of lifeless things. "You're going to get Curtis, and bring him back," said Mrs. Wye.

"I think I might," said Margaret. The flowers were huge and stalky, and aggressively pretty. "It depends on Curtis."

"You want Curtis all to yourself."

"Is that wrong?" Margaret was glad she had the flowers to fuss with. "Does someone like Curtis belong to the world?"

"Good heavens, who cares about 'the world,' Margaret. Thinking that way is something men made up, to make them feel important. 'I am doing this not for myself, but for the world.' " Mrs. Wye had just then adopted a marvelous voice, Alfred Hitchcock doing General MacArthur, and Margaret laughed.

She was excited. In less than an hour she was due at the airport. Not long after that, an hour and a half or so, she would be with Curtis.

"Men need to feel important," said Mrs. Wye. "What I need is to feel that I can take care of my life without much help."

Margaret told her that she was doing wonderfully, and while Mrs. Wye heard Margaret, and acknowledged what she said with a smile, Mrs. Wye seemed to feel that Margaret's compliment was trifling and unneeded. Mrs. Wye managed to stand, and found her way to the vase of flowers.

"Once I had an affair with a very famous director," said Mrs. Wye, looking at Margaret with wide eyes that said: I have never told this to anyone, not as I am telling you. "If I told you his name you would recognize it at once. Very famous. Handsome in his way. You know how men can have that big, angular, beaky look and still have grace."

Mrs. Wye continued to shift the flower stalks in the crystal vase, drops of water falling from time to time on the surface of the table. "It was a secret. I was married at the time, and so was he, and I detested it for happening, because despite what you hear about Hollywood and actresses, so many of us were normal."

Mrs. Wye exaggerated the word *normal,* the word taking on moral weight. Margaret thought that the word *normal* had gone out of fashion, that wanting to be stable, healthily typical had long been undesirable.

"Do you know what the attraction was?" said Mrs. Wye.

It was not a merely rhetorical question. Margaret was expected to ask, and she did.

"Romance," said Mrs. Wye, with a whisper that caught all the magic, all the candlelight and twilight of the word.

Mrs. Wye looked, suddenly, very tired. She accepted Margaret's help over to the sofa again, and took a deep breath, like someone who has been marching up a long hill.

"It was romantic," said Mrs. Wye in a very different voice, quiet, confessional. "Even the secrecy of it, the shame, the fact I knew I was doing wrong. I loved it."

"That's quite understandable," said Margaret, feeling at once understanding and inexperienced.

"The other night there was a special on Channel Nine about this director. If you stop and look at the television schedule you'll know everything. Well, I watched it."

Margaret leaned forward with an encouraging expression.

"The narrator, quite a good voice, one of those American voices that really make you proud to hear the language spoken, was saying the most complete nonsense."

"Things that weren't true?"

"He said that in his films, the director is still alive. That the legacy an artist leaves the world is a piece of the artist still alive among us. And I thought *how untrue this is.* The word immortal was used. This director's immortal enthusiasm for such and such.''

''It's just a manner of speaking—''

''I remember this man, this famous man. I remember the way he laughed, rather like a mule, and the way he would forget to comb the back of his hair so that it stuck out. I remember his love for cherry tomatoes, how he'd eat them stem and all. He was like a horse in some ways, this man. He hated reptiles and he loved Cole Porter. And he's gone. He's entirely gone. And all of his wonderful works—and they are wonderful—do nothing to keep him alive.''

''Please be careful,'' said Margaret after a long silence. ''If anything happened to you. . . .''

''What if Curtis wants to stay right where he is?'' said Mrs. Wye. ''What if he's still not well enough to leave the doctor?''

There were photographers at the airport, not many, but enough. ''Do you think it's right that you should disturb your husband's therapy like this?'' said a thin, intense woman, holding out a tape recorder the way, in other times, one might have extended a pack of cigarettes.

''Mrs. Newns, what is it that worries you, exactly?'' said a small man with a dark mustache and very white teeth, a person who looked much taller and younger on the video screen.

''How long will *your* therapy with Dr. Patterson last?'' asked another reporter.

Margaret chose to ignore the questions as celebrities learn to do, pretending that she wasn't hearing them. Someone wished her luck, and Margaret did smile in return. This was a mistake, probably, because it brought the same questions all over again. She made a show of confidence, of being sure that she was doing what anyone in her position would do.

It was clear to Margaret, however, that many people might think her visit unnecessary and unwise. People would understand her motives, but they might think her overanxious, lacking faith in the famous doctor.

It seemed like a long flight to Margaret, the small corporate jet descending at last over the strikingly empty landscape, the wrinkled hillsides, the stark stream-wrinkles, subject matter Georgia O'Keeffe had savored, and, Margaret saw now, had painted because she'd had no choice. This countryside commanded, defeated. Margaret realized how little she knew about desert.

She was so close to Curtis now.

A steward explained that as soon as they landed they would have to take off again. "They don't want any visitors at all," said the steward with a smile, as though this was good news.

"That's very strange, isn't it," she said, sipping some cherry-flavored Calistoga water because it was a drink Curtis liked.

"That's the way it is." He spoke in a southern accent, and, now that the short flight was nearly over, seemed eager to impart something of himself. The network logo was emblazoned on his jacket pocket, and the man was manicured, polished, tailored, so that the residue of regional accent seemed an affectation.

"It doesn't strike you as peculiar?"

"Red Patterson can make up the rules. Why not? Listen—he's got a lot of responsibility on his shoulders. That's what people don't realize. An average person couldn't even begin to understand what goes on in the mind of someone like that. I imagine that if you—well, maybe not you, but me, for sure—were to live twenty-four hours with the kinds of cares and worries Red Patterson has—we'd probably implode under the weight."

"Do you really think so?"

The steward made a single, silent *ha* in response: are you kidding?

As they descended, Margaret fumbled half-aware for her seatbelt. They were falling from the sky, in that gliding, controlled way of aircraft, and the desert looked featureless. Where was this famous oasis, this estate she had heard so much about?

"You stick it together like this," he said, fastening the seatbelt for her. She was so taken with the barren desert, brass-yellow in the afternoon light, that she could not take her eyes away from the view out the window.

"The work that goes on here is for the good of mankind," said the steward.

Margaret looked into his eyes for a hint of irony, of knowing exaggeration.

Already she felt reassured. The place was real—as though this had been the reason for her fear. How could she have doubted? There were palm trees and a wall, and the large, oval buildings she knew must be airplane hangars. They were on the ground, and Margaret experienced that exhilaration that arrival so often gave her, destination evolving from idea, to hope, to solid, sun-soaked fact, fact with asphalt and concrete and distant, arcing leaves and alluring shadows.

So close to Curtis.

But it was not Curtis who stepped from the shadow of the palm trees and strode toward her.

It was the doctor himself.

There were several fine cracks in the landing strip, and a line of red ants worked their way from one of them. There was a sprinkler running somewhere. From a great distance water touched her.

For a moment she was disappointed, but then she swept herself forward. She embraced the doctor, and he kissed her.

"It's so wonderful to see you here, Margaret," he said.

39

His kiss was not a surprise. It was pleasant, brotherly, a light touch. It silenced her.

"You'll want a tour of the garden," he said. When she did not respond at once, he added, "Everyone sees the garden first."

"You make it sound like I have no choice," she said.

He laughed. "Why would you want a choice?"

Odd, she told herself, that at the very beginning the doctor told her how little freedom she had.

She tried to console herself that Curtis had been secure in a beautiful place.

"You'd be surprised how much time I sit right here in the water," Patterson said, when they had returned to the side of the pool. "Sometimes I spend so much time in the water I turn into a giant prune."

Margaret had noticed this tendency in men before, joking cheerfulness as a barrier against what had to be said. She felt that it was awkward to ask, but it was time. "I want to see Curtis."

He led her to a chair beside the shimmering water. The reflection cast white wrinkles over his shirt front. "You're going to be enchanted with the new painting," said the doctor. "I certainly am."

She felt the sharpest disappointment. Curtis knew that she was here, and he didn't want to see her.

Patterson must have read the feeling in her eyes. "Curtis loves you," he said.

This was so exactly what she needed to hear that she could not speak.

"Maybe I doubted that, at first, although I don't know why. Any man would love you," he said with a smile. "But as Curtis and I worked it became clear that he really wanted to be with you, and that I was not going to be able to help nearly as much as I had hoped."

"I want to be with him. That's all I want." She meant that this was all she wanted in her life.

It was as if she had not spoken. "And it was obvious to me finally, just in the last day or two, that what we need here is you."

She allowed herself to make the proper response. "I'm so glad."

"It's true that in many ways your marriage was barren."

She felt tears start. *No,* she told herself. *No tears.*

"But I think we all endure a form of imprisonment," he said, "trapped in our sex, enslaved by our bodies. Don't you?"

She recovered her poise. "I'm so grateful for everything you've done."

"Can you wait one more night?" he asked. "One more night before seeing Curtis?"

The grill at the bottom of the pool was an ugly, slotted thing, blistered with rust. "It doesn't seem fair."

"No, it hardly does. But now with you here in the walls of the estate—I think the painting will thrive."

The painting. She began to hate it. "I can't interrupt the painting," she said, feeling disheartened and hopeful at once. She had a brief and vivid fantasy of running through the halls of the big house, calling out for Curtis. He might be able to see her, even now, from one of the upper windows. To just see him, just for a moment, that was all she wanted.

She had the strongest impression, as she sat there, that the two of them were absolutely alone in the desert. This was hardly likely, she knew, in an estate as elaborate as this. She gazed at the famous countenance before her. Hadn't he worn makeup before? Now he looked tanned, confident, the man she had seen in so many magazines, so many videos. He looked full of life, a man who had never been troubled by anything.

"I'm so thankful," she said, feeling childish and powerless as she spoke.

"Once I thought I saw a scorpion there, right where your foot is now. But it was only an empty shell. They moult."

"I have to wait, don't I? I don't have any choice."

He smiled. He opened his hands, and then closed them, softly, the way he would catch something he did not want to kill.

40

In chess, her father had written, *we need more eyes than this common, everyday vision. Even that sublime, additional seat of vision, the third eye, is not enough. We need the many eyes of a spider, to watch what stands before us on the board, and also what does not.*

It was cool inside. "You'll like your room," said Patterson. "It's the biggest bedroom in the house, and my favorite."

"You must have a large staff here," Margaret said.

"Not anymore," he said. "I had to sacrifice them, for the greater solitude."

Margaret did not want to take another step. *How can Curtis stand it here?* she wondered. The garden was paradise, but the house was bulky and dead, random corridors, and the odd, dry smell of unused rooms.

It had struck her before how little actual mental telepathy there was in the world. Her father had been dying and she had been at a librarian's convention in New Orleans, signing copies of one of her books. Even when the desk clerk had handed her the slip with her keys the *Urgent—call home* had not triggered any particular anxiety, only the annoyance that her mother was interrupting her professional life. Later, she had felt guilt and shock that she'd had so little premonition.

Now she was so close to the man she loved, and she felt no intimation where in the house he might be, or what he might be feeling.

Patterson showed her works of art, views of the desert out large

245

windows, and a screening room like a tiny theater at the end of one
corridor, the smell of the room dry, like freshly ironed cotton. He
showed her a Picasso, a lovely crayon mother and child. He said
that he felt a little guilty about having art all the way out here, where
so few people could see it.

Patterson was giving her a tour, but also, perhaps, showing her
that the place was too big for her to even think of searching it. The
message seemed to be: to search is to lose, to think is to forget.
"The story is that Ernest Hemingway and Gary Cooper stood on
this balcony and shot the branches off that Joshua tree over there,"
he said.

"It still has its branches," said Margaret.

Patterson laughed, shrugged. "I think it's missing a few."

Margaret had always felt, without really examining the belief, that
there were two kinds of people. There were ordinary people, who
shopped at supermarkets and had favorite television shows, checked
books out of the library and bought frozen food.

Then there was the other, much smaller set of people, the people
who mattered. Curtis was one of these people, and so was Red Patterson. These people had inner qualities that made them more actual
than most people, their lives more colorful, their passions more important. And, because of the respect and even awe people in general
felt for such figures, they had an extra dimension that most people
did not possess.

Margaret did not think of herself as a nonentity, and by no means
thought of herself as drab and lightweight. But compared with the
famous artist and this famous psychiatrist she was merely another
human being.

There had to be a reason that she had created Earl the Duck, and
given him so little character. So when she walked beside Red Patterson and felt afraid, she tried to argue the feeling away. This tight-
ness in her throat, this feeling that the walls were narrowing around
her, were sensations that had to be ignored.

The doctor unlocked a door, and let it swing open.

The bedroom had curtains that would have suited an opera house,
mauve with tasseled gold braid, a style that did not match the bare,
Western decor of the other rooms she had seen.

But it did suit the house in a way, she realized. It was amusing—
this was the best room of a brothel. The mirrors were everywhere,
antique, age-flecked. She turned her head, and there were Margarets

and Red Pattersons, sliced and cast downward into an infinity of chambers.

"No mirrors on the ceiling, though," said Patterson. Sometimes he seemed to know what she was thinking. "This room is a tribute to vanity, not sex." He ran his fingers through his hair, appraising his reflection. The glass of the mirrors had yellowed with age, a tint that softened shapes, altering colors gently but in a way that displeased, like smog.

She carried only an overnight bag. It looked out of place when she put it down on the bed, casual and contemporary.

"I'll leave you here," he said, and she had the oddest feeling that he expected her to say *No, please stay.*

"I'd like something to drink," she said, although she was not thirsty.

She was relieved when there was a knock at the door and a man she had not met stood there with a tray.

So, she thought, there is a staff here after all.

She introduced herself. "Yes, Mrs. Newns, I know who you are," said the man.

He was a solid-looking individual, of medium height, and he looked at her without a smile. He should have been dressed in something black and white, she thought, something formal. He wore clean, pressed cottons, soft-grays, tans. "We've been looking forward to having you at Owl Springs."

He put the tray on a side table, and stood for a moment looking at the teapot. Although his movements were deft, sure-handed, Margaret could not suppress the thought that he was not used to carrying trays and serving beverages.

"Where is my husband staying?" she asked.

Typical of me, she chided herself. To boldly go where anyone with a brain would shut up.

He did not look at her but moved the teapot minutely. He had blond, curly hair on his hands. He shifted a lid, peered in to look at the sugar cubes, and took long enough, she thought, to count every one.

It was plain the man was not going to answer her question. She tried again, making herself sound offhand. "Just out of curiosity, because it's been so long." She did not sound offhand at all; she could not keep the feeling from her voice.

"He's doing very well," said the man.

"Does my husband come down for dinner very often?" she said.

"Mr. Newns is very happy here," he said.

"Is he?"

The man looked at her, and then he laughed, a little, quiet laugh, a laugh that was inhaled rather than exhaled, the laugh of a man who was used to private jokes. Margaret laughed a little, too; she couldn't help it. It seemed courteous and appropriate, even though she felt she had understood only a part of the punch line.

But then, she realized, there was nothing to laugh about.

"My name is Don Bishop," the man was saying. "I owe everything to Dr. Patterson."

"And you would do anything in the world to help him."

He did not quite meet her eyes. Many men had faces like this, pleasant masks. Such men often found speech unfamiliar, and resented being forced by circumstance to communicate. "You shouldn't try to disturb Dr. Patterson's work," he said.

When he was gone, she tried to tell herself that she did not really feel trapped. She tried to convince herself that she was going to enjoy this insane place. She hurried to the curtains, ready to be amused at her worries.

The windows were blank, dark. They were shuttered, heavy oak boards that, even when she got the sash up and fought the fastenings, would not open. She felt all the breathable air vanish from the room.

The hook free, the wooden coverings stayed as they were, weathered into place, baked solid by sun.

She pounded the barrier with her fists, and then gathered herself and gave the shutters a kick, hard, with the flat of her foot.

They swung free, and she pushed them all the way open, as far as they could go, until the desert was there, open and empty, mirage consuming the horizon.

Escape was possible, if she survived the jump without breaking an ankle on the sharp stones. But then there would be that flat, solid heat to trek through, and she could feel the heat even now, kneading the air. She closed the shutters, hating the way the dry wood met with a quiet sound, bone on bone.

I should just relax, she told herself. I'm getting upset about nothing.

She tiptoed from her room. She had the strangest feeling that this was what Patterson wanted her to do. *We'll put the rat in the maze, and see what it sniffs out.* She was down the hall, hurrying, putting her ear to one door after another. She was lost within a minute, confounded by the sameness of the doors, the solemn, beamed ceilings, the silence.

Curtis—I'm here.

There was only the silence, and her sense of feeling both helpless and ridiculous. When she found herself standing outside the mirrored room at last she hesitated, wanting to delay her entrance into this chamber, this maze of reflections, each image marked by the figure of a woman looking back, into the tunnel that held her.

They sat beside the pool. It was late, the air cool, scented with the mulch and flowers hidden by the dark.

"There is one aspect of Curtis's life that I still have to explore," said Patterson.

"If I can help you. . . ." said Margaret.

He liked the way she looked. "I need to get to know you, Margaret. It's necessary, and it will be a pleasure."

"A mutual pleasure," she said, sounding more hopeful than sure of herself.

What name will I have for you, thought Patterson. What pet name when I know you well?

Bishop served them a light supper there under the palms, a delicious shrimp curry, very mild, served over rice, and sangria in one of the big hand-thrown pitchers from Guadalajara. Bishop was a decent cook, but his sangria was heavenly, made with lemons from here in the oasis, a delicate citrus that had grown more like a vine than a tree.

"It's beautiful here," said Margaret.

"Some people don't like it," said Patterson.

"It's so peaceful."

"I think that's what some of the singers and politicians didn't like. It was too quiet. Too remote."

"How far away are we?"

"From what?" he asked.

"From help. If anyone should need it."

"But we wouldn't really need help, out here."

She smiled, and he laughed. What an amusing idea, he made his eyes say.

"But," she said, "if I had an attack of appendicitis or—"

"I was a pretty fair surgeon," said Patterson. "And could very easily perform an adequate procedure here on the estate."

"But certainly you'd need—"

"I was joking. Of course I wouldn't actually perform surgery here." He rolled his eyes. "I want you to realize how self-contained we are. How complete."

She smiled, with perhaps less enthusiasm than he thought appropriate.

"Bishop can fly you anywhere you want. And if Bishop is away, I can do the flying. Victorville is less than a hundred miles away, and Palm Springs, and San Bernardino."

"And the famous owls," she asked, "the ones the spring is named after—will I see any of them?"

"The owls are around," said Patterson, "but you won't see them. The elf owl, *micrathene whitneyi.* The smallest owl in North America. Devotedly nocturnal."

It was going to be delicious, thought Patterson, having her here.

She found it as she was getting ready to go to bed, not expecting sleep, but prepared to spend the night's wait as comfortably as possible. She was wearing a nightshirt Curtis had given her, a replica 1927 New York Yankees jersey. It was not a very accurate replica, Margaret thought, having been modified to look comfortable and even sexy, slit up the sides. She had brought it to please Curtis, hoping to spend this night with him. Now she wore it out of loyalty, waiting, convinced that all would be well.

She put her hand under the pillow, and there was a manila envelope, with something heavy inside, the envelope's clasp bent and crooked.

She opened the envelope carefully, with considerable suspicion, and yet also with that instinctive optimism she so often felt when she opened a package: *is it a gift?*

But she did not like this.

It isn't intended for me, thought Margaret. It was a handgun, shiny, its handle inlaid with mother-of-pearl. An automatic, thought Margaret. Someone must have left it here by mistake.

On the outside of the envelope there was hurried, feminine handwriting, a single sentence.

I think Curtis is dead.

41

The steward asked what would he like to drink and Bruno said he wanted a bourbon over ice. He was a little surprised at himself. He did not usually drink bourbon. He told himself that he had no intention of returning to the U.S. anytime soon, so that this was something of a farewell tipple.

Bruno had an ability that he prized in himself. He could simply allow himself to forget anything that was unpleasant or difficult. He could wrestle a worry onto the freight elevator of his psyche, press the well-worn *down* button and the loathsome preoccupation, whatever it might be, would descend from sight. If Margaret was going to be difficult and foolish, that was her problem.

The seat beside him was occupied by a young man who looked about old enough to be excited about video games but who turned out to be an author and something of a scholar, working on an article about the excavations under Saint Peter's Basilica. Bruno introduced himself, and the young author gave him that look of exaggerated awe, that *no kidding* expression that indicates delight and at the same time mocks it, one of those American responses Bruno was certain must have been learned from television.

The young historian shook Bruno's hand and said his own name, which Bruno could not quite catch—it sounded like ''Beanpole Nonsense.''

A national endowment of some sort, it seemed, had funded a fairly luxurious visit to the Holy City so that the article could be finished.

''I recognized you right away,'' said the young author.

"Sometimes I think I should travel in some sort of disguise," said Bruno, who had no intention of traveling in any sort of disguise under any circumstance.

"You're used to this," said young Mr. Nonsense. "People look at you and say—hey it's him."

Bruno made an airy wave of the hand. He was used to it, or he wasn't—what difference did it make?

The young man assured Bruno that the skeletal remains archaeologists had discovered under the basilica were almost certainly those of the historical Peter. "A robust man of about sixty, with his feet missing," said the blond historian, as though sharing the most delightful news imaginable.

"His feet having been cut off, I imagine, by the Romans," said Bruno, sipping bourbon.

"I think the Romans were much more brutal than we realize," said the child-scholar. "If they wanted to get you down off a cross they just cut off most of you, and who knows what they did with what stayed nailed on."

"My favorite martyr," said Bruno, "is Saint Agnes. I think because I live so near her church."

"The woman who grew so much hair."

"You know the story," said Bruno with a smile, disappointed that he could not tell the tale himself.

Smart Mr. Nonsense sensed this. "Not very well," he said.

Bruno told the story, one of his favorite Roman legends, of the young lady who would not give in to a Roman centurion, or perhaps it was a senator—Bruno could not remember the tale so well, after all. She was stripped naked before a crowd, in an unlikely last stage of failed seduction, and to protect her virgin body from the unruly gaze of hundreds her hair grew, in an instant, long enough to flow down over her body, all the way to the paving stones.

The site of this miracle was her church in the Piazza Navona. Bruno had often wandered in out of the heat and sat in the semidarkness before the altar that displayed what Bruno assumed must be her skull. Matters were a little confused—her remains were generally thought to rest in Sant'Agnese fuori le Mura, some miles away on the Via Nomentana. The altar Bruno visited displayed a delicate, small skull in a box, a relic not so much of an innocent woman, as of brutal persecution. It was also a reminder that the other, grander miracle the Christians were expecting—the dead returned to quickness and flesh—had not yet taken place.

"She is the patron saint of virgins," Bruno concluded, feeling that his recounting of the legend had taken an odd turn. He had begun the story in a flippant tone, intending to make the story little more than a humorous impossibility. But now he felt that while this particular miracle was pure fable, other miracles might not be.

The miracle of a work of art, he thought. The miracle of a man in a room standing before an empty surface, and transforming it. The miracle of day after day, stitching night to night with its golden thread.

"I'm all 'Hey, I'm sitting here next to Bruno Kraft.' I know I'm going to think of a million questions to ask you as soon as I get off the plane."

That's how even the scholarly young talk these days, thought Bruno. The young sound so colloquial and offhand.

"I wrote an article about you once," said the young scholar.

Bruno arched his brow in an unspoken, really?

"A review, actually. It was in *Connoisseur,* discussing the video you made about Cézanne."

"Good heavens, I remember—"

"I thought it was incredible."

"Cézanne was a sort of person we don't have anymore."

"That's what you said in the video."

"What else did I say?" asked Bruno.

"You said that what we are is not as important as what we 'engender upon life.' What an incredible phrase."

"You're Stevenot Brawnson."

"Yes, of course." He laughed. "You're just figuring out who I am."

"Stupid of me."

"I'm not that important."

It would be unkind to agree in so many words. "You're not at all what I thought you would be."

"A disappointment."

"No, young. I'm growing deaf."

"It's the air-pressure in these planes. You can't hear a fucking thing."

Bruno smiled. Nice the way everyone worked *fucking* into their vocabulary these days, just like in the movies. Stevenot Brawnson was not so young after all, and the slang was all an affectation. His father had endowed a college and supplied it with a library.

Still, Stevenot was likable. American men were almost always likable, adaptable, easygoing, slow to give or take offense. This man had a smile like Curtis's, and had the same way of speaking, a smart person choosing to be simple.

Stevenot was asking about Curtis. He was asking about the new painting. "People are going to line up around the block," he said.

Don't think about Curtis, Bruno warned himself. Don't think about anything. Just sit here and have some more Kentucky whisky, and let life approach you from afar.

It was fine to be in Rome again, a warm summer storm just evaporating, puddles everywhere.

Bruno was exhausted. It was a mercy to be outside the apartment, fumbling in his pocket for the key.

The apartment had a glass door, a translucent pane that distorted the view and made the interior of the apartment look like an absence, a drowned world lost to the clatter and chatter of the street, the jumble of parked Vespas, the hammer-taps of craftsmen in the furniture design shops up and down the street.

Bruno could just barely see through the glass door, and into the promising shadow of the apartment. There was movement there, the passing of a figure inside, a flash. Bruno could not deny the thought: someone naked.

He put the impression out of his mind. He twisted the key, stepped across the threshold, and greeted Andy with, "Home is the hunter."

Andy was on his feet, twisting a cloth in his hands, and Bruno nearly asked him what on earth was the matter.

There was a blanket on the floor, a blue woolen afghan, and a photographer's light was set up in the corner, beside one of the terracotta gargoyles. The light swept the blanket, which held, in the folds and contours of the fabric, the imprint of a body. There was the sound of a footstep upstairs.

"So," said Bruno. His carryon bag was suddenly heavy, but he did not want to put it down.

Andy hesitated. "I'm working, Bruno."

"Discipline is very important, especially for an artist."

"We were right in the middle. But it's good to see you. How was California?"

"I can imagine the subject. Not quite one of your glossies of the baked goods of the Jewish Quarter this time, is it?"

"Just getting a little work in." Andy sounded apologetic, but barely. He was wiping a lens with the cloth in his hand and looked sharply at the blanket on the floor.

Lines from a dozen farces occurred to Bruno. *Don't let me interrupt* seemed most appropriate, followed by its opposite, *Forgive me for interrupting,* followed, in these all-but-forgotten comedies, by a lover leaping out of hiding wearing inappropriate clothing, oversized boxer shorts or something garishly flowered.

Because it should be funny. It should be something to accept with a debonair laugh, and Bruno could toss down his coat and his overnight bag and go out for a cup of coffee. Besides, perhaps it was innocent. Perhaps Andy had branched out into nude but demure photos, the sort of brawn one saw on calendars.

"Just do whatever you want to when I'm gone," said Bruno, "because it certainly doesn't matter to me at all."

"Taking pictures," said Andy, with the pointed deliberate slowness he might have used on someone who spoke little English.

"That's right. Take pictures of whatever you want and whomever you want right here on the floor."

"I will," said Andy.

"Good. I encourage it. You want to take pictures of boys you pick up at the Piazza Barberini. Big boys with hard-ons. It's fine with me, Andy, because I realize I'm fat and old and that you and I don't have much together. I have my career—that's all that matters to me. Why shouldn't you have your career too? I love it. It's so good to see you happy."

"I'm glad you feel that way," said Andy.

The model clumped down the stairs, evidently deciding that departing invisibly and silently was out of the question. "Hello, how are you," said the youth, his words in a burst, hardly sounding like a greeting or a question, schoolbook English marched forth under pressure. He wore something vaguely military, wrinkled khaki, heavy boots. He was fastening a snap.

He was a black-haired shepherd-type, a model for a Renaissance David, a young Christ dazzling the elders, and everyone else. Bruno could find a dozen like him on a Saturday night off Via Sistina among the gypsy children looking for pockets to pick.

Bruno stormed up the stairs, and the model shrank against the wall to let him past. Bruno threw open the bedroom shutters. He grabbed a handful of Andy's clothing from a drawer, and tossed it from the window. The trousers unfolded, spun around into a tight wad, and plummeted, followed by a T-shirt, a single sock.

The model looked up from the street, his expression one of earnest curiosity, wondering at Bruno's anger, or trying to guess what would fly out of the window next, and then the youth mounted one of the motorscooters, just out of sight. There was the cough of a starter, and then the brazen rattle of the Vespa as it caught, swung up the street, and was gone.

"You're overreacting, Bruno," said Andy from the bedroom door.

Two shoppers paused in the street below to comment to each other on the sight of jockey shorts hurled in their general direction.

"You're embarrassing yourself," said Andy.

Bruno stopped for a moment to relish his anger. "You have no business talking to me that way," said Bruno very quietly.

"You're tired. You look awful."

"Thank you, Andy," said Bruno.

"We'll talk when you feel better."

The calm of Andy's voice made Bruno furious. He threw an entire drawer, tugged from the frame of the dresser, onto the window sill. The small pink geranium there withstood a load of polo shirts.

Andy stood for a moment, saying nothing, challenging Bruno to offer an apology, an explanation.

"You have no idea," said Andy.

There had always been something bright about Andy, but his enthusiasms had been those of the moment, humming a recent tune, repeating the latest Hollywood gossip. This empty quickness was interlaced with surprising moments of common sense, and it was this contradiction in Andy that sometimes made Bruno realize how little he knew about his friend and lover, and how little he had wanted to know. To know more was to care more, and it was always silently understood that Andy would be a part of Bruno's life a few weeks, a few months. And yet, they had already known each other the better part of a year.

Andy slipped downstairs like someone going out for a pack of cigarettes. Bruno followed him. Andy gathered up his camera, thrust it into the camera bag, and with an air of quiet decision ignored the sight of his clothes flung out upon the cobblestones and made his way, in no apparent hurry, down to the Via di Monte Brianzo, where he turned right, toward Via Condotti and the Spanish Steps, out of Bruno's life.

The phone was ringing.

It was an editor in London, a newspaper needing an update on their Curtis Newns' file obituary. "I know it's quite a bit to ask.

The one we have now had him marrying Margaret Darcy, and all the interesting events since then aren't even mentioned.''

Bruno found his voice. "There have been some interesting changes—''

"We were thinking that what we will need is something more retrospective, something sweeping and summing-up, in the light of the loss of *Skyscape*, from the point of view of an authority like yourself. . . .''

"Naturally.''

"But then I was thinking that we should wait until the new painting is done.''

It sounded like a statement, but it wasn't.

"I'm sure that I can write something new,'' said Bruno. "Or at least begin it. We'll have plenty of time to revise Curtis's obituary. He has years ahead of him.''

"We were thinking it might be best to have something early rather than later. I wasn't catching you at a bad time, just now?''

"No. Well, just got in. Traffic. Humid. Sticky, actually, and hot. But fine.''

The editor paused long enough to seem polite, and then continued, "And a paragraph or two on the importance of Red Patterson—''

"Of course.''

"Is the painting going to actually belong to Red Patterson?'' asked the editor.

The question shocked Bruno. Bruno had assumed that a painting by Curtis Newns would belong to the world of art.

"As a gift,'' said the editor, "from patient to doctor.''

"I think it's too early to speculate,'' said Bruno.

"Some people will be thinking that you gave your opinion on the painting for a consideration, to raise its value.''

Bruno was speechless.

"Or in exchange for setting up a sale to a prearranged buyer,'' said the editor breezily. "For a fee.''

I have never been, thought Bruno, quite cynical enough. God knows I've tried. But this editor was a far more accomplished cynic, and Bruno felt humbled. The truth sounded so supercilious he was almost embarrassed. "I gave my professional opinion for the sake of the painting, and for Curtis's sake—''

"And because you believe Red Patterson can do anything he wants to do,'' said the editor, without, as far as Bruno could tell, the smallest trace of irony.

42

The phone rang again and it was Renata San Pablo.

"I want the painting," she said.

Bruno explained to her that her galleries represented Curtis, and that naturally she would have a chance to handle the painting once it was a finished work, and not a mere sketch.

"I mean I want it personally—to own it."

"A painting like that should be shared with the public, don't you think?"

"Is that what Red Patterson thinks?"

Bruno admitted that he was not entirely certain what Patterson thought about anything.

"He's going to put the painting on television and say that Curtis gave it to him," said Renata. "I know what Patterson's all about."

"There's a lot of work to be done," said Bruno, "before we have what you and I would call a real work of art."

"You compared it to *Skyscape.* You practically came right out and called it a masterpiece."

"I was so happy," said Bruno, "to see Curtis at least beginning something—"

Then, to keep Bruno off-balance, she changed the subject. She wanted Bruno to start to work on a video of Curtis, "Better than that ratty thing you did on Cézanne."

"The video that won all those awards."

"You sound funny, Bruno."

Bruno protested. He felt wonderful, ready for anything.

"Honestly, Bruno, you can con just about everybody, but I know you. I want you to *work* on the Curtis Newns video, not just say what everybody can see with their own eyes. What sort of man *is* Curtis? Insight, Bruno, not talk. Tell us what it was that Patterson was able to do, how nothing worked except the Red Patterson touch."

"What you want me to do is make a video about Red Patterson."

"People want to know."

He did not want to hear Renata's voice. He had a print of the original *Skyscape* in the apartment. He could illuminate it with the photographer's lamp Andy had left behind.

She was still talking, but he thanked Renata for calling and hung up.

He was gazing at the picture, the small universe that the youthful Curtis Newns had created.

Bruno had written that if da Vinci had taken a look at one of Turner's sea and sky panoramas, and decided to show the world how a master would handle the subject, the Renaissance genius would have painted something like *Skyscape*.

The phone was ringing again. Bruno let it ring, and when the answering machine kicked in, whoever it was hung up.

In the famous, now lost masterpiece, landscape was absent but implied, humanity invisible but alive in every signature of paint. This print was a scaled-down version of the original, but even so it had power.

There was something wrong with the work-in-progress at Owl Springs, something that Bruno had not sensed at first glance.

Bruno folded Andy's clothes, gathering them from the street. People passed by, quietly enjoying the sight.

Bruno folded the clothes tenderly. He remembered how his mother would squint into the wind as she hung out the wash, the quiet happiness of the chore tucking every small detail of the landscape into place. The clothespins had hung in a canvas bag, the green stripes of the bag faded, the weight of the pins satisfying to the hand.

I could call up Owl Springs now, and find out how things are going, talk to Margaret.

If I were Andy, thought Bruno, and I left the life of Bruno Kraft, and marched off into the streets of Rome, where would I go? They had met in the Borghese Gardens. Bruno had been out for a stroll on a Sunday afternoon, drinking a can of Coca-Cola through a thin straw and wishing so many of the white cement mock-classical busts were not damaged, noses and sometimes entire faces smashed. He had heard a voice say, "They do that sort of thing everywhere," and there had stood Andy, lean, freckled, in the sort of shirt so many men were wearing just then, a sweatshirt with artfully torn-off sleeves.

Bruno called Owl Springs.

A voice answered on the second ring. It took patience, like playing a card game with a very young child, but at last Bruno got some information out of her. The Owl Springs phone was being answered in Burbank. There was no way of contacting Red Patterson "at this particular time, sir."

"I was just there," said Bruno, "visiting Dr. Patterson, and I think—"

"Mr. Kraft," said the operator, breaking into just a little bit of personality. "I thought I recognized your voice. I have to tell you we've been given very definite instructions not to bother the Springs with any sort of call at all, although I can sure take a message and see that—"

That was not necessary, said Bruno.

Bruno didn't have to search. He *knew* where Andy was.

Andy was in Bruno's favorite spot, outside the Pantheon, ostentatiously brooding over a double espresso. He gave Bruno a look that Bruno recognized—Bruno's own bored stare.

Andy was pretty good at it.

"I'm sorry," said Bruno.

Andy made one of Bruno's gestures: what use were apologies?

"You expected me to show up," said Bruno.

"It's all so much trouble," said Andy.

Bruno knew what he meant: people, relationships. It all took so much.

Andy gave Bruno a measuring look. "You're out of breath."

"You're very important to me," said Bruno.

Andy performed another Bruno gesture: maybe, maybe not.

"I'm changing. Places have always been more important to me than people," said Bruno. "And paintings. You take a city and fill it with art, and I fall in love with it. Look at this place." He indicated the huge, brooding building before them, the great Roman structure enduring, commanding, as though what people were amounted to nothing compared with what people created.

I'd spot a fake in an instant.

Bruno had been deceived by no one, ever. Well, there was that time in Athens with that manuscript that was supposed to be one of the lost books of Plutarch, his life of Heracles. He had known at the time he was being reckless, so it didn't really count. The paper panned out, too, passed a cathode-ray test at the British Museum. The thing was papyrus, real Egyptian proto-paper. And the fragments of Latin? Well, he had taken a risk. He knew enough Latin to tell it was about the infant Heracles strangling the serpents, the snakes Hera sent to kill him in his crib. It was one of the basic problems of being a demi-god: you had to have an unusual birth, or a fantastic problem in early childhood. And as for the rest of us, the merely-human?

He got cheated. The paper was ancient dunnage, shipper's packing stolen along with some fragments of a Rhodian Hermes some decades ago, a long-filed and forgotten theft, until the wrinkled leaves showed up with ink that radiated the wrong spectrum under the guiding touch of a British Museum technician.

But he knew Curtis's brushstroke as he knew the handwriting of his own father. Bruno gazed at the Pantheon. "The paint was put on thin, and it was put on quickly," Bruno said. "It was very dry."

"So?"

"There was a smell of turpentine in the room, almost overpowering."

"Maybe Curtis left the can open."

"There were brushes soaking. Curtis was always very neat. His studios were always clean, paintings put away."

"Maybe," said Andy, "Red Patterson wanted you to think Curtis was working that very day."

"Why would he want to do that?"

"Maybe something has happened to Curtis," said Andy, as though it didn't matter much.

"It would be a disaster for Patterson."

"Not really."

"I thought you admired Patterson."

"I *love* Red Patterson," said Andy. "But you should watch more of his videos. He believes we can do anything we want if we really understand what we are. You can make money if you open your mind. You can walk away from drugs if you want to, or cigarettes, or compulsive gambling. You don't need years of psycho-babble.

Things are really pretty simple. If your life is dark, turn on the light.
Miracles happen. We can be anything we want.''

"But nobody really *believes* that.''

"All it takes is faith,'' said Andy. "You just have to get out of
the boat and walk across the water.''

"This is your philosophy, Andy? Or are you pretending to be
obnoxious, just to make me suffer?''

"You're so dumb,'' said Andy.

"Red Patterson would paint a fake Curtis Newns, and try to pass
it off?''

"It wouldn't be a fake. Jesus, Bruno, you're really kind of a
blockhead, you know that? It would be a new painting, a hybrid
work of wonder.''

" 'Work of wonder'?''

Andy shrugged. "It's one of his phrases. Don't you know *anything*
about Red Patterson?''

"You're describing a monster.''

"Famous people don't live in the same world as the rest of us,''
said Andy. There was a yellow Bic lighter at Andy's elbow, and a
pack of Marlboros. Andy picked up the lighter and put it in his pants
pocket, shifting sideways in his seat.

"But he couldn't get away with it.''

"Sure he could. People would understand.''

Bruno ignored the waiter at his side. "The art world would be
outraged.''

"But Patterson could care less about the art world. To him, whatever happens out there is just great, as long as he ends up with a
painting. Don't you remember that time he had that actor, the one
who was a bionic policeman in that movie, and the man had hysterical hoarseness?''

Bruno closed his eyes and opened them again. Andy had always
known so much more about popular culture.

Andy continued, "The actor was about to lose out on that role in
that movie where the CIA hired an invisible man. Big part, big
movie. And he went on *Red Patterson Live,* and the results were
great. Even when some people said that Patterson ended up doing
some of the dubbing, it didn't matter. People loved it. There was a
book about it, *Voice in the Wilderness,* by Red Patterson and someone. I guarantee you that a Patterson/Newns painting would be worth
more money than anything Curtis would paint by himself.''

"But people would hate it," cried Bruno. He stood, and the waiter gave a slight bow and vanished.

"No, Bruno. You really don't know anything. Art people would hate it. Museums would hate it. But everyone else would be wild about it."

"But if Patterson did something like that he'd be exposed as a—" Bruno stopped himself. What an old-fashioned-sounding word *fraud* was.

"He's a famous wonderful television doctor," said Andy in a tone of reason, "and he just almost got assassinated. People *love* Red Patterson."

Bruno couldn't say this: Patterson could finish the painting himself, if he had to.

Andy was being gentle, like a considerate teacher. "Don't take it so seriously. Curtis is just another artist. We're all artists, inside."

Bruno tried to adopt something like his usual tone. "If Curtis is dead my career is on a stretcher, heading for the morgue."

"Don't be silly. You'll be the big name when it comes to Curtis as long as you live. Maybe you could join forces with Red Patterson, and make a video on unlocking the artist within."

Bruno felt heavy, a man made of lead. He felt that he had over-looked something vital, and now realized what it was.

He had been worried about the painting, worried about Curtis. Red Patterson was all that mattered. "I shouldn't have let Margaret go out there."

Andy picked up the cigarettes and worked them into his shirt pocket. "You've got to be kidding. You know Red Patterson is supposed to be a fantastic lover."

"Why did Red Patterson seem so interested in having me look at the painting and authenticate it?"

"I'm sure he was pleased. It makes him look good. Besides, in Patterson's eyes you're still important. He respects you. But—" Andy shrugged.

"People aren't that stupid."

Andy gave him a smile. "The people on television are the people who matter."

Bruno had no answer to that.

"Look over there," said Andy. "That couple—they recognize you. She's trying to get the man to come over and get your autograph in the guidebook. Think what it would be like if you were Red Patterson."

Bruno closed his eyes again. Swallows were squealing overhead, their cries spiraling, citadels sketched in the air. "The painting doesn't matter. Margaret doesn't matter. I don't matter—"

"Yes, you do. Because you've been on television. But Red Patterson is—" Andy gestured, indicating the Pantheon, the buildings, the city around them, the capitol of emperors and saints, of human beings turned into gods.

Andy looked different, now, his chest deeper, his eyes brighter. Andy was full of life, just as Bruno felt himself growing more and more empty.

"The future belongs to people like Red Patterson," said Andy, sounding carefree, as though that was not only inevitable, but good.

The couple was Dutch, and she and her husband were sorry to interrupt. Bruno signed their guidebook, on a blank page under a scab of glue where the map had been removed.

The couple thanked Bruno, and departed.

"But Bruno," Andy was saying, getting up, ready to leave. "You have to tell me—what is he really like?"

43

Margaret found herself on her knees, holding the envelope in her hands. The prongs of the envelope's clasp were askew, the glue of the flap unmoistened.

She tried to tell herself that this was only some sort of brutal joke. Someone, an anonymous scribbler, was trying to frighten her. It was ridiculous to take it seriously.

The words stopped everything, canceled every other thought.

She watched her hand move. She reached into the envelope. She let the pistol lie across the flat of her palm, and there was an instant in which she thought—or tried to think—it must be a toy.

Her face stared back, half-aware, from the mirror. The mirror was flawed with tarnish stains, and the infinity effect, the nautilus-chambered spill of Margarets and envelopes and handguns mocked her.

You should have given up a long time ago, her mother would have said. It was always hopeless where Curtis was concerned. You were always going to be too late.

She dressed quickly, tugging on running shoes, leaving her base-ball shirt on so that it hung down, covering the pistol thrust into the front pocket of her jeans. It fit snugly, as though designed to be hidden in a pocket just like that, tucked away with just a little awkwardness in the way it felt, like carrying rolls of pennies in a pocket on the way to the bank.

The mirrored door to the hallway was locked. That was hardly a surprise. It made sense. *Oh, by the way, take this key and make sure Margaret is locked in so we can forget her for the night.*

She opened the window and the shutters, and felt herself standing at the edge of a void. She could not see the desert. She could smell it.

She hoisted herself onto the sill. The scent, fine and dry, swirled around her as it mixed with the air conditioning. *She won't try jumping out that window, little slip of a thing like that.* She knew that it was best not to think, to get it over with fast. She pushed off, into the dark.

There was enough time to wonder as she fell. How would she avoid hurting herself? A wind rose upward from the land she could not see, and she felt herself drifting, beginning to tumble sideways.

She sprawled.

She stood. She fell again, and when she was on her feet a second time she staggered to the wall of the villa and leaned against it for support. The wall was warm, stored heat at her cheek, at the bare skin of her arms.

They had been right. Anyone who jumped out of the bedroom window was in trouble. She tried to tell herself she wasn't hurt. She sensed an absence. There was something metallic on the stones, and she groped. She closed her hand around the gun, and worked it back into her pocket.

She ran, stumbling over stones, and found her way around the big house, all the way to the entrance of the garden. The pool light was still on, an azure glitter through the black stalks of trees.

Her breathing was loud. In the desert you can hear things far off, she told herself. She was no secret. Anyone could hear her panting like this.

Ahead of her, across the black of the landing strip apron, shined a light from one of the hangars, or from a garage. The light played out across the asphalt, and grease spots glistened. There were two sources of light, two interiors she could barely make out from here.

She was beginning to feel a delayed effect from her jump. She limped, and ran as hard and fast as she could, so she could reach the source of the light before her legs failed completely.

She made it to the garage. There was a car in the bright interior, all chrome and windshield in the sudden illumination as she slipped through the gap in the door.

She warned herself not to make a sound, but she couldn't help it. She was inside the car, reaching for the ignition, but the key was missing.

She was out of the car, out of the garage, stumbling, all the way to the next source of light. She was through the doorway, into the bright light of the hangar, halted by what she saw.

She had not expected to see so many. Airplanes waited, living things under the light from the metal-beamed ceiling. She had the impression of a war that had been stilled and captured, and stored here, of adventure kept, as hands cup a butterfly, power and freedom awaiting some distant morning.

The aircraft seemed to be living things, animation suspended, propellers still, each fuselage canted upward, and she had the impression that this was a boy's fantasy played out, a youth's love of the sky given its own playground.

There was something moving over by a workbench. Shadows pulsed. She sought the half-shelter of a Shell oil drum, and then approached the bench. It was only a moth, a big, chalky set of wings, chiming almost inaudibly off a lightbulb.

"We could always take one up," said Red Patterson.

She turned and felt for the gun in her pocket to be sure it was there. She backed away from him, all the way against a corrugated aluminum wall.

He stepped through the doorway. He looked younger than he had earlier, dressed in a white shirt and pants like hers, jeans, except that his had a tear at one knee. There was a smudge of paint on one of his knuckles, bright yellow.

"I was in the studio," he said. "Bishop told me you had flown, and I didn't believe it. I had to see for myself."

"I won't be able to wait until tomorrow," Margaret said.

"You don't know how many people I've seen with that trapped expression, the look of a jackrabbit in the headlights. It's the beginning of your future. You see it coming, and you're afraid of it. Tell me what you want to know."

"Where is Curtis?"

"I saw the message Loretta Lee left you." He paused, and when she said nothing, continued, "She shouldn't have tried to frighten you like that. What really concerns me is I think I know what she left in the envelope. It left an impression in the paper, the definite outline of something that could get you into serious trouble." He paused, giving her time to respond. Then he said, "I am worried about you, Margaret."

"I have to see him."

"Tomorrow," he said.

"I remember you saying on one of your shows that there is always only today."

"Without trust there really isn't going to be any future, Margaret. It's your inability to have faith in life that is crippling you. Are you all right? I meant *cripple* metaphorically, but you actually hurt yourself, didn't you? I'm so sorry. It pains me to see you suffering. I've got something that'll make you feel a whole lot better."

He was so relaxed, and so sure, that she had to doubt herself. "I want to be sure that Curtis is still alive."

"Of course you do. But stop and think for a moment. Why wouldn't he be alive?"

There was an instant of chagrin. Red Patterson looked so confident. Margaret felt herself waver. How could she think like this?

"This is a Ryan S-T," said Patterson. "Built about 1937. One hundred and twenty-five horsepower. Dual controls, front and back, open cockpits. Lovely plane. Over there we have the Lockheed Vega. Amelia Earhart flew one of these. It was the holder of several transcontinental speed records. A sweet piece of work. Over there we have the Stinson 105 Voyager. Bishop's been reconditioning this plane, but basically he never stops working."

He was gazing dreamily at the aircraft. Now he turned to look at her. The moth continued to worry the light, and there was another sound, somewhere off among the shadowy aircraft. A footfall, she thought. Or another moth.

"There's something magic about art," he said. "I don't mean the old, used-up magic, superstition. I mean the other kind—the kind that works. If a special work of art is destroyed we feel much worse than if several people we have never met are lost in a boating accident somewhere."

Patterson picked up one end of an airhose, pink rubber tipped with bright brass. He wound the hose into a tight series of circles, and hung it on a hook. "You blow up some art in Florence and people are aghast. You blow up some people and we can't help but think that the individuals can be replaced."

He's talking about Curtis, she thought.

"We're wrong, of course," he said. "The people are alive and precious. But the art is sacred to us, out of another world. Not just a historical world. I mean out of the other world of the psyche, a world we don't really understand."

"If I knew he was still alive," she said, choosing not to speak his name. "If I could just see him."

He gave her a look of compassion. "I've come to an understanding out here in recent weeks, Margaret. A wonderful understanding about life, and about myself. Just as a work of art is more important than a human being, so am I more important than you are. Because I am a kind of work of art, a creation of my own time just as surely as Michelangelo's *Moses* is a creation of his. As much as I love you, and Curtis, I am more important than either one of you."

Margaret worked the pistol out of her pocket, and held it in both hands. The weapon drew itself upward, until it aimed itself at Red Patterson's chest.

Red Patterson had a sudden hungry look. He lost all appearance of confidence. Even so, he could smile. "Loretta Lee's gift to the future," he said.

She held the gun. She did not speak.

"You're going to be so embarrassed when you realize what's been happening here. Besides, those pistols are more complicated than you think. A gun like that sometimes has two safeties, and then, if you're lucky and you get it working right, someone's dead. They're horrible things, really. Put it down."

Curtis.

"Margaret, do you realize what people will think if you shoot me? Do you realize how hated you'll be by so many people, all over the world?"

He lost that starved look in his eyes. "You won't do it, because you know that it would be like destroying the works of Monet, say, with the squeeze of a trigger, or demolishing the architecture of Rome with the push of a button. That's what it would be like, Margaret. You aren't alive the way I am. And you know it."

"I know Curtis is dead." She was weeping, her breath broken, but she held the gun steady.

Patterson spread his arms casually, at ease: how do you know a thing like that? Or maybe he meant: what difference does it make?

The blow knocked her down. The pistol made a shiny spinning blur across the floor, and Patterson stopped it with his foot.

She tried to get up but couldn't move. She was hurt. She couldn't breathe.

Bishop knelt beside her. His eyes were without feeling, looking into hers as if into a defective device. He was panting, rubbing his shoulder where he had slammed into her.

"That wasn't necessary," said Patterson, soothingly.

Patterson picked up the gun. The doctor held out his hand, and helped her to her feet. He turned the pistol around, butt-forward. He gave it back to her. Her hand accepted it. For a moment they both held the gun, their eyes locked.

Then he released the pistol. Until then it had been impossible to trust him. Until then she was ready to kill him. But now, with the metal of the gun warm from her hand, and from his, she knew that the weapon might as well be a toy.

"You win, Margaret," he said.

As she left the hangar, and walked through the darkness under the loud stars, she understood what she had nearly done. She had nearly killed Red Patterson, and the thought of it was nauseating.

She left the gun beside the swimming pool, the surface of the water shivering as a creature touched it and then fled on invisible wings.

44

He was glad Margaret put the gun down in a nice safe place.

The sprinkler was on again, over by the ornamental orange trees. The water came on and off, on its own. Patterson didn't know what to do about it. The breath of the water, wafting through the air, made them all pause to let it drift over them.

Suddenly, the sprinkler ceased its chatter, and the cool mist was gone. Everything was computerized, and the computer wasn't working very well.

There were never any moths out here, and yet there they were, all over the place, even over the pool, dogfighting the big knob of the light among the palm leaves.

Patterson was feeling sorry for Bishop. Maybe Bishop missed Loretta Lee. This had been an incident-rich environment, and Bishop really was more of maintenance sort of guy, fix it and sign-off. Bishop was tagging along, far behind them, like a hound sure that his master was about to hurt someone, anyone.

Inside, the house felt cool, almost chilly.

After we look at the painting, thought Patterson, maybe we'll have a celebratory drink and light a fire. He'd stack some of that cedar in the downstairs fireplace, that wood that burned with such fragrance, and add a little Georgia fatwood. And we'll make love, actual love, not that carnal jig I used to do with Loretta Lee, that meat pogo she and I used to do. This will be an act of real love. Because there was no doubt: Margaret is going to be won tonight. Patterson knew that his accomplishment here would be incomplete without Margaret opening up and taking him in, and loving him.

It was freezing in here, he thought. The air conditioner must be set way too low. Maybe it was broken. He'd have Bishop take a look. You send the staff away, and you are naturally going to run into a malfunction or two.

"Do you need a sweater?" he asked.

Margaret said that she didn't, but she must be lying, because she was folding her arms as she hurried behind him down the hall. She was wearing a pair of jeans and a baseball shirt, and here he was in a T-shirt. It was one of those nice T's, the ones he picked out when *Vogue* was going to do that story on him, and wanted him to look casual but put together. They were all-cotton and tailored, T-shirts for Olympus.

He recognized the tune he was humming under his breath and laughed. It was an early theme for his show, a jazzy little piece that played as the credits rolled until Patterson said that applause was the only intro/outro he wanted.

"How did you know?" she asked. "That I had left the bedroom?"

Patterson liked the way her hesitation made the question come out in sections. He was not about to get into matters of video cameras and two-way mirrors. Those naughty studio heads—their voyeurism had proved useful at last.

"You don't know much about guns, do you?" asked Patterson, in the tone of someone sharing a joke. It was a nice way to switch subjects.

"I'm glad I don't," she said in a soft voice.

"Guns," said Patterson, in the tone of amused disdain with which his father might have said *women.*

But the sight of the gun had shaken him more than he wanted to admit. He was named after a martyr, he quipped to himself, but he was in no hurry to become one.

His poor mother had always been out of her league. She had come out of the Midwest to act, and she had appeared as a stagecoach passenger and a girlfriend's girlfriend, and it wasn't the wear and tear of the movie business that made her quit, but some inner sense in the woman that she had lost something by appearing on the screen. His mother had died of the flu, an Asiatic variety that most people survived. He had her photograph somewhere, posed with one foot on the step of a buckboard beside the squinting, impatient Walter Brennan.

The *Stephen* on his birth certificate was her insistence at a touch of tradition. Patterson suspected that the martyr's name was an attempt at something cosmetic, a dash of devotional makeup in a world of press kits and quickie divorces.

Jesus, it was cold.

"When I recognized what sort of person I actually was, a lot of things became very simple for me," said Patterson. "I realized that I didn't have to confine myself anymore behind the little structures most people erect for themselves. I was free to be what I was destined to be, and it was like arriving from a crowded, overpopulated place, out into a clean, bare fertile wilderness. I cannot begin to tell you how happy I am."

He paused to measure her reaction. He was telling her the truth, but sometimes the truth crawls out of the Precambrian seas with a few too many legs.

He couldn't read her expression. At least with Loretta Lee you could see trouble coming. He was at the door of the studio, shivering, inserting the key.

He was careful to put the key back into his pocket. A key could be as powerful as a gun, and this one was color-coded, sporting a dot of Loretta Lee's Carnival Blush nail polish so he could tell it from the others.

Patterson was a little nervous. He wasn't apprehensive, and he was confident, but still—it was the first time this stage of the painting had been seen by anyone else. Sometimes in front of a special audience you feel it, that flutter. You can't help it. The size of the room hushed them, the spaciousness of the studio—and the sheet-draped presence at the far end of the room.

There was the painting, under its shroud. Their footsteps resounded. The turpentine smell was strong. Even here it felt like winter.

"He's been painting," said Margaret in a hushed voice.

She was a remarkable woman, but she didn't seem to quite understand. Perhaps he was expecting too much of her, moving too quickly. It was like that last show, the session with Curtis, great television but terrible therapy, the miracle dying, time running out.

There at the side table was the pallet, and Curtis's knife, the blade blistered with paint.

"What happened here?" asked Margaret.

He did not quite understand her question.

"Did we just interrupt him?" she asked.

Patterson smiled, gave her a flash of the capped teeth. It was like running through a rehearsal, the special guest not knowing how to read the cue cards, and Patterson acting calm, encouraging. *Only a retard sounds like a retard on my show.*

"Curtis never leaves his paints like this," she said, "tossed around on a table."

"Stand over there," said Patterson. "Right there. That's where you'll get the best view." In the TV studio they had marks on the floor; you never had to wonder where you were supposed to stand.

He felt like a conjuror biding time as his audience filed into its seats. That's what Paul Angevin had called him, *psychiatry's first stage magician.*

The room was getting unbearably cold, degree by degree. The entire house was stuck on *freeze.* At last she was following his instructions, and standing in the middle of the room. *Just walk to the middle of the stage, stand on the little yellow dot, and say hello to the world.* He reached up and pinched a corner of the cloth. He knew how to time his movements for the best effect.

He waited three heartbeats. You always wait that long if you have a surprise on camera, one beat for people to realize they are alive, two to let them be aware that they are still alive, and three so they begin to wonder if anything is ever going to happen.

He whisked the sheet away.

The muslin billowed, rose upward, and then drifted down, where it spilled across the floor. Margaret's hair was blown lightly by the movement of the air.

We have a wonderful surprise for today's special guest.

Now she could see. She could see the painting, and all she was doing was standing there. She took a long time. Had she turned into a pillar of salt? *Hello, Margaret, are you still there?*

But Patterson told himself to be patient. It took time, and Patterson had plenty of that.

Margaret could not understand what she was looking at.

Then she did understand, and she raised her hands to her face. She wanted to close her eyes, but she could not.

She took one slow step after another. She reached out to touch it, but then drew her fingers back again, as though from a thing that could hurt her.

Because the thing *was* dangerous. She sensed that he expected her to say something, but she could not trust herself to speak.

"It's not done. It's going to develop," said Patterson. "But I think it's 'coming into the room,' as they say, don't you?"

Margaret leaped for the table, and seized the knife. It took two stabs—the canvas was tough. She forced the knife into the cloth. She ripped the painting, the paint-stiff canvas slashing with a thunderous shudder. As Patterson grappled with her she found further strength and pierced the painting again, and this time when Patterson dragged her away the knife dragged downward.

The painting was violated with a slashed X that gradually fell open as Patterson held her, the splashes of paint giving way to an empty gap.

Patterson buckled over, as though he had been stabbed himself, gutted with the knife.

She held the knife toward Red Patterson, point forward. She was panting so hard each word came out separate. "Where is Curtis?"

Patterson gazed at the painting. He turned to look at her. He hit her with his open hand. It was a loud smack, but he knew she wasn't hurt, not yet.

Her mind observed everything in segments, each movement a separate, hasty icon, like early cinema. He was going to hit her again, she thought, but he didn't. He lifted one hand. He lifted the other, and the two hands joined at her throat. She had a vision of frantic eyes, white teeth, a blur. She stabbed him.

Once—quick in, quick out.

The knife slithered over ribs, and between them, and made a high, meaty whisper. The blade came away, and Patterson released her. He gazed down at his shirt, and at his hand. He looked at her, amazed.

Nothing happened in a hurry. Like a man practicing an ugly tango, he reeled backward. Tubes of paint fell, scattered.

Patterson waded, an underwater figure. Margaret retreated, until she found herself at the far wall, one hand warm with sticky fluid.

Patterson straightened. He held onto the table, and took a breath, let it out. He did it again, his lips shaped like a kiss. He did not bother with her for the moment. All his attention was on the painting, its empty gap wide open, now, the canvas hanging all the way to the floor.

Thank God, she thought. He isn't really hurt—not badly. There was a rent in his T-shirt and a splash of red, but nothing worse. He's fine. You didn't really stab him.

His voice was a whisper. "You hurt the painting."

Bishop was there, urging Patterson to sit down. "You're going to be okay," said Bishop. "It's okay, don't worry," trying to help Patterson, but the doctor waved him off.

Patterson was not looking at Bishop, or at Margaret. He was looking at the painting. He walked like someone afraid the floorboards were rotten, and might break under each step. He touched the rips in the canvas, picking up the fallen flag of the art work.

Patterson stayed like that a long while, studying the canvas. Bishop hurried away, and when he returned he carried a doctor's bag, an old-fashioned black grip.

Margaret remained where she was. She clung to the knife, sticky though it was, clotted with paint and blood.

"Well, this has been an exciting little meeting," said Patterson, his voice philosophical, almost lighthearted. "You gave me just a little bit of a surprise, Margaret."

Thank God I still have the knife, she thought.

"Don't you realize that Curtis Newns is the kind of man who doesn't matter anymore?" said Patterson. He was searching through his bag. He found a hypodermic.

Don't waste your time talking to him, Margaret told herself. Just get out. Get out, and get far away from this place.

Patterson held his side for a moment. He seemed to take a merely academic interest in his wound. "The knife cut into the intercostal muscles," Patterson said. "It doesn't hurt yet. Interesting. I dealt a good deal with knife wounds when I was starting out. You so much as nick an intestine—major problems. But other parts of the body can be stuck through and through and it's little more than a circus stunt."

Margaret looked upon Patterson with a certain horror. She *had* stabbed him, and the wound was fairly deep, and yet there he was, giving another *Red Patterson Live*. "The blood is just a vast, watery organ. The only thing that really hurts me is the painting."

His face was gleaming with sweat, despite the cold. "Curtis Newns was an artist from the time when people thought there was a separation between the artist and the rest of us, just as people used to think there was a difference between priest and supplicant." The needle glittered. The chemical in the hypodermic squirted, a thin probe like a hummingbird's tongue.

The place was icy cold and there was a hole in his side.

Bishop had that sick look again. Patterson got tired of looking at a face like that. It was time to move fast, and Bishop was unsteady.

After the shot he didn't feel the wound at all. It had started to hurt, and so something out of the department of analgesics was just the ticket.

"Do you remember," Patterson continued, turning to Bishop, "the other plan, the one I talked about a long time ago? The one we decided wouldn't be fair, but a lot more fun."

The painting was wrecked. He was sick at the sight. Well, maybe you could find an art restorer to do a Frankenstein on it, but it was agony to see it the way it was now. They would just have to repair it. That was all—just spend a few dollars. It was simple, really.

Once he had done his show right after a technician had suffered a coronary, actually turned blue, impervious to Patterson's efforts, which were vigorous and sufficient to bring anyone back to life who wasn't determined to head toward the Light on a permanent basis. And Patterson had done the show, helping a set of triplets reconcile themselves to their abusive drunkard dad. A good show, higher than usual in the ratings.

He couldn't keep his hands from shaking. Jesus, she was a dangerous woman. He had been almost ready to start *loving* this woman. She was there against the wall, big-eyed and panting. He was going to do the world a favor.

"I think you should go lie down," said Bishop, his voice sounding strained. "I'll call someone."

Patterson was incredulous. Bishop never expressed hesitation, always thought the way Patterson wanted him to think.

"Don't worry," said Patterson. He spoke sweetly, the way you'd talk to a boy. "We'll carry on just the way we always have. You and I, Bishop. I think, and you act. Remember that. We'll want to call London, talk to the people who were restoring *Skyscape* when it was burned. Tell them we need their professional services, only this time no barbecue."

Patterson gave Margaret a smile. A really good one, love-at-first-sight quality, the kind he had given Loretta Lee when they met, the woman looking like something out of a catalog, *for the man who has everything.* At least Loretta Lee had understood a little bit about what he had in mind, the way he thought, the way he really was.

He told Margaret, "You wanted to leave, all the while. Even now that's what you want. You want to go away and get help. So that's what you are going to do. No need to worry. Everything's fine. I'm going to fly you out of here. No, don't be afraid. Look at her, Bishop—she's afraid. The poor little woman thinks you and I are going to hurt her. And we're not. We are just going to help her get exactly what she wants."

He shouldn't have swung at her. That gave her a hint how he felt, broke the professional surface just a little too obviously.

The woman held the knife. She didn't say a word. This had never happened on the show. If it had, he would have loved it. Blood on his shirt, each breath making a funny noise. A body mike would have picked up that sound, broadcast it, and everyone would have seen him with a wound, carrying on like it didn't bother him at all.

45

Margaret felt like a woman naked against a wall, stripped before a crowd.

Odd, thought Patterson, how a homicidal woman can look so sexy.

"Margaret," he said, in his most reassuring voice. "Take it easy—we're friends here."

Fortunately, thought Patterson, the muscles weren't stiffening, although he was feeling something like an out-of-body sensation. Maybe he was slipping into shock. It was almost pleasant.

Margaret held herself against the wall of the studio. You could see her eyes not making sense of what they saw. It was really enough to break your heart, to see how frightened she was.

Patterson put his hands out in the classic pose of looking completely harmless, patting the air. He continued this pantomime until he got close.

Margaret made a cut through the air. Patterson shrank back a step, shrugging: hey, what's the problem? He held both hands up.

She had a good grip on the knife. That was the problem. She was good with it, too, kept her balance despite herself, stayed centered.

Bishop unsnapped something at his belt. He produced a can of Mace, held it out like bug spray in front of him and said that he didn't want to use it. Which was putting it mildly, thought Patterson.

"Don't," said Patterson.

Margaret made another lunge with the knife, and almost got Patterson again.

"Don't squirt that in here, for God's sake," said Patterson.

Margaret was quick with the knife, whipping it through the air so close he heard the pretty whistle it made.

Bishop squirted the Mace.

The effect stunned all three of them. Margaret was down on the floor, blinded. Patterson was almost blind himself, the entire vision/reflex package paralyzed. It was worse for Margaret, but they were all crawling.

They got out into the hall, a tangle of arms and legs and tears. Bishop held her out in the hall and Patterson gave her a shot of sodium pentothal. At least, that's what he hoped it was, but it was hard to get visual confirmation of any object, out there in the freezing corridor, the whites of Margaret's eyes red from the Mace, her face a mask of tears and mucus. Patterson hurt her a little bit more than he had to with the needle, probing the cephalic vein right there on the surface.

She was yelling. She hung onto everything they passed, furniture, posts, even dragged a Navajo rug for awhile. They dragged her down one hall after another, and finally got her out by the swimming pool.

Bishop held her. Patterson plunged his head into the water to clear it, and he felt a lot better. It was amazing, though, how suddenly you could feel so tired.

Margaret was feeling the full effect by then, her mouth agape, arms and legs all over the place.

"You aren't really going to do it," said Bishop. "Are you? You're just playing around, right?"

"Don't think, Bishop."

"I have to know you aren't really going to do it."

Take her up there and lose her, you mean? No, Bishop, you pathetic little shit, I'm going to give her a chance to land on her feet from five thousand feet up. That shouldn't be much of a problem for this little lady, should it?

"Don't do that to her, Dr. Patterson," said Bishop. The man started to beg. "Do like you did with Loretta Lee and with—"

Until Patterson's eyes burned into Bishop, and Bishop couldn't stand it any more. Bishop shut up.

They worked hard, leaning into the hangar door until it opened all the way. They wheeled the Ryan out. The sky was changing color, stars starting to fade. It happened while you watched, It was dawn.

Patterson was up in the forward cockpit with Curtis Newns's knife, sawing away at the safety belt, nylon high-test knit that made the same squeak against the steel that a ligament makes.

The knife was going blunt, and the belt was tough, or both. He only had to cut through one, and he was thankful for that. When he had the buckle strap cut away, he threw it out of the plane and half fell out of the fuselage.

Margaret was moving around. They had put her in a nice place over by the garage, with a folded-up tarp for a pillow. She was crawling around like a beetle in the growing light but not going far.

Patterson was having little breaks in his consciousness, frames cut out of the film. He hated to repeat himself. "You're doing fine, Bishop." *Fine for a guy so catatonic with guilt before I met you that you would have starved yourself to death.* "Just do what I tell you."

Bishop apparently thought that Patterson meant do *only* what he was told to do, because the mechanic stood there as Patterson gasped, trying to lift Margaret off the asphalt.

She planted an elbow in his mouth, groggily, only half-aware. She was a small, shapely woman but just now she weighed enough to make him put her down for a second. "Don't bother helping me," said Patterson sarcastically. "I can do this all by myself."

They got her into the forward cockpit, and she sank down so you could barely see one hand sticking up out of it.

Patterson climbed into the rear cockpit, and it was a real act of will to make it all the way up and in, feeling the way he did.

Jesus, it felt good to be there, fastening the safety belt with a hand that was greasy with blood, so much blood that Patterson had to consider whether the endothoracic fascia had been damaged. No wonder he was feeling light-headed. His neck was puffy, and his breath sounded like wind in an underground cavern. *Hey, what's a collapsed lung to Red Patterson?*

Bishop chocked the right wheel. He called, "Switch off." Patterson called out, in response, "Switch off," and advanced the throttle halfway. Bishop pulled the wooden prop through several times to prime the engine. Then Bishop set the prop, stepped back, and called "Contact."

Patterson set the ignition switch and called, "Contact," retarding the throttle to just above idle and pulling the stick back to keep the tail down when the engine started. Bishop stepped forward and pulled the prop down hard and the engine coughed, starting. It ran rough at first, then smoothed out as Patterson advanced the throttle.

Patterson had another tiny blackout, another loss of continuity with the general march of events. Margaret was stirring in the passenger seat in front of him. He didn't have much time.

Taxiing a vintage plane like this, a tail-dragger, meant that he had
to lean out of the cockpit and taxi down toward the strip in a series
of S's. It didn't hurt very much to lean out like that, but he did
begin to wonder about the severity of his wound.

He didn't have much feeling in his fingers. By the time he reached
the beginning of the runway he was aware of a leak in his side,
through his ribs, every time he took a deep breath. The engine was
going to be warm before long. He checked the wind sock, a flaccid
thing on a pole, and ran the engine to full RPM, checked the magne-
tos, pulled the throttle back to idle.

And then he saw her.

It was wonderful, but it also gave him the feeling that things
weren't right. There was a figure in the very early dawn, close, at
the edge of the landing strip, a person he immediately recognized.
He was delighted. It was madness, he knew. He should be angry to
see her staggering along, but he couldn't help it; he was pleased to
see her.

Loretta Lee looked awful. He wanted to laugh. He wanted to call
out to her that she looked terrible, her hair stringy and her face
blistered but that she looked wonderful to him. It was a miracle to
see her there, finding her way toward him, and he gave her a wave,
trying to climb from his seat.

When Loretta Lee started shooting it didn't make any sense for a
second. The little thirty-two caliber automatic made pops he couldn't
hear because of the sound of the engine, and there was the smoke-
ring effect of the gun.

She was missing, one bullet snapping through the air like spit way
ahead of the plane. You could actually see the bullet for a fraction
of a second, a flash in the early sun.

He fell back into the leather upholstery, the smell of years of
engine oil surrounding him in what he knew was the safety and
power of the aircraft.

Margaret was struggling, slowly, out of her seat. Patterson moved
the controls quickly from stop to stop to make sure there was nothing
binding. Then they were rolling, and this was always the most exciting time, heading off down the runway thinking *we're off.*

Maybe he lost consciousness for an instant. The aircraft lurched
in a subtle, awkward way. Loretta Lee was on the wing of the plane.
The plane wasn't sounding good. The engine wasn't as warm as it
should have been, and they were not that far off the ground, Patterson
flying badly, the aircraft yawing, working to stay in the air.

Were they far enough off the runway so that when Loretta Lee let go it would kill her? She was on her belly, inexorably slipping off of the wing. She called something to Margaret and Margaret called back, but Patterson was sure they couldn't hear each other over the sound of the engine.

Loretta Lee slithered gradually off the wing, the silvery, doped surface nothing to hang on to. Margaret was half in, half out of the plane. She hung on, fighting now to get back in, fighting to stay where she was.

Loretta Lee skittered down the wing, about to fall off. Margaret was about to spill out of the cockpit. They were nearly out of runway when the plane touched down again, Patterson working to slow it just enough so Loretta Lee would let go. He didn't want to hurt Loretta Lee. He wanted Loretta Lee to be safe and happy.

Margaret had one sensation: they were going up, fast. Then they were hesitating. They were falling back again, the wheels bouncing off the runway. The engine was loud. She had to let go and hit ground now, as the surface tore along beneath her.

Did she let go, Margaret wondered? Did she let go, and let the airplane leave her behind, or did she dream it, as she dreamed the sunlight, the asphalt, the color of stones?

Patterson must have lost something somewhere, lost consciousness again for another moment, because when he was aware again they were in the air. The engine torque was pulling the plane to the left, and the warm air of the land was lifting them, the aircraft sweeping upward.

46

Patterson let the Ryan slip sideways, banking again. He applied the rudder and the tail of the plane swung out, and there was that faintly sickening feeling of altitude being lost. The plane was about to stall. The altimeter was spinning downward. Patterson arrested the fall, and got the white hands of the dial to begin crawling upward again.

The aircraft sputtered and made a little roller-coaster leap. The early morning thermals off the desert floor were rising, and the aircraft bucked the strata of heat.

As a pilot he was a little rusty, but he dipped the plane easily down, and rolled the aircraft over on its back and held it there. Camel-yellow desert swung over his head, and stayed there, quaking, a living thing.

This was where Margaret would find herself without a seatbelt, out of the cockpit, standing straight in the air that tore upward around her.

But nothing happened. With the blood ballooning upward into his head he realized that Margaret was not in the passenger seat, slumped down beyond his vision. She was not in the plane at all.

He must have lost consciousness again for a split second as he rolled the plane; he thought she must have fallen out during that moment. He reassured himself. Surely that's what happened.

He rolled the plane once more, doing a clumsy job of it, the plane standing on one wing, wanting to fall, aerodynamically about as fit as a ball rolling off a table. He got the aircraft on its back, losing direction, and getting upright again, the horizon slanted up, rocking back, Patterson tasting blood in his mouth.

He wanted to be sure.

It was time to stop the action, time to step out of the airplane, and stand on a wrinkle of air, freeze the frame and hold the plane upside down. He wanted to look into the passenger seat up ahead of him and see whether or not this agile and unpredictable woman was cowering there—or had she fallen out into the air like a cooperative passenger, or was there some other droll possibility.

He circled the estate, Owl Springs a dark jewel surrounded by a void. There were the red tiles of the roof, the dark sentries of the chimneys. There was the landing strip. He told himself that he couldn't see what was happening down there. Then—there was a figure, Loretta Lee looking up, her arm cocked.

The desert would not stay flat. One moment it was off one wing, the next it was off the other. The landing strip moved around, too. Left alone, desert would claim the runway in a few years. He sneezed and there was blood all over his hands.

It had been a surprise when he was learning to fly: it isn't all that easy to find a runway, approach it, descend, and touch the gear at the right angle. He descended now, below one thousand feet. He was still way too high. Owl Springs was eleven feet above sea level. He centered the landing strip, and then reduced the airspeed, almost to the point of a stall. It was one of the first rules of flight—*to go down, slow down.*

There was Margaret, not far from Loretta Lee. Poor Margaret was a crumpled figure on the strip. He aimed, ready to bring the plane down on top of her. It was going to be easy—he'd crunch her with the landing gear, smear her all over the asphalt, and take off again having barely kissed the floor. He steadied the plane, and let it slip downward.

Loretta Lee flung herself over Margaret's body. Patterson pulled up. The aircraft was about to stall. One wing tipped downward, nearly brushing the asphalt.

He climbed, swung wide, and was about to come down again when he saw Loretta Lee dragging Margaret away.

He felt the knife wound sucking air, and slate-gray lung solids sprayed from the hole and onto the fabric of his T-shirt. He spread the lips of the wound, and what he saw made him almost black out again.

There are many veins in the lungs, many arteries. And tubes for the passage of air. He could no longer pretend to himself that he was going to be all right without help. The Ryan's Menasco four-cylinder was far from the noisiest engine in existence, but it was loud enough to keep him from hearing the air whistling in and out of his side.

We have a special guest on today's show. Hold your applause until you see who it is, and then you'll not only want to applaud—you'll want to give your life to this man, your actual life so he can fulfill his destiny.

This man knew power and what it could do, and he did something with it, ladies and gentlemen. Don't ask yourself to try not to love this man because you don't have any choice. Here he is, let's give him all our futures, everything we have so he can stand there with the Michelangelos and the Caesars and the Buddhas and everyone anyone has ever thought was divine—ladies and gentleman, on silver wings, Stephen Patterson.

Patterson knew how to play this. The best plan was to make it over the San Bernardinos to Ontario and call the network to organize a press briefing by one o'clock, which would be in time for the late afternoon news on the East Coast. Or maybe make it to Vegas. That was a good plan, too. He'd be able to speak from a hospital bed with a nose tube, whether he needed one or not, minutes away from the operating room, maybe an IV rehydrating him, or by that time a transfusion—he wasn't sure how much type O he was losing down there in the abdominal cavity.

He would be more confident if he had some feeling in his hands.

The desert was pink, except where the rocks and alluvial fans cast shadows. Patterson knew where to look, but even so he couldn't see them, the couple on the camping trip there by the dead lake.

He had expected this, but it was still a surprise: You really couldn't see them from the air. The lost campers out by the dry lake had been just sitting there while we went on with our lives. We suffered disappointment and saw harm come to people we loved, regained hope and planned a future and, eventually lost it, in a world where to be immortal is to be gone.

Maybe he could see just a little wink of light off a side mirror or a window, although Patterson wasn't even sure of that as he pulled up the aircraft's nose, letting the altimeter's hands spin, that little clock face that told you how high you were, as though altitude and time were the same thing.

He let the altitude ride up to eight thousand feet. And then higher.

It was cool up here, so far from the desert. When he was over ten thousand he could feel the thin air, the light-headed joy of the oxygen-poor sky.

The painting still existed. The fact that it was cut now—ripped, gashed—made it all the more authentic. Only important art was attacked, just as only important people were assassinated. And the painting was beautiful. The only thing in his life that mattered.

He'd get to Burbank, call Bruno Kraft, and the word would be out. Margaret Darcy Newns has just slashed the new, Patterson/Newns *Skyscape*.

Why did she do that, people would ask. Jealousy? Hysteria? She always was a little headstrong, wasn't she? Marrying the famous artist, insisting on forcing her way into Owl Springs, trespassing on the infinite patience of Red Patterson.

After all he tried to do. People would kill her. Absolutely destroy the poor girl. She didn't know what she was up against.

It was getting colder. Morning was a red sore, not a presence, an absence, a wound where something has been cut out. Patterson aimed into the rising sun.

47

Curtis was trying to open his eyes. That should have been easy, but it was like erasing the darkness. Light was imperfect, and the natural appearance of an hour was black. Color was added to the world, cosmetic, extra, like a radio left on in an empty room.

Margaret was not happy, but he could not tell what she was saying. He wanted to call out to her, like a man crying from an anchored raft in the middle of a lake.

"There's nothing to worry about," he wanted to say.

But on waking, when Curtis tried to call out, he could not make a sound.

He could only think her name, and after awhile he knew he must have dreamed. The oak beams above him were all he would ever see, and they were handsome. He only wished that he could show them to Margaret, the way someone had hewn the stout timbers and how hands had hoisted them, lifted them as far as they remained to this day, keeping out the sky.

When he was a boy, staying with the woman who sold greeting cards by mail, he would go into Woolworth's and look at the gold-fish. The fish lived in plastic bags, bags no bigger than sandwich wrappers. The individual fish, one in each bag, were each confined in a pouch of water so small every time they turned they stroked the side of the plastic container with their mouths.

The fish had fascinated him, so much that he felt somehow guilty about visiting the five-and-dime so often, and took to buying things he did not really want, a small multicolored tablet of scratch paper, or a miniature globe that was also a pencil sharpener. Curtis felt now how it would feel to stroke the plastic, turn after turn, the touch of dead confinement the only remaining pleasure.

He was working on a painting in his mind. Not a version of the painting that had burned. He no longer enjoyed the memory of that work, the famous ''masterpiece,'' painted by a young man who had never fully understood that he shared life with other souls.

This new painting, the one he created in his mind, was a painting of Margaret, nude, looking out of the canvas with an expression of recognition. It was the way she acted when he came home early, and she was sitting at her desk. His first thought was that he was interrupting her. But she had always given him this look of unmistakable welcome, surprise linked with happiness.

Ruskin had written that if you could draw a sphere you could draw anything. Curtis knew that a sphere was easy to render, charcoal on paper. What was difficult was absence, drawing a portrait so that the city outside the studio was implied, its sounds, the traffic, the laughter of children.

He dreamed again. There was a boy's toy, an airplane with a propeller driven by a rubber band. You wound the rubber band by turning the prop, and when the rubber band was twisted and knotted with tension, the thing was ready to fly.

When he woke, he wondered if he could hear an airplane. Eventually he would sleep and not awaken. That was how far this path led. And it was a path, as definite as the heart-line in a palm, as clear as lace, as the living mapwork of ivy.

He wanted to see her once more.

It was cold, and he could not move his arms to pull up a blanket.

He fought against what held him, puzzled as before at how far he had fallen from a height he could no longer recall.

''What's he doing?'' said Loretta Lee.

Margaret lay still on the airstrip. There was the sound of an airplane, a metal mosquito. The noise was getting louder.

''Bishop, what's he doing?'' said Loretta Lee.

There was no answer. Maybe I'm hurt, thought Margaret, maybe I'm not.

The airplane noise was very loud.

Loretta Lee fell over Margaret, holding on to her, saying she was sorry but she had to.

The airplane was on top of them. There was shadow when the

aircraft blocked the light. There was a whisk of wind. The engine noise filled her body. Then the sound of the motor receded, climbing.

Loretta Lee got to her feet. Margaret stayed where she was, sprawled on the asphalt. It had a smell, this plain of sandpaper. It was clean and sun-cured. She was not sure where she was, only that shadows stretched from the palm trees almost all the way to where she lay.

There was a comic strip in her head, one of those episodic narratives, talking faces, frowns, urgent calls. She had hung from the airplane, clinging, and when it rebounded off the airstrip she had let go.

"He's coming back," said Loretta Lee.

Margaret's mind was full of color. She was on her feet. She left blood on the asphalt. There was the sound of the airplane, sweeping back, around, approaching again.

They hobbled to the shelter of the trees.

Bishop touched Loretta Lee on the arm to get her attention, and gave her a canteen. Loretta Lee drank, water flowing down the corners of her mouth, dripping onto the asphalt. Margaret drank, too.

Margaret leaned against the stone wall. She was conscious and she was breathing. She sniffed and she tasted blood, her sinus cavities, her throat, full of fluid. She spat and there was blood on the sun-bleached surface.

Margaret's vision was still bleary from the spray that had crippled. The sound of the airplane swung wide, diminished. Loretta Lee left her side, and stood gazing upward. Margaret limped out of the shadow to look upward, too. The silver aircraft looked bright and innocent, something a child would delight in.

The plane faded into silence.

"He's going to come back, and I'm going to have to shoot him," said Loretta Lee. She began to weep. "He shouldn't have done that." Her voice was torn. "He shouldn't have put me out in the desert."

"He's cut pretty bad," said Bishop. "When he gets a chance to think about it he'll come back here." He spoke like someone who did not so much understand things as balance them out.

Loretta Lee drank from the canteen again, and then let it drop.

"I'll pack the wound," Bishop was saying. "And I'll fly him out myself. To Palm Springs. They have the best hospital."

"You're basically just a boy, aren't you Bishop?" said Loretta Lee. "Just a boy, forty-eight years old."

Bishop did not answer.

"He doesn't need you anymore," said Loretta Lee.

Bishop rubbed one arm thoughtfully. Loretta Lee, dark and blistered, looked up at the empty sky.

Margaret found her way to the gate. Her legs were only partially under her control, wobbly, unsteady.

Her left arm was weak. She kept it close to her body as she tried to run. The pool was calm in the morning light, several fronds lying at the bottom of the pool like large black feathers.

Margaret was in the house. Bishop followed her.

"I didn't take her all the way out into the desert," Bishop was saying. "Because I wanted her to survive. If I took her all the way out where Paul Angevin was, she wouldn't have made it."

Margaret only partly understood what Bishop was saying. She turned and took hold of the man's shoulder with her good hand.

"Where is he?" she asked.

"People don't understand what it's like out there," said Bishop.

"Where is Curtis?"

"The doctor'll be back in a couple of minutes," he said. "He's got so many people who'd do anything for him."

She grabbed the man's shirt, tearing the pocket.

They were in the studio, at the end of the room. There was still an eye-smarting trace of Mace in the air. Bishop tried the door. "The keys are with Dr. Patterson," said Bishop, as though that settled it.

"We'll break it down," said Margaret.

Bishop made a calming gesture. "We don't want to rush into anything," he said. His face was still a mask, but the look of pleasant competence had been replaced by one of doubt. "A door like this— we shouldn't do anything we might regret later on."

"Open it."

"We will," he said. "We'll get the door open." His eyes looked hurt, as though surprised that she would doubt his ability. "But Dr. Patterson is going to want to know why we didn't just wait for him."

Margaret grabbed him again, the fabric of the shirt making another tearing sound.

"What are you going to tell him when he comes back?" Bishop was saying. There was no anger in his voice, only a need.

"Do what she tells you," said Loretta Lee from across the room.

Loretta Lee stood still. The gun in her hand gave her a certain authority, although she gave no indication that she knew it was there.

Bishop's eyes narrowed. He considered Margaret. He considered Loretta Lee. "I'll tell him I had no choice," he said.

"That's true," said Loretta Lee.

Bishop and Loretta Lee left. They were not gone long, but Margaret was alone with the barrier, the door that would not open. She pressed against it, listening, telling Curtis that she was there.

There was no sound from inside. The room might be empty. The place could be filled with things long lost but, for the moment, useless, dusty furniture, blank canvas.

Bishop and Loretta Lee returned with a long crowbar, a crowbar longer than he was tall, a classic lever out of a physics lesson.

"Found this in the desert," Bishop said, inserting the curved end of the iron into the crack in the door. "Maybe a year ago. Out near Trona, near the dry lake. Belonged to the railroad, I would imagine," he said. "No telling how old."

Margaret wanted to take the iron in her own hands, because there was something deliberate and at the same time thoughtless in the man's behavior, a person so baffled by events that he clung to empty fact.

Or perhaps it was Bishop's way of consoling himself that although he did the bidding of two women, he did it in his own way, at his own pace. The door did not splinter, but the lines between the boards that made up the door began to show white against the walnut-stained oak. Bishop grunted, and the door did not move or shiver, except to part where the door met the jamb.

The muscles in his arms were taut. He planted his feet, and pulled again, saying, as he worked, "Iron like this doesn't get old. You keep it from rusting—"

The door burst. Something metal, part of the lock, Margaret surmised, sang off the ceiling.

The smell of the room was vaguely medicinal. The place was like a hospital room, a room that had been thoughtfully decorated with Mexican wool rugs and palm leaves and art books stacked, with hopeful disorder, beside the hospital bed.

In the bed was an unshaven figure, a person she nearly could not recognize. The man was asleep, his lips moving like someone suffering a bad dream.

Margaret held Curtis, weeping, calling to him.

"I couldn't do it anymore," said Curtis. His voice was an urgent whisper, sometimes breaking into a rasp. "I couldn't work."

Margaret told him not to talk. She would take care of everything.

But he continued, "I saw the paints go transparent. All I could see was the empty canvas behind the colors." The emptiness, he thought, that is always there. "So I had to quit, and there was nothing he could do to help me."

He held her as though he was afraid that she was not real.

"You know what I have to do," she said.

As though it were alive, he thought. As though the work of art had become a thing that could take life.

He met her eyes.

Loretta Lee watched Margaret gather in the torn, color-splashed sail of the painting.

"What's she doing?" asked Bishop.

"Don't move," said Loretta Lee. "Stay where you are."

Her voice was calm, and Margaret looked up, expecting to see the gun pointing at her. But it was pointing at Bishop, and Bishop turned like a man in pain, and felt his way toward a chair.

He sat. "I won't let you do this," he said in a voice without strength.

Margaret made her way quickly down the stairs. Her fingers were glazed with a substance like dried cocoa, her own blood. She found old sheets of newspaper in a wicker basket, yellowed classified ads. The match heads were pastel colors, pink, mint green. She broke one match, and then another. At last one of the matches was alight.

The canvas beside her on the floor, she worked carefully, touching the white flame to a wad of newspaper. The paper began to burn. As it burned the wad of paper began to loosen, opening, an ugly blossom.

She let the fire grow, fed by kindling and lengths of sweet-smelling wood, wood so dense with sap that it glistened. When she tried to roll up the canvas, crumbs of paint fell onto the floor. The painting was bulky, heavy, and it shifted in her grasp.

Patterson might be here now, she knew—climbing from the aircraft, running through the heat.

It was an effort, the thing buckling, fighting back. The canvas threw itself open in the big fireplace, suffocating the flame. The fire was out.

You didn't want to let it burn, something in her said. Look at it, how seductive it is, wanting you to reach in and pull it free. *Go ahead—it's not too late.* The splashes of color were distorted by their position in the fireplace. This new painting was a semblance, a disguise, but even a disguise can flow, pleasing the eye. It wasn't going to burn. Flame couldn't harm a thing like this.

She thrust an iron poker into the middle of the canvas, and kept it there.

A single trellis of smoke rose in one corner of the blackened fireplace. Where Margaret had gashed the painting there was a curl of flame. A folded-over corner straightened, flaring. Fire ate a further hole. The painting made a sound, a whisper, a sputtering whistle. She stepped back, letting the poker fall.

The full conflagration was so sudden it shook the air in the room. There was a flash, and the painting was gone.

48

Before the sheriff's deputies arrived, when it was not clear what was going to happen next, Margaret heard the sound of a car from outside, beyond the trees. She thought it must be help, but when she looked up at the sound of a footstep it was only Loretta Lee with some knowledge quiet in her eyes.

"Bishop's gone," said Loretta Lee.

Margaret was sitting beside Curtis, helping him eat. Tomato juice and crackers had seemed easiest in his condition, and she held the glass of juice so he could take another drink. The Saltines made crumbs and she brushed the flakes of flour and the salt from the pillow.

"Bishop loves Dr. Patterson so much," said Loretta Lee.

Margaret was the authority now. There was power in the house, and it belonged to her. Loretta Lee waited for her response. "What harm can he do?" asked Margaret.

"A lot of harm," said Loretta Lee, in a voice that sounded unafraid. "To all of us."

All the way there Margaret was by his side. Deputy sheriffs in their pea-green uniforms and cowboy hats did not try to separate them. Medics did their work, apologizing to both of them for interrupting.

They flew together, under the thudding prop of a helicopter, the desert falling away from them. It was replaced by a different sort of desert, empty river beds and golf courses, with shaved patches for sand traps and white plumes where sprinklers plied water. There were streets of houses among green lawns.

                        *   *   *

Curtis wanted to have a view, and so they gave him one.

There was a strip of Palm Springs grass. There was a parking lot, a range of mountains, and sky.

But, having been given a view, Curtis ignored it. He followed Margaret with his eyes as she brought him water, a cloth to moisten his lips. There was talk of pneumonia, and blood clots in his legs from injuries that were slow to heal.

But more than one doctor commented that he was not doing so badly, considering what he had been through.

She stayed with him through a cavalcade of doctors and nurses, the white smocks of technicians and the green smocks of orderlies. Margaret did not want to leave his side, but she had to.

She had unfinished work.

The room was filled with men and women in a hurry, medical personnel, guards, administrators.

She was introduced to a short man in a blue suit. He did security, he said, for the network. He had worked briefly with Red Patterson, but it had not gone well; Patterson had found him irritating. Poole offered this revelation as though it did not interest him much.

"They kicked me upstairs," said Poole. "The usual sort of consolation. Now I get to worry about a lot of things at once."

She listened to Poole with a polite expression, but did not feel moved to respond to him beyond a few soft-spoken remarks. Her press conference was in three minutes. She kept her eye on the clock on the wall, a circle with numerals as black and joyless as the glyphs in an eye chart.

"So," said Poole at last, "the question of the hour, aside from the health of Mr. Newns, is—"

"Where is Red Patterson?" she said.

"Exactly."

"No, I'm asking you," said Margaret. "Where is he?"

Poole's suit was the sort that does not go out of fashion. He buttoned one of the jacket's black buttons, then unbuttoned it again. He seemed unhappy to have to trouble her, and Margaret liked him for that. Margaret wore the only thing available in her overnight bag, an outfit her mother would have termed *plain but pretty*: silk blouse, stylishly wrinkled, cotton blend slacks, all the moderately dressy clothing she had taken to Owl Springs.

"He's missing," said Poole.

"You'll find him."

"I have to ask you if you know where he went."

"The sheriffs were all very nice," said Margaret. "I told them what I knew." She had even confessed to a little bit of a stab with a knife, in self-defense. There had been many questions, but somehow there was little surprise. Perhaps it was the way Margaret told it, or the fact that Loretta Lee related the same story.

"We have a question or two more to ask," said Poole.

"Curtis is expected to be all right. Thank you for asking."

Poole gave a smile. He was a sweet-looking little man, she thought.

"What happened out there?" he asked.

She considered the question. "Did you like Dr. Patterson?"

Poole took a moment. "I liked him a lot. Even though we didn't get along. Why?"

She could imagine Patterson finding this man irritating. He was insistent, but quiet, and he wanted to do his job.

Poole waited for Margaret to respond, but she turned away from him.

"And this other man, Donald Morton Bishop," he said. "What do you know about him?"

"Nothing."

"Any idea where he was heading when he left?"

"No idea, Mr. Poole."

"He might have gone to meet Patterson in the desert somewhere."

"That's possible."

"Why do I have the feeling you know a lot you don't want to share with me tonight?"

Margaret liked that little fillip, *tonight*. That was the way waitresses kept their questions from sounding too straightforward. *Anything more I can get you tonight?*

Poole spoke as though to the wall. "You don't have to talk to the media. You don't have to do anything you don't want to do. The network's going to issue a further statement."

"What sort of statement?" said Margaret, her tone so flat it came out not sounding like a question. She was looking in a mirror. She looked good, she thought. Not so plain after all.

"You're going to cooperate with investigative agencies, and we'll have further statements in a few days. We think the best thing is to say nothing. Nothing slanderous."

"What are you afraid of?"

The man laughed, showing his teeth. "I personally am not afraid of anything. It's just that if you go out there with that particular story and expect people to change their minds about Red Patterson. . . ."

It was time. She took a peek through the swinging doors. There was an army out there, videocams and microphones, a hungry corps of people who were up at one o'clock in the morning. They had been at the hospital all day, and while Palm Springs was pleasant in January, this was the dead of summer. They couldn't all fit into the air-conditioned building. There was an international corps of irritated, articulate people growing increasingly frayed.

"You can just tell them all to take a walk. You don't owe them anything," said Poole.

"You couldn't protect Red Patterson the man," she said, "so now you guard his reputation."

"It's entirely up to you, Mrs. Newns. But you have to realize that you can't really just go out there and say anything you feel like saying. . . ." His voice died.

Margaret said, "Watch me."

Margaret stood in the hospital cafeteria. There was a tangle of microphones, some of them taped together, held to the podium with hastily applied duct tape so that the ends of the adhesive strips crept over the edge of the podium like a Halloween spider.

Margaret was bandaged, under her clothes, painted with antiseptic, coddled with painkillers. They like this, all these reporters, she thought. They act efficient and professional, but this is what they love to do.

You learn to ignore everyone, her father had said. They are not friends, and they are not enemies. You see the chessboard, and what plays the game isn't you, not your desire to win, not your desire to avoid losing. What plays the game is the game—chess playing chess.

Margaret told the crowd what had happened.

She knew that he would turn up soon in Las Vegas or San Bernardino with a story of his own, a story everyone would prefer to Margaret's. You don't kill a man like Patterson with a paint-crusted knife.

She told the truth. And to her surprise, people believed it. Even their questions reassured her. How was Curtis feeling? What happened to the painting? What did she feel about Red Patterson now?

Margaret saw the power in being the first to escape the wilderness with the truth. Their loyalty to Patterson was thin. Patterson was absent. She was not. She told them that Curtis had been trusting and that Patterson had deceived them all.

She even began to feel a little sorry for Red Patterson as she spoke. These people didn't love him. They prized something else, the effervescence of the moment, the living, dying yeast of a name.

Bruno was just coming through the door with Andy after a delicious meal of *abbacchio* served in a casserole with anchovies, and just a modest splash of chianti. It was evening, and raining.

There might have been thunder, or it might have been a jumbo jet in the distance, it was hard to tell. The rain made the far-off sounds of Rome seem closer than ever, the motorcycles, the footsteps, the greetings of pedestrians, the tinkle of fork against plate as someone fed the cats in the street.

The phone was ringing.

Bruno listened to the voice, a television reporter in Los Angeles, a woman he knew slightly. He must have been out, she said; she had left three messages.

She talked, reading from a bulletin, the sort of pleasant voice Bruno associated with dental hygienists.

The news stunned Bruno, and he enjoyed the thrill. It was such a relief, in a horrible way. And Curtis, he asked, a little breathlessly? Was the artist still ... And the painting?

Ah, well, the painting.

But even that was not undiluted disaster. Imagine the difficulty of saying something about a painting that had become not a masterpiece but something created by the contemporary worship of—

Jesus, maybe I'm going to end up looking like a fake, thought Bruno. Maybe they'll think I was in collusion with Red Patterson. He felt a little sick.

"What is it?" Andy was mouthing at him from where he stood, leaning next to a terra-cotta cherub.

"Nothing," said Bruno.

Well, almost nothing. Curtis nearly starved to death, the painting destroyed, Red Patterson missing. "Turn on the television," said Bruno. And he added, "Upstairs."

"So we'll need a statement," said the California voice.

Bruno wanted to tell a small lie, slip just a little pinkie ring onto the truth. He wanted to say that he expected this all along, and he was half convinced that he had. Hadn't he always despised Red Patterson?

"Patterson was able to help many people," Bruno heard himself saying. "He was not an evil man." Those past-tense verbs had a way of marching in, unexpectedly, jack-booted and final. "He was a man who believed in life. But he had life confused with himself." He paused.

"That's your statement?" asked the L.A. voice.

"Margaret Darcy Newns is a brave woman," said Bruno, sounding, he thought, both airy and solemn.

Good Lord, he didn't know where this stuff was coming from. He should have written something down and called her back.

"That's it?" said the voice from television, sounding just a little bit peeved.

And I, thought Bruno, am more like Red Patterson than I would like to be.

"In ancient times," said Bruno, "when a Caesar was declared divine, people must have known that the individual emperor was not actually immortal, but they worshipped him anyway. Because we need to worship. We do it happily, instinctively, with very little hesitation. And why not?"

There was a mock-courteous pause. "If we could maybe backtrack just a little bit," said the woman on the phone.

Bruno sat. It was really raining outside now. People ran up the street, laughing. He was struck by a thought that impressed him.

He tried it out. "Hasn't it occurred to you that I might have guessed this was happening?"

"You knew something was going on but you didn't tell any of the authorities?"

She didn't believe him. The woman owed everything to a nose-job and a B.A. in broadcasting from UCLA, and here she was doubting Bruno Kraft.

"What did you say happened to Dr. Patterson?" asked Bruno.

Margaret spent the night sitting beside Curtis, telling him stories to make him laugh, true stories, the memories of her girlhood, and it was like meeting Curtis all over again, but this time trusting herself the way she never had before.

Outside, the moon passed over the mountains. They could not see the moon, but only the light it cast, opening canyons and then closing them as the moon fell westward and the night lost its hold.

49

Sometimes the starling flew back and forth within the apartment, perching on the back of a chair. Margaret worried at such times that he would collide with the sliding glass door, or with one of the windows.

But over the months the bird escaped harm from the limits of his world, and he learned to imitate an ever-widening variety of sounds—motors, bells, distant calls of other birds. Sometimes the bird alighted on the bathroom sink before its own reflection, but the starling did not appear to notice the black, dappled image in the mirror.

Loretta Lee called occasionally from her new home on Catalina Island, where she spent time reading books she ordered by water taxi from the mainland, waiting for the past to die before she went on with her life.

"The trouble is, Bishop always kept secrets," said Loretta Lee. "Now all he has to keep is himself. He'll be real good at that."

"For some reason I'm not anxious," said Margaret.

"I am," said Loretta Lee.

"Why? He wouldn't hurt you when he had the chance."

"I'm not thinking about me," said Loretta Lee.

From time to time Margaret saw someone who looked like Bishop. The figure watched her as she entered Davies Hall for a concert, or as she took part in a panel on children's literature. At the end of a row of books at the library she'd see a compact figure edging behind a bookcase, stepping through the door to the reference room, where, when Margaret followed, there would be nothing but empty tables, the lights going off and on to signal it was time to close.

Police visited. A body had been discovered in the desert around Owl Springs, a half-remembered TV producer named Paul Angevin. Other bodies were discovered shortly afterward, two campers and their mini-pickup.

She received polite calls from reporters, sharing bits of news. The Range Rover had been found in San Jose. Bishop's sister, a tax accountant in Ukiah, said she had not heard from her brother in nine years. Margaret was to call if she had any idea where Bishop might be. There were many questions.

Margaret was never uneasy when she saw one of these men who might be Bishop. She was glad, and only after the man turned off into the crowd, into the haze at the end of the street, did she think that Bishop might be watching her, might be stalking her, might be waiting to do her harm.

It was hard for her to be afraid of anything, even though she and Curtis waited for word of Patterson. Margaret wanted to hurry away from the attractive chatter, the smiles, the business of coffee or champagne and find Bishop, and take his hand.

Curtis was troubled by dreams of confinement, and fretted over Patterson's fate. But he was not afraid any longer, and it struck Margaret that Patterson had helped Curtis in some way that defied understanding.

Red Patterson's plane was missing for eleven months.

One week before the opening of Curtis's new exhibit, Patterson's aircraft was discovered. There it was on the news, a crumpled pair of wings in the Nevada desert.

Margaret called to Curtis, but he could not hear her. She hurried to the hall and called again.

The televised view rocked slightly, as the helicopter that supported the camera jockeyed from one angle to another. Figures stood beside the wrecked plane, casting short, stumpy shadows.

There were no remains of Red Patterson.

Curtis sat on the sofa and said nothing.

"Maybe he made it out of the desert," said Margaret.

He put his arm around her, and kissed her.

"It's possible," she said, not quite believing it.

"That's not," said Curtis, "what he wanted."

"You wanted to think of him riding a horse on an island somewhere, snorkeling, looking at the tropical fish."

"He helped me," said Curtis. "You were right to hate the painting—but when I think of him working to finish it I understand something about him. I wish he could be alive, somewhere, and happy. I look off the balcony, and I half expect to see him.''

In the air, he meant. Walking in the air.

When she remembered the painting she could not see it clearly in her mind. What she saw when she woke with a start before dawn was not a work that disturbed her. What she saw was a painting of peculiar beauty surrendering itself to flame.

That was the night Bishop resurfaced.

They went out to Lulu, a restaurant which, if you arrived late enough, was fairly quiet. Curtis needed to have what he called ''a change of walls.'' They both knew what Curtis was waiting for, and sitting in the penthouse while the televised news played scenes of violence, storms and riots, was a strain on both of them.

It was closing time, nearly, and mesquite smoke was in everyone's eyes, offering something like privacy. A few diners glanced their way, and heads were put together, whispers exchanged, but most people were oblivious.

Curtis wasn't hungry, eating salad and drinking black coffee, and Margaret had a chocolate whiskey cake that reminded her of her favorite recipe for truffles. It was possible to pretend to forget, for a few minutes, the televised image of the shiny wings fractured on the desert floor.

They stopped on their way out to say hello to people they knew slightly, a movie director and his wife, and they enjoyed the cool night air outside, aware of how smoky their clothes smelled. Low clouds were smudged and blotted with color, reflecting the city lights.

There was light from streetlights, light from the restaurant, big, sloppy carpets of artificial illumination. There was light from a billboard across the street, smiling people surrounded by blank white.

There was a small crowd on the sidewalk. It was a part of town that blended nightclubs with small offices, warehouses with condos. Margaret glanced over her shoulder, certain that she sensed something, but there were only the unilluminated headlights of parked cars, the embers of glowing cigarettes, figures huddling together in the cool midnight.

Curtis asked her if there was anything wrong. She made no response, only looked back once more. Some silhouette was familiar, some movement caught her.

No, she was ready to say. There's nothing wrong.

And there he was.

There was Bishop, sidestepping a couple talking, laughing together in the light that fell from the restaurant. Margaret experienced no hesitation, no catch in her breath. She was happy to see him. He had that aging boy's mask for a face, and he looked at her with a glint of something like brotherly affection. He had lost weight, and his hair was boot-camp short.

The event was slow, choppy. Bishop crooked his body to extract an object from within his clothing, and the gesture was that of a wino tugging out his half-liter.

He pulled a gun, and she saw it happening just before it actually took place. There was a little worm of reflection along the barrel of the gun, and light in Bishop's eyes. He aimed at Curtis, but then changed his mind, or perhaps the gun decided for him. The pistol turned as a hunting thing turns, a moray eel nosing blood. There was a sensation of both clarity and confusion, *this isn't happening* conflicting with *this is real.*

Bishop moved with the deliberate command she had seen in traffic police: *I am in charge here.* He brought the handgun up so the black pupil of the weapon was leveled at Margaret's face.

Curtis had one hand up, as though he could catch the bullet in the air. But Margaret could read Bishop's eyes.

There was a report so loud, so sharp, that it was more than a single gunshot. Something essential in the hour vanished, the way lightning burns a vacuum through air, but there was a ragged second when nothing happened. Curtis was a silhouette, and Bishop himself had lost all power to move.

No one, Margaret told herself.

The gun fell, an ugly, iron clatter. Margaret put one foot on the weapon, and held the pilot in her arms. Bishop was silent, sobbing.

No one is hurt.

People stood from where the sound of the shot had dropped them, half-crouches, hiding places behind cars, like figures in a photograph given unsteady freedom.

Bishop couldn't hurt us.

There was a hole in a plate-glass window. There was another in a far wall inside, above an empty table, surrounded by a patch of freshly dislodged plaster.

Bishop was trying to talk, but he couldn't.

Tell me, said Margaret, or she wanted to say. She knew. There was no other reason for Bishop to strike, no other reason for him to deliberately fail.

"They found him," said Bishop.

50

Margaret was going to be late.

First of all there was a protest on the Golden Gate Bridge, a group against the Rape of Forests, as far as Margaret could make out. There was a burst of static on the radio, and it obliterated the news for a moment. Five cars had stopped in the lanes going north, and people were out of the cars with bullhorns.

Margaret could not actually see this, but heard about it on KCBS. What she did see was halted traffic, everywhere. According to "Traffic and Weather Together" all the approaches to the bridge were blocked and the Bay Bridge was suffering, too, three stalls and something jackknifed.

It was late afternoon and Curtis's show was set to open in exactly one hour. Margaret was stuck in traffic, burning out the clutch, probably, although Curtis had said they would buy a new car.

This was an important afternoon, and it was going all wrong. Something electrical had blown up on Taylor Street, a transformer, according to the radio. Nobody was hurt but the possible long-term health effects from PCPs meant that authorities were cautious. Workers painting lines on Van Ness had encountered an elderly driver, and white paint had spread across two lanes. A former president was giving a speech at the Commonwealth Club.

A dog barked at Margaret, hanging out a car window. It was a collie with small, alert, uncomprehending eyes, yapping at Margaret until she asked it very gently to please be quiet. The dog looked ashamed, and tucked back into its car.

*   *   *

But she wasn't late.

Margaret reached the gallery. There was already a crowd on Sutter Street, hired security directing traffic, setting up barriers, smiling at Margaret as she passed them. Someone said, "That's her!" This happened all the time, lately. Strangers smiled and said hello.

Margaret ran into Renata San Pablo in the elevator.

Margaret told Renata how wonderful it was to see her.

It had been Renata's contention that Margaret, in her anguish, had committed a crime, burning a work of singular importance. Strangely, this simply added to the luster of this particular show. Margaret had, in the public eye, taken on the aura of both savior and destroyer, and people seemed to regard her with a mix of affection and awe.

"Curtis is so gorgeous!" said Renata. "It's bliss to look at him!"

What could Margaret think of saying but, "Thank you"?

"You *will* make Curtis sell them, won't you? When he feels ready to, of course."

"Curtis is happy to show these drawings. But he doesn't want to let them go."

"But isn't that *wrong,* Margaret? Isn't that *selfish?* You know it is."

The elevator opened, but neither Renata nor Margaret made a move to leave it. "They belong to Curtis," said Margaret.

"But they should belong to all of us," said Renata.

Curtis was smiling, and gave Margaret a huge hug, picking her up off the carpet as he did so.

It made Margaret self-conscious, still, to see so many drawings of her own naked body. She lifted her hand to touch an earring, as though the feel of the lapis lazuli wing would reassure her that it was all right to be nude, and in such abandon, before strangers.

Loretta Lee had turned the drawings over to Curtis and Margaret that day as they awaited the arrival of the sheriff's department. She had told the artist that Patterson had found them in the living room of the house in Marin, the morning after the shooting, but then, in private with Margaret, Loretta Lee confessed that she herself had found them in the foyer of the house, and taken good care of them, following Patterson's advice once he learned of the existence of "all those cute little Margaret behinds."

Bruno was there. Margaret had not spoken to him for many months, not since he visited the hospital in Palm Springs just before

Curtis was released. Even then, her smile had been strained, her words few. She had trouble forgiving him.

Andy was taking pictures, favoring those shots which had Curtis and Bruno together, but there still were no members of the public, only what Curtis called "the chosen few and their fleas."

"He was probably committing suicide," said Renata to a small gathering of her hand-chosen. "By disappearing way off where he knew everyone would have to come out and find him." People were surprised that Patterson was dead, although not saddened. His vanishing act had been intriguing. His mere remains lacked any further magic.

There was a photograph of a body in magazines and newspapers. The image had been shocking, days ago, but it was accepted now. The body was sunbaked, the eyes closed, the posture like that of a man meditating. The surrounding terrain was scattered stone, gravel as lifeless as the Martian surface.

Some people claimed that this corpse was not Red Patterson, in fact, but someone else. The medical examiner, however, was definite. It was Red Patterson, and he had suffered a stab wound to the chest. That he had survived long enough to find his way that far out in the desert, so far from his aircraft, was something of a miracle.

Public response to Patterson's death had been tempered by Bruno Kraft's comments in several interviews. Just as no jury would convict Margaret, Bruno said, no art lover could ultimately blame her. But how much of the painting would have been completed, Bruno wondered, if Margaret had stayed in San Francisco? How much had Margaret's visit to Owl Springs forced Patterson's hand?

"We're about to let in the people," said Renata San Pablo.

"Don't," said Bruno. "Let's just stay here together for a moment."

"People," said Renata, as she might have said *pustules,* "get irritated if they have to wait."

Curtis put his arm around Margaret, for strength, although whether to take it or give it was not clear.

"I stand corrected. We certainly don't want to keep people waiting, do we?" said Bruno.

The place was, suddenly, crowded and happy.

Margaret remembered how she had felt, while this drawing was being sketched onto the paper, how the sun had felt, and how they had made love. Curtis was here at her side now, and yet she wondered what had happened to her, how she had been so lucky to see her image re-created on a sheet of paper.

"Now you are immortal," said Bruno, indicating the drawings around them.

When she closed her eyes she could still see desert, the rise and fall, the eternal stone. She wanted to laugh. She wanted to tell Bruno something he might not understand. When Curtis drew these pictures, she would have said, he loved her, as he did now, his hand in hers.

Renata was describing the relatively poor quality of Patterson's collection, which she would personally not even consider buying. "That means she's fallen in love with it," said Curtis.

"You don't like it here, do you?" asked Margaret.

"All these people—" He shrugged.

Margaret knew. The avalanche that sweeps the world each day leaves survivors. It leaves them with something else, not their past, and no promise of a future. People have the brief circle of daylight, and they have each other.

Margaret and Curtis left when no one could see, their escape momentarily blocked by the arrival of video equipment and two local television celebrities. Margaret pulled him along by one hand. They took the stairs, leaped three steps at a time, and were out in the street, out in the traffic.

They strolled up Sutter Street, passing their reflections in the shop windows, their images elongated, shortened, or trembling as a truck rumbled behind them in the street.

"Bruno was going to show his new video," said Curtis. "The one Renata commissioned, the one all about the 'Margaret Series.' "

"We can go back, if you want," she said teasingly.

"Do you think they've noticed we're gone?" he asked.

"By now."

"Do you think they'll send someone after us?"

She laughed. "Of course."

"We'd better run," said Curtis.

They stayed where they were. Curtis ran a finger along her lips, like a man drawing lips onto a canvas. That is how it felt, as though his touch created not simply her response, but her body, his whisper loud in her ear as he put his arms around her, people parting around them on the sidewalk, not seeing them, or seeing them and passing by, a world in a hurry to get home.